Fritz Reuter Leiber

The World of Dystopia

OK Publishing 2021

*Fritz Reuter Leiber*
# The World of Dystopia

Apocalyptic & Post-Apocalyptic Stories of Fritz Leiber

Published by

Books

- Advanced Digital Solutions & High-Quality book Formatting -

musaicumbooks@okpublishing.info

2021 OK Publishing

ISBN 978-80-272-7919-7

# Contents

# The Creature from Cleveland Depths

*Here is a modern tale of an inner-directed sorcerer and an outer-directed sorcerer's apprentice... a tale of —* The Creature from Cleveland Depths

"Come on, Gussy," Fay prodded quietly, "quit stalking around like a neurotic bear and suggest something for my invention team to work on. I enjoy visiting you and Daisy, but I can't stay aboveground all night."

"If being outside the shelters makes you nervous, don't come around any more," Gusterson told him, continuing to stalk. "Why doesn't your invention team think of something to invent? Why don't you? Hah!" In the "Hah!" lay triumphant condemnation of a whole way of life.

"We do," Fay responded imperturbably, "but a fresh viewpoint sometimes helps."

"I'll say it does! Fay, you burglar, I'll bet you've got twenty people like myself you milk for free ideas. First you irritate their bark and then you make the rounds every so often to draw off the latex or the maple gloop."

Fay smiled. "It ought to please you that society still has a use for you outre inner-directed types. It takes something to make a junior executive stay aboveground after dark, when the missiles are on the prowl."

"Society can't have much use for us or it'd pay us something," Gusterson sourly asserted, staring blankly at the tankless TV and kicking it lightly as he passed on.

"No, you're wrong about that, Gussy. Money's not the key goad with you inner-directeds. I got that straight from our Motivations chief."

"Did he tell you what we should use instead to pay the grocer? A deep inner sense of achievement, maybe? Fay, why should I do any free thinking for Micro Systems?"

"I'll tell you why, Gussy. Simply because you get a kick out of insulting us with sardonic ideas. If we take one of them seriously, you think we're degrading ourselves, and that pleases you even more. Like making someone laugh at a lousy pun."

Gusterson held still in his roaming and grinned. "That the reason, huh? I suppose my suggestions would have to be something in the line of ultra-subminiaturized computers, where one sinister fine-etched molecule does the work of three big bumbling brain cells?"

"Not necessarily. Micro Systems is branching out. Wheel as free as a rogue star. But I'll pass along to Promotion your one molecule-three brain cell sparkler. It's a slight exaggeration, but it's catchy."

"I'll have my kids watch your ads to see if you use it and then I'll sue the whole underworld." Gusterson frowned as he resumed his stalking. He stared puzzledly at the antique TV. "How about inventing a plutonium termite?" he said suddenly. "It would get rid of those stockpiles that are worrying you moles to death."

Fay grimaced noncommittally and cocked his head.

"Well, then, how about a beauty mask? How about that, hey? I don't mean one to repair a woman's complexion, but one she'd wear all the time that'd make her look like a 17-year-old sexpot. That'd end *her* worries."

"Hey, that's for me," Daisy called from the kitchen. "I'll make Gusterson suffer. I'll make him crawl around on his hands and knees begging my immature favors."

"No, you won't," Gusterson called back. "You having a face like that would scare the kids. Better cancel that one, Fay. Half the adult race looking like Vina Vidarsson is too awful a thought."

"Yah, you're just scared of making a million dollars," Daisy jeered.

"I sure am," Gusterson said solemnly, scanning the fuzzy floor from one murky glass wall to the other, hesitating at the TV. "How about something homey now, like a flock of little prickly cylinders that roll around the floor collecting lint and flub? They'd work by electricity, or at a pinch cats could bat 'em around. Every so often they'd be automatically herded together and the lint cleaned off the bristles."

"No good," Fay said. "There's no lint underground and cats are *verboten*. And the above-ground market doesn't amount to more moneywise than the state of Southern Illinois. Keep it grander, Gussy, and more impractical-you can't sell people merely useful ideas." From his hassock in the center of the room he looked uneasily around. "Say, did that violet tone in the glass come from the high Cleveland hydrogen bomb or is it just age and ultraviolet, like desert glass?"

"No, somebody's grandfather liked it that color," Gusterson informed him with happy bitterness. "I like it too-the glass, I mean, not the tint. People who live in glass houses can see the stars-especially when there's a window-washing streak in their germ-plasm."

"Gussy, why don't you move underground?" Fay asked, his voice taking on a missionary note. "It's a lot easier living in one room, believe me. You don't have to tramp from room to room hunting things."

"I like the exercise," Gusterson said stoutly.

"But I bet Daisy'd prefer it underground. And your kids wouldn't have to explain why their father lives like a Red Indian. Not to mention the safety factor and insurance savings and a crypt church within easy slidewalk distance. Incidentally, we see the stars all the time, better than you do-by repeater."

"Stars by repeater," Gusterson murmured to the ceiling, pausing for God to comment. Then, "No, Fay, even if I could afford it-and stand it —I'm such a bad-luck Harry that just when I got us all safely stowed at the N minus 1 sublevel, the Soviets would discover an earthquake bomb that struck from below, and I'd have to follow everybody back to the treetops. *Hey! How about bubble homes in orbit around earth?* Micro Systems could subdivide the world's most spacious suburb and all you moles could go ellipsing. Space is as safe as there is: no air, no shock waves. Free fall's the ultimate in restfulness-great health benefits. Commute by rocket-or better yet stay home and do all your business by TV-telephone, or by waldo if it were that sort of thing. Even pet your girl by remote control-she in her bubble, you in yours, whizzing through vacuum. Oh, damn-damn-*damn-damn*-DAMN!"

He was glaring at the blank screen of the TV, his big hands clenching and unclenching.

"Don't let Fay give you apoplexy-he's not worth it," Daisy said, sticking her trim head in from the kitchen, while Fay inquired anxiously, "Gussy, what's the matter?"

"Nothing, you worm!" Gusterson roared, "Except that an hour ago I forgot to tune in on the only TV program I've wanted to hear this year —*Finnegans Wake* scored for English, Gaelic and brogue. Oh, damn-*damn*-DAMN!"

"Too bad," Fay said lightly. "I didn't know they were releasing it on flat TV too."

"Well, they were! Some things are too damn big to keep completely underground. And I had to forget! I'm always doing it —I miss everything! Look here, you rat," he blatted suddenly at Fay, shaking his finger under the latter's chin, "I'll tell you what you can have that ignorant team of yours invent. They can fix me up a mechanical secretary that I can feed orders into and that'll remind me when the exact moment comes to listen to TV or phone somebody or mail in a story or write a letter or pick up a magazine or look at an eclipse or a new orbiting station or fetch the kids from school or buy Daisy a bunch of flowers or whatever it is. It's got to be something that's always with me, not something I have to go and consult or that I can get sick of and put down somewhere. And it's got to remind me forcibly enough so that I take notice and don't just shrug it aside, like I sometimes do even when Daisy reminds me of things. That's what your stupid team can invent for me! If they do a good job, I'll pay 'em as much as fifty dollars!"

"That doesn't sound like anything so very original to me," Fay commented coolly, leaning back from the wagging finger. "I think all senior executives have something of that sort. At least, their secretary keeps some kind of file...."

"I'm not looking for something with spiked falsies and nylons up to the neck," interjected Gusterson, whose ideas about secretaries were a trifle lurid. "I just want a mech reminder-that's all!"

"Well, I'll keep the idea in mind," Fay assured him, "along with the bubble homes and beauty masks. If we ever develop anything along those lines, I'll let you know. If it's a beauty mask, I'll bring Daisy a pilot model-to use to scare strange kids." He put his watch to his ear. "Good lord, I'm going to have to cut to make it underground before the main doors close. Just ten minutes to Second Curfew! 'By, Gus. 'By, Daze."

Two minutes later, living room lights out, they watched Fay's foreshortened antlike figure scurrying across the balding ill-lit park toward the nearest escalator.

Gusterson said, "Weird to think of that big bright space-poor glamor basement stretching around everywhere underneath. Did you remind Smitty to put a new bulb in the elevator?"

"The Smiths moved out this morning," Daisy said tonelessly. "They went underneath."

"Like cockroaches," Gusterson said. "Cockroaches leavin' a sinkin' apartment building. Next the ghosts'll be retreatin' to the shelters."

"Anyhow, from now on we're our own janitors," Daisy said.

He nodded. "Just leaves three families besides us loyal to this glass death trap. Not countin' ghosts." He sighed. Then, "You like to move below, Daisy?" he asked softly, putting his arm lightly across her shoulders. "Get a woozy eyeful of the bright lights and all for a change? Be a rat for a while? Maybe we're getting too old to be bats. I could scrounge me a company job and have a thinking closet all to myself and two secretaries with stainless steel breasts. Life'd be easier for you and a lot cleaner. And you'd sleep safer."

"That's true," she answered and paused. She ran her fingertip slowly across the murky glass, its violet tint barely perceptible against a cold dim light across the park. "But somehow," she said, snaking her arm around his waist, "I don't think I'd sleep happier-or one bit excited."

Three weeks later Fay, dropping in again, handed to Daisy the larger of the two rather small packages he was carrying.

"It's a so-called beauty mask," he told her, "complete with wig, eyelashes, and wettable velvet lips. It even breathes-pinholed elastiskin with a static adherence-charge. But Micro Systems had nothing to do with it, thank God. Beauty Trix put it on the market ten days ago and it's already started a teen-age craze. Some boys are wearing them too, and the police are yipping at Trix for encouraging transvestism with psychic repercussions."

"Didn't I hear somewhere that Trix is a secret subsidiary of Micro?" Gusterson demanded, rearing up from his ancient electric typewriter. "No, you're not stopping me writing, Fay-it's the gut of evening. If I do any more I won't have any juice to start with tomorrow. I got another of my insanity thrillers moving. A real id-teaser. In this one not only all the characters are crazy but the robot psychiatrist too."

"The vending machines are jumping with insanity novels," Fay commented. "Odd they're so popular."

Gusterson chortled. "The only way you outer-directed moles will accept individuality any more even in a fictional character, without your superegos getting seasick, is for them to be crazy. Hey, Daisy! Lemme see that beauty mask!"

But his wife, backing out of the room, hugged the package to her bosom and solemnly shook her head.

"A hell of a thing," Gusterson complained, "not even to be able to see what my stolen ideas look like."

"I got a present for you too," Fay said. "Something you might think of as a royalty on all the inventions someone thought of a little ahead of you. Fifty dollars by your own evaluation." He held out the smaller package. "Your tickler."

"My *what?*" Gusterson demanded suspiciously.

"Your tickler. The mech reminder you wanted. It turns out that the file a secretary keeps to remind her boss to do certain things at certain times is called a tickler file. So we named this a tickler. Here."

Gusterson still didn't touch the package. "You mean you actually put your invention team to work on that nonsense?"

"Well, what do you think? Don't be scared of it. Here, I'll show you."

As he unwrapped the package, Fay said, "It hasn't been decided yet whether we'll manufacture it commercially. If we do, I'll put through a voucher for you-for 'development consultation' or something like that. Sorry no royalty's possible. Davidson's squad had started to work up the identical idea three years ago, but it got shelved. I found it on a snoop through the closets. There! Looks rich, doesn't it?"

On the scarred black tabletop was a dully gleaming silvery object about the size and shape of a cupped hand with fingers merging. A tiny pellet on a short near-invisible wire led off from it. On the back was a punctured area suggesting the face of a microphone; there was also a window with a date and time in hours and minutes showing through and next to that four little buttons in a row. The concave underside of the silvery "hand" was smooth except for a central area where what looked like two little rollers came through.

"It goes on your shoulder under your shirt," Fay explained, "and you tuck the pellet in your ear. We might work up bone conduction on a commercial model. Inside is an ultra-slow fine-wire recorder holding spool that runs for a week. The clock lets you go to any place on the 7-day wire and record a message. The buttons give you variable speed in going there, so you don't waste too much time making a setting. There's a knack in fingering them efficiently, but it's easily acquired."

Fay picked up the tickler. "For instance, suppose there's a TV show you want to catch tomorrow night at twenty-two hundred." He touched the buttons. There was the faintest whirring.

The clock face blurred briefly three times before showing the setting he'd mentioned. Then Fay spoke into the punctured area: "Turn on TV Channel Two, you big dummy!" He grinned over at Gusterson. "When you've got all your instructions to yourself loaded in, you synchronize with the present moment and let her roll. Fit it on your shoulder and forget it. Oh, yes, and it literally does tickle you every time it delivers an instruction. That's what the little rollers are for. Believe me, you can't ignore it. Come on, Gussy, take off your shirt and try it out. We'll feed in some instructions for the next ten minutes so you get the feel of how it works."

"I don't want to," Gusterson said. "Not right now. I want to sniff around it first. My God, it's small! Besides everything else it does, does it think?"

"Don't pretend to be an idiot, Gussy! You know very well that even with ultra-sub-micro nothing quite this small can possibly have enough elements to do any thinking."

Gusterson shrugged. "I don't know about that. I think bugs think."

Fay groaned faintly. "Bugs operate by instinct, Gussy," he said. "A patterned routine. They do not scan situations and consequences and then make decisions."

"I don't expect bugs to make decisions," Gusterson said. "For that matter I don't like people who go around alla time making decisions."

"Well, you can take it from me, Gussy, that this tickler is just a miniaturized wire recorder and clock...and a tickler. It doesn't do anything else."

"Not yet, maybe," Gusterson said darkly. "Not this model. Fay, I'm serious about bugs thinking. Or if they don't exactly think, they feel. They've got an interior drama. An inner glow. They're conscious. For that matter, Fay, I think all your really complex electronic computers are conscious too."

"Quit kidding, Gussy."

"Who's kidding?"

"You are. Computers simply aren't alive."

"What's alive? A word. I think computers are conscious, at least while they're operating. They've got that inner glow of awareness. They sort of...well...meditate."

"Gussy, computers haven't got any circuits for meditating. They're not programmed for mystical lucubrations. They've just got circuits for solving the problems they're on."

"Okay, you admit they've got problem-solving circuits-like a man has. I say if they've got the equipment for being conscious, they're conscious. What has wings, flies."

"Including stuffed owls and gilt eagles and dodoes-and wood-burning airplanes?"

"Maybe, under some circumstances. There *was* a wood-burning airplane. Fay," Gusterson continued, wagging his wrists for emphasis, "I really think computers are conscious. They just don't have any way of telling us that they are. Or maybe they don't have any *reason* to tell us, like the little Scotch boy who didn't say a word until he was fifteen and was supposed to be deaf and dumb."

"Why didn't he say a word?"

"Because he'd never had anything to say. Or take those Hindu fakirs, Fay, who sit still and don't say a word for thirty years or until their fingernails grow to the next village. If Hindu fakirs can do that, computers can!"

Looking as if he were masticating a lemon, Fay asked quietly, "Gussy, did you say you're working on an insanity novel?"

Gusterson frowned fiercely. "Now you're kidding," he accused Fay. "The dirty kind of kidding, too."

"I'm sorry," Fay said with light contrition. "Well, now you've sniffed at it, how about trying on Tickler?" He picked up the gleaming blunted crescent and jogged it temptingly under Gusterson's chin.

"Why should I?" Gusterson asked, stepping back. "Fay, I'm up to my ears writing a book. The last thing I want is something interrupting me to make me listen to a lot of junk and do a lot of useless things."

"But, dammit, Gussy! It was all your idea in the first place!" Fay blatted. Then, catching himself, he added, "I mean, you were one of the first people to think of this particular sort of instrument."

"Maybe so, but I've done some more thinking since then." Gusterson's voice grew a trifle solemn. "Inner-directed worthwhile thinkin'. Fay, when a man forgets to do something, it's because he really doesn't want to do it or because he's all roiled up down in his unconscious. He ought to take it as a danger signal and investigate the roiling, not hire himself a human or mech reminder."

"Bushwa," Fay retorted. "In that case you shouldn't write memorandums or even take notes."

"Maybe I shouldn't," Gusterson agreed lamely. "I'd have to think that over too."

"Ha!" Fay jeered. "No, I'll tell you what your trouble is, Gussy. You're simply scared of this contraption. You've loaded your skull with horror-story nonsense about machines sprouting minds and taking over the world-until you're even scared of a simple miniaturized and clocked recorder." He thrust it out.

"Maybe I am," Gusterson admitted, controlling a flinch. "Honestly, Fay, that thing's got a gleam in its eye as if it had ideas of its own. Nasty ideas."

"Gussy, you nut, it hasn't *got* an eye."

"Not now, no, but it's got the gleam-the eye may come. It's the Cheshire cat in reverse. If you'd step over here and look at yourself holding it, you could see what I mean. But I don't think computers *sprout* minds, Fay. I just think they've *got* minds, because they've got the mind elements."

"Ho, ho!" Fay mocked. "Everything that has a material side has a mental side," he chanted. "Everything that's a body is also a spirit. Gussy, that dubious old metaphysical dualism went out centuries ago."

"Maybe so," Gusterson said, "but we still haven't anything but that dubious dualism to explain the human mind, have we? It's a jelly of nerve cells and it's a vision of the cosmos. If that isn't dualism, what is?"

"I give up. Gussy, are you going to try out this tickler?"

"No!"

"But dammit, Gussy, we made it just for you! —practically."

"Sorry, but I'm not coming near the thing."

"Zen come near me," a husky voice intoned behind them. "Tonight I vant a man."

Standing in the door was something slim in a short silver sheath. It had golden bangs and the haughtiest snub-nosed face in the world. It slunk toward them.

"My God, Vina Vidarsson!" Gusterson yelled.

"Daisy, that's terrific," Fay applauded, going up to her.

She bumped him aside with a swing of her hips, continuing to advance. "Not you, Ratty," she said throatily. "I vant a real man."

"Fay, I suggested Vina Vidarsson's face for the beauty mask," Gusterson said, walking around his wife and shaking a finger. "Don't tell me Trix just happened to think of that too."

"What else could they think of?" Fay laughed. "This season sex means VV and nobody else." An odd little grin flicked his lips, a tic traveled up his face and his body twitched slightly. "Say, folks, I'm going to have to be leaving. It's exactly fifteen minutes to Second Curfew. Last time I had to run and I got heartburn. When *are* you people going to move downstairs? I'll leave Tickler, Gussy. Play around with it and get used to it. 'By now."

"Hey, Fay," Gusterson called curiously, "have you developed absolute time sense?"

Fay grinned a big grin from the doorway-almost too big a grin for so small a man. "I didn't need to," he said softly, patting his right shoulder. "My tickler told me."

He closed the door behind him.

As side-by-side they watched him strut sedately across the murky chilly-looking park, Gusterson mused, "So the little devil had one of those nonsense-gadgets on all the time and I never noticed. Can you beat that?" Something drew across the violet-tinged stars a short bright line that quickly faded. "What's that?" Gusterson asked gloomily. "Next to last stage of missile-here?"

"Won't you settle for an old-fashioned shooting star?" Daisy asked softly. The (wettable) velvet lips of the mask made even her natural voice sound different. She reached a hand back of her neck to pull the thing off.

"Hey, don't do that," Gusterson protested in a hurt voice. "Not for a while anyway."

"Hokay!" she said harshly, turning on him. "Zen down on your knees, dog!"

# III

It was a fortnight and Gusterson was loping down the home stretch on his 40,000-word insanity novel before Fay dropped in again, this time promptly at high noon.

Normally Fay cringed his shoulders a trifle and was inclined to slither, but now he strode aggressively, his legs scissoring in a fast, low goosestep. He whipped off the sunglasses that all moles wore topside by day and began to pound Gusterson on the back while calling boisterously, "How are you, Gussy Old Boy, Old Boy?"

Daisy came in from the kitchen to see why Gusterson was choking. She was instantly grabbed and violently bussed to the accompaniment of, "Hiya, Gorgeous! Yum-yum! How about ad-libbing that some weekend?"

She stared at Fay dazedly, rasping the back of her hand across her mouth, while Gusterson yelled, "Quit that! What's got into you, Fay? Have they transferred you out of R & D to Company Morale? Do they line up all the secretaries at roll call and make you give them an eight-hour energizing kiss?"

"Ha, wouldn't you like to know?" Fay retorted. He grinned, twitched jumpingly, held still a moment, then hustled over to the far wall. "Look out there," he rapped, pointing through the violet glass at a gap between the two nearest old skyscraper apartments. "In thirty seconds you'll see them test the new needle bomb at the other end of Lake Erie. It's educational." He began to count off seconds, vigorously semaphoring his arm. "...Two...three...Gussy, I've put through a voucher for two yards for you. Budgeting squawked, but I pressured 'em."

Daisy squealed, "Yards! —are those dollar thousands?" while Gusterson was asking, "Then you're marketing the tickler?"

"Yes. Yes," Fay replied to them in turn. "...Nine...ten..." Again he grinned and twitched. "Time for noon Com-staff," he announced staccato. "Pardon the hush box." He whipped a pancake phone from under his coat, clapped it over his face and spoke fiercely but inaudibly into it, continuing to semaphore. Suddenly he thrust the phone away. "Twenty-nine...thirty... Thar she blows!"

An incandescent streak shot up the sky from a little above the far horizon and a doubly dazzling point of light appeared just above the top of it, with the effect of God dotting an "i".

"Ha, that'll skewer espionage satellites like swatting flies!" Fay proclaimed as the portent faded. "Bracing! Gussy, where's your tickler? I've got a new spool for it that'll razzle-dazzle you."

"I'll bet," Gusterson said drily. "Daisy?"

"You gave it to the kids and they got to fooling with it and broke it."

"No matter," Fay told them with a large sidewise sweep of his hand. "Better you wait for the new model. It's a six-way improvement."

"So I gather," Gusterson said, eyeing him speculatively. "Does it automatically inject you with cocaine? A fix every hour on the second?"

"Ha-ha, joke. Gussy, it achieves the same effect without using any dope at all. Listen: a tickler reminds you of your duties and opportunities-your chances for happiness and success! What's the obvious next step?"

"Throw it out the window. By the way, how do you do that when you're underground?"

"We have hi-speed garbage boosts. The obvious next step is you give the tickler a heart. It not only tells you, it warmly persuades you. It doesn't just say, 'Turn on the TV Channel Two, Joyce program,' it *brills* at you, 'Kid, Old Kid, race for the TV and flip that Two Switch! There's a great show coming through the pipes this second plus ten-you'll enjoy the hell out of yourself! Grab a ticket to ecstasy!'"

"My God," Gusterson gasped, "are those the kind of jolts it's giving you now?"

"Don't you get it, Gussy? You never load your tickler except when you're feeling buoyantly enthusiastic. You don't just tell yourself what to do hour by hour next week, you sell yourself on it. That way you not only make doubly sure you'll obey instructions but you constantly reinoculate yourself with your own enthusiasm."

"I can't stand myself when I'm that enthusiastic," Gusterson said. "I feel ashamed for hours afterwards."

"You're warped-all this lonely sky-life. What's more, Gussy, think how still more persuasive some of those instructions would be if they came to a man in his best girl's most bedroomy voice, or his doctor's or psycher's if it's that sort of thing-or Vina Vidarsson's! By the way, Daze, don't wear that beauty mask outside. It's a grand misdemeanor ever since ten thousand teen-agers rioted through Tunnel-Mart wearing them. And VV's sueing Trix."

"No chance of that," Daisy said. "Gusterson got excited and bit off the nose." She pinched her own delicately.

"I'd no more obey my enthusiastic self," Gusterson was brooding, "than I'd obey a Napoleon drunk on his own brandy or a hopped-up St. Francis. Reinoculated with my own enthusiasm? I'd die just like from snake-bite!"

"Warped, I said," Fay dogmatized, stamping around. "Gussy, having the instructions persuasive instead of neutral turned out to be only the opening wedge. The next step wasn't so obvious, but I saw it. Using subliminal verbal stimuli in his tickler, a man can be given constant supportive euphoric therapy 24 hours a day! And it makes use of all that empty wire. We've revived the ideas of a pioneer dynamic psycher named Dr. Coué. For instance, right now my tickler is saying to me-in tones too soft to reach my conscious mind, but do they stab into the unconscious! —'Day by day in every way I'm getting sharper and sharper.' It alternates that with 'gutsier and gutsier' and...well, forget that. Coué mostly used 'better and better' but that seems too general. And every hundredth time it says them out loud and the tickler gives me a brush-just a faint cootch-to make sure I'm keeping in touch."

"That third word-pair," Daisy wondered, feeling her mouth reminiscently. "Could I guess?"

Gusterson's eyes had been growing wider and wider. "Fay," he said, "I could no more use my mind for anything if I knew all that was going on in my inner ear than if I were being brushed down with brooms by three witches. Look here," he said with loud authority, "you got to stop all this-it's crazy. Fay, if Micro'll junk the tickler, I'll think you up something else to invent-something real good."

"Your inventing days are over," Fay brilled gleefully. "I mean, you'll never equal your masterpiece."

"How about," Gusterson bellowed, "an anti-individual guided missile? The physicists have got small-scale antigravity good enough to float and fly something the size of a hand grenade. I can smell that even though it's a back-of-the-safe military secret. Well, how about keying such a missile to a man's finger-prints —or brainwaves, maybe, or his unique smell! —so it can spot and follow him around then target in on him, without harming anyone else? Long-distance assassination-and the stinkingest gets it! Or you could simply load it with some disgusting goo and key it to teen-agers as a group-that'd take care of them. Fay, doesn't it give you a rich warm kick to think of my midget missiles buzzing around in your tunnels, seeking out evil-doers, like a swarm of angry wasps or angelic bumblebees?"

"You're not luring me down any side trails," Fay said laughingly. He grinned and twitched, then hurried toward the opposite wall, motioning them to follow. Outside, about a hundred yards beyond the purple glass, rose another ancient glass-walled apartment skyscraper. Beyond, Lake Erie rippled glintingly.

"Another bomb-test?" Gusterson asked.

Fay pointed at the building. "Tomorrow," he announced, "a modern factory, devoted solely to the manufacture of ticklers, will be erected on that site."

"You mean one of those windowless phallic eyesores?" Gusterson demanded. "Fay, you people aren't even consistent. You've got all your homes underground. Why not your factories?"

"Sh! Not enough room. And night missiles are scarier."

"I know that building's been empty for a year," Daisy said uneasily, "but how —?"

"Sh! Watch! *Now!*"

The looming building seemed to blur or fuzz for a moment. Then it was as if the lake's bright ripples had invaded the old glass a hundred yards away. Wavelets chased themselves up and down the gleaming walls, became higher, higher...and then suddenly the glass cracked all over to tiny fragments and fell away, to be followed quickly by fragmented concrete and plastic and plastic piping, until all that was left was the nude steel framework, vibrating so rapidly as to be almost invisible against the gleaming lake.

Daisy covered her ears, but there was no explosion, only a long-drawn-out low crash as the fragments hit twenty floors below and dust whooshed out sideways.

"Spectacular!" Fay summed up. "Knew you'd enjoy it. That little trick was first conceived by the great Tesla during his last fruity years. Research discovered it in his biog-we just made the dream come true. A tiny resonance device you could carry in your belt-bag attunes itself to the natural harmonic of a structure and then increases amplitude by tiny pushes exactly in time. Just like soldiers marching in step can break down a bridge, only this is as if it were being done by one marching ant." He pointed at the naked framework appearing out of its own blur and said, "We'll be able to hang the factory on that. If not, we'll whip a mega-current through it and vaporize it. No question the micro-resonator is the neatest sweetest wrecking device going. You can expect a lot more of this sort of efficiency now that mankind has the tickler to enable him to use his full potential. What's the matter, folks?"

Daisy was staring around the violet-walled room with dumb mistrust. Her hands were trembling.

"You don't have to worry," Fay assured her with an understanding laugh. "This building's safe for a month more at least." Suddenly he grimaced and leaped a foot in the air. He raised a clawed hand to scratch his shoulder but managed to check the movement. "Got to beat it, folks," he announced tersely. "My tickler gave me the grand cootch."

"Don't go yet," Gusterson called, rousing himself with a shudder which he immediately explained: "I just had the illusion that if I shook myself all my flesh and guts would fall off my shimmying skeleton, Brr! Fay, before you and Micro go off half cocked, I want you to know there's one insuperable objection to the tickler as a mass-market item. The average man or woman won't go to the considerable time and trouble it must take to load a tickler. He simply hasn't got the compulsive orderliness and willingness to plan that it requires."

"We thought of that weeks ago," Fay rapped, his hand on the door. "Every tickler spool that goes to market is patterned like wallpaper with one of five designs of suitable subliminal supportive euphoric material. 'Ittier and ittier,' 'viriler and viriler' —you know. The buyer is robot-interviewed for an hour, his personalized daily routine laid out and thereafter templated on his weekly spool. He's strongly urged next to take his tickler to his doctor and psycher for further instruction-imposition. We've been working with the medical profession from the start. They love the tickler because it'll remind people to take their medicine on the dot...and rest and eat and go to sleep just when and how doc says. This is a big operation, Gussy —a biiiiiig operation! 'By!"

Daisy hurried to the wall to watch him cross the park. Deep down she was a wee bit worried that he might linger to attach a micro-resonator to *this* building and she wanted to time him. But Gusterson settled down to his typewriter and began to bat away.

"I want to have another novel started," he explained to her, "before the ant marches across this building in about four and a half weeks...or a million sharp little gutsy guys come swarming out of the ground and heave it into Lake Erie."

Early next morning windowless walls began to crawl up the stripped skyscraper between them and the lake. Daisy pulled the black-out curtains on that side. For a day or two longer their thoughts and conversations were haunted by Gusterson's vague sardonic visions of a horde of tickler-energized moles pouring up out of the tunnels to tear down the remaining trees, tank the atmosphere and perhaps somehow dismantle the stars-at least on this side of the world-but then they both settled back into their customary easy-going routines. Gusterson typed. Daisy made her daily shopping trip to a little topside daytime store and started painting a mural on the floor of the empty apartment next theirs but one.

"We ought to lasso some neighbors," she suggested once. "I need somebody to hold my brushes and admire. How about you making a trip below at the cocktail hours, Gusterson, and picking up a couple of girls for a starter? Flash the old viriler charm, cootch them up a bit, emphasize the delights of high living, but make sure they're compatible roommates. You could pick up that two-yard check from Micro at the same time."

"You're an immoral money-ravenous wench," Gusterson said absently, trying to dream of an insanity beyond insanity that would make his next novel a real id-rousing best-vender.

"If that's your vision of me, you shouldn't have chewed up the VV mask."

"I'd really prefer you with green stripes," he told her. "But stripes, spots, or sun-bathing, you're better than those cocktail moles."

Actually both of them acutely disliked going below. They much preferred to perch in their eyrie and watch the people of Cleveland Depths, as they privately called the local sub-suburb, rush up out of the shelters at dawn to work in the concrete fields and windowless factories, make their daytime jet trips and freeway jaunts, do their noon-hour and coffee-break guerrilla practice, and then go scurrying back at twilight to the atomic-proof, brightly lit, vastly exciting, claustrophobic caves.

Fay and his projects began once more to seem dreamlike, though Gusterson did run across a cryptic advertisement for ticklers in *The Manchester Guardian*, which he got daily by facsimile. Their three children reported similar ads, of no interest to young fry, on the TV and one afternoon they came home with the startling news that the monitors at their subsurface school had been issued ticklers. On sharp interrogation by Gusterson, however, it appeared that these last were not ticklers but merely two-way radios linked to the school police station transmitter.

"Which is bad enough," Gusterson commented later to Daisy. "But it'd be even dirtier to think of those clock-watching superegos being strapped to kids' shoulders. Can you imagine Huck Finn with a tickler, tellin' him when to tie up the raft to a tow-head and when to take a swim?"

"I bet Fay could," Daisy countered. "When's he going to bring you that check, anyhow? Iago wants a jetcycle and I promised Imogene a Vina Kit and then Claudius'll have to have something."

Gusterson scowled thoughtfully. "You know, Daze," he said, "I got a feeling Fay's in the hospital, all narcotized up and being fed intravenously. The way he was jumping around last time, that tickler was going to cootch him to pieces in a week."

As if to refute this intuition, Fay turned up that very evening. The lights were dim. Something had gone wrong with the building's old transformer and, pending repairs, the two remaining occupied apartments were making do with batteries, which turned bright globes to mysterious amber candles and made Gusterson's ancient typewriter operate sluggishly.

Fay's manner was subdued or at least closely controlled and for a moment Gusterson thought he'd shed his tickler. Then the little man came out of the shadows and Gusterson saw the large bulge on his right shoulder.

"Yes, we had to up it a bit sizewise," Fay explained in clipped tones. "Additional super-features. While brilliantly successful on the whole, the subliminal euphorics were a shade too effective. Several hundred users went hoppity manic. We gentled the cootch and qualified the subliminals-you know, 'Day by day in every way I'm getting sharper *and more serene'* —but a stabilizing influence was still needed, so after a top-level conference we decided to combine Tickler with Moodmaster."

"My God," Gusterson interjected, "do they have a machine now that does that?"

"Of course. They've been using them on ex-mental patients for years."

"I just don't keep up with progress," Gusterson said, shaking his head bleakly. "I'm falling behind on all fronts."

"You ought to have your tickler remind you to read Science Service releases," Fay told him. "Or simply instruct it to scan the releases and-no, that's still in research." He looked at Guster-son's shoulder and his eyes widened. "You're not wearing the new-model tickler I sent you," he said accusingly.

"I never got it," Gusterson assured him. "Postmen deliver top-side mail and parcels by throwing them on the high-speed garbage boosts and hoping a tornado will blow them to the right addresses." Then he added helpfully, "Maybe the Russians stole it while it was riding the whirl-winds."

"That's not a suitable topic for jesting," Fay frowned. "We're hoping that Tickler will mobilize the full potential of the Free World for the first time in history. Gusterson, you are going to have to wear a ticky-tick. It's becoming impossible for a man to get through modern life without one."

"Maybe I will," Gusterson said appeasingly, "but right now tell me about Moodmaster. I want to put it in my new insanity novel."

Fay shook his head. "Your readers will just think you're behind the times. If you use it, under-play it. But anyhow, Moodmaster is a simple physiotherapy engine that monitors bloodstream chemicals and body electricity. It ties directly into the bloodstream, keeping blood, sugar, et cetera, at optimum levels and injecting euphrin or depressin as necessary-and occasionally a touch of extra adrenaline, as during work emergencies."

"Is it painful?" Daisy called from the bedroom.

"Excruciating," Gusterson called back. "Excuse it, please," he grinned at Fay. "Hey, didn't I suggest cocaine injections last time I saw you?"

"So you did," Fay agreed flatly. "Oh by the way, Gussy, here's that check for a yard I promised you. Micro doesn't muzzle the ox."

"Hooray!" Daisy cheered faintly.

"I thought you said it was going to be for two." Gusterson complained.

"Budgeting always forces a last-minute compromise," Fay shrugged. "You have to learn to accept those things."

"I love accepting money and I'm glad any time for three feet," Daisy called agreeably. "Six feet might make me wonder if I weren't an insect, but getting a yard just makes me feel like a gangster's moll."

"Want to come out and gloat over the yard paper, Toots, and stuff it in your diamond-embroidered net stocking top?" Gusterson called back.

"No, I'm doing something to that portion of me just now. But hang onto the yard, Guster-son."

"Aye-aye, Cap'n," he assured her. Then, turning back to Fay, "So you've taken the Dr. Coué repeating out of the tickler?"

"Oh, no. Just balanced it off with depressin. The subliminals are still a prime sales-point. All the tickler features are cumulative, Gussy. You're still underestimating the scope of the device."

"I guess I am. What's this 'work-emergencies' business? If you're using the tickler to inject drugs into workers to keep them going, that's really just my cocaine suggestion modernized and I'm putting in for another thou. Hundreds of years ago the South American Indians chewed coca leaves to kill fatigue sensations."

"That so? Interesting-and it proves priority for the Indians, doesn't it? I'll make a try for you, Gussy, but don't expect anything." He cleared his throat, his eyes grew distant and, turning his head a little to the right, he enunciated sharply, "Pooh-Bah. Time: Inst oh five. One oh five seven. Oh oh. Record: Gussy coca thou budget. Cut." He explained, "We got a voice-cued setter now on the deluxe models. You can record a memo to yourself without taking off your shirt. Incidentally, I use the ends of the hours for trifle-memos. I've already used up the fifty-nines and eights for tomorrow and started on the fifty-sevens."

"I understood most of your memo," Gusterson told him gruffly. "The last 'Oh oh' was for seconds, wasn't it? Now I call that crude-why not microseconds too? But how do you remember where you've made a memo so you don't rerecord over it? After all, you're rerecording over the wallpaper all the time."

"Tickler beeps and then hunts for the nearest information-free space."

"I see. And what's the Pooh-Bah for?"

Fay smiled. "Cut. My password for activating the setter, so it won't respond to chance numerals it overhears."

"But why Pooh-Bah?"

Fay grinned. "Cut. And you a writer. It's a literary reference, Gussy. Pooh-Bah (cut!) was Lord High Everything Else in *The Mikado*. He had a little list and nothing on it would ever be missed."

"Oh, yeah," Gusterson remembered, glowering. "As I recall it, all that went on that list was the names of people who were slated to have their heads chopped off by Ko-Ko. Better watch your step, Shorty. It may be a back-handed omen. Maybe all those workers you're puttin' ticklers on to pump them full of adrenaline so they'll overwork without noticin' it will revolt and come out some day choppin' for your head."

"Spare me the Marxist mythology," Fay protested. "Gussy, you've got a completely wrong slant on Tickler. It's true that most of our mass sales so far, bar government and army, have been to large companies purchasing for their employees —"

"Ah-ha!"

" —but that's because there's nothing like a tickler for teaching a new man his job. It tells him from instant to instant what he must do-while he's already on the job and without disturbing other workers. Magnetizing a wire with a job pattern is the easiest thing going. And you'd be astonished what the subliminals do for employee morale. It's this way, Gussy: most people are too improvident and unimaginative to see in advance the advantages of ticklers. They buy one because the company strongly suggests it and payment is on easy installments withheld from salary. They find a tickler makes the work day go easier. The little fellow perched on your shoulder is a friend exuding comfort and good advice. The first thing he's set to say is 'Take it easy, pal.'

"Within a week they're wearing their tickler 24 hours a day-and buying a tickler for the wife, so she'll remember to comb her hair and smile real pretty and cook favorite dishes."

"I get it, Fay," Gusterson cut in. "The tickler is the newest fad for increasing worker efficiency. Once, I read somewheres, it was salt tablets. They had salt-tablet dispensers everywhere, even in air-conditioned offices where there wasn't a moist armpit twice a year and the gals sweat only champagne. A decade later people wondered what all those dusty white pills were for. Sometimes they were mistook for tranquilizers. It'll be the same way with ticklers. Somebody'll open a musty closet and see jumbled heaps of these gripping-hand silvery gadgets gathering dust curls and —"

"They will not!" Fay protested vehemently. "Ticklers are not a fad-they're history-changers, they're Free-World revolutionary! Why, before Micro Systems put a single one on the market, we'd made it a rule that every Micro employee had to wear one! If that's not having supreme confidence in a product —"

"Every employee except the top executives, of course," Gusterson interrupted jeeringly. "And that's not demoting you, Fay. As the R & D chief most closely involved, you'd naturally have to show special enthusiasm."

"But you're wrong there, Gussy," Fay crowed. "Man for man, our top executives have been more enthusiastic about their personal ticklers than any other class of worker in the whole outfit."

Gusterson slumped and shook his head. "If that's the case," he said darkly, "maybe mankind deserves the tickler."

"I'll say it does!" Fay agreed loudly without thinking. Then, "Oh, can the carping, Gussy. Tickler's a great invention. Don't deprecate it just because you had something to do with its genesis. You're going to have to get in the swim and wear one."

"Maybe I'd rather drown horribly."

"Can the gloom-talk too! Gussy, I said it before and I say it again, you're just scared of this new thing. Why, you've even got the drapes pulled so you won't have to look at the tickler factory."

"Yes, I am scared," Gusterson said. "Really sca...AWP!"

Fay whirled around. Daisy was standing in the bedroom doorway, wearing the short silver sheath. This time there was no mask, but her bobbed hair was glitteringly silvered, while her legs, arms, hands, neck, face-every bit of her exposed skin-was painted with beautifully even vertical green stripes.

"I did it as a surprise for Gusterson," she explained to Fay. "He says he likes me this way. The green glop's supposed to be smudgeproof."

Gusterson did not comment. His face had a rapt expression. "I'll tell you why your tickler's so popular, Fay," he said softly. "It's not because it backstops the memory or because it boosts the ego with subliminals. It's because it takes the hook out of a guy, it takes over the job of withstanding the pressure of living. See, Fay, here are all these little guys in this subterranean rat race with atomic-death squares and chromium-plated reward squares and enough money if you pass Go almost to get to Go again-and a million million rules of the game to keep in mind. Well, here's this one little guy and every morning he wakes up there's all these things he's got to keep in mind to do or he'll lose his turn three times in a row and maybe a terrible black rook in iron armor'll loom up and bang him off the chessboard. But now, look, now he's got his tickler and he tells his sweet silver tickler all these things and the tickler's got to remember them. Of course he'll have to do them eventually but meanwhile the pressure's off him, the hook's out of his short hairs. He's shifted the responsibility...."

"Well, what's so bad about that?" Fay broke in loudly. "What's wrong with taking the pressure off little guys? Why shouldn't Tickler be a super-ego surrogate? Micro's Motivations chief noticed that positive feature straight off and scored it three pluses. Besides, it's nothing but a gaudy way of saying that Tickler backstops the memory. Seriously, Gussy, what's so bad about it?"

"I don't know," Gusterson said slowly, his eyes still far away. "I just know it feels bad to me." He crinkled his big forehead. "Well for one thing," he said, "it means that a man's taking orders from something else. He's got a kind of master. He's sinking back into a slave psychology."

"He's only taking orders from himself," Fay countered disgustedly. "Tickler's just a mech reminder, a notebook, in essence no more than the back of an old envelope. It's no master."

"Are you absolutely sure of that?" Gusterson asked quietly.

"Why, Gussy, you big oaf—" Fay began heatedly. Suddenly his features quirked and he twitched. "'Scuse me, folks," he said rapidly, heading for the door, "but my tickler told me I gotta go."

"Hey Fay, don't you mean you told your tickler to tell you when it was time to go?" Gusterson called after him.

Fay looked back in the doorway. He wet his lips, his eyes moved from side to side. "I'm not quite sure," he said in an odd strained voice and darted out.

Gusterson stared for some seconds at the pattern of emptiness Fay had left. Then he shivered. Then he shrugged. "I must be slipping," he muttered. "I never even suggested something for him to invent." Then he looked around at Daisy, who was still standing poker-faced in her doorway.

"Hey, you look like something out of the Arabian Nights," he told her. "Are you supposed to be anything special? How far do those stripes go, anyway?"

"You could probably find out," she told him coolly. "All you have to do is kill me a dragon or two first."

He studied her. "My God," he said reverently, "I really have all the fun in life. What do I do to deserve this?"

"You've got a big gun," she told him, "and you go out in the world with it and hold up big companies and take yards and yards of money away from them in rolls like ribbon and bring it all home to me."

"Don't say that about the gun again," he said. "Don't whisper it, don't even think it. I've got one, dammit-thirty-eight caliber, yet-and I don't want some psionic monitor with two-way clairaudience they haven't told me about catching the whisper and coming to take the gun away from us. It's one of the few individuality symbols we've got left."

Suddenly Daisy whirled away from the door, spun three times so that her silvered hair stood out like a metal coolie hat, and sank to a curtsey in the middle of the room.

"I've just thought of what I am," she announced, fluttering her eyelashes at him. "I'm a sweet silver tickler with green stripes."

# V

Next day Daisy cashed the Micro check for ten hundred silver smackers, which she hid in a broken radionic coffee urn. Gusterson sold his insanity novel and started a new one about a mad medic with a hiccupy hysterical chuckle, who gimmicked Moodmasters to turn mental patients into nymphomaniacs, mass murderers and compulsive saints. But this time he couldn't get Fay out of his mind, or the last chilling words the nervous little man had spoken.

For that matter, he couldn't blank the underground out of his mind as effectively as usually. He had the feeling that a new kind of mole was loose in the burrows and that the ground at the foot of their skyscraper might start humping up any minute.

Toward the end of one afternoon he tucked a half dozen newly typed sheets in his pocket, shrouded his typer, went to the hatrack and took down his prize: a miner's hard-top cap with electric headlamp.

"Goin' below, Cap'n," he shouted toward the kitchen.

"Be back for second dog watch," Daisy replied. "Remember what I told you about lassoing me some art-conscious girl neighbors."

"Only if I meet a piebald one with a taste for Scotch-or maybe a pearl gray biped jaguar with violet spots," Gusterson told her, clapping on the cap with a We-Who-Are-About-To-Die gesture.

Halfway across the park to the escalator bunker Gusterson's heart began to tick. He resolutely switched on his headlamp.

As he'd known it would, the hatch robot whirred an extra and higher-pitched ten seconds when it came to his topside address, but it ultimately dilated the hatch for him, first handing him a claim check for his ID card.

Gusterson's heart was ticking like a sledgehammer by now. He hopped clumsily onto the escalator, clutched the moving guard rail to either side, then shut his eyes as the steps went over the edge and became what felt like vertical. An instant later he forced his eyes open, unclipped a hand from the rail and touched the second switch beside his headlamp, which instantly began to blink whitely, as if he were a civilian plane flying into a nest of military jobs.

With a further effort he kept his eyes open and flinchingly surveyed the scene around him. After zigging through a bombproof half-furlong of roof, he was dropping into a large twilit cave. The blue-black ceiling twinkled with stars. The walls were pierced at floor level by a dozen archways with busy niche stores and glowing advertisements crowded between them. From the archways some three dozen slidewalks curved out, tangenting off each other in a bewildering multiple cloverleaf. The slidewalks were packed with people, traveling motionless like purposeful statues or pivoting with practiced grace from one slidewalk to another, like a thousand toreros doing veronicas.

The slidewalks were moving faster than he recalled from his last venture underground and at the same time the whole pedestrian concourse was quieter than he remembered. It was as if the five thousand or so moles in view were all listening-for what? But there was something else that had changed about them —a change that he couldn't for a moment define, or unconsciously didn't want to. Clothing style? No...My God, they weren't all wearing identical monster masks? No...Hair color?...Well....

He was studying them so intently that he forgot his escalator was landing. He came off it with a heel-jarring stumble and bumped into a knot of four men on the tiny triangular hold-still. These four at least sported a new style-wrinkle: ribbed gray shoulder-capes that made them look as if their heads were poking up out of the center of bulgy umbrellas or giant mushrooms.

One of them grabbed hold of Gusterson and saved him from staggering onto a slidewalk that might have carried him to Toledo.

"Gussy, you dog, you must have esped I wanted to see you," Fay cried, patting him on the elbows. "Meet Davidson and Kester and Hazen, colleagues of mine. We're all Micro-men." Fay's companions were staring strangely at Gusterson's blinking headlamp. Fay explained rapidly, "Mr. Gusterson is an insanity novelist. You know, I-D."

"Inner-directed spells *id*," Gusterson said absently, still staring at the interweaving crowd beyond them, trying to figure out what made them different from last trip. "Creativity fuel. Cranky. Explodes through the parietal fissure if you look at it cross-eyed."

"Ha-ha," Fay laughed. "Well, boys, I've found my man. How's the new novel perking, Gussy?"

"Got my climax, I think," Gusterson mumbled, still peering puzzledly around Fay at the slide-standers. "Moodmaster's going to come alive. Ever occur to you that 'mood' is 'doom' spelled backwards? And then...." He let his voice trail off as he realized that Kester and Davidson and Hazen had made their farewells and were sliding into the distance. He reminded himself wryly that nobody ever wants to hear an author talk-he's much too good a listener to be wasted that way. Let's see, was it that everybody in the crowd had the same facial expression...? Or showed symptoms of the same disease...?

"I was coming to visit you, but now you can pay me a call," Fay was saying. "There are two matters I want to —"

Gusterson stiffened. "My God, *they're all hunchbacked*!" he yelled.

"Shh! Of course they are," Fay whispered reprovingly. "They're all wearing their ticklers. But you don't need to be insulting about it."

"*I'm gettin' out o' here.*" Gusterson turned to flee as if from five thousand Richard the Thirds.

"Oh no you're not," Fay amended, drawing him back with one hand. Somehow, underground, the little man seemed to carry more weight. "You're having cocktails in my thinking box. Be-sides, climbing a down escaladder will give you a heart attack."

In his home habitat Gusterson was about as easy to handle as a rogue rhinoceros, but away from it-and especially if underground-he became more like a pliable elephant. All his bones dropped out through his feet, as he described it to Daisy. So now he submitted miserably as Fay surveyed him up and down, switched off his blinking headlamp ("That coalminer caper is corny, Gussy.") and then-surprisingly-rapidly stuffed his belt-bag under the right shoulder of Gusterson's coat and buttoned the latter to hold it in place.

"So you won't stand out," he explained. Another swift survey. "You'll do. Come on, Gussy. I got lots to brief you on." Three rapid paces and then Gusterson's feet would have gone out from under him except that Fay gave him a mighty shove. The small man sprang onto the slidewalk after him and then they were skimming effortlessly side by side.

Gusterson felt frightened and twice as hunchbacked as the slidestanders around him-morally as well as physically.

Nevertheless he countered bravely, "I got things to brief *you* on. I got six pages of cautions on ti —"

"Shh!" Fay stopped him. "Let's use my hushbox."

He drew out his pancake phone and stretched it so that it covered both their lower faces, like a double yashmak. Gusterson, his neck pushing into the ribbed bulge of the shoulder cape so he could be cheek to cheek with Fay, felt horribly conspicuous, but then he noticed that none of the slidestanders were paying them the least attention. The reason for their abstraction occurred to him. They were listening to their ticklers! He shuddered.

"I got six pages of caution on ticklers," he repeated into the hot, moist quiet of the pancake phone. "I typed 'em so I wouldn't forget 'em in the heat of polemicking. I want you to read every word. Fay, I've had it on my mind ever since I started wondering whether it was you or your tickler made you duck out of our place last time you were there. I want you to —"

"Ha-ha! All in good time." In the pancake phone Fay's laugh was brassy. "But I'm glad you've decided to lend a hand, Gussy. This thing is moving faaaasst. Nationwise, adult underground ticklerization is 90 per cent complete."

"I don't believe that," Gusterson protested while glaring at the hunchbacks around them. The slidewalk was gliding down a low glow-ceiling tunnel lined with doors and advertisements.

Rapt-eyed people were pirouetting on and off. "A thing just can't develop that fast, Fay. It's against nature."

"Ha, but we're not in nature, we're in culture. The progress of an industrial scientific culture is geometric. It goes n-times as many jumps as it takes. More than geometric-exponential. Confidentially, Micro's Math chief tells me we're currently on a fourth-power progress curve trending into a fifth."

"You mean we're goin' so fast we got to watch out we don't bump ourselves in the rear when we come around again?" Gusterson asked, scanning the tunnel ahead for curves. "Or just shoot straight up to infinity?"

"Exactly! Of course most of the last power and a half is due to Tickler itself. Gussy, the tickler's already eliminated absenteeism, alcoholism and aboulia in numerous urban areas-and that's just one letter of the alphabet! If Tickler doesn't turn us into a nation of photo-memory constant-creative-flow geniuses in six months, I'll come live topside."

"You mean because a lot of people are standing around glassy-eyed listening to something mumbling in their ear that it's a good thing?"

"Gussy, you don't know progress when you see it. Tickler is the greatest invention since language. Bar none, it's the greatest instrument ever devised for integrating a man into all phases of his environment. Under the present routine a newly purchased tickler first goes to government and civilian defense for primary patterning, then to the purchaser's employer, then to his doctor-psycher, then to his local bunker captain, then to *him*. *Everything* that's needful for a man's welfare gets on the spools. Efficiency cubed! Incidentally, Russia's got the tickler now. Our dip-satellites have photographed it. It's like ours except the Commies wear it on the left shoulder...but they're two weeks behind us developmentwise and they'll never close the gap!"

Gusterson reared up out of the pancake phone to take a deep breath. A sulky-lipped sylph-figured girl two feet from him twitched-medium cootch, he judged-then fumbled in her belt-bag for a pill and popped it in her mouth.

"Hell, the tickler's not even efficient yet about little things," Gusterson blatted, diving back into the privacy-yashmak he was sharing with Fay. "Whyn't that girl's doctor have the Mood-master component of her tickler inject her with medicine?"

"Her doctor probably wants her to have the discipline of pill-taking —or the exercise," Fay answered glibly. "Look sharp now. Here's where we fork. I'm taking you through Micro's postern."

A ribbon of slidewalk split itself from the main band and angled off into a short alley. Guster-son hardly felt the constant-speed juncture as they crossed it. Then the secondary ribbon speeded up, carrying them at about 30 feet a second toward the blank concrete wall in which the alley ended. Gusterson prepared to jump, but Fay grabbed him with one hand and with the other held up toward the wall a badge and a button. When they were about ten feet away the wall whipped aside, then whipped shut behind them so fast that Gusterson wondered mo-mentarily if he still had his heels and the seat of his pants.

Fay, tucking away his badge and pancake phone, dropped the button in Gusterson's vest pocket. "Use it when you leave," he said casually. "That is, if you leave."

Gusterson, who was trying to read the Do and Don't posters papering the walls they were passing, started to probe that last sinister supposition, but just then the ribbon slowed, a swing-ing door opened and closed behind them and they found themselves in a luxuriously furnished thinking box measuring at least eight feet by five.

"Hey, this is something," Gusterson said appreciatively to show he wasn't an utter yokel. Then, drawing on research he'd done for period novels, "Why, it's as big as a Pullman car compartment, or a first mate's cabin in the War of 1812. You really must rate."

Fay nodded, smiled wanly and sat down with a sigh on a compact overstuffed swivel chair. He let his arms dangle and his head sink into his puffed shoulder cape. Gusterson stared at him. It was the first time he could ever recall the little man showing fatigue.

"Tickler currently does have one serious drawback," Fay volunteered. "It weighs 28 pounds. You feel it when you've been on your feet a couple of hours. No question we're going to give the next model that antigravity feature you mentioned for pursuit grenades. We'd have had it in this model except there were so many other things to be incorporated." He sighed again. "Why, the scanning and decision-making elements alone tripled the mass."

"Hey," Gusterson protested, thinking especially of the sulky-lipped girl, "do you mean to tell me all those other people were toting two stone?"

Fay shook his head heavily. "They were all wearing Mark 3 or 4. I'm wearing Mark 6," he said, as one might say, "I'm carrying the genuine Cross, not one of the balsa ones."

But then his face brightened a little and he went on. "Of course the new improved features make it more than worth it...and you hardly feel it at all at night when you're lying down...and if you remember to talcum under it twice a day, no sores develop...at least not very big ones...."

Backing away involuntarily, Gusterson felt something prod his right shoulderblade. Ripping open his coat, he convulsively plunged his hand under it and tore out Fay's belt-bag...and then set it down very gently on the top of a shallow cabinet and relaxed with the sigh of one who has escaped a great, if symbolic, danger. Then he remembered something Fay had mentioned. He straightened again.

"Hey, you said it's got scanning and decision-making elements. That means your tickler thinks, even by your fancy standards. And if it thinks, it's conscious."

"Gussy," Fay said wearily, frowning, "all sorts of things nowadays have S&DM elements. Mail sorters, missiles, robot medics, high-style mannequins, just to name some of the Ms. They 'think,' to use that archaic word, but it's neither here nor there. And they're certainly not conscious."

"Your tickler thinks," Gusterson repeated stubbornly, "just like I warned you it would. It sits on your shoulder, ridin' you like you was a pony or a starved St. Bernard, and now it thinks."

"Suppose it does?" Fay yawned. "What of it?" He gave a rapid sinuous one-sided shrug that made it look for a moment as if his left arm had three elbows. It stuck in Gusterson's mind, for he had never seen Fay use such a gesture and he wondered where he'd picked it up. Maybe imitating a double-jointed Micro Finance chief? Fay yawned again and said, "Please, Gussy, don't disturb me for a minute or so." His eyes half closed.

Gusterson studied Fay's sunken-cheeked face and the great puff of his shoulder cape.

"Say, Fay," he asked in a soft voice after about five minutes, "are you meditating?"

"Why, no," Fay responded, starting up and then stifling another yawn. "Just resting a bit. I seem to get more tired these days, somehow. You'll have to excuse me, Gussy. But what made you think of meditation?"

"Oh, I just got to wonderin' in that direction," Gusterson said. "You see, when you first started to develop Tickler, it occurred to me that there was one thing about it that might be real good even if you did give it S&DM elements. It's this: having a mech secretary to take charge of his obligations and routine in the real world might allow a man to slide into the other world, the world of thoughts and feelings and intuitions, and sort of ooze around in there and accomplish things. Know any of the people using Tickler that way, hey?"

"Of course not," Fay denied with a bright incredulous laugh. "Who'd want to loaf around in an imaginary world and take a chance of *missing out on what his tickler's doing?* —I mean, on what his tickler has in store for him-what he's *told* his tickler to have in store for him."

Ignoring Gusterson's shiver, Fay straightened up and seemed to brisken himself. "Ha, that little slump did me good. A tickler *makes* you rest, you know-it's one of the great things about it. Pooh-Bah's kinder to me than I ever was to myself." He buttoned open a tiny refrigerator and took out two waxed cardboard cubes and handed one to Gusterson. "Martini? Hope you don't mind drinking from the carton. Cheers. Now, Gussy old pal, there are two matters I want to take up with you —"

"Hold it," Gusterson said with something of his old authority. "There's something I got to get off my mind first." He pulled the typed pages out of his inside pocket and straightened them. "I told you about these," he said. "I want you to read them before you do anything else. Here."

Fay looked toward the pages and nodded, but did not take them yet. He lifted his hands to his throat and unhooked the clasp of his cape, then hesitated.

"You wear that thing to hide the hump your tickler makes?" Gusterson filled in. "You got better taste than those other moles."

"Not to hide it, exactly," Fay protested, "but just so the others won't be jealous. I wouldn't feel comfortable parading a free-scanning decision-capable Mark 6 tickler in front of people who can't buy it-until it goes on open sale at twenty-two fifteen tonight. Lot of shelterfolk won't be sleeping tonight. They'll be queued up to trade in their old tickler for a Mark 6 almost as good as Pooh-Bah."

He started to jerk his hands apart, hesitated again with an oddly apprehensive look at the big man, then whirled off the cape.

Gusterson sucked in such a big gasp that he hiccuped. The right shoulder of Fay's jacket and shirt had been cut away. Thrusting up through the neatly hemmed hole was a silvery gray hump with a one-eyed turret atop it and two multi-jointed metal arms ending in little claws.

It looked like the top half of a pseudo-science robot —a squat evil child robot, Gusterson told himself, which had lost its legs in a railway accident-and it seemed to him that a red fleck was moving around imperceptibly in the huge single eye.

"I'll take that memo now," Fay said coolly, reaching out his hand. He caught the rustling sheets as they slipped from Gusterson's fingers, evened them up very precisely by tapping them on his knee... and then handed them over his shoulder to his tickler, which clicked its claws around either margin and then began rather swiftly to lift the top sheet past its single eye at a distance of about six inches.

"The first matter I want to take up with you, Gussy," Fay began, paying no attention whatsoever to the little scene on his shoulder, " —or warn you about, rather-is the imminent ticklerization of schoolchildren, geriatrics, convicts and topsiders. At three zero zero tomorrow ticklers become mandatory for all adult shelterfolk. The mop-up operations won't be long in coming-in fact, these days we find that the square root of the estimated time of a new development is generally the best time estimate. Gussy, I strongly advise you to start wearing a tickler now. And Daisy and your moppets. If you heed my advice, your kids will have the jump on your class. Transition and conditioning are easy, since Tickler itself sees to it."

Pooh-Bah leafed the first page to the back of the packet and began lifting the second past his eye —a little more swiftly than the first.

"I've got a Mark 6 tickler all warmed up for you," Fay pressed, "*and* a shoulder cape. You won't feel one bit conspicuous." He noticed the direction of Gusterson's gaze and remarked, "Fascinating mechanism, isn't it? Of course 28 pounds are a bit oppressive, but then you have to remember it's only a way-station to free-floating Mark 7 or 8."

Pooh-Bah finished page two and began to race through page three.

"But I wanted *you* to read it," Gusterson said bemusedly, staring.

"Pooh-Bah will do a better job than I could," Fay assured him. "Get the gist without losing the chaff."

"But dammit, it's all about *him*," Gusterson said a little more strongly. "He won't be objective about it."

"A better job," Fay reiterated, "*and* more fully objective. Pooh-Bah's set for full precis. Stop worrying about it. He's a dispassionate machine, not a fallible, emotionally disturbed human misled by the will-o'-the-wisp of consciousness. Second matter: Micro Systems is impressed by your contributions to Tickler and will recruit you as a senior consultant with a salary and thinking box as big as my own, family quarters to match. It's an unheard-of high start. Gussy, I think you'd be a fool —"

He broke off, held up a hand for silence, and his eyes got a listening look. Pooh-Bah had finished page six and was holding the packet motionless. After about ten seconds Fay's face broke into a big fake smile. He stood up, suppressing a wince, and held out his hand. "Gussy," he said loudly, "I am happy to inform you that all your fears about Tickler are so much thistledown. My word on it. There's nothing to them at all. Pooh-Bah's precis, which he's just given to me, proves it."

"Look," Gusterson said solemnly, "there's one thing I want you to do. Purely to humor an old friend. But I want you to do it. *Read that memo yourself.*"

"Certainly I will, Gussy," Fay continued in the same ebullient tones. "I'll read it —" he twitched and his smile disappeared —"a little later."

"Sure," Gusterson said dully, holding his hand to his stomach. "And now if you don't mind, Fay, I'm goin' home. I feel just a bit sick. Maybe the ozone and the other additives in your shelter air are too heady for me. It's been years since I tramped through a pine forest."

"But Gussy! You've hardly got here. You haven't even sat down. Have another martini. Have a seltzer pill. Have a whiff of oxy. Have a —"

"No, Fay, I'm going home right away. I'll think about the job offer. *Remember to read that memo.*"

"I will, Gussy, I certainly will. You know your way? The button takes you through the wall. 'By, now."

He sat down abruptly and looked away. Gusterson pushed through the swinging door. He tensed himself for the step across onto the slowly-moving reverse ribbon. Then on a impulse he pushed ajar the swinging door and looked back inside.

Fay was sitting as he'd left him, apparently lost in listless brooding. On his shoulder Pooh-Bah was rapidly crossing and uncrossing its little metal arms, tearing the memo to smaller and smaller shreds. It let the scraps drift slowly toward the floor and oddly writhed its three-elbowed left arm... and then Gusterson knew from whom, or rather from what, Fay had copied his new shrug.

## VII

When Gusterson got home toward the end of the second dog watch, he slipped aside from Daisy's questions and set the children laughing with a graphic enactment of his slidestanding technique and a story about getting his head caught in a thinking box built for a midget physicist. After supper he played with Imogene, Iago and Claudius until it was their bedtime and thereafter was unusually attentive to Daisy, admiring her fading green stripes, though he did spend a while in the next apartment, where they stored their outdoor camping equipment.

But the next morning he announced to the children that it was a holiday-the Feast of St. Gusterson-and then took Daisy into the bedroom and told her everything.

When he'd finished she said, "This is something I've got to see for myself."

Gusterson shrugged. "If you think you've got to. I say we should head for the hills right now. One thing I'm standing on: the kids aren't going back to school."

"Agreed," Daisy said. "But, Gusterson, we've lived through a lot of things without leaving home altogether. We lived through the Everybody-Six-Feet-Underground-by-Christmas campaign and the Robot Watchdog craze, when you got your left foot half chewed off. We lived through the Venomous Bats and Indoctrinated Saboteur Rats and the Hypnotized Monkey Paratrooper scares. We lived through the Voice of Safety and Anti-Communist Somno-Instruction and Rightest Pills and Jet-Propelled Vigilantes. We lived through the Cold-Out, when you weren't supposed to turn on a toaster for fear its heat would be a target for prowl missiles and when people with fevers were unpopular. We lived through —"

Gusterson patted her hand. "You go below," he said. "Come back when you've decided this is different. Come back as soon as you can anyway. I'll be worried about you every minute you're down there."

When she was gone-in a green suit and hat to minimize or at least justify the effect of the faded stripes-Gusterson doled out to the children provender and equipment for a camping expedition to the next floor. Iago led them off in stealthy Indian file. Leaving the hall door open Gusterson got out his .38 and cleaned and loaded it, meanwhile concentrating on a chess problem with the idea of confusing a hypothetical psionic monitor. By the time he had hid the revolver again he heard the elevator creaking back up.

Daisy came dragging in without her hat, looking as if she'd been concentrating on a chess problem for hours herself and just now given up. Her stripes seemed to have vanished; then Gusterson decided this was because her whole complexion was a touch green.

She sat down on the edge of the couch and said without looking at him, "Did you tell me, Gusterson, that everybody was quiet and abstracted and orderly down below, especially the ones wearing ticklers, meaning pretty much everybody?"

"I did," he said. "I take it that's no longer the case. What are the new symptoms?"

She gave no indication. After some time she said, "Gusterson, do you remember the Doré illustrations to the *Inferno*? Can you visualize the paintings of Hieronymous Bosch with the hordes of proto-Freudian devils tormenting people all over the farmyard and city square? Did you ever see the Disney animations of Moussorgsky's witches' sabbath music? Back in the foolish days before you married me, did that drug-addict girl friend of yours ever take you to a genuine orgy?"

"As bad as that, hey?"

She nodded emphatically and all of a sudden shivered violently. "Several shades worse," she said. "If they decide to come topside —" She shot up. "Where are the kids?"

"Upstairs campin' in the mysterious wilderness of the 21st floor," Gusterson reassured her. "Let's leave 'em there until we're ready to —"

He broke off. They both heard the faint sound of thudding footsteps.

"They're on the stairs," Daisy whispered, starting to move toward the open door. "But are they coming from up or down?"

"It's just one person," judged Gusterson, moving after his wife. "Too heavy for one of the kids."

The footsteps doubled in volume and came rapidly closer. Along with them there was an agonized gasping. Daisy stopped, staring fearfully at the open doorway. Gusterson moved past her. Then he stopped too.

Fay stumbled into view and would have fallen on his face except he clutched both sides of the doorway halfway up. He was stripped to the waist. There was a little blood on his shoulder. His narrow chest was arching convulsively, the ribs standing out starkly, as he sucked in oxygen to replace what he'd burned up running up twenty flights. His eyes were wild.

"They've taken over," he panted. Another gobbling breath. "Gone crazy." Two more gasps. "Gotta stop 'em."

His eyes filmed. He swayed forward. Then Gusterson's big arms were around him and he was carrying him to the couch.

Daisy came running from the kitchen with a damp cool towel. Gusterson took it from her and began to mop Fay off. He sucked in his own breath as he saw that Fay's right ear was raw and torn. He whispered to Daisy, "Look at where the thing savaged him."

The blood on Fay's shoulder came from his ear. Some of it stained a flush-skin plastic fitting that had two small valved holes in it and that puzzled Gusterson until he remembered that Moodmaster tied into the bloodstream. For a second he thought he was going to vomit.

The dazed look slid aside from Fay's eyes. He was gasping less painfully now. He sat up, pushing the towel away, buried his face in his hands for a few seconds, then looked over the fingers at the two of them.

"I've been living in a nightmare for the last week," he said in a taut small voice, "knowing the thing had come alive and trying to pretend to myself that it hadn't. Knowing it was taking charge of me more and more. Having it whisper in my ear, over and over again, in a cracked little rhyme that I could only hear every hundredth time, 'Day by day, in every way, you're learning to listen...and *obey*. Day by day —'"

His voice started to go high. He pulled it down and continued harshly, "I ditched it this morning when I showered. It let me break contact to do that. It must have figured it had complete control of me, mounted or dismounted. I think it's telepathic, and then it did some, well, rather unpleasant things to me late last night. But I pulled together my fears and my will and I ran for it. The slidewalks were chaos. The Mark 6 ticklers showed some purpose, though I couldn't tell you what, but as far as I could see the Mark 3s and 4s were just cootching their mounts to death-Chinese feather torture. Giggling, gasping, choking...gales of mirth. People are dying of laughter...ticklers!...the irony of it! It was the complete lack of order and sanity and that let me get topside. There were things I saw —" Once again his voice went shrill. He clapped his hand to his mouth and rocked back and forth on the couch.

Gusterson gently but firmly laid a hand on his good shoulder. "Steady," he said. "Here, swallow this."

Fay shoved aside the short brown drink. "We've got to stop them," he cried. "Mobilize the topsiders-contact the wilderness patrols and manned satellites-pour ether in the tunnel airpumps-invent and crash-manufacture missiles that will home on ticklers without harming humans-SOS Mars and Venus-dope the shelter water supply-do something! Gussy, you don't realize what people are going through down there every second."

"I think they're experiencing the ultimate in outer-directedness," Gusterson said gruffly.

"Have you no heart?" Fay demanded. His eyes widened, as if he were seeing Gusterson for the first time. Then, accusingly, pointing a shaking finger: "*You invented the tickler, George Gusterson! It's all your fault! You've got to do something about it!*"

Before Gusterson could retort to that, or begin to think of a reply, or even assimilate the full enormity of Fay's statement, he was grabbed from behind and frog-marched away from Fay and something that felt remarkably like the muzzle of a large-caliber gun was shoved in the small of his back.

Under cover of Fay's outburst a huge crowd of people had entered the room from the hall-eight, to be exact. But the weirdest thing about them to Gusterson was that from the first instant he had the impression that only one mind had entered the room and that it did not reside in any of the eight persons, even though he recognized three of them, but in something that they were carrying.

Several things contributed to this impression. The eight people all had the same blank expression-watchful yet empty-eyed. They all moved in the same slithery crouch. And they had all taken off their shoes. Perhaps, Gusterson thought wildly, they believed he and Daisy ran a Japanese flat.

Gusterson was being held by two burly women, one of them quite pimply. He considered stamping on her toes, but just at that moment the gun dug in his back with a corkscrew movement.

The man holding the gun on him was Fay's colleague Davidson. Some yards beyond Fay's couch, Kester was holding a gun on Daisy, without digging it into her, while the single strange man holding Daisy herself was doing so quite decorously—a circumstance which afforded Gusterson minor relief, since it made him feel less guilty about not going berserk.

Two more strange men, one of them in purple lounging pajamas, the other in the gray uniform of a slidewalk inspector, had grabbed Fay's skinny upper arms, one on either side, and were lifting him to his feet, while Fay was struggling with such desperate futility and gibbering so pitifully that Gusterson momentarily had second thoughts about the moral imperative to go berserk when menaced by hostile force. But again the gun dug into him with a twist.

Approaching Fay face-on was the third Micro-man Gusterson had met yesterday-Hazen. It was Hazen who was carrying-quite reverently or solemnly-or at any rate very carefully the object that seemed to Gusterson to be the mind of the little storm troop presently desecrating the sanctity of his own individual home.

All of them were wearing ticklers, of course-the three Micro-men the heavy emergent Mark 6s with their clawed and jointed arms and monocular cephalic turrets, the rest lower-numbered Marks of the sort that merely made Richard-the-Third humps under clothing.

The object that Hazen was carrying was the Mark 6 tickler Gusterson had seen Fay wearing yesterday. Gusterson was sure it was Pooh-Bah because of its air of command, and because he would have sworn on a mountain of Bibles that he recognized the red fleck lurking in the back of its single eye. And Pooh-Bah alone had the aura of full conscious thought. Pooh-Bah alone had mana.

It is not good to see an evil legless child robot with dangling straps bossing-apparently by telepathic power-not only three objects of its own kind and five close primitive relatives, but also eight human beings...and in addition throwing into a state of twitching terror one miserable, thin-chested, half-crazy research-and-development director.

Pooh-Bah pointed a claw at Fay. Fay's handlers dragged him forward, still resisting but more feebly now, as if half-hypnotized or at least cowed.

Gusterson grunted an outraged, "Hey!" and automatically struggled a bit, but once more the gun dug in. Daisy shut her eyes, then firmed her mouth and opened them again to look.

Seating the tickler on Fay's shoulder took a little time, because two blunt spikes in its bottom had to be fitted into the valved holes in the flush-skin plastic disk. When at last they plunged home Gusterson felt very sick indeed-and then even more so, as the tickler itself poked a tiny pellet on a fine wire into Fay's ear.

The next moment Fay had straightened up and motioned his handlers aside. He tightened the straps of his tickler around his chest and under his armpits. He held out a hand and someone gave him a shoulderless shirt and coat. He slipped into them smoothly, Pooh-Bah dexterously using its little claws to help put its turret and body through the neatly hemmed holes. The small storm troop looked at Fay with deferential expectation. He held still for a moment, as if thinking, and then walked over to Gusterson and looked him in the face and again held still.

Fay's expression was jaunty on the surface, agonized underneath. Gusterson knew that he wasn't thinking at all, but only listening for instructions from something that was whispering on the very threshold of his inner ear.

"Gussy, old boy," Fay said, twitching a depthless grin, "I'd be very much obliged if you'd answer a few simple questions." His voice was hoarse at first but he swallowed twice and corrected that. "What exactly did you have in mind when you invented ticklers? What exactly are they supposed to be?"

"Why, you miserable —" Gusterson began in a kind of confused horror, then got hold of himself and said curtly, "They were supposed to be mech reminders. They were supposed to record memoranda and —"

Fay held up a palm and shook his head and again listened for a space. Then, "That's how ticklers were supposed to be of use to humans," he said. "I don't mean that at all. I mean how ticklers were supposed to be of use to themselves. Surely you had some notion." Fay wet his lips. "If it's any help," he added, "keep in mind that it's not Fay who's asking this question, but Pooh-Bah."

Gusterson hesitated. He had the feeling that every one of the eight dual beings in the room was hanging on his answer and that something was boring into his mind and turning over his next thoughts and peering at and under them before he had a chance to scan them himself. Pooh-Bah's eye was like a red searchlight.

"Go on," Fay prompted. "What were ticklers supposed to be-for themselves?"

"Nothin'," Gusterson said softly. "Nothin' at all."

He could feel the disappointment well up in the room-and with it a touch of something like panic.

This time Fay listened for quite a long while. "I hope you don't mean that, Gussy," he said at last very earnestly. "I mean, I hope you hunt deep and find some ideas you forgot, or maybe never realized you had at the time. Let me put it to you differently. What's the place of ticklers in the natural scheme of things? What's their aim in life? Their special reason? Their genius? Their final cause? What gods should ticklers worship?"

But Gusterson was already shaking his head. He said, "I don't know anything about that at all."

Fay sighed and gave simultaneously with Pooh-Bah the now-familiar triple-jointed shrug. Then the man briskened himself. "I guess that's as far as we can get right now," he said. "Keep thinking, Gussy. Try to remember something. You won't be able to leave your apartment — I'm setting guards. If you want to see me, tell them. Or just think-In due course you'll be questioned further in any case. Perhaps by special methods. Perhaps you'll be ticklerized. That's all. Come on, everybody, let's get going."

The pimply woman and her pal let go of Gusterson, Daisy's man loosed his decorous hold, Davidson and Kester sidled away with an eye behind them and the little storm troop trudged out.

Fay looked back in the doorway. "I'm sorry, Gussy," he said and for a moment his old self looked out of his eyes. "I wish I could —" A claw reached for his ear, a spasm of pain crossed his face, he stiffened and marched off. The door shut.

Gusterson took two deep breaths that were close to angry sobs. Then, still breathing stentorously, he stamped into the bedroom.

"What —?" Daisy asked, looking after him.

He came back carrying his .38 and headed for the door.

"What are you up to?" she demanded, knowing very well.

"I'm going to blast that iron monkey off Fay's back if it's the last thing I do!"

She threw her arms around him.

"Now lemme go," Gusterson growled. "I gotta be a man one time anyway."

As they struggled for the gun, the door opened noiselessly, Davidson slipped in and deftly snatched the weapon out of their hands before they realized he was there. He said nothing, only smiled at them and shook his head in sad reproof as he went out.

Gusterson slumped. "I *knew* they were all psionic," he said softly. "I just got out of control now-that last look Fay gave us." He touched Daisy's arm. "Thanks, kid."

He walked to the glass wall and looked out desultorily. After a while he turned and said, "Maybe you better be with the kids, hey? I imagine the guards'll let you through."

Daisy shook her head. "The kids never come home until supper. For the next few hours they'll be safer without me."

Gusterson nodded vaguely, sat down on the couch and propped his chin on the base of his palm. After a while his brow smoothed and Daisy knew that the wheels had started to turn inside and the electrons to jump around-except that she reminded herself to permanently cross out those particular figures of speech from her vocabulary.

After about half an hour Gusterson said softly, "I think the ticklers are so psionic that it's as if they just had one mind. If I were with them very long I'd start to be part of that mind. Say something to one of them and you say it to all."

Fifteen minutes later: "They're not crazy, they're just newborn. The ones that were creating a cootching chaos downstairs were like babies kickin' their legs and wavin' their eyes, tryin' to see what their bodies could do. Too bad their bodies are us."

Ten minutes more: "I gotta do something about it. Fay's right. It's all my fault. He's just the apprentice; I'm the old sorcerer himself."

Five minutes more, gloomily: "Maybe it's man's destiny to build live machines and then bow out of the cosmic picture. Except the ticklers need us, dammit, just like nomads need horses."

Another five minutes: "Maybe somebody could dream up a purpose in life for ticklers. Even a religion-the First Church of Pooh-Bah Tickler. But I hate selling other people spiritual ideas and that'd still leave ticklers parasitic on humans...."

As he murmured those last words Gusterson's eyes got wide as a maniac's and a big smile reached for his ears. He stood up and faced himself toward the door.

"What are you intending to do now?" Daisy asked flatly.

"I'm merely goin' out an' save the world," he told her. "I may be back for supper and I may not."

## VIII

Davidson pushed out from the wall against which he'd been resting himself and his two-stone tickler and moved to block the hall. But Gusterson simply walked up to him. He shook his hand warmly and looked his tickler full in the eye and said in a ringing voice, "Ticklers should have bodies of their own!" He paused and then added casually, "Come on, let's visit your boss."

Davidson listened for instructions and then nodded. But he watched Gusterson warily as they walked down the hall.

In the elevator Gusterson repeated his message to the second guard, who turned out to be the pimply woman, now wearing shoes. This time he added, "Ticklers shouldn't be tied to the frail bodies of humans, which need a lot of thoughtful supervision and drug-injecting and can't even fly."

Crossing the park, Gusterson stopped a hump-backed soldier and informed him, "Ticklers gotta cut the apron string and snap the silver cord and go out in the universe and find their own purposes." Davidson and the pimply woman didn't interfere. They merely waited and watched and then led Gusterson on.

On the escaladder he told someone, "It's cruel to tie ticklers to slow-witted snaily humans when ticklers can think and live...ten thousand times as fast," he finished, plucking the figure from the murk of his unconscious.

By the time they got to the bottom, the message had become, "Ticklers should have a planet of their own!"

They never did catch up with Fay, although they spent two hours skimming around on slide-walks, under the subterranean stars, pursuing rumors of his presence. Clearly the boss tickler (which was how they thought of Pooh-bah) led an energetic life. Gusterson continued to deliver his message to all and sundry at 30-second intervals. Toward the end he found himself doing it in a dreamy and forgetful way. His mind, he decided, was becoming assimilated to the communal telepathic mind of the ticklers. It did not seem to matter at the time.

After two hours Gusterson realized that he and his guides were becoming part of a general movement of people, a flow as mindless as that of blood corpuscles through the veins, yet at the same time dimly purposeful-at least there was the feeling that it was at the behest of a mind far above.

The flow was topside. All the slidewalks seemed to lead to the concourses and the escaladders. Gusterson found himself part of a human stream moving into the tickler factory adjacent to his apartment-or another factory very much like it.

Thereafter Gusterson's awarenesses were dimmed. It was as if a bigger mind were doing the remembering for him and it were permissible and even mandatory for him to dream his way along. He knew vaguely that days were passing. He knew he had work of a sort: at one time he was bringing food to gaunt-eyed tickler-mounted humans working feverishly in a production line-human hands and tickler claws working together in a blur of rapidity on silvery mechanisms that moved along jumpily on a great belt; at another he was sweeping piles of metal scraps and garbage down a gray corridor.

Two scenes stood out a little more vividly.

A windowless wall had been knocked out for twenty feet. There was blue sky outside, its light almost hurtful, and a drop of many stories. A file of humans were being processed. When one of them got to the head of the file his (or her) tickler was ceremoniously unstrapped from his shoulder and welded onto a silvery cask with smoothly pointed ends. The result was something that looked-at least in the case of the Mark 6 ticklers-like a stubby silver submarine, child size. It would hum gently, lift off the floor and then fly slowly out through the big blue gap. Then the next tickler-ridden human would step forward for processing.

The second scene was in a park, the sky again blue, but big and high with an argosy of white clouds. Gusterson was lined up in a crowd of humans that stretched as far as he could see, row on irregular row. Martial music was playing. Overhead hovered a flock of little silver submarines, lined up rather more orderly in the air than the humans were on the ground. The music rose to a heart-quickening climax. The tickler nearest Gusterson gave (as if to say, "And now-who knows?") a triple-jointed shrug that stung his memory. Then the ticklers took off straight up on their new and shining bodies. They became a flight of silver geese … of silver midges … and the humans around Gusterson lifted a ragged cheer.…

That scene marked the beginning of the return of Gusterson's mind and memory. He shuffled around for a bit, spoke vaguely to three or four people he recalled from the dream days, and then headed for home and supper-three weeks late, and as disoriented and emaciated as a bear coming out of hibernation.

Six months later Fay was having dinner with Daisy and Gusterson. The cocktails had been poured and the children were playing in the next apartment. The transparent violet walls brightened, then gloomed, as the sun dipped below the horizon.

Gusterson said, "I see where a spaceship out beyond the orbit of Mars was holed by a tickler. I wonder where the little guys are headed now?"

Fay started to give a writhing left-armed shrug, but stopped himself with a grimace.

"Maybe out of the solar system altogether," suggested Daisy, who'd recently dyed her hair fire-engine red and was wearing red leotards.

"They got a weary trip ahead of them," Gusterson said, "unless they work out a hyper-Einsteinian drive on the way."

Fay grimaced again. He was still looking rather peaked. He said plaintively, "Haven't we heard enough about ticklers for a while?"

"I guess so," Gusterson agreed, "but I get to wondering about the little guys. They were so serious and intense about everything. I never did solve their problem, you know. I just shifted it onto other shoulders than ours. No joke intended," he hurried to add.

Fay forbore to comment. "By the way, Gussy," he said, "have you heard anything from the Red Cross about that world-saving medal I nominated you for? I know you think the whole concept of world-saving medals is ridiculous, especially when they started giving them to all heads of state who didn't start atomic wars while in office, but —"

"Nary a peep," Gusterson told him. "I'm not proud, Fay. I could use a few world-savin' medals. I'd start a flurry in the old-gold market. But I don't worry about those things. I don't have time to. I'm busy these days thinkin' up a bunch of new inventions."

"Gussy!" Fay said sharply, his face tightening in alarm, "Have you forgotten your promise?"

"'Course not, Fay. My new inventions aren't for Micro or any other firm. They're just a legitimate part of my literary endeavors. Happens my next insanity novel is goin' to be about a mad inventor."

# The Night of the Long Knives

## Chapter 1

> Any man who saw you, or even heard your footsteps must be ambushed, stalked and killed, whether needed for food or not. Otherwise, so long as his strength held out, he would be on your trail.
> —The Twenty-Fifth Hour,
> *by Herbert Best*

I was one hundred miles from Nowhere-and I mean that literally-when I spotted this girl out of the corner of my eye. I'd been keeping an extra lookout because I still expected the other undead bugger left over from the murder party at Nowhere to be stalking me.

I'd been following a line of high-voltage towers all canted over at the same gentlemanly tipsy angle by an old blast from the Last War. I judged the girl was going in the same general direction and was being edged over toward my course by a drift of dust that even at my distance showed dangerous metallic gleams and dark humps that might be dead men or cattle.

She looked slim, dark topped, and on guard. Small like me and like me wearing a scarf loosely around the lower half of her face in the style of the old buckaroos.

We didn't wave or turn our heads or give the slightest indication we'd seen each other as our paths slowly converged. But we were intensely, minutely watchful —I knew I was and she had better be.

Overhead the sky was a low dust haze, as always. I don't remember what a high sky looks like. Three years ago I think I saw Venus. Or it may have been Sirius or Jupiter.

The hot smoky light was turning from the amber of midday to the bloody bronze of evening.

The line of towers I was following showed the faintest spread in the direction of their canting-they must have been only a few miles from blast center. As I passed each one I could see where the metal on the blast side had been eroded-vaporized by the original blast, mostly smoothly, but with welts and pustules where the metal had merely melted and run. I supposed the lines the towers carried had all been vaporized too, but with the haze I couldn't be sure, though I did see three dark blobs up there that might be vultures perching.

From the drift around the foot of the nearest tower a human skull peered whitely. That is rather unusual. Years later now you still see more dead bodies with the meat on them than skeletons. Intense radiation has killed their bacteria and preserved them indefinitely from decay, just like the packaged meat in the last advertisements. In fact such bodies are one of the signs of a really hot drift-you avoid them. The vultures pass up such poisonously hot carrion too-they've learned their lesson.

Ahead some big gas tanks began to loom up, like deformed battleships and flat-tops in a smoke screen, their prows being the juncture of the natural curve of the off-blast side with the massive concavity of the on-blast side.

None of the three other buggers and me had had too clear an idea of where Nowhere had been-hence, in part, the name-but I knew in a general way that I was somewhere in the Death-lands between Porter County and Ouachita Parish, probably much nearer the former.

It's a real mixed-up America we've got these days, you know, with just the faintest trickle of a sense of identity left, like a guy in the paddedest cell in the most locked up ward in the whole loony bin. If a time traveler from mid Twentieth Century hopped forward to it across the few intervening years and looked at a map of it, if anybody has a map of it, he'd think that the map had run-that it had got some sort of disease that had swollen a few tiny parts beyond all bounds, paper tumors, while most of the other parts, the parts he remembered carrying names in such big print and showing such bold colors, had shrunk to nothingness.

To the east he'd see Atlantic Highlands and Savannah Fortress. To the west, Walla Walla Territory, Pacific Palisades, and Los Alamos-and there he'd see an actual change in the coastline, I'm told, where three of the biggest stockpiles of fusionables let go and opened Death Valley to the sea-so that Los Alamos is closer to being a port. Centrally he'd find Porter County and Manteno Asylum surprisingly close together near the Great Lakes, which are tilted and spilled out a bit toward the southwest with the big quake. South-centrally: Ouachita Parish inching up the Mississippi from old Louisiana under the cruel urging of the Fisher Sheriffs.

Those he'd find and a few, a very few other places, including a couple I suppose I haven't heard of. Practically all of them would surprise him-no one can predict what scraps of a blasted nation are going to hang onto a shred of organization and ruthlessly maintain it and very slowly and very jealously extend it.

But biggest of all, occupying practically all the map, reducing all those swollen localities I've mentioned back to tiny blobs, bounding most of America and thrusting its jetty pseudopods everywhere, he'd see the great inkblot of the Deathlands. I don't know how else than by an area of solid, absolutely unrelieved black you'd represent the Deathlands with its multicolored radioactive dusts and its skimpy freightage of lonely Deathlanders, each bound on his murderous, utterly pointless, but utterly absorbing business-an area where names like Nowhere, It, Anywhere, and the Place are the most natural thing in the world when a few of us decide to try to pad down together for a few nervous months or weeks.

As I say, I was somewhere in the Deathlands near Manteno Asylum.

The girl and me were getting closer now, well within pistol or dart range though beyond any but the most expert or lucky knife throw. She wore boots and a weathered long-sleeved shirt and jeans. The black topping was hair, piled high in an elaborate coiffure that was held in place by twisted shavings of bright metal. A fine bug-trap, I told myself.

In her left hand, which was closest to me, she carried a dart gun, pointed away from me, across her body. It was the kind of potent tiny crossbow you can't easily tell whether the spring is loaded. Back around on her left hip a small leather satchel was strapped to her belt. Also on the same side were two sheathed knives, one of which was an oddity-it had no handle, just the bare tang. For nothing but throwing, I guessed.

I let my own left hand drift a little closer to my Banker's Special in its open holster-Ray Baker's great psychological weapon, though (who knows?) the two .38 cartridges it contained might actually fire. The one I'd put to the test at Nowhere had, and very lucky for me.

She seemed to be hiding her right arm from me. Then I spotted the weapon it held, one you don't often see, a stevedore's hook. She *was* hiding her right hand, all right, she had the long sleeve pulled down over it so just the hook stuck out. I asked myself if the hand were perhaps covered with radiation scars or sores or otherwise disfigured. We Deathlanders have our vanities. I'm sensitive about my baldness.

Then she let her right arm swing more freely and I saw how short it was. She had no right hand. The hook was attached to the wrist stump.

I judged she was about ten years younger than me. I'm pushing forty, I think, though some people have judged I'm younger. No way of my knowing for sure. In this life you forget trifles like chronology.

Anyway, the age difference meant she would have quicker reflexes. I'd have to keep that in mind.

The greenishly glinting dust drift that I'd judged she was avoiding swung closer ahead. The girl's left elbow gave a little kick to the satchel on her hip and there was a sudden burst of irregular ticks that almost made me start. I steadied myself and concentrated on thinking whether I should attach any special significance to her carrying a Geiger counter. Naturally it wasn't the sort of thinking that interfered in any way with my watchfulness-you quickly lose the habit of that kind of thinking in the Deathlands or you lose something else.

It could mean she was some sort of greenhorn. Most of us old-timers can visually judge the heat of a dust drift or crater or rayed area more reliably than any instrument. Some buggers claim they just feel it, though I've never known any of the latter too eager to navigate in unfamiliar country at night-which you'd think they'd be willing to do if they could feel heat blind.

But she didn't look one bit like a tenderfoot-like for instance some citizeness newly banished from Manteno. Or like some Porter burgher's unfaithful wife or troublesome girlfriend whom he'd personally carted out beyond the ridges of cleaned-out hot dust that help guard such places, and then abandoned in revenge or from boredom-and they call themselves civilized, those cultural queers!

No, she looked like she *belonged* in the Deathlands. But then why the counter?

Her eyes might be bad, real bad. I didn't think so. She raised her boot an extra inch to step over a little jagged fragment of concrete. No.

Maybe she was just a born double-checker, using science to back up knowledge based on experience as rich as my own or richer. I've met the super-careful type before. They mostly get along pretty well, but they tend to be a shade too slow in the clutches.

Maybe she was *testing* the counter, planning to use it some other way or trade it for something.

Maybe she made a practice of traveling by night! Then the counter made good sense. But then why use it by day? Why reveal it to me in any case?

Was she trying to convince me that she was a greenhorn? Or had she hoped that the sudden noise would throw me off guard? But who would go to the trouble of carrying a Geiger counter for such devious purposes? And wouldn't she have waited until we got closer before trying the noise gambit?

Think-shmink —it gets you nowhere!

She kicked off the counter with another bump of her elbow and started to edge in toward me faster. I turned the thinking all off and gave my whole mind to watchfulness.

Soon we were barely more than eight feet apart, almost within lunging range without even the preliminary one-two step, and still we hadn't spoken or looked straight at each other, though being that close we'd had to cant our heads around a bit to keep each other in peripheral vision. Our eyes would be on each other steadily for five or six seconds, then dart forward an instant to check for rocks and holes in the trail we were following in parallel. A cultural queer from one of the "civilized" places would have found it funny, I suppose, if he'd been able to watch us perform in an arena or from behind armor glass for his exclusive pleasure.

The girl had eyebrows as black as her hair, which in its piled-up and metal-knotted savagery called to mind African queens despite her typical pale complexion-very little ultraviolet gets through the dust. From the inside corner of her right eye socket a narrow radiation scar ran up between her eyebrows and across her forehead at a rakish angle until it disappeared under a sweep of hair at the upper left corner of her forehead.

I'd been smelling her, of course, for some time.

I could even tell the color of her eyes now. They were blue. It's a color you never see. Almost no dusts have a bluish cast, there are few blue objects except certain dark steels, the sky never gets very far away from the orange range, though it is green from time to time, and water reflects the sky.

Yes, she had blue eyes, blue eyes and that jaunty scar, blue eyes and that jaunty scar and a dart gun and a steel hook for a right hand, and we were walking side by side, eight feet apart, not an inch closer, still not looking straight at each other, still not saying a word, and I realized that the initial period of unadulterated watchfulness was over, that I'd had adequate opportunity to inspect this girl and size her up, and that night was coming on fast, and that here I was, once again, back with *the problem of the two urges*.

I could try either to kill her or go to bed with her.

I know that at this point the cultural queers (and certainly our imaginary time traveler from mid Twentieth Century) would make a great noise about not understanding and not believing in the genuineness of the simple urge to murder that governs the lives of us Deathlanders. Like detective-story pundits, they would say that a man or woman murders for gain, or concealment of crime, or from thwarted sexual desire or outraged sexual possessiveness-and maybe they would list a few other "rational" motives-but not, they would say, just for the simple sake of murder, for the sure release and relief it gives, for the sake of wiping out one recognizable bit more (the closest bit we can, since those of us with the courage or lazy rationality to wipe out ourselves have long since done so) —wiping out one recognizable bit more of the whole miserable, unutterably disgusting human mess. Unless, they would say, a person is completely insane, which is actually how all outsiders view us Deathlanders. They can think of us in no other way.

I guess cultural queers and time travelers simply *don't* understand, though to be so blind it seems to me that they have to overlook much of the history of the Last War and of the subsequent years, especially the mushrooming of crackpot cults with a murder tinge: the werewolf gangs, the Berserkers and Amuckers, the revival of Shiva worship and the Black Mass, the machine wreckers, the kill-the-killers movements, the new witchcraft, the Unholy Creepers, the Unconsciousers, the radioactive blue gods and rocket devils of the Atomites, and a dozen other groupings clearly prefiguring Deathlander psychology. Those cults had all been as unpredictable as Thuggee or the Dancing Madness of the Middle Ages or the Children's Crusade, yet they had happened just the same.

But cultural queers are good at overlooking things. They have to be, I suppose. They think they're humanity growing again. Yes, despite their laughable warpedness and hysterical crippledness, they actually believe-each howlingly different community of them-that they're the new Adams and Eves. They're all excited about themselves and whether or not they wear fig leaves. They don't carry with them, twenty-four hours a day, like us Deathlanders do, the burden of all that was forever lost.

Since I've gone this far I'll go a bit further and make the paradoxical admission that even us Deathlanders don't really understand our urge to murder. Oh, we have our rationalizations of it, just like everyone has of his ruling passion-we call ourselves junkmen, scavengers, gangrene surgeons; we sometimes believe we're doing the person we kill the ultimate kindness, yes and get slobbery tearful about it afterwards; we sometimes tell ourselves we've finally found and are rubbing out the one man or woman who was responsible for everything; we talk, mostly to ourselves, about the aesthetics of homicide; we occasionally admit, but only each to himself alone, that we're just plain nuts.

But we don't really understand our urge to murder, we only *feel* it.

At the hateful sight of another human being, we feel it begins to grow in us until it becomes an overpowering impulse that jerks us, like a puppet is jerked by its strings, into the act itself or its attempted commission.

Like I was feeling it grow in me now as we did this parallel deathmarch through the reddening haze, me and this girl and our problem. This girl with the blue eyes and the jaunty scar.

The problem of the *two* urges, I said. The other urge, the sexual, is one that I know all cultural queers (and certainly our time traveler) would claim to know all about. Maybe they do. But I wonder if they understand how intense it can be with us Deathlanders when it's the only release (except maybe liquor and drugs, which we seldom can get and even more rarely dare use) —the only complete release, even though a brief one, from the overpowering loneliness and from the tyranny of the urge to kill.

To embrace, to possess, to glut lust on, yes even briefly to love, briefly to shelter in-that was good, that was a relief and release to be treasured.

But it couldn't last. You could draw it out, prop it up perhaps for a few days, for a month even (though sometimes not for a single night) —you might even start to talk to each other a little, after a while-but it could never last. The glands always tire, if nothing else.

Murder was the only *final* solution, the only *permanent* release. Only us Deathlanders know how good it feels. But then after the kill the loneliness would come back, redoubled, and after a while I'd meet another hateful human...

*Our* problem of the two urges. As I watched this girl slogging along parallel to me, as I kept constant watch on her of course, I wondered how *she* was feeling the two urges. Was she attracted to the ridgy scars on my cheeks half revealed by my scarf? —to me they have a pleasing symmetry. Was she wondering how my head and face looked without the black felt skullcap low-visored over my eyes? Or was she thinking mostly of that hook swinging into my throat under the chin and dragging me down?

I couldn't tell. She looked as poker-faced as I was trying to.

For that matter, I asked myself, how was *I* feeling the two urges? —how was I feeling them as I watched this girl with the blue eyes and the jaunty scar and the arrogantly thinned lips that asked to be smashed, and the slender throat? —and I realized that there was no way to describe that, not even to myself. I could only feel the two urges grow in me, side by side, like monstrous twins, until they would simply be too big for my taut body and one of them would have to get out fast.

I don't know which one of us started to slow down first, it happened so gradually, but the dust puffs that rise from the ground of the Deathlands under even the lightest treading became smaller and smaller around our steps and finally vanished altogether, and we were standing still. Only then did I notice the obvious physical trigger for our stopping. An old freeway ran at right angles across our path. The shoulder by which we'd approached it was sharply eroded, so that the pavement, which even had a shallow cave eroded under it, was a good three feet above the level of our path, forming a low wall. From where I'd stopped I could almost reach out and touch the rough-edged smooth-topped concrete. So could she.

We were right in the midst of the gas tanks now, six or seven of them towered around us, squeezed like beer cans by the decade-old blast but their metal looking sound enough until you became aware of the red light showing through in odd patterns of dots and dashes where vaporization or later erosion had been complete. Almost but not quite lace-work. Just ahead of us, right across the freeway, was the six-storey skeletal structure of an old cracking plant, sagged like the power towers away from the blast and the lower storeys drifted with piles and ridges and smooth gobbets of dust.

The light was getting redder and smokier every minute.

With the cessation of the physical movement of walking, which is always some sort of release for emotions, I could feel the twin urges growing faster in me. But that was all right, I told myself-this was the crisis, as she must realize too, and that should key us up to bear the urges a little longer without explosion.

I was the first to start to turn my head. For the first time I looked straight into her eyes and she into mine. And as always happens at such times, a third urge appeared abruptly, an urge momentarily as strong as the other two-the urge to speak, to tell and ask all about it. But even as I started to phrase the first crazily happy greeting, my throat lumped, as I'd known it would, with the awful melancholy of all that was forever lost, with the uselessness of any communication, with the impossibility of recreating the past, our individual pasts, any pasts. And as it always does, the third urge died.

I could tell she was feeling that ultimate pain just like me. I could see her eyelids squeeze down on her eyes and her face lift and her shoulders go back as she swallowed hard.

She was the first to start to lay aside a weapon. She took two sidewise steps toward the freeway and reached her whole left arm further across her body and laid the dart gun on the concrete and drew back her hand from it about six inches. At the same time looking at me hard-fiercely angrily, you'd say-across her left shoulder. She had the experienced duelist's trick of seeming to look into my eyes but actually focussing on my mouth. I was using the same gimmick myself-it's tiring to look straight into another person's eyes and it can put you off guard.

My left side was nearest the wall so I didn't for the moment have the problem of reaching across my body. I took the same sidewise steps she had and using just two fingers, very gingerly —*disarmingly*, I hoped —I lifted my antique firearm from its holster and laid it on the concrete and drew back my hand from it all the way. Now it was up to her again, or should be. Her hook was going to be quite a problem, I realized, but we needn't come to it right away.

She temporized by successively unsheathing the two knives at her left side and laying them beside the dart gun. Then she stopped and her look told me plainly that it was up to me.

Now I am a bugger who believes in carrying *one perfect knife* —otherwise, I know for a fact, you'll go knife-happy and end up by weighing yourself down with dozens, literally. So I am naturally very reluctant to get out of touch in any way with Mother, who is a little rusty along the sides but made of the toughest and most sharpenable alloy steel I've ever run across.

Still, I was most curious to find out what she'd do about that hook, so I finally laid Mother on the concrete beside the .38 and rested my hands lightly on my hips, all ready to enjoy myself-at least I hoped I gave that impression.

She smiled, it was almost a nice smile-by now we'd let our scarves drop since we weren't raising any more dust-and then she took hold of the hook with her left hand and started to unscrew it from the leather-and-metal base fitting over her stump.

Of course, I told myself. And her second knife, the one without a grip, must be that way so she could screw its tang into the base when she wanted a knife on her right hand instead of a hook. I ought to have guessed.

I grinned my admiration of her mechanical ingenuity and immediately unhitched my knapsack and laid it beside my weapons. Then a thought occurred to me. I opened the knapsack and moving my hand slowly and very openly so she'd have no reason to suspect a ruse, I drew out a blanket and, trying to show her both sides of it in the process, as if I were performing some damned conjuring trick, dropped it gently on the ground between us.

She unsnapped the straps on her satchel that fastened it to her belt and laid it aside and then she took off her belt too, slowly drawing it through the wide loops of weathered denim. Then she looked meaningfully at my belt.

I had to agree with her. Belts, especially heavy-buckled ones like ours, can be nasty weapons. I removed mine. Simultaneously each belt joined its corresponding pile of weapons and other belongings.

She shook her head, not in any sort of negation, and ran her fingers into the black hair at several points, to show me it hid no weapon, then looked at me questioningly. I nodded that I was satisfied —I hadn't seen anything run out of it, by the way. Then she looked up at my black skullcap and she raised her eyebrows and smiled again, this time with a spice of mocking anticipation.

In some ways I hate to part with that headpiece more than I do with Mother. Not really because of its sandwiched lead-mesh inner lining-if the rays haven't baked my brain yet they never will and I'm sure that the patches of lead mesh sewed into my pants over my loins give a lot more practical protection. But I was getting real attracted to this girl by now and there are times when a person must make a sacrifice of his vanity. I whipped off my stylish black felt and tossed it on my pile and dared her to laugh at my shiny egg top.

Strangely she didn't even smile. She parted her lips and ran her tongue along the upper one. I gave an eager grin in reply, an incautiously wide one, and she saw my plates flash.

My plates are something rather special though they are by no means unique. Back toward the end of the Last War, when it was obvious to any realist how bad things were going to be, though not how strangely terrible, a number of people, like myself, had all their teeth jerked and replaced with durable plates. I went some of them one better. My plates were stainless steel biting and chewing ridges, smooth continuous ones that didn't attempt to copy individual teeth. A person who looks closely at a slab of chewing tobacco, say, I offer him will be puzzled by the smoothly curved incision, made as if by a razor blade mounted on the arm of a compass. Magnetic powder buried in my gums makes for a real nice fit.

This sacrifice was worse than my hat and Mother combined, but I could see the girl expected me to make it and would take no substitutes, and in this attitude I had to admit that she showed very sound judgment, because I keep the incisor parts of those plates filed to razor sharpness. I have to be careful about my tongue and lips but I figure it's worth it. With my dental scimitars I can in a wink bite out a chunk of throat and windpipe or jugular, though I've never had occasion to do so yet.

For the first minute it made me feel like an old man, a real dodderer, but by now the attraction this girl had for me was getting irrational. I carefully laid the two plates on top of my knapsack.

In return, as a sort of reward you might say, she opened her mouth wide and showed me what was left of her own teeth-about two-thirds of them, a patchwork of tartar and gold.

We took off our boots, pants and shirts, she watching very suspiciously —I knew she'd been skeptical of my carrying only one knife.

Oddly perhaps, considering how touchy I am about my baldness, I felt no sensitivity about revealing the lack of hair on my chest and in fact a sort of pride in displaying the slanting radiation scars that have replaced it, though they are crawling keloids of the ugliest, bumpiest sort. I guess to me such scars are tribal insignia-one-man and one-woman tribes of course. No question but that the scar on the girl's forehead had been the first focus of my desire for her and it still added to my interest.

By now we weren't staying as perfectly on guard or watching each other's clothing for concealed weapons as carefully as we should —I know I wasn't. It was getting dark fast, there wasn't much time left, and the other interest was simply becoming too great.

We were still automatically careful about how we did things. For instance the way we took off our pants was like ballet, simultaneously crouching a little on the left foot and whipping the right leg out of its sheath in one movement, all ready to jump without tripping ourselves if the other person did anything funny, and then skinning down the left pants-leg with a movement almost as swift.

But as I say it was getting too late for perfect watchfulness, in fact for any kind of effective watchfulness at all. The complexion of the whole situation was changing in a rush. The possibilities of dealing or receiving death-along with the chance of the minor indignity of cannibalism, which some of us practice-were suddenly gone, all gone. It was going to be all right this time, I was telling myself. This was the time it would be different, this was the time love would last, this was the time lust would be the firm foundation for understanding and trust, this time there would be really safe sleeping. This girl's body would be home for me, a beautiful tender inexhaustibly exciting home, and mine for her, for always.

As she threw off her shirt, the last darkly red light showed me another smooth slantwise scar, this one around her hips, like a narrow girdle that has slipped down a little on one side.

# Chapter 2

Murder most foul, as in the best it is;

But this most foul, strange and unnatural.

—Hamlet

When I woke the light was almost full amber and I could feel no flesh against mine, only the blanket under me. I very slowly rolled over and there she was, sitting on the corner of the blanket not two feet from me, combing her long black hair with a big, wide-toothed comb she'd screwed into the leather-and-metal cap over her wrist stump.

She'd put on her pants and shirt, but the former were rolled up to her knees and the latter, though tucked in, wasn't buttoned.

She was looking at me, contemplating me you might say, quite dreamily but with a faint, easy smile.

I smiled back at her.

It was lovely.

Too lovely. There had to be something wrong with it.

There was. Oh, nothing big. Just a solitary trifle-nothing worth noticing really.

But the tiniest solitary things can sometimes be the most irritating, like *one* mosquito.

When I'd first rolled over she'd been combing her hair straight back, revealing a wedge of baldness following the continuation of her forehead scar deep back across her scalp. Now with a movement that was swift though not hurried-looking she swept the mass of her hair forward and to the left, so that it covered the bald area. Also her lips straightened out.

I was hurt. She shouldn't have hidden her bit of baldness, it was something we had in common, something that brought us closer. And she shouldn't have stopped smiling at just that moment. Didn't she realize I loved that blaze on her scalp just as much as any other part of her, that she no longer had any need to practice vanity in front of me?

Didn't she realize that as soon as she stopped smiling, her contemplative stare became an insult to me? What right had she to stare, critically I felt sure, at my bald head? What right had she to know about the nearly-healed ulcer on my left shin? —that was a piece of information worth a man's life in a fight. What right had she to cover up, anyways, while I was still naked? She ought to have waked me up so that we could have got dressed as we'd undressed, together. There were lots of things wrong with her manners.

Oh, I know that if I'd been able to think calmly, maybe if I'd just had some breakfast or a little coffee inside me, or even if there'd been some hot breakfast to eat at that moment, I'd have recognized my irritation for the irrational, one-mosquito surge of negative feeling that it was.

Even without breakfast, if I'd just had the knowledge that there was a reasonably secure day ahead of me in which there'd be an opportunity for me to straighten out my feelings, I wouldn't have been irked, or at least being irked wouldn't have bothered me terribly.

But a sense of security is an even rarer commodity in the Deathlands than a hot breakfast.

Given just the ghost of a sense of security and/or some hot breakfast, I'd have told myself that she was merely being amusingly coquettish about her bald streak and her hair, that it was natural for a woman to try to preserve some mystery about herself in front of the man she beds with.

But you get leery of any kind of mystery in the Deathlands. It makes you frightened and angry, like it does an animal. Mystery is for cultural queers, strictly. The only way for two people to get along together in the Deathlands, even for a while, is never to hide anything and never to make a move that doesn't have an immediate clear explanation. You can't talk, you see, certainly not at first, and so you can't explain anything (most explanations are just lies and dreams, anyway), so you have to be doubly careful and explicit about everything you do.

This girl wasn't being either. Right now, on top of her other gaucheries, she was unscrewing the comb from her wrist-an unfriendly if not quite a hostile act, as anyone must admit.

Understand, please, I wasn't *showing* any of these negative reactions of mine any more than she was showing hers, except for her stopping smiling. In fact *I hadn't* stopped smiling, I was playing the game to the hilt.

But inside me everything was stewed up and the other urge had come back and presently it would begin to grow again. That's the trouble, you know, with sex as a solution to the problem of the two urges. It's fine while it lasts but it wears itself out and then you're back with Urge Number One and you have nothing left to balance it with.

Oh, I wouldn't kill this girl today, I probably wouldn't seriously think of killing her for a month or more, but Old Urge Number One would be there and growing, mostly under cover, all the time. Of course there were things I could do to slow its growth, lots of little gimmicks, in fact —I was pretty experienced at this business.

For instance, I could take a shot at talking to her pretty soon. For a catchy starter, I could tell her about Nowhere, how these five other buggers and me found ourselves independently skulking along after this scavenging expedition from Porter, how we naturally joined forces in that situation, how we set a pitfall for their alky-powered jeep and wrecked it and them, how when our haul turned out to be unexpectedly big the four of us left from the kill chummied up and padded down together and amused each other for a while and played games, you might say. Why, at one point we even had an old crank phonograph going and read some books. And, of course, how when the loot gave out and the fun wore off, we had our murder party and I survived along with, I think, a bugger named Jerry-at any rate, he was gone when the blood stopped spurting, and I'd had no stomach for tracking him, though I probably should have.

And in return she could tell me how she had killed off her last set of girlfriends, or boyfriends, or friend, or whatever it was.

After that, we could have a go at exchanging news, rumors and speculations about local, national and world events. Was it true that Atlantic Highlands had planes of some sort or were they from Europe? Were they actually crucifying the Deathlanders around Walla Walla or only nailing up their dead bodies as dire warnings to others such? Had Manteno made Christianity compulsory yet, or were they still tolerating Zen Buddhists? Was it true that Los Alamos had been completely wiped out by plague, but the area taboo to Deathlanders because of the robot guards they'd left behind-metal guards eight feet tall who tramped across the white sands, wailing? Did they still have free love in Pacific Palisades? Did she know there'd been a pitched battle fought by expeditionary forces from Ouachita and Savannah Fortress? Over the loot of Birmingham, apparently, after yellow fever had finished off that principality. Had she rooted out any "observers" lately? —some of the "civilized" communities, the more "scientific" ones, try to maintain a few weather stations and the like in the Deathlands, camouflaging them elaborately and manning them with one or two impudent characters to whom we give a hard time if we uncover them. Had she heard the tale that was going around that South America and the French Riviera had survived the Last War absolutely untouched? —and the obviously ridiculous rider that they had blue skies there and saw stars every third night? Did she think that subsequent conditions were showing that the Earth actually had plunged into an interstellar dust cloud coincidentally with the start of the Last War (the dust cloud used as a cover for the first attacks, some said) or did she still hold with the majority that the dust was solely of atomic origin with a little help from volcanoes and dry spells? How many green sunsets had she seen in the last year?

After we'd chewed over those racy topics and some more like them, and incidentally got bored with guessing and fabricating, we might, if we felt especially daring and conversation were going particularly well, even take a chance on talking a little about our childhoods, about how things were before the Last War (though she was almost too young for that) —about the *little* things we remembered-the big things were much too dangerous topics to venture on and sometimes even the little memories could suddenly twist you up as if you'd swallowed lye.

But after that there wouldn't be anything left to talk about. Anything you'd risk talking about, that is. For instance, no matter how long we talked, it was very unlikely that we'd either of us tell the other anything complete or very accurate about how we lived from day to day, about our techniques of surviving and staying sane or at least functional-that would be too imprudent, it would go too much against the grain of any player of the murder game. Would I tell her, or anyone, about how I worked the ruses of playing dead and disguising myself as a woman, about my trick of picking a path just before dark and then circling back to it by a pre-surveyed route, about the chess games I played with myself, about the bottle of green, terribly hot-looking powder I carried to sprinkle behind me to bluff off pursuers? A fat chance of my revealing things like that!

And when all the talk was over, what would it have gained us? Our minds would be filled with a lot of painful stuff better kept buried-meaningless hopes, scraps of vicarious living in "cultured" communities, memories that were nothing but melancholy given concrete form. The melancholy is easiest to bear when it's the diffused background for everything; and all garbage is best kept in the can. Oh yes, our talking would have gained us a few more days of infatuation, of phantom security, but those we could have-almost as many of them, at any rate-without talking.

For instance things were smoothing over already between her and me again and I no longer felt quite so irked. She'd replaced the comb with an inoffensive-looking pair of light pliers and was doing up her hair with the metal shavings. And I was acting as if content to watch her, as in a way I was. I'd still made no move to get dressed.

She looked real sweet, you know, primping herself that way. Her face was a little flat, but it was young, and the scar gave it just the fillip it needed.

But what was going on behind that forehead right now, I asked myself? I felt real psychic this morning, my mind as clear as a bottle of White Rock you find miraculously unbroken in a blasted tavern, and the answers to the question I'd asked myself came effortlessly.

She was telling herself she'd got herself a man again, a man who was adequate in the primal clutch (I gave myself that pat on the back), and that she wouldn't have to be plagued and have her safety endangered by *that* kind of mind-dulling restlessness and yearning for a while.

She was lightly playing around with ideas about how she'd found a home and a protector, knowing she was kidding herself, that it was the most gimcracky feminine make-believe, but enjoying it just the same.

She was sizing me up, deciding in detail just what I went for in a woman, what whetted my interest, so she could keep that roused as long as seemed desirable or prudent to her to continue our relation.

She was kicking herself, only lightly to begin with, because she hadn't taken any precautions-because we who've escaped hot death against all reasonable expectations by virtue of some incalculable resistance to the ills of radioactivity, quite often find we've escaped sterility too. If she should become pregnant, she was telling herself, then she had a real sticky business ahead of her where no man could be trusted for a second.

And because she was thinking of this and because she was obviously a realistic Deathlander, she was reminding herself that a woman is basically less impulsive and daring and resourceful than a man and so had always better be sure she gets in the first blow. She would be thinking that I was a realist myself and a smart man, one able to understand her predicament quite clearly-and because of that a much sooner danger to her. She was feeling Old Number One Urge starting to grow in her again and wondering whether it mightn't be wisest to give it the hot-house treatment.

That is the trouble with a clear mind. For a little while you see things as they really are and you can accurately predict how they're going to shape the future ... and then suddenly you realize you've predicted yourself a week or a month into the future and you can't live the intervening time any more because you've already imagined it in detail. People who live in communities, even the cultural queers of our maimed era, aren't much bothered by it-there must be some sort of blinkers they hand you out along with the key to the city-but in the Deathlands it's a fairly common phenomenon and there's no hiding from it.

Me and my clear mind! —once again it had done me out of days of fun, changed a thoroughly-explored love affair into a one night stand. Oh, there was no question about it, this girl and I were finished, right this minute, as of now, because she was just as psychic as I was this morning and had sensed every last thing that I'd been thinking.

With a movement smooth enough not to look rushed I swung into a crouch. She was on her knees faster than that, her left hand hovering over the little set of tools for her stump, which like any good mechanic she'd lined up neatly on the edge of the blanket-the hook, the comb, a long telescoping fork, a couple of other items, and the knife. I'd grabbed a handful of blanket, ready to jerk it from under her. She'd seen that I'd grabbed it. Our gazes dueled.

There was a high-pitched whine over our heads! Quite loud from the start, though it sounded as if it were very deep up in the haze. It swiftly dropped in pitch and volume.

The top of the skeletal cracking plant across the freeway glowed with St. Elmo's fire! Three times it glowed that way, so bright we could see the violet-blue flames of it reaching up despite the full amber daylight.

The whine died away but in the last moment, paradoxically, it seemed to be coming closer!

This shared threat-for any unexpected event is a threat in the Deathlands and a mysterious event doubly so-put a stop to our murder game. The girl and I were buddies again, buddies to be relied on in a pinch, for the duration of the threat at least. No need to say so or to reassure each other of the fact in any way, it was taken for granted. Besides, there was no time. We had to use every second allowed us in getting ready for whatever was coming.

First I grabbed up Mother. Then I relieved myself-fear made it easy. Then I skinned into my pants and boots, slapped in my teeth, thrust the blanket and knapsack into the shallow cave under the edge of the freeway, looking around me all the time so as not to be surprised from any quarter.

Meanwhile the girl had put on her boots, located her dart gun, unscrewed the pliers from her stump, put the knife in, and was arranging her scarf so it made a sling for the maimed arm —I wondered why but had no time to waste guessing, even if I'd wanted to, for at that moment a small dull silver plane, beetle-shaped more than anything else, loomed out of the haze beyond the cracking plant and came silently drifting down toward us.

The girl thrust her satchel into the cave and along with it her dart gun. I caught her idea and tucked Mother into my pants behind my back.

I'd thought from the first glimpse of it that the plane was disabled —I guess it was its silence that gave me the idea. This theory was confirmed when one of its very stubby wings or vanes touched a corner pillar of the cracking plant. The plane was moving in too slow a glide to be wrecked, in fact it was moving in a slower glide than I would have believed possible-but then it's many years since I have seen a plane in flight.

It wasn't wrecked but the little collision it around twice in a lazy circle and it landed on the freeway with a scuffing noise not fifty feet from us. You couldn't exactly say it had crashed in, but it stayed at an odd tilt. It looked crippled all right.

An oval door in the plane opened and a man dropped lightly out on the concrete. And what a man! He was nearer seven feet tall than six, close-cropped blond hair, face and hands richly tanned, the rest of him covered by trim garments of a gleaming gray. He must have weighed as much as the two of us together, but he was beautifully built, muscular yet supple-seeming. His face looked brightly intelligent and even-tempered and kind.

Yes, kind! —damn him! It wasn't enough that his body should fairly glow with a health and vitality that was an insult to our seared skins and stringy muscles and ulcers and half-rotted stomachs and half-arrested cancers, he had to look kind too-the sort of man who would put you to bed and take care of you, as if you were some sort of interesting sick fox, and maybe even say a little prayer for you, and all manner of other abominations.

I don't think I could have endured my fury standing still. Fortunately there was no need to. As if we'd rehearsed the whole thing for hours, the girl and I scrambled up onto the freeway and scurried toward the man from the plane, cunningly swinging away from each other so that it would be harder for him to watch the two of us at once, but not enough to make it obvious that we attended an attack from two quarters.

We didn't run though we covered the ground as fast as we dared-running would have been too much of a give-away too, and the Pilot, which was how I named him to myself, had a strange-looking small gun in his right hand. In fact the way we moved was part of our act —I dragged one leg as if it were crippled and the girl faked another sort of limp, one that made her approach a series of half curtsies. Her arm in the sling was all twisted, but at the same time she was accidently showing her breasts —I remember thinking *you won't distract this breed bull that way, sister, he probably has a harem of six-foot heifers.* I had my head thrown back and my hands stretched out supplicatingly. Meanwhile the both of us were babbling a blue streak. I was rapidly croaking something like, "Mister for God's sake save my pal he's hurt a lot worse'n I am not a hundred yards away he's dyin' mister he's dyin' o' thirst his tongue's black'n all swole up oh save him mister save my pal he's not a hundred yards away he's dyin' mister dyin' —" and she was singsonging an even worse rigamarole about how "they" were after us from Porter and going to crucify us because we believed in science and how they'd already impaled her mother and her ten-year-old sister and a lot more of the same.

It didn't matter that our stories didn't fit or make sense, the babble had a convincing tone and getting us closer to this guy, which was all that counted. He pointed his gun at me and then I could see him hesitate and I thought exultingly *it's a lot of healthy meat you got there, mister, but it's tame meat, mister, tame!*

He compromised by taking a step back and sort of hooting at us and waving us off with his left hand, as if we were a couple of stray dogs.

It was greatly to our advantage that we'd acted without hesitation, and I don't think we'd have been able to do that except that we'd been all set to kill each other when he dropped in. Our muscles and nerves and minds were keyed for instant ruthless attack. And some "civilized" people still say that the urge to murder doesn't contribute to self-preservation!

We were almost close enough now and he was steeling himself to shoot and I remember wondering for a split second what his damn gun did to you, and then me and the girl had started the alternation routine. I'd stop dead, as if completely cowed by the threat of his weapon, and as he took note of it she'd go in a little further, and as his gaze shifted to her she'd stop dead and I'd go in another foot and then try to make my halt even more convincing as his gaze darted back to me. We worked it perfectly, our rhythm was beautiful, as if we were old dancing partners, though the whole thing was absolutely impromptu.

Still, I honestly don't think we'd ever have got him if it hadn't been for the distraction that came just then to help us. I could tell, you see, that he'd finally steeled himself and we still weren't quite close enough. He wasn't as tame as I'd hoped. I reached behind me for Mother, determined to do a last-minute rush and leap anyway, when there came this sick scream.

I don't know how else to describe it briefly. It was a scream, feminine for choice, it came from some distance and the direction of the old cracking plant, it had a note of anguish and warning, yet at the same time it was weak and almost faltering you might say and squeaky at the end, as if it came from a person half dead and a throat choked with phlegm. It had all those qualities or a wonderful mimicking of them.

And it had quite an effect on our boy in gray for in the act of shooting me down he started to turn and look over his shoulder.

Oh, it didn't altogether stop him from shooting me. He got me partly covered again as I was in the middle of my lunge. I found out what his gun did to you. My right arm, which was the part he'd covered, just went dead and I finished my lunge slamming up against his iron knees, like a highschool kid trying to block out a pro footballer, with the knife slipping uselessly away from my fingers.

But in the blessed meanwhile the girl had lunged too, not with a slow slash, thank God, but with a high, slicing thrust aimed arrow-straight for a point just under his ear.

She connected and a fan of blood sprayed her full in the face.

I grabbed my knife with my left hand as it fell, scrambled to my feet, and drove the knife at his throat in a round-house swing that happened to come handiest at the time. The point went through his flesh like nothing and jarred against his spine with a violence that I hoped would shock into nervous insensibility the stoutest medulla oblongata and prevent any dying reprisals on his part.

I got my wish, in large part. He swayed, straightened, dropped his gun, and fell flat on his back, giving his skull a murderous crack on the concrete for good measure. He lay there and after a half dozen gushes the bright blood quit pumping strongly out of his neck.

Then came the part that was like a dying reprisal, though obviously not being directed by him as of now. And come to think of it, it may have had its good points.

The girl, who was clearly a most cool-headed cuss, snatched for his gun where he'd dropped it, to make sure she got it ahead of me. She snatched, yes-and then jerked back, letting off a sizable squeal of pain, anger, and surprise.

Where we'd seen his gun hit the concrete there was now a tiny incandescent puddle. A rill of blood snaked out from the pool around his head and touched the whitely glowing puddle and a jet of steam sizzled up.

Somehow the gun had managed to melt itself in the moment of its owner dying. Well, at any rate that showed it hadn't contained any gunpowder or ordinary chemical explosives, though I already knew it operated on other principles from the way it had been used to paralyze me. More to the point, it showed that the gun's owner was the member of a culture that believed in taking very complete precautions against its gadgets falling into the hands of strangers.

But the gun fusing wasn't quite all. As the girl and me shifted our gaze from the puddle, which was cooling fast and now glowed red like the blood-as we shifted our gaze back from the puddle to the dead man, we saw that at three points (points over where you'd expect pockets to be) his gray clothing had charred in small irregularly shaped patches from which threads of black smoke were twisting upward.

Just at that moment, so close as to make me jump in spite of years of learning to absorb shocks stoically-right at my elbow it seemed to (the girl jumped too, I may say) —a voice said, "Done a murder, hey?"

Advancing briskly around the skewily grounded plane from the direction of the cracking plant was an old geezer, a seasoned, hard-baked Deathlander if I ever saw one. He had a shock of bone-white hair, the rest of him that showed from his weathered gray clothing looked fried by the sun's rays and others to a stringy crisp, and strapped to his boots and weighing down his belt were a good dozen knives.

Not satisfied with the unnerving noise he'd made already, he went on brightly, "Neat job too, I give you credit for that, but why the hell did you have to set the guy afire?"

# Chapter 3

We are always, thanks to our human nature, potential criminals. None of us stands outside humanity's black collective shadow.

—The Undiscovered Self,
*by Carl Jung*

Ordinarily scroungers who hide around on the outskirts until the killing's done and then come in to share the loot get what they deserve-wordless orders, well backed up, to be on their way at once. Sometimes they even catch an after-clap of the murder urge, if it hasn't all been expended on the first victim or victims. Yet they *will* do it, trusting I suppose to the irresistible glamor of their personalities. There were several reasons why we didn't at once give Pop this treatment.

In the first place we didn't neither of us have our distance weapons. My revolver and her dart gun were both tucked in the cave back at the edge of the freeway. And there's one bad thing about a bugger so knife-happy he lugs them around by the carload-he's generally good at tossing them. With his dozen or so knives Pop definitely outgunned us.

Second, we were both of us without the use of an arm. That's right, the both of us. My right arm still dangled like a string of sausages and I couldn't yet feel any signs of it coming undead. While she'd burned her fingers badly grabbing at the gun —I could see their red-splotched tips now as she pulled them out of her mouth for a second to wipe the Pilot's blood out of her eyes. All she had was her stump with the knife screwed to it. Me, I can throw a knife left-handed if I have to, but you bet I wasn't going to risk Mother that way.

Then I'd no sooner heard Pop's voice, breathy and a little high like an old man's will get, than it occurred to me that he must have been the one who had given the funny scream that had distracted the Pilot's attention and let us get him. Which incidentally made Pop a quick thinker and imaginative to boot, and meant that he'd helped on the killing.

Besides all that, Pop did not come in fawning and full of extravagant praise, as most scroungers will. He just assumed equality with us right from the start and he talked in an absolutely matter-of-fact way, neither praising nor criticizing one bit-too damn matter-of-fact and open, for that matter, to suit my taste, but then I have heard other buggers say that some old men are apt to get talkative, though I had never worked with or run into one myself. Old people are very rare in the Deathlands, as you might imagine.

So the girl and me just scowled at him but did nothing to stop him as he came along. Near us, his extra knives would be no advantage to him.

"Hum," he said, "looks a lot like a guy I murdered five years back down Los Alamos way. Same silver monkey suit and almost as tall. Nice chap too-was trying to give me something for a fever I'd faked. That his gun melted? My man didn't smoke after I gave him his quietus, but then it turned out he didn't have any metal on him. I wonder if this chap —" He started to kneel down by the body.

"Hands off, Pop!" I gritted at him. That was how we started calling him Pop.

"Why sure, sure," he said, staying there on one knee. "I won't lay a finger on him. It's just that I've heard the Alamosers have it rigged so that any metal they're carrying melts when they die, and I was wondering about this boy. But he's all yours, friend. By the way, what's your name, friend?"

"Ray," I snarled. "Ray Baker." I think the main reason I told him was that I didn't want him calling me "friend" again. "You talk too much, Pop."

"I suppose I do, Ray," he agreed. "What's your name, lady?"

The girl just sort of hissed at him and he grinned at me as if to say, "Oh, women!" Then he said, "Why don't you go through his pockets, Ray? I'm real curious."

"Shut up," I said, but I felt that he'd put me on the spot just the same. I was curious about the guy's pockets myself, of course, but I was also wondering if Pop was alone or if he had somebody with him, and whether there was anybody else in the plane or not-things like that, too many things. At the same time I didn't want to let on to Pop how useless my right arm was-if I'd just get a twinge of feeling in that arm, I knew I'd feel a lot more confident fast. I knelt down across the body from him, started to lay Mother aside and then hesitated.

The girl gave me an encouraging look, as if to say, "I'll take care of the old geezer." On the strength of her look I put down Mother and started to pry open the Pilot's left hand, which was clenched in a fist that looked a mite too big to have nothing inside it.

The girl started to edge behind Pop, but he caught the movement right away and looked at her with a grin that was so knowing and yet so friendly, and yet so pitying at the same time-with the pity of the old pro for even the seasoned amateur-that in her place I think I'd have blushed myself, as she did now ... through the streaks of the Pilot's blood.

"You don't have to worry none about me, lady," he said, running a hand through his white hair and incidentally touching the pommel of one of the two knives strapped high on the back of his jacket so he could reach one over either shoulder. "I quit murdering some years back. It got to be too much of a strain on my nerves."

"Oh yeah?" I couldn't help saying as I pried up the Pilot's index finger and started on the next. "Then why the stab-factory, Pop?"

"Oh you mean those," he said, glancing down at his knives. "Well, the fact is, Ray, I carry them to impress buggers dumber than you and the lady here. Anybody wants to think I'm still a practicing murderer I got no objections. Matter of sentiment, too, I just hate to part with them-they bring back important memories. And then-you won't believe this, Ray, but I'm going to tell you just the same-guys just up and give me their knives and I doubly hate to part with a gift."

I wasn't going to say "Oh yeah?" again or "Shut up!" either, though I certainly wished I could turn off Pop's spigot, or thought I did. Then I felt a painful tingling shoot down my right arm. I smiled at Pop and said, "Any other reasons?"

"Yep," he said. "Got to shave and I might as well do it in style. A new blade every day in the fortnight is twice as good as the old ads. You know, it makes you keep a knife in fine shape if you shave with it. What you got there, Ray?"

"You were wrong, Pop," I said. "He did have some metal on him that didn't melt."

I held up for them to see the object I'd extracted from his left fist: a bright steel cube measuring about an inch across each side, but it felt lighter than if it were solid metal. Five of the faces looked absolutely bare. The sixth had a round button recessed in it.

From the way they looked at it neither Pop nor the girl had the faintest idea of what it was. I certainly hadn't.

"Had he pushed the button?" the girl asked. Her voice was throaty but unexpectedly refined, as if she'd done no talking at all, not even to herself, since coming to the Deathlands and so retained the cultured intonations she'd had earlier, whenever and wherever that had been. It gave me a funny feeling, of course, because they were the first words I'd heard her speak.

"Not from the way he was holding it," I told her. "The button was pointed up toward his thumb but the thumb was on the outside of his fingers." I felt an unexpected satisfaction at having expressed myself so clearly and I told myself not to get childish.

The girl slitted her eyes. "Don't you push it, Ray," she said.

"Think I'm nuts?" I told her, meanwhile sliding the cube into the smaller pocket of my pants, where it fit tight and wouldn't turn sideways and the button maybe get pressed by accident. The tingling in my right arm was almost unbearable now, but I was getting control over the muscles again.

"Pushing that button," I added, "might melt what's left of the plane, or blow us all up." It never hurts to emphasize that you may have another weapon in your possession, even if it's just a suicide bomb.

"There was a man pushed another button once," Pop said softly and reflectively. His gaze went far out over the Deathlands and took in a good half of the horizon and he slowly shook his head. Then his face brightened. "Did you know, Ray," he said, "that I actually met that man? Long afterwards. You don't believe me, I know, but I actually did. Tell you about it some other time."

I almost said, "Thanks, Pop, for sparing me at least for a while," but I was afraid that would set him off again. Besides, it wouldn't have been quite true. I've heard other buggers tell the yarn of how they met (and invariably rubbed out) the actual guy who pushed the button or buttons that set the fusion missiles blasting toward their targets, but I felt a sudden curiosity as to what Pop's version of the yarn would be. Oh well, I could ask him some other time, if we both lived that long. I started to check the Pilot's pockets. My right hand could help a little now.

"Those look like mean burns you got there, lady," I heard Pop tell the girl. He was right. There were blisters easy to see on three of the fingertips. "I've got some salve that's pretty good," he went on, "and some clean cloth. I could put on a bandage for you if you wanted. If your hand started to feel poisoned you could always tell Ray here to slip a knife in me."

Pop was a cute gasser, you had to admit. I reminded myself that it was Pop's business to play up to the both of us, charm being the secret weapon of all scroungers.

The girl gave a harsh little laugh. "Very well," she said, "but we will use my salve, I know it works for me." And she started to lead Pop to where we'd hidden our things.

"I'll go with you," I told them, standing up.

It didn't look like we were going to have any more murders today-Pop had got through the preliminary ingratiations pretty well and the girl and me had had our catharsis-but that would be no excuse for any such stupidity as letting the two of them get near my .38.

Strolling to the cave and back I eased the situation a bit more by saying, "That scream you let off, Pop, really helped. I don't know what gave you the idea, but thanks."

"Oh that," he said. "Forget about it."

"I won't," I told him. "You may say you've quit killing, but helped on a do-in today."

"Ray," he said a little solemnly, "if it'll make you feel any happier, I'll take a bit of the responsibility for every murder that's been done since the beginning of time."

I looked at him for a while. Then, "Pop, you're not by any chance the religious type?" I asked suddenly.

"Lord, no," he told us.

That struck me as a satisfactory answer. God preserve me from the religious type! We have quite a few of those in the Deathlands. It generally means that they try to convert you to something before they kill you. Or sometimes afterwards.

We completed our errands. I felt a lot more secure with Old Financier's Friend strapped to my middle. Mother is wonderful but she is not enough.

I dawdled over inspecting the Pilot's pockets, partly to give my right hand time to come back all the way. And to tell the truth I didn't much enjoy the job —a corpse, especially such a handsome cadaver as this, just didn't go with Pop's brand of light patter.

Pop did up the girl's hand in high style, bandaging each finger separately and then persuading her to put on a big left-hand work glove he took out of his small pack.

"Lost the right," he explained, "which was the only one I ever used anyway. Never knew until now why I kept this. How does it feel, Alice?"

I might have known he'd worm her name out of her. It occurred to me that Pop's ideas of scrounging might extend to Alice's favors. The urge doesn't die out when you get old, they tell me. Not completely.

He'd also helped her replace the knife on her stump with the hook.

By that time I'd poked into all the Pilot's pockets I could get at without stripping him and found nothing but three irregularly shaped blobs of metal, still hot to the touch. Under the charred spots, of course.

I didn't want the job of stripping him. Somebody else could do a little work, I told myself. I've been bothered by bodies before (as who hasn't, I suppose?) but this one was really beginning to make me sick. Maybe I was cracking up, it occurred to me. Murder is a very wearing business, as all Deathlanders know, and although some crack earlier than others, all crack in the end.

I must have been showing how I was feeling because, "Cheer up, Ray," Pop said. "You and Alice have done a big murder —I'd say the subject was six foot ten-so you ought to be happy. You've drawn a blank on his pockets but there's still the plane."

"Yeah, that's right," I said, brightening a little. "There's still the stuff in the plane." I knew there were some items I couldn't hope for, like .38 shells, but there'd be food and other things.

"Nuh-uh," Pop corrected me. "I said *the plane*. You may have thought it's wrecked, but I don't. Have you taken a real gander at it? It's worth doing, believe me."

I jumped up. My heart was suddenly pounding. I was glad of an excuse to get away from the body, but there was a lot more in my feelings than that. I was filled with an excitement to which I didn't want to give a name because it would make the let-down too great.

One of the wide stubby wings of the plane, raking downward so that its tip almost touched the concrete, had hidden the undercarriage of the fuselage from our view. Now, coming around the wing, I saw that *there was no undercarriage*.

I had to drop to my hands and knees and scan around with my cheek next to the concrete before I'd believe it. *The "wrecked" plane was at all points at least six inches off the ground.*

I got to my feet again. I was shaking. I wanted to talk but I couldn't. I grabbed the leading edge of the wing to stop from falling. The whole body of the plane gave a fraction of an inch and then resisted my leaning weight with lazy power, just like a gyroscope.

"Antigravity," I croaked, though you couldn't have heard me two feet. Then my voice came back. "Pop, Alice! They got antigravity! Antigravity-and it's working!"

Alice had just come around the wing and was facing me. She was shaking too and her face was white like I knew mine was. Pop was politely standing off a little to one side, watching us curiously. "Told you you'd won a real prize," he said in his matter-of-fact way.

Alice wet her lips. "Ray," she said, "we can get away."

Just those four words, but they did it. Something in me unlocked-no, exploded describes it better.

"We can go places!" I almost shouted.

"Beyond the dust," she said. "Mexico City. South America!" She was forgetting the Death-lander's cynical article of belief that the dust never ends, but then so was I. It makes a difference whether or not you've got a means of doing something.

"Rio!" I topped her with. "The Indies. Hong Kong. Bombay. Egypt. Bermuda. The French Riviera!"

"Bullfights and clean beds," she burst out with. "Restaurants. Swimming pools. Bathrooms!"

"Skindiving," I took it up with, as hysterical as she was. "Road races and roulette tables."

"Bentleys and Porsches!"

"Aircoups and DC4s and Comets!"

"Martinis and hashish and ice cream sodas!"

"Hot food! Fresh coffee! Gambling, smoking, dancing, music, drinks!" I was going to add *women*, but then I thought of how hard-bitten little Alice would look beside the dream creatures I had in mind. I tactfully suppressed the word but I filed the idea away.

I don't think either of us knew exactly what we were saying. Alice in particular I don't believe was old enough to have experienced almost any of the things the words referred to. They were mysterious symbols of long-interdicted delights spewing out of us.

"Ray," Alice said, hurrying to me, "let's get aboard."

"Yes," I said eagerly and then I saw a little problem. The door to the plane was a couple of feet above our heads. Whoever hoisted himself up first-or got hoisted up, as would have to be the case with Alice on account of her hand-would be momentarily at the other's mercy. I guess it occurred to Alice too because she stopped and looked at me. It was a little like the old teaser about the fox, the goose, and the corn.

Maybe, too, we were both a little scared the plane was booby-trapped.

Pop solved the problem in the direct way I might have expected of him by stepping quietly between us, giving a light leap, catching hold of the curving sill, chinning himself on it, and scrambling up into the plane so quickly that we'd hardly have had time to do anything about it if we'd wanted to. Pop couldn't be much more than a bantamweight, even with all his knives. The plane sagged an inch and then swung up again.

As Pop disappeared from view I backed off, reaching for my .38, but a moment later he stuck out his head and grinned down at us, resting his elbows on the sill.

"Come on up," he said. "It's quite a place. I promise not to push any buttons 'til you get here, though there's whole regiments of them."

I grinned back at Pop and gave Alice a boost up. She didn't like it, but she could see it had to be her next. She hooked onto the sill and Pop caught hold of her left wrist below the big glove and heaved.

Then it was my turn. I didn't like it. I didn't like the idea of those two buggers poised above me while my hands were helpless on the sill. But I thought *Pop's a nut. You can trust a nut, at least a little ways, though you can't trust nobody else.* I heaved myself up. It was strange to feel the plane giving and then bracing itself like something alive. It seemed to have no trouble accepting our combined weight, which after all was hardly more than half again the Pilot's.

Inside the cabin was pretty small but as Pop had implied, oh my! Everything looked soft and smoothly curved, like you imagine your insides being, and almost everything was a restfully dull silver. The general shape of it was something like the inside of an egg. Forward, which was the larger end, were a couple of screens and a wide viewport and some small dials and the button brigades Pop had mentioned, lined up like blank typewriter keys but enough for writing Chinese.

Just aft of the instrument panel were two very comfortable-looking strange low seats. They seemed to be facing backwards until I realized they were meant to be knelt into. The occupant, I could see, would sort of sprawl forward, his hands free for button-pushing and such. There were spongy chinrests.

Aft was a tiny instrument panel and a kind of sideways seat, not nearly so fancy. The door by which we'd entered was to the side, a little aft.

I didn't see any indications of cabinets or fixed storage spaces of any kinds, but somehow stuck to the walls here and there were quite a few smooth blobby packages, mostly dull silver too, some large, some small-valises and handbags, you might say.

All in all, it was a lovely cabin and, more than that, it seemed lived in. It looked as if it had been shaped for, and maybe by one man. It had a personality you could feel, a strong but warm personality of its own.

Then I realized whose personality it was. I almost got sick-so close to it I started telling myself it must be something antigravity did to your stomach.

But it was all too interesting to let you get sick right away. Pop was poking into two of the large mound-shaped cases that were sitting loose and open on the right-hand seat, as if ready for emergency use. One had a folded something with straps on it that was probably a parachute. The second had I judged a thousand or more of the inch cubes such as I'd pried out of the Pilot's hand, all neatly stacked in a cubical box inside the soft outer bag. You could see the one-cube gap where he'd taken the one.

I decided to take the rest of the bags off the walls and open them, if I could figure out how. The others had the same idea, but Alice had to take off her hook and put on her pliers, before she could make progress. Pop helped her. There was room enough for us to do these things without crowding each other too closely.

By the time Alice was set to go I'd discovered the trick of getting the bags off. You couldn't pull them away from the wall no matter what force you used, at least I couldn't, and you couldn't even slide them straight along the walls, but if you just gave them a gentle counterclockwise twist they came off like nothing. Twisting them clockwise glued them back on. It was very strange, but I told myself that if these boys could generate antigravity fields they could create screwy fields of other sorts.

It also occurred to me to wonder if "these boys" came from Earth. The Pilot had looked human enough, but these accomplishments didn't —not by my standards for human achievement in the Age of the Deaders. At any rate I had to admit to myself that my pet term "cultural queer" did not describe to my own satisfaction members of a culture which could create things like this cabin. Not that I liked making the admission. It's hard to admit an exception to a pet gripe against things.

The excitement of getting down and opening the Christmas packages saved me from speculating too much along these or any other lines.

I hit a minor jackpot right away. In the same bag were a compass, a catalytic pocket lighter, a knife with a saw-tooth back edge that made my affection for Mother waver, a dust mask, what looked like a compact water-filtration unit, and several other items adding up to a deluxe Deathlands Survival Kit.

There were some goggles in the kit I didn't savvy until I put them on and surveyed the landscape out the viewport. A nearby dust drift I knew to be hot glowed green as death in the slightly smoky lenses. Wow! Those specs had Geiger counters beat a mile and I privately bet myself they worked at night. I stuck them in my pocket quick.

We found bunches of tiny electronics parts —I think they were; spools of magnetic tape, but nothing to play it on; reels of very narrow film with frames much too small to see anything at all unmagnified; about three thousand cigarettes in unlabeled transparent packs of twenty-we lit up quick, using my new lighter; a picture book that didn't make much sense because the views might have been of tissue sections or starfields, we couldn't quite decide, and there were no captions to help; a thin book with ricepaper pages covered with Chinese characters —*that* was a puzzler; a thick book with nothing but columns of figures, all zeros and ones and nothing else; some tiny chisels; and a mouth organ. Pop, who'd make a point of just helping in the hunt, appropriated that last item —I might have known he would, I told myself. Now we could expect "Turkey in the Straw" at odd moments.

Alice found a whole bag of what were women's things judging from the frilliness of the garments included. She set aside some squeeze-packs and little gadgets and elastic items right away, but she didn't take any of the clothes. I caught her measuring some kind of transparent chemise against herself when she thought we weren't looking; it was for a girl maybe six sizes bigger.

And we found food. Cans of food that was heated up inside by the time you got the top rolled off, though the outside could still be cool to the touch. Cans of boneless steak, boneless chops, cream soup, peas, carrots, and fried potatoes-they weren't labeled at all but you could generally guess the contents from the shape of the can. Eggs that heated when you touched them and were soft-boiled evenly and barely firm by the time you had the shell broke. And small plastic bottles of strong coffee that heated up hospitably too-in this case the tops did a five-second hesitation in the middle of your unscrewing them.

At that point as you can imagine we let the rest of the packages go and had ourselves a feast. The food ate even better than it smelled. It was real hard for me not to gorge.

Then as I was slurping down my second bottle of coffee I happened to look out the viewport and see the Pilot's body and the darkening puddle around it and the coffee began to taste, well, not bad, but sickening. I don't think it was guilty conscience. Deathlanders outgrow those if they ever have them to start with; loners don't keep consciences-it takes cultures to give you those and make them work. Artistic inappropriateness is the closest I can come to describing what bothered me. Whatever it was, it made me feel lousy for a minute.

About the same time Alice did an odd thing with the last of *her* coffee. She slopped it on a rag and used it to wash her face. I guess she'd caught a reflection of herself with the blood smears. She didn't eat any more after that either. Pop kept on chomping away, a slow feeder and appreciative.

To be doing something I started to inspect the instrument panel and right away I was all excited again. The two screens were what got me. They showed shadowy maps, one of North America, the other of the World. The first one was a whole lot like the map I'd been imagining earlier-faint colors marked the small "civilized" areas including one in Eastern Canada and another in Upper Michigan that must be "countries" I didn't know about, and the Deathlands were real dark just as I'd always maintained they should be!

South of Lake Michigan was a brightly luminous green point that must be where we were, I decided. And for some reason the colored areas representing Los Alamos and Atlantic Highlands were glowing brighter than the others-they had an active luminosity. Los Alamos was blue, Atla-Hi violet. Los Alamos was shown having more territory than I expected. Savannah Fortress for that matter was a whole *lot* bigger than I'd have made it, pushing out pseudopods west and northeast along the coast, though its red didn't have the extra glow. But its growth-pattern reeked of imperialism.

The World screen showed dim color patches too, but for the moment I was more interested in the other.

The button armies marched right up to the lower edge of the screens and right away I got the crazy hunch that they were connected with spots on the map. Push the button for a certain spot and the plane would go there! Why, one button even seemed to have a faint violet nimbus around it (or else my eyes were going bad) as if to say, "Push me and we go to Atlantic Highlands."

A crazy notion as I say and no sensible way to handle a plane's navigation according to any standards I could imagine, but then as I've also said this plane didn't seem to be designed according to any standards but rather in line with one man's ideas, including his whims.

At any rate that was my hunch about the buttons and the screens. It tantalized rather than helped, for the only button that seemed to be marked in any way was the one (guessing by color) for Atlantic Highlands, and I certainly didn't want to go there. Like Alamos, Atla-Hi has the reputation for being a mysteriously dangerous place. Not openly mean and death-on-Deathlanders like Walla Walla or Porter, but buggers who swing too close to Atla-Hi have a way of never turning up again. You never expect to see again two out of three buggers who pass in the night, but for three out of three to keep disappearing is against statistics.

Alice was beside me now, scanning things over too, and from the way she frowned and what not I gathered she had caught my hunch and also shared my puzzlement.

Now was the time, all right, when we needed an instruction manual and not one in Chinese neither!

Pop swallowed a mouthful and said, "Yep, now'd be a good time to have him back for a minute, to explain things a bit. Oh, don't take offense, Ray, I know how it was for you and for you too, Alice. I know the both of you *had* to murder him, it wasn't a matter of free choice, it's the way us Deathlanders are built. Just the same, it'd be nice to have a way of killing 'em and keeping them on hand at the same time. I remember feeling that way after murdering the Alamoser I told you about. You see, I come down with the very fever I'd faked and almost died of it, while the man who could have cured me easy wouldn't do nothing but perfume the landscape with the help of a gang of anaerobic bacteria. Stubborn single-minded cuss!"

The first part of that oration started up my sickness again and irked me not a little. Dammit, what right had Pop to talk about how all us Deathlanders *had to* kill (which was true enough and by itself would have made me cotton to him) if as he'd claimed earlier *he'd* been able to quit killing? Pop was, an old hypocrite, I told myself-he'd helped murder the Pilot, he'd admitted as much-and Alice and me'd be better off if we bedded the both of them down together. But then the second part of what Pop said so made me want to feel pleasantly sorry for myself and laugh at the same time that I forgave the old geezer. Practically everything Pop said had that reassuring touch of insanity about it.

So it was Alice who said, "Shut up, Pop" —and rather casually at that-and she and me went on to speculate and then to argue about which buttons we ought to push, if any and in what order.

"Why not just start anywhere and keep pushing 'em one after another? —you're going to have to eventually, may as well start now," was Pop's light-hearted contribution to the discussion. "Got to take some chances in this life." He was sitting in the back seat and still nibbling away like a white-topped mangy old squirrel.

Of course Alice and me knew more than that. We kept making guesses as to how the buttons worked and then backing up our guesses with hot language. It was a little like two savages trying to decide how to play chess by looking at the pieces. And then the old escape-to-paradise theme took hold of us again and we studied the colored blobs on the World screen, trying to decide which would have the fanciest accommodations for blase ex-murderers. On the North America screen too there was an intriguing pink patch in southern Mexico that seemed to take in old Mexico City and Acapulco too.

"Quit talking and start pushing," Pop prodded us. "This way you're getting nowhere fast. I can't stand hesitation, it riles my nerves."

Alice thought you ought to push ten buttons at once, using both hands, and she was working out patterns for me to try. But I was off on a kick about how we should darken the plane to see if any of the other buttons glowed beside the one with the Atla-Hi violet.

"Look here, you killed a big man to get this plane," Pop broke in, coming up behind me. "Are you going to use it for discussion groups or are you going to fly it?"

"Quiet," I told him. I'd got a new hunch and was using the dark glasses to scan the instrument panel. They didn't show anything.

"Dammit, I can't stand this any more," Pop said and reached a hand and arm between us and brought it down on about fifty buttons, I'd judge.

The other buttons just went down and up, but the Atla-Hi button went down and stayed down.

The violet blob of Atla-Hi on the screen got even brighter in the next few moments.

The door closed with a tiny thud.

We took off.

# Chapter 4

> Any man who deals in murder, must have very incorrect ways of think-
> ing, and truly inaccurate principles.
> —*Thomas de Quincey in*
> Murder Considered as One of the Fine Arts

For that matter we took off *fast* with the plane swinging to beat hell. Alice and me was in the two kneeling seats and we hugged them tight, but Pop was loose and sort of rattled around the cabin for a while-and serve him right!

On one of the swings I caught a glimpse of the seven dented gas tanks, looking like dull crescents from this angle through the orange haze and getting rapidly smaller as they hazed out.

After a while the plane levelled off and quit swinging, and a while after that my image of the cabin quit swinging too. Once again I just managed to stave off the vomits, this time the vomits from natural causes. Alice looked very pale around the gills and kept her face buried in the chinrest of her chair.

Pop ended up right in our faces, sort of spread-eagled against the instrument panel. In getting himself off it he must have braced his hands against half the buttons at one time or another and I noticed that none of them went down a fraction. They were *locked*. It had probably happened automatically when the Atla-Hi button got pushed.

I'd have stopped him messing around in that apish way, but with the ultra-queasy state of my stomach I lacked all ambition and was happy just not to be smelling him so close.

I still wasn't taking too great an interest in things as I idly watched the old geezer rummaging around the cabin for something that got misplaced in the shake-up. Eventually he found it —a small almond-shaped can. He opened it. Sure enough it turned out to have almonds in it. He fitted himself in the back seat and munched them one at a time. Ish!

"Nothing like a few nuts to top off with," he said cheerfully.

I could have cut his throat even more cheerfully, but the damage had been done and you think twice before you kill a person in close quarters when you aren't absolutely sure you'll be able to dispose of the body. How did I know I'd be able to open the door? I remember philosophizing that Pop ought at least to have broke an arm so he'd be as badly off as Alice and me (though for that matter my right arm was fully recovered now) but he was all in one piece. There's no justice in events, that's for sure.

The plane ploughed along silently through the orange soup, though there was really no way to tell it was moving now-until a skewy spindle shape loomed up ahead and shot back over the viewport. I think it was a vulture. I don't know how vultures manage to operate in the haze, which ought to cancel their keen eyesight, but they do. It shot past *fast*.

Alice lifted her face out of the sponge stuff and began to study the buttons again. I heaved myself up and around a little and said, "Pop, Alice and me are going to try to work out how this plane navigates. This time we don't want no interference." I didn't say a word more about what he'd done. It never does to hash over stupidities.

"That's perfectly fine, go right ahead," he told me. "I feel calm as a kitten now we're going somewheres. That's all that ever matters with me." He chuckled a bit and added, "You got to admit I gave you and Alice something to work with," but then he had the sense to shut up tight.

We weren't so chary of pushing buttons this time, but ten minutes or so convinced us that you couldn't push any of the buttons any more, they *were* all locked down-all locked except for maybe one, which we didn't try at first for a special reason.

We looked for other controls-sticks, levers, pedals, finger-holes and the like. There weren't any. Alice went back and tried the buttons on Pop's minor console. They were locked too. Pop looked interested but didn't say a word.

We realized in a general way what had happened, of course. Pushing the Atla-Hi button had set us on some kind of irreversible automatic. I couldn't imagine the why of gimmicking a plane's controls like that, unless maybe to keep loose children or prisoners from being able to mess things up while the pilot took a snooze, but there were a lot of whys to this plane that didn't seem to have any standard answers.

The business of taking off on irreversible automatic had happened so neatly that I naturally wondered whether Pop might not know more about navigating this plane than he let on, a whole lot more in fact, and the seemingly idiotic petulance of his pushing all the buttons have been a shrewd cover for pushing the Atla-Hi button. But if Pop had been acting he'd been acting beautifully, with a serene disregard for the chances of breaking his own neck. I decided this was a possibility I could think about later and maybe act on then, after Alice and me had worked through the more obvious stuff.

The reason we hadn't tried the one button yet was that it showed a green nimbus, just like the Atla-Hi button had had a violet nimbus. Now there was no green on either of the screens except for the tiny green star that I had figured stood for the plane and it didn't make sense to go where we already were. And if it meant some other place, some place not shown on the screens, you bet we weren't going to be too quick about deciding to go there. It might not be on Earth.

Alice expressed it by saying, "My namesake was always a little too quick at responding to those DRINK ME cues."

I suppose she thought she was being cryptic, but I fooled her. "*Alice in Wonderland?*" I asked. She nodded, and gave me a little smile, not at all like one of the EAT ME smiles she'd given me last evening.

It is funny how crazily happy a little touch of the intellectual past like that can make you feel-and how horribly uncomfortable a moment later.

We both started to study the North America screen again and almost at once we realized that it had changed in one small particular. The green star had twinned. Where there had been one point of green light there were now two, very close together like the double star in the handle of the Dipper. We watched it for a while. The distance between the two stars grew perceptibly greater. We watched it for a while longer, considerably longer. It became clear that the position of the more westerly star on the screen was fixed, while the more easterly star was moving east toward Atla-Hi with about the speed of the tip of the minute hand on a wrist watch (two inches an hour, say). The pattern began to make sense.

I figured it this way: the moving star must stand for the plane, the other green dot must stand for where the plane had just been. For some reason the spot on the freeway by the old cracking plant was recognized as a marked locality by the screen. Why I don't know. It reminded me of the old "X Marks the Spot" of newspaper murders, but that would be getting very fancy. Anyway the spot we'd just taken off from was so marked and in that case the button with the green nimbus...

"Hold tight, everybody," I said to Alice, grudgingly including Pop in my warning. "I got to try it."

I gripped my seat with my knees and one arm and pushed the green button. It pushed.

The plane swung around in a level loop, not too tight to disturb the stomach much, and steadied out again.

I couldn't judge how far we'd swung but Alice and me watched the green stars and after about a minute she said, "They're getting closer," and a little while later I said, "Yeah, for sure."

I scanned the board. The green button-the cracking-plant button, to call it that-was locked down of course. The Atla-Hi button was up, glowing violet. All the other buttons were still up and *locked* up —I tried them all again.

It was clear as day used to be. We could either go to Atla-Hi or we could go back where we'd started from. There was no third possibility.

It was a little hard to take. You think of a plane as freedom, as something that will carry you anywhere in the world you choose to go, especially any paradise, and then you find yourself worse limited than if you'd stayed on the ground-at least that was the way it was happening to us.

But Alice and me were realists. We knew it wouldn't help to wail. We were up against another of those "two" problems, the problem of two destinations, and we had to choose ours.

*If we go back*, I thought, *we can trek on somewhere-anywhere-richer by the loot from the plane, especially that Survival Kit. Trek on with some loot we'll mostly never understand and with the knowledge that we are leaving a plane that can fly, that we are shrinking back from an unknown adventure.*

Also if we go back there's something else we'll have to face, something we'll have to live with for a little while at least that won't be nice to live with after this cozily personal cabin, something that shouldn't bother me at all but, dammit, it does.

Alice made the decision for us and at the same time showed she was thinking about the same thing as me.

"I don't want to have to smell him, Ray," she said. "I am not going back to keep company with that filthy corpse. I'd rather anything than that." And she pushed the Atla-Hi button again and as the plane started to swing she looked at me defiantly as if to say I'd reverse the course again over her dead body.

"Don't tense up," I told her. "I want a new shake of the dice myself."

"You know, Alice," Pop said reflectively, "it was the smell of my Alamoser got to me too. I just couldn't bear it. I couldn't get away from it because my fever had me pinned down, so there was nothing left for me to do but go crazy. No Atla-Hi for me, just Bug-land. My mind died, though not my memory. By the time I'd got my strength back I'd started to be a new bugger. I didn't know no more about living than a newborn babe, except I knew I couldn't go back-go back to murdering and all that. My new mind knew that much though otherwise it was just a blank. It was all very funny."

"And then I suppose," Alice cut in, her voice corrosive with sarcasm, "you hunted up a wandering preacher, or perhaps a kindly old hermit who lived on hot manna, and he showed you the blue sky!"

"Why no, Alice," Pop said. "I told you I don't go for religion. As it happens, I hunted me up a couple of murderers, guys who were worse cases then myself but who'd wanted to quit because it wasn't getting them nowhere and who'd found, I'd heard, a way of quitting, and the three of us had a long talk together."

"And they told you the great secret of how to live in the Deathlands without killing," Alice continued acidly. "Drop the nonsense, Pop. It can't be done."

"It's hard, I'll grant you," Pop said. "You have to go crazy or something almost as bad-in fact, maybe going crazy is the easiest way. But it can be done and, in the long run, murder is even harder."

I decided to interrupt this idle chatter. Since we were now definitely headed for Atla-Hi and there was nothing to do until we got there, unless one of us got a brainstorm about the controls, it was time to start on the less obvious stuff I'd tabled in my mind.

"Why are you on this plane, Pop?" I asked sharply. "What do you figure on getting out of Alice and me? —and I don't mean the free meals."

He grinned. His teeth were white and even-plates, of course. "Why, Ray," he said, "I was just giving Alice the reason. I like to talk to murderers, practicing murderers preferred. I need to —*have* to talk to 'em, to keep myself straight. Otherwise I might start killing again and I'm not up to that any more."

"Oh, so you get your kicks at second hand, you old peeper," Alice put in but, "Quit lying, Pop," I said. "About having quit killing, for one thing. In my books, which happen to be the old books in this case, the accomplice is every bit as guilty as the man with the slicer. You helped us kill the Pilot by giving that funny scream and you know it."

"Who says I did?" Pop countered, rearing up a little. "I never said so. I just said, 'Forget it.'" He hesitated a moment, studying me. Then he said, "I wasn't the one gave that scream. In fact, I'd have stopped it if I'd have been able."

"Who did then?"

Again he studied me as he hesitated. "I'm not telling," he said, settling back.

"Pop!" I said, sharp again. "Buggers who pad together tell everything."

"Oh yeah," he agreed, smiling. "I remember saying that to quite a few guys in my day. It's a very restful comradely sentiment. I killed every last one of 'em, too."

"You may have, Pop," I granted, "but we're two to one."

"So you are," he agreed softly, looking the both of us over. I knew what he was thinking—that Alice still had just her pliers on and that in these close quarters his knives were as good as my gun.

"Give me your right hand, Alice," I said. Without taking my eyes off Pop I reached the knife without a handle out of her belt and then I started to unscrew the pliers out of her stump.

"Pop," I said as I did so, "you may have quit killing for all I know. I mean you may have quit killing clean decent Deathland style. But I don't believe one bit of that guff about having to talk to murderers to keep your mind sweet. Furthermore —"

"It's true though," he interrupted. "I got to keep myself reminded of how lousy it feels to be a murderer."

"So?" I said. "Well, here's one person who believes you've got a more practical reason for being on this plane. Pop, what's the bounty Atla-Hi gives you for every Deathlander you bring in? What would it be for two live Deathlanders? And what sort of reward would they pay for a lost plane brought in? Seems to me they might very well make you a citizen for that."

"Yes, even give you your own church," Alice added with a sort of wicked gaiety. I squeezed her stump gently to tell her let me handle it.

"Why, I guess you can believe that if you want to," Pop said and let out a soft breath. "Seems to me you need a lot of coincidences and happenstances to make that theory hold water, but you sure can believe it if you want to. I got no way, Ray, to prove to you I'm telling the truth except to say I am."

"Right," I said and then I threw the next one at him real fast. "What's more, Pop, weren't you traveling in this plane to begin with? That cuts a happenstance. Didn't you hop out while we were too busy with the Pilot to notice and just *pretend* to be coming from the cracking plant? Weren't the buttons locked because you were the Pilot's prisoner?"

Pop creased his brow thoughtfully. "It could have been that way," he said at last. "Could have been—according to the evidence as you saw it. It's quite a bright idea, Ray. I can almost see myself skulking in this cabin, while you and Alice —"

"You were skulking somewhere," I said. I finished screwing in the knife and gave Alice back her hand. "I'll repeat it, Pop," I said. "We're two to one. You'd better talk."

"Yes," Alice added, disregarding my previous hint. "You may have given up fighting, Pop, but I haven't. Not fighting, nor killing, nor anything in between those two. Any least thing." My girl was being her most pantherish.

"Now who says I've given up *fighting*?" Pop demanded, rearing a little again. "You people assume too much, it's a dangerous habit. Before we have any trouble and somebody squawks about me cheating, let's get one thing straight. If anybody jumps me I'll try to disable them, I'll try to hurt them in any way short of killing, and that means hamstringing and rabbit-punching and everything else. Every least thing, Alice. And if they happen to die while I'm honestly just trying to hurt them in a way short of killing, then I won't grieve too much. My conscience will be reasonably clear. Is that understood?"

I had to admit that it was. Pop might be lying about a lot of things, but I just didn't believe he was lying about this. And I already knew Pop was quick for his age and strong enough. If Alice and me jumped him now there'd be blood let six different ways. You can't jump a man who has a dozen knives easy to hand and not expect that to happen, two to one or not. We'd get him in the end but it would be gory.

"And now," Pop said quietly, "I *will* talk a little if you don't mind. Look here, Ray …Alice … the two of you are confirmed murderers, I know you wouldn't tell me nothing different, and being such you both know that there's nothing in murder in the long run. It satisfies a hunger and maybe gets you a little loot and it lets you get on to the next killing. But that's all, absolutely all. Yet you got to do it because it's the way you're built. The urge is there, it's an overpowering urge, and you got nothing to oppose it with. You feel the Big Grief and the Big Resentment, the dust is eating at your bones, you can't stand the city squares-the Porterites and Mantenors and such-because you know they're whistling in the dark and it's a dirty tune, so you go on killing. But if there were a decent practical way to quit, you'd take it. At least I think you would. When you still thought this plane could take you to Rio or Europe you felt that way, didn't you? You weren't planning to go there as murderers, were you? You were going to leave your trade behind."

It was pretty quiet in the cabin for a couple of seconds. Then Alice's thin laugh sliced the silence. "We were dreaming then," she said. "We were out of our heads. But now you're talking about practical things, as you say. What do you expect us to do if we quit our trade, as you call it-go into Walla Walla or Ouachita and give ourselves up? I might lose more than my right hand at Ouachita this time-that was just on suspicion."

"Or Atla-Hi," I added meaningfully. "Are you expecting us to admit we're murderers when we get to Atla-Hi, Pop?"

The old geezer smiled and thinned his eyes. "Now that wouldn't accomplish much, would it? Most places they'd just string you up, maybe after tickling your pain nerves a bit, or if it was Manteno they might put you in a cage and feed you slops and pray over you, and would that help you or anybody else? If a man or woman quits killing there's a lot of things he's got to straighten out-first his own mind and feelings, next he's got to do what he can to make up for the murders he's done-help the next of kin if any and so on-then he's got to carry the news to other killers who haven't heard it yet. He's got no time to waste being hanged. Believe me, he's got work lined up for him, work that's got to be done mostly in the Deathlands, and it's the sort of work the city squares can't help him with one bit, because they just don't understand us murderers and what makes us tick. We have to do it ourselves."

"Hey, Pop," I cut in, getting a little interested in the argument (there wasn't anything else to get interested in until we got to Atla-Hi or Pop let down his guard), "I dig you on the city squares (I call 'em cultural queers) and what sort of screwed-up fatheads they are, but just the same for a man to quit killing he's got to quit lone-wolfing it. He's got to belong to a community, he's got to have a culture of some sort, no matter how disgusting or nutsy."

"Well," Pop said, "don't us Deathlanders have a culture? With customs and folkways and all the rest? A very tight little culture, in fact. Nutsy as all get out, of course, but that's one of the beauties of it."

"Oh sure," I granted him, "but it's a culture based on murder and devoted wholly to murder. Murder is our way of life. That gets your argument nowhere, Pop."

"Correction," he said. "Or rather, re-interpretation." And now for a little while his voice got less old-man harsh and yet bigger somehow, as if it were more than just Pop talking. "Every culture," he said, "is a way of growth as well as a way of life, because the first law of life is growth. Our Deathland culture is devoted to growing *through* murder *away from* murder. That's my thought. It's about the toughest way of growth anybody was ever asked to face up to, but it's a way of growth just the same. A lot bigger and fancier cultures never could figure out the answer to the problem of war and killing —*we* know that, all right, we inhabit their grandest failure. Maybe us Deathlanders, working with murder every day, unable to pretend that it isn't part of every one of us, unable to put it out of our minds like the city squares do-maybe us Deathlanders are the ones to do that little job."

"But hell, Pop," I objected, getting excited in spite of myself, "even if we got a culture here in the Deathlands, a culture that can grow, it ain't a culture that can deal with repentant murderers. In a *real* culture a murderer feels guilty and confesses and then he gets hanged or imprisoned a long time and that squares things for him and everybody. You need religion and courts and hangmen and screws and all the rest of it. I don't think it's enough for a man just to say he's sorry and go around glad-handing other killers —*that* isn't going to be enough to wipe out his sense of guilt."

Pop squared his eyes at mine. "Are you so fancy that you have to have a sense of guilt, Ray?" he demanded. "Can't you just see when something's lousy? A sense of guilt's a luxury. Of course it's not enough to say you're sorry-you're going to have to spend a good part of the rest of your life making up for what you've done ... and what you will do, too! But about hanging and prisons-was it ever proved those were the right thing for murderers? As for religion now-some of us who've quit killing are religious and a lot of us (me included) aren't; and some of the ones that are religious figure (maybe because there's no way for them to get hanged) that they're damned eternally-but that doesn't stop them doing good work. I ask you now, is any little thing like being damned eternally a satisfactory excuse for behaving like a complete rat?"

That did it, somehow. That last statement of Pop's appealed so much to me and was completely crazy at the same time, that I couldn't help warming up to him. Don't get me wrong, I didn't really fall for his line of chatter at all, but I found it fun to go along with it-so long as the plane was in this shuttle situation and we had nothing better to do.

Alice seemed to feel the same way. I guess any bugger that could kid religion the way Pop could got a little silver star in her books. Bronze, anyway.

Right away the atmosphere got easier. To start with we asked Pop to tell us about this "us" he kept mentioning and he said it was some dozens (or hundreds-nobody had accurate figures) of killers who'd quit and went nomading around the Deathlands trying to recruit others and help those who wanted to be helped. They had semi-permanent meeting places where they tried to get together at pre-arranged dates, but mostly they kept on the go, by twos and threes or-more rarely-alone. They were all men so far, at least Pop hadn't heard of any women members, but-he assured Alice earnestly-he would personally guarantee that there would be no objections to a girl joining up. They had recently taken to calling themselves Murderers Anonymous, after some pre-war organization Pop didn't know the original purpose of. Quite a few of them had slipped and gone back to murdering again, but some of these had come back after a while, more determined than ever to make a go of it.

"We welcomed 'em, of course," Pop said. "We welcome everybody. Everybody that's a genuine murderer, that is, and says he wants to quit. Guys that aren't blooded yet we draw the line at, no matter how fine they are."

Also, "We have a lot of fun at our meetings," Pop assured us. "You never saw such high times. Nobody's got a right to go glooming around or pull a long face just because he's done a killing or two. Religion or no religion, pride's a sin."

Alice and me ate it all up like we was a couple of kids and Pop was telling us fairy tales. That's what it all was, of course, a fairy tale —a crazy mixed-up fairy tale. Alice and me knew there could be no fellowship of Deathlanders like Pop was describing-it was impossible as blue sky-but it gave us a kick to pretend to ourselves for a while to believe in it.

Pop could talk forever, apparently, about murder and murderers and he had a bottomless bag of funny stories on the same topic and character vignettes-the murderers who were forever wanting their victims to understand and forgive them, the ones who thought of themselves as little kings with divine rights of dispensing death, the ones who insisted on laying down (chastely) beside their finished victims and playing dead for a couple of hours, the ones who weren't so chaste, the ones who could only do their killings when they were dressed a certain way (and the troubles they had with their murder costumes), the ones who could only kill people with certain traits or of a certain appearance (red-heads, say, or people who read books, or who couldn't carry tunes, or who used bad language), the ones who always mixed sex and murder and the ones who believed that murder was contaminated by the least breath of sex, the sticklers and the Sloppy Joes, the artists and the butchers, the ax- and stiletto-types, the *compulsives* and the *repulsives*-honestly, Pop's portraits from life added up to a Dance of Death as good as anything the Middle Ages ever produced and they ought to have been illustrated like those by some great artist. Pop told us a lot about his own killings too. Alice and me was interested, but neither of us wasn't tempted into making parallel revelations about ourselves. Your private life's your own business, I felt, as close as your guts, and no joke's good enough to justify revealing a knot of it.

Not that we talked about nothing but murder while we were bulleting along toward Atla-Hi. The conversation was free-wheeling and we got onto all sorts of topics. For instance, we got to talking about the plane and how it flew itself-or levitated itself, rather. I said it must generate an antigravity field that was keyed to the body of the plane but nothing else, so that *we* didn't feel lighter, nor any of the objects in the cabin-it just worked on the dull silvery metal-and I proved my point by using Mother to shave a little wisp of metal off the edge of the control board. The curlicue stayed in the air wherever you put it and when you moved it you could feel the faintest sort of gyroscopic resistance. It was very strange.

Pop pointed out it was a little like magnetism. A germ riding on an iron filing that was traveling toward the pole of a big magnet wouldn't feel the magnetic pull-it wouldn't be operating on him, only on the iron-but just the same the germ'd be carried along with the filing and feel its acceleration and all, provided he could hold on-but for that purpose you could imagine a tiny cabin in the filing. "That's what we are," Pop added. "Three germs, jumbo size."

Alice wanted to know why an antigravity plane should have even the stubbiest wings or a jet for that matter, for we remembered now we'd noticed the tubes, and I said it was maybe just a reserve system in case the antigravity failed and Pop guessed it might be for extra-fast battle maneuvering or even for operating outside the atmosphere (which hardly made sense, as I proved to him).

"If we're a battle plane, where's our guns?" Alice asked. None of us had an answer.

We remembered the noise the plane had made before we saw it. It must have been using its jets then. "And do you suppose," Pop asked, "that it was something from the antigravity that made electricity flare out of the top of the cracking plant? Like to have scared the pants off me!" No answer to that either.

Now was a logical time, of course, to ask Pop what he knew about the cracking plant and just who had done the scream if not him, but I figured he still wouldn't talk; as long as we were acting friendly there was no point in spoiling it.

We guessed around a little, though, about where the plane came from. Pop said Alamos, I said Atla-Hi, Alice said why not from both, why couldn't Alamos and Atla-Hi have some sort of treaty and the plane be traveling from the one to the other. We agreed it might be. At least it fitted with the Atla-Hi violet and the Alamos blue being brighter than the other colors.

"I just hope we got some sort of anti-collision radar," I said. I guessed we had, because twice we'd jogged in our course a little, maybe to clear the Alleghenies. The easterly green star was by now getting pretty close to the violet blot of Atla-Hi. I looked out at the orange soup, which was *one* thing that hadn't changed a bit so far, and I got to wishing like a baby that it wasn't there and to thinking how it blanketed the whole Earth (stars over the Riviera? —don't make me laugh!) and I heard myself asking, "Pop, did you rub out that guy that pushed the buttons for all this?"

"Nope," Pop answered without hesitation, just as if it hadn't been four hours or so since he'd mentioned the point. "Nope, Ray. Fact is I welcomed him into our little fellowship about six months back. This is *his* knife here, this horn-handle in my boot, though he never killed with it. He claimed he'd been tortured for years by the thought of the millions and millions he'd killed with blast and radiation, but now he was finding peace at last because he was where he belonged, with the murderers, and could start to do something about it. Several of the boys didn't want to let him in. They claimed he wasn't a real murderer, doing it by remote control, no matter how many he bumped off."

"I'd have been on their side," Alice said, thinning her lips.

"Yep," Pop continued, "they got real hot about it. *He* got hot too and all excited and offered to go out and kill somebody with his bare hands right off, or try to (he's a skinny little runt), if that's what he had to do to join. We argued it over, I pointed out that we let ex-soldiers count the killings they'd done in service, and that we counted poisonings and booby traps and such too-which are remote-control killings in a way-so eventually we let him in. He's doing good work. We're fortunate to have him."

"Do you think he's really the guy who pushed the buttons?" I asked Pop.

"How should I know?" Pop replied. "He claims to be."

I was going to say something about people who faked confessions to get a little easy glory, as compared to the guys who were really guilty and would sooner be chopped up than talk about it, but at that moment a fourth voice started talking in the plane. It seemed to be coming out of the violet patch on the North America screen. That is, it came from the general direction of the screen at any rate and my mind instantly tied it to the violet patch at Atla-Hi. It gave us a fright, I can tell you. Alice grabbed my knee with her pliers (she changed again), harder than she'd intended, I suppose, though I didn't let out a yip —I was too defensively frozen.

The voice was talking a language I didn't understand at all that went up and down the scale like atonal music.

"Sounds like Chinese," Pop whispered, giving me a nudge.

"It *is* Chinese. Mandarin," the screen responded instantly in the purest English-at least that was how I'd describe it. Practically Boston. "Who are you? And where is Grayl? Come in, Grayl."

I knew well enough who Grayl must be-or rather, have been. I looked at Pop and Alice. Pop grinned, maybe a mite feebly this time, I thought, and gave me a look as if to say, "*You* want to handle it?"

I cleared my throat. Then, "We've taken over for Grayl," I said to the screen.

"Oh." The screen hesitated, just barely. Then, "Do any of 'you' speak Mandarin?"

I hardly bothered to look at Pop and Alice. "No," I said.

"Oh." Again a tiny pause. "Is Grayl aboard the plane?"

"No." I said.

"Oh. Incapacitated in some way, I suppose?"

"Yes," I said, grateful for the screen's tactfulness, unintentional or not.

"But you have taken over for him?" the screen pressed.

"Yes," I said, swallowing. I didn't know what I was getting us into, things were moving too fast, but it seemed the merest sense to act cooperative.

"I'm very glad of that," the screen said with something in its tone that made me feel funny —I guess it was sincerity. Then it said, "Is the —" and hesitated, and started again with "Are the blocks aboard?"

I thought. Alice pointed at the stuff she dumped out of the other seat. I said. "There's a box with a thousand or so one-inch underweight steel cubes in it. Like a child's blocks, but with buttons in them. Alongside a box with a parachute."

"That's what I mean," the screen said and somehow, maybe because whoever was talking was trying to hide it, I caught a note of great relief.

"Look," the screen said, more rapidly now, "I don't know how much you know, but we may have to work very fast. You aren't going to be able to deliver the steel cubes to us directly. In fact you aren't going to be able to land in Atlantic Highlands at all. We're sieged in by planes and ground forces of Savannah Fortress. All our aircraft, such as haven't been destroyed, are pinned down. You're going to have to parachute the blocks to a point as near as possible to one of our ground parties that's made a sortie. We'll give you a signal. I hope it will be later-nearer here, that is-but it may be sooner. Do you know how to fight the plane you're in? Operate its armament?"

"No," I said, wetting my lip.

"Then that's the first thing I'd best teach you. Anything you see in the haze from now on will be from Savannah. You must shoot it down."

# Chapter 5

And we are here as on a darkling plain
Swept with confused alarms of struggle and flight,

Where ignorant armies clash by night.

—Dover Beach,
by Matthew Arnold

I am not going to try to describe point by point all that happened the next half hour because there was too much of it and it involved all three of us, sometimes doing different things at the same time, and although we were told a lot of things, we were seldom if ever told the why of them, and through it all was the constant impression that we were dealing with human beings (I almost left out the "human" and I'm still not absolutely sure whether I shouldn't) of vastly greater scope-and probably intelligence too-than ourselves.

And that was just the *basic* confusion, to give it a name. After a while the situation got more difficult, as I'll try to tell in due course.

To begin with, it was extremely weird to plunge from a rather leisurely confab about a fairy-tale fellowship of non-practicing murderers into a shooting war between a violet blob and a dark red puddle on a shadowy fluorescent map. The voice didn't throw any great shining lights on this topic, because after the first-and perhaps unguarded-revelation, we learned little more of the war between Atla-Hi and Savannah Fortress and nothing of the reasons behind it. Presumably Savannah was the aggressor, reaching out north after the conquest of Birmingham, but even that was just a guess. It is hard to describe how shadowy it all felt to me; there were some minutes while my mind kept mixing up the whole thing with what I'd read long ago about the Civil War: Savannah was Lee, Atla-Hi was Grant, and we had been dropped spang into the middle of the second Battle of the Wilderness.

Apparently the Savannah planes had some sort of needle ray as part of their armament-at any rate I was warned to watch out for "swinging lines in the haze, like straight strings of pink stars" and later told to aim at the sources of such lines. And naturally I guessed that the steel cubes must be some crucial weapon for Atla-Hi, or ammunition for a weapon, or parts for some essential instrument like a giant computer, but the voice ignored my questions on that point and didn't fall into the couple of crude conversational traps I tried to set. We were to drop the cubes when told, that was all. Pop had the box of them closed again and rigged to the parachute-he took over that job because Alice and me were busy with other things when the instructions on that came through-and he was told how to open the door of the plane for the drop (you just held your hand steadily on a point beside the door), but, as I say, that was all.

Naturally it occurred to me that once we had made the drop, Atla-Hi would have no more use for us and might simply let us be destroyed by Savannah or otherwise-perhaps *want* us to be destroyed-so that it might be wisest for us to refuse to make the drop when the signal came and hang onto those myriad steel cubes as our only bargaining point. Still, I could see no advantage to refusing *before* the signal came. I'd have liked to discuss the point with Alice and maybe Pop too, but apparently everything we said, even whispered, could be overheard by Atla-Hi. (We never did determine, incidentally, whether Atla-Hi could *see* into the cabin of the plane also. I don't believe they could, though they sure had it bugged for sound.)

All in all, we found out almost nothing about Atla-Hi. In fact, three witless germs traveling in a cabin in an iron filing wasn't a bad description of us at all. As I often say of my deductive faculties-think-shmink! But Atla-Hi (always meaning, of course, the personality behind the voice from the screen) found out all it wanted about us-and apparently knew a good deal to start with. For one thing, they must have been tracking our plane for some time, because they guessed it was on automatic and that we could reverse its course but nothing else. Though they seemed under the impression that we could reverse its course to Los Alamos, not the cracking plant. Here obviously I did get a nugget of new data, though it was just about the only one. For a moment the voice from the screen got real unguarded-anxious as it asked, "Do you know if it is true that they have stopped dying at Los Alamos, or are they merely broadcasting that to cheer us up?"

I answered, "Oh yes, they're all fine," to that, but I couldn't have made it very convincing, because the next thing I knew the voice was getting me to admit that we'd only boarded the plane somewhere in the Central Deathlands. I even had to describe the cracking plant and freeway and gas tanks—I couldn't think of a lie that mightn't get us into as much trouble as the truth-and the voice said, "Oh, did Grayl stay there?" and I said, "Yes," and braced myself to do some more admitting, or some heavy lying, as the inspiration took me.

But the voice continued to skirt around the question of what exactly had happened to Grayl. I guess they knew well enough we'd bumped him off, but didn't bring it up because they needed our cooperation-they were handling us like children or savages, you see.

One pretty amazing point-Atla-Hi apparently knew something about Pop's fairy-tale fellowship of non-practicing murderers, because when he had to speak up, while he was getting instructions on preparing the stuff for the drop, the voice said, "Excuse me, but you sound like one of those M. A. boys."

Murderers Anonymous, Pop had said some of their boys called their unorganized organization.

"Yep, I am," Pop admitted uncomfortably.

"Well, a word of advice then, or perhaps I only mean gossip," the screen said, for once getting on a side track. "Most of our people do not believe you are serious about it, although you may think that you are. Our skeptics (which includes all but a very few of us) split quite evenly between those who think that the M. A. spirit is a terminal psychotic illusion and those who believe it is an elaborate ruse in preparation for some concerted attack on cities by Deathlanders."

"Can't say that I blame the either of them," was Pop's only comment. "I think I'm nuts myself and a murderer forever." Alice glared at him for that admission, but it seemed to do us no damage. Pop really did seem out of his depth though during this part of our adventure, more out of his depth than even Alice and me —I mean, as if he could only really function in the Deathland with Deathlanders and wanted to get anything else over quickly.

I think one reason Pop was that way was that he was feeling very intensely something I was feeling myself: a sort of sadness and bewilderment that beings as smart as the voice from the screen sounded should still be fighting wars. Murder, as you must know by now, I can understand and sympathize with deeply, but war? —no!

Oh, I can understand cultural queers fighting city squares and even get a kick out of it and whoop 'em on, but these Atla-Hi and Alamos folk seemed a different sort of cat altogether (though I'd only come to that point of view today) —the kind of cat that ought to have outgrown war or thought its way around it. Maybe Savannah Fortress had simply forced the war on them and they had to defend themselves. I hadn't contacted any Savannans-they might be as blood-simple as the Porterites. Still, I don't know that it's always a good excuse that somebody else forced you into war. That sort of justification can keep on until the end of time. But who's a germ to judge?

A minute later I was feeling doubly like a germ and a very lowly one, because the situation had just got more difficult and depressing too-the thing had happened that I said I'd tell you about in due course.

The voice was just repeating its instructions to Pop on making the drop, when it broke off of a sudden and a second voice came in, a deep voice with a sort of European accent (not Chinese, oddly)—not talking *to* us, I think, but to the first voice and overlooking or not caring that we could hear.

"*Also* tell them," the second voice said, "that we will blow them out of the sky the instant they stop obeying us! If they should hesitate to make the drop or if they should put a finger on the button that reverses their course, then—*pouf!* Such brutes understand only the language of force. *Also* warn them that the blocks are atomic grenades that will blow them out of the sky too if—"

"Dr. Kovalsky, will you permit me to point out—" the first voice interrupted, getting as close to expressing irritation as I imagine it ever allowed itself to do. Then both voices cut off abruptly and the screen was silent for ten seconds or so. I guess the first voice thought it wasn't nice for us to overhear Atla-Hi bickering with itself, even if the second voice didn't give a damn (any more than a farmer would mind the pigs overhearing him squabble with his hired man; of course this guy seemed to overlook that we were killer-pigs, but there wasn't anything we could do in that line just now except get burned up).

When the screen came on again, it was just the first voice talking once more, but it had something to say that was probably the result of a rapid conference and compromise.

"Attention, everyone! I wish to inform you that the plane in which you are traveling can be exploded-melted in the air, rather-if we activate a certain control at this end. We will *not* do so, now or subsequently, if you make the drop when we give the signal and if you remain on your present course until then. Afterwards you will be at liberty to reverse your course and escape as best you may. Let me re-emphasize that when you told me you had taken over for Grayl I accepted that assertion in full faith and still so accept it. Is that all fully understood?"

We all told him "Yes," though I don't imagine we sounded very happy about it, even Pop. However I did get that funny feeling again that the voice was being really sincere-an illusion, I supposed, but still a comforting one.

Now while all these things were going on, believe it or not, and while the plane continued to bullet through the orange haze-which hadn't shown any foreign objects in it so far, thank God, even vultures, let alone "straight strings of pink stars"—I was receiving a cram course in gunnery! (Do you wonder I don't try to tell this part of my story consecutively?)

It turned out that Alice had been brilliantly right about one thing: if you pushed some of the buttons simultaneously in patterns of five they unlocked and you could play on them like organ keys. Two sets of five keys, played properly, would rig out a sight just in front of the viewport and let you aim and fire the plane's main gun in any forward direction. There was a rearward firing gun too, that you aimed by changing over the World Screen to a rear-view TV window, but we didn't get around to mastering that one. In fact, in spite of my special talents it was all I could do to achieve a beginner's control over the main gun, and I wouldn't have managed even that except that Alice, from the thinking she'd been doing about patterns of five, was quick at understanding from the voice's descriptions which buttons were meant. She couldn't work them herself of course, what with her stump and burnt hand, but she could point them out for me.

After twenty minutes of drill I was a gunner of sorts, sprawled in the right-hand kneeling seat and intently scanning the onrushing orange haze which at last was beginning to change toward the bronze of evening. If something showed up in it I'd be able to make a stab at getting a shot in. Not that I knew what my gun fired-the voice wasn't giving away any unnecessary data.

Naturally I had asked why didn't the voice teach me to fly the plane so that I could maneuver in case of attack, and naturally the voice had told me it was out of the question-much too difficult and besides they wanted us on a known course so they could plan better for the drop and recovery. (I think maybe the voice would have given me some hints-and maybe even told me more about the steel cubes too and how much danger we were in from them-if it hadn't been for the second voice, which presumably had issued from a being who was keeping watch to make sure among other things that the first voice didn't get soft-hearted.)

So there I was being a front gunner. Actually a part of me was getting a big bang out of it-from antique Banker's Special to needle cannon (or whatever it was) —but at the same time another part of me was disgusted with the idea of acting like I belonged to a live culture (even a smart, unqueer one) and working in a war (even just so as to get out of it fast), while a third part of me-one that I normally keep down-was very simply horrified.

Pop was back by the door with the box and 'chute, ready to make the drop.

Alice had no duties for the moment, but she'd suddenly started gathering up food cans and packing them in one bag —I couldn't figure out at first what she had in mind. Orderly house-wife wouldn't be exactly my description of her occupational personality.

Then of course everything had to happen at once.

The voice said, "Make the drop!"

Alice crossed to Pop and thrust out the bag of cans toward him, writhing her lips in silent "talk" to tell him something. She had a knife in her burnt hand too.

But I didn't have time to do any lip-reading, because just then a glittering pink asterisk showed up in the darkening haze ahead —a whole half dozen straight lines spreading out from a blank central spot, as if a super-fast gigantic spider had laid in the first strands of its web.

Wind whistled as the door of the plane started to open.

I fought to center my sight on the blank central spot, which drifted toward the left.

One of the straight lines grew dazzlingly bright.

I heard Alice whisper fiercely, "Drop *these!*" and the part of my mind that couldn't be applied to gunnery instantly deduced that she'd had some last-minute inspiration about dropping a bunch of cans instead of the steel cubes.

I got the sight centered and held down the firing combo. The thought flashed to me: *it's a city you're firing at, not a plane*, and I flinched.

The dazzlingly pink line dipped down toward me.

Behind me, the sound of a struggle. Alice snarling and Pop giving a grunt.

Then all at once a scream from Alice, a big whoosh of wind, a flash way ahead (where I'd aimed), a spatter of hot metal inside the cabin, a blinding spot in the middle of the World Screen, a searing beam inches from my neck, an electric shock that lifted me from my seat and ripped at my consciousness!

When I came to (if I really ever was out-seconds later, at most) there were no more pink lines. The haze was just its disgustingly tawny evening self with black spots that were only after-images. The cabin stunk of ozone, but wind funneling through a hole in the one-time World Screen was blowing it out fast enough-Savannah had gotten in one lick, all right. And we were falling, the plane was swinging down like a crippled bird —I could feel it and there was no use kidding myself.

But staring at the control panel wouldn't keep us from crashing if that was in the cards. I looked around and there were Pop and Alice glaring at each other across the closing door. He looked mean. She looked agonized and was pressing her burnt hand into her side with her elbow as if he'd stamped on the hand, maybe. I didn't see any blood though. I didn't see the box and 'chute either, though I did see Alice's bag of groceries. I guessed Pop had made the drop.

Now, it occurred to me, was a bully time for Voice Two to melt the plane-if he hadn't already tried. My first thought had been that the spatter of hot metal had come from the Savannah craft spitting us, but there was no way to be sure.

I looked around at the viewport in time to see rocks and stunted trees jump out of the haze. *Good old Ray*, I thought, *always in at the death*. But just then the plane took a sickening bounce, as if its antigravity had only started to operate within yards of the ground. Another lurching fall and another bounce, less violent. A couple of repetitions of that, each one a little gentler, and then we were sort of bumping along on an even keel with the rocks and such sliding past fast about a hundred feet below, I judged. We'd been spoiled for altitude work, it seemed, but we could still cripple along in some sort of low-power repulsion field.

I looked at the North America screen and the buttons, wondering if I should start us back west again or leave us set on Atla-Hi and see what the hell happened-at the moment I hardly cared what else Savannah did to us. I needn't have wasted the mental energy. The decision was made for me. As I watched, the Atla-Hi button jumped up by itself and the button for the cracking plant went down and there was some extra bumping as we swung around.

Also, the violet patch of Atla-Hi went real dim and the button for it no longer had a violet nimbus. The Los Alamos blue went dull too. The cracking-plant dot glowed a brighter green-that was all.

All except for one thing. As the violet dimmed I thought I heard Voice One very faintly (not as if speaking directly but as if the screen had heard and remembered-not a voice but the fluorescent ghost of one): "Thank you and good luck!"

# Chapter 6

Many a man has dated his ruin from some murder or other that perhaps he thought little of at the time.

—Thomas de Quincey

"And a long merry siege to you, sir, and roast rat for Christmas!" I responded, very out loud and rather to my surprise.

"War! How I hate war!" —that was what Pop exploded with. He didn't exactly dance in senile rage-he was still keeping too sharp a watch on Alice-but his voice sounded that way.

"Damn you, Pop!" Alice contributed. "And you too, Ray! We might have pulled something, but you had to go obedience-happy." Then her anger got the better of her grammar, or maybe Pop and me was corrupting it. "Damn the both of you!" she finished.

It didn't make much sense, any of it. We were just cutting loose, I guess, after being scared to say anything for the last half hour.

I said to Alice, "I don't know what you could have pulled, except the chain on us." To Pop I remarked, "You may hate war, but you sure helped that one along. Those grenades you dropped will probably take care of a few hundred Savannans."

"That's what you always say about me, isn't it?" he snapped back. "But I don't suppose I should expect any kinder interpretation of my motives." To Alice he said, "I'm sorry I had to slap your burnt fingers, sister, but you can't say I didn't warn you about my low-down tactics." Then to me again: "I *do* hate war, Ray. It's just murder on a bigger scale, though some of the boys give me an argument there."

"Then why don't you go preach against war in Atla-Hi and Savannah?" Alice demanded, still very hot but not quite so bitter.

"Yeah, Pop, how about it?" I seconded.

"Maybe I should," he said, thoughtful all at once. "They sure need it." Then he grinned. "Hey, how'd this sound: HEAR THE WORLD-FAMOUS MURDERER POP TRUMBULL TALK AGAINST WAR. WEAR YOUR STEEL THROAT PROTECTORS. Pretty good, hey?"

We all laughed at that, grudgingly at first, then with a touch of wholeheartedness. I think we all recognized that things weren't going to be very cheerful from here on in and we'd better not turn up our noses at the feeblest fun.

"I guess I didn't have anything very bright in mind," Alice admitted to me, while to Pop she said, "All right, I forgive you for the present."

"Don't!" Pop said with a shudder. "I hate to think of what happened to the last bugger made the mistake of forgiving me."

We looked around and took stock of our resources. It was time we did. It was getting dark fast, although we were chasing the sun, and there weren't any cabin lights coming on and we sure didn't know of any way of getting any.

We wadded a couple of satchels into the hole in the World Screen without trying to probe it. After a while it got warmer again in the cabin and the air a little less dusty. Presently it started to get too smoky from the cigarettes we were burning, but that came later.

We screwed off the walls the few storage bags we hadn't inspected. They didn't contain nothing of consequence, not even a flashlight.

I had one last go at the buttons, though there weren't any left with nimbuses on them-the darker it got, the clearer that was. Even the Atla-Hi button wouldn't push now that it had lost its violet halo. I tried the gunnery patterns, figuring to put in a little time taking pot shots at any mountains that turned up, but the buttons that had been responding so well a few minutes ago refused to budge. Alice suggested different patterns, but none of them worked. That console was really locked-maybe the shot from Savannah was partly responsible, though Atla-Hi remote-locking things was explanation enough.

"The buggers!" I said. "They didn't have to tie us up *this* tight. Going east we at least had a choice-forward or back. Now we got none."

"Maybe we're just as well off," Pop said. "If Atla-Hi had been able to do anything more for us-that is, if they hadn't been sieged in, I mean-they'd sure as anything have pulled us in. Pull the plane in, I mean, and picked us out of it-with a big pair of tweezers, likely as not. And contrary to your flattering opinion of my preaching (which by the way none of the religious boys in my outfit share-they call me 'that misguided old atheist'), I don't think none of us would go over big at Atla-Hi."

We had to agree with him there. I couldn't imagine Pop or Alice or even me cutting much of a figure (even if we weren't murder-pariahs) with the pack of geniuses that seemed to make up the Atla-Alamos crowd. The Double-A Republics, to give them a name, might have their small-brain types, but somehow I didn't think so. There must be more than one Edison-Einstein, it seemed to me, back of antigravity and all the wonders in this plane and the other things we'd gotten hints of. Also, Grayl had seemed bred for brains as well as size, even if us small mammals had cooked his goose. And none of the modern "countries" had more than a few thousand population yet, I was pretty sure, and that hardly left room for a dumbbell class. Finally, too, I got hold of a memory I'd been reaching for the last hour-how when I was a kid I'd read about some scientists who learned to talk Mandarin just for kicks. I told Alice and Pop.

"And if *that's* the average Atla-Alamoser's idea of mental recreation," I said, "well, you can see what I mean."

"I'll grant you they got a monopoly of brains," Pop agreed. "Not sense, though," he added doggedly.

"Intellectual snobs," was Alice's comment. "I know the type and I detest it." ("You *are* sort of intellectual, aren't you?" Pop told her, which fortunately didn't start a riot.)

Still, I guess all three of us found it fun to chew over a bit the new slant we'd gotten on two (in a way, three) of the great "countries" of the modern world. (And as long as we thought of it as fun, we didn't have to admit the envy and wistfulness that was behind our wisecracks.)

I said, "We've always figured in a general way that Alamos was the remains of a community of scientists and technicians. Now we know the same's true of the Atla-Hi group. They're the Brookhaven survivors."

"Manhattan Project, don't you mean?" Alice corrected.

"Nope, that was in Colorado Springs," Pop said with finality.

I also pointed out that a community of scientists would educate for technical intelligence, maybe breed for it too. And being a group picked for high I. Q. to begin with, they might make startlingly fast progress. You could easily imagine such folk, unimpeded by the boobs, creating a wonder world in a couple of generations.

"They got their troubles though," Pop reminded me and that led us to speculating about the war we'd dipped into. Savannah Fortress, we knew, was supposed to be based on some big atomic plants on the river down that way, but its culture seemed to have a fiercer ingredient than Atla-Alamos. Before we knew it we were, musing almost romantically about the plight of Atla-Hi, besieged by superior and (it was easy to suppose) barbaric forces, and maybe distant Los Alamos in a similar predicament-Alice reminded me how the voice had asked if they were still dying out there. For a moment I found myself fiercely proud that I had been able to strike a blow against evil aggressors. At once, of course, then, the revulsion came.

"This is a hell of a way," I said, "for three so-called realists to be mooning about things."

"Yes, especially when your heroes kicked us out," Alice agreed.

Pop chuckled. "Yep," he said, "they even took Ray's artillery away from him."

"You're wrong there, Pop," I said, sitting up. "I still got one of the grenades-the one the pilot had in his fist." To tell the truth I'd forgotten all about it and it bothered me a little now to feel it snugged up in my pocket against my hip bone where the skin is thin.

"You believe what that old Dutchman said about the steel cubes being atomic grenades?" Pop asked me.

"I don't know," I said, "He sure didn't sound enthusiastic about telling us the truth about anything. But for that matter he sounded mean enough to tell the truth figuring we'd think it was a lie. Maybe this *is* some sort of baby A-bomb with a fuse timed like a grenade." I got it out and hefted it. "How about I press the button and drop it out the door? Then we'll know." I really felt like doing it-restless, I guess.

"Don't be a fool, Ray," Alice said.

"Don't tense up, I won't," I told her. At the same time I made myself the little promise that if I ever got to feeling restless, that is, restless and *bad*, I'd just go ahead and punch the button and see what happened-sort of leave my future up to the gods of the Deathlands, you might say.

"What makes you so sure it's a weapon?" Pop asked.

"What else would it be," I asked him, "that they'd be so hot on getting them in the middle of a war?"

"I don't know for sure," Pop said. "I've made a guess, but I don't want to tell it now. What I'm getting at, Ray, is that your first thought about anything you find-in the world outside or in your own mind-is that it's a weapon."

"Anything worthwhile in your mind is a weapon!" Alice interjected with surprising intensity.

"You see?" Pop said. "That's what I mean about the both of you. That sort of thinking's been going on a long time. Cave man picks up a rock and right away asks himself, 'Who can I brain with this?' Doesn't occur to him for several hundred thousand years to use it to start building a hospital."

"You know, Pop," I said, carefully tucking the cube back in my pocket, "you *are* sort of preachy at times."

"Guess I am," he said. "How about some grub?"

It was a good idea. Another few minutes and we wouldn't have been able to see to eat, though with the cans shaped to tell their contents I guess we'd have managed. It was a funny circumstance that in this wonder plane we didn't even know how to turn on the light-and a good measure of our general helplessness.

We had our little feed and lit up again and settled ourselves. I judged it would be an overnight trip, at least to the cracking plant-we weren't making anything like the speed we had been going east. Pop was sitting in back again and Alice and I lay half hitched around on the kneeling seats, which allowed us to watch each other. Pretty soon it got so dark we couldn't see anything of each other but the glowing tips of the cigarettes and a bit of face around the mouth when the person took a deep drag. They were a good idea, those cigarettes-kept us from having ideas about the other person starting to creep around with a knife in his hand.

The North America screen still glowed dimly and we could watch our green dot trying to make progress. The viewport was dead black at first, then there came the faintest sort of bronze blotch that very slowly shifted forward and down. The Old Moon, of course, going west ahead of us.

After a while I realized what it was like-an old Pullman car (I'd traveled in one once as a kid) or especially the smoker of an old Pullman, very late at night. Our crippled antigravity, working on the irregularities of the ground as they came along below, made the ride rhythmically bumpy, you see. I remembered how lonely and strange that old sleeping car had seemed to me as a kid. This felt the same. I kept waiting for a hoot or a whistle. It was the sort of loneliness that settles in your bones and keeps working at you.

"I recall the first man I ever killed —" Pop started to reminisce softly.

"Shut up!" Alice told him. "Don't you ever talk about anything but murder, Pop?"

"Guess not," he said. "After all, it's the only really interesting topic there is. Do you know of another?"

It was silent in the cabin for a long time after that. Then Alice said, "It was the afternoon before my twelfth birthday when they came into the kitchen and killed my father. He'd been wise, in a way, and had us living at a spot where the bombs didn't touch us or the worst fallout. But he hadn't counted on the local werewolf gang. He'd just been slicing some bread-homemade from our own wheat (Dad was great on back to nature and all) —but he laid down the knife.

"Dad couldn't see any object or idea as a weapon, you see-that was his great weakness. Dad couldn't even see weapons as weapons. Dad had a philosophy of cooperation, that was his name for it, that he was going to explain to people. Sometimes I think he was glad of the Last War, because he believed it would give him his chance.

"But the werewolves weren't interested in philosophy and although their knives weren't as sharp as Dad's they didn't lay them down. Afterwards they had themselves a meal, with me for dessert. I remember one of them used a slice of bread to sop up blood like gravy. And another washed his hands and face in the cold coffee..."

She didn't say anything else for a bit. Pop said softly, "That was the afternoon, wasn't it, that the fallen angels ..." and then just said, "My big mouth."

"You were going to say 'the afternoon they killed God?'" Alice asked him. "You're right, it was. They killed God in the kitchen that afternoon. That's how I know he's dead. Afterwards they would have killed me too, eventually, except —"

Again she broke off, this time to say, "Pop, do you suppose I can have been thinking about myself as the Daughter of God all these years? That that's why everything seems so intense?"

"I don't know," Pop said. "The religious boys say we're all children of God. I don't put much stock in it-or else God sure has some lousy children. Go on with your story."

"Well, they would have killed me too, except the leader took a fancy to me and got the idea of training me up for a Weregirl or She-wolf Deb or whatever they called it."

"That was my first experience of ideas as weapons. He got an idea about me and I used it to kill him. I had to wait three months for my opportunity. I got him so lazy he let me shave him. He bled to death the same way as Dad."

"Hum," Pop commented after a bit, "that was a chiller, all right. I got to remember to tell it to Bill-it was somebody killing his mother that got *him* started. Alice, you had about as good a justification for your first murder as any I remember hearing."

"Yet," Alice said after another pause, with just a trace of the old sarcasm creeping back into her voice, "I don't suppose you think I was right to do it?"

"Right? Wrong? Who knows?" Pop said almost blusteringly. "Sure you were justified in a whole pack of ways. Anybody'd sympathize with you. A man often has fine justification for the first murder he commits. But as you must know, it's not that the first murder's always so bad in itself as that it's apt to start you on a killing spree. Your sense of values gets shifted a tiny bit and never shifts back. But you know all that and who am I to tell you anything, anyway? I've killed men because I didn't like the way they spit. And may very well do it again if I don't keep watching myself and my mind ventilated."

"Well, Pop," Alice said, "I didn't always have such dandy justification for my killings. Last one was a moony old physicist-he fixed me the Geiger counter I carry. A silly old geek —I don't know how he survived so long. Maybe an exile or a runaway. You know, I often attach myself to the elderly do-gooder type like my father was. Or like you, Pop."

Pop nodded. "It's good to know yourself," he said.

There was a third pause and then, although I hadn't exactly been intending to, I said, "Alice had justification for her first murder, personal justification that an ape would understand. I had no personal justification at all for mine, yet I killed about a million people at a modest estimate. You see, I was the boss of the crew that took care of the hydrogen missile ticketed for Moscow, and when the ticket was finally taken up I was the one to punch it. My finger on the firing button, I mean."

I went on, "Yeah, Pop, I was one of the button-pushers. There were really quite a few of us, of course-that's why I get such a laugh out of stories about being or rubbing out the *one* guy who pushed all the buttons."

"That so?" Pop said with only mild-sounding interest. "In that case you ought to know —"

We didn't get to hear right then who I ought to know because I had a fit of coughing and we realized the cigarette smoke was getting just too thick. Pop fixed the door so it was open a crack and after a while the atmosphere got reasonably okay though we had to put up with a low lonely whistling sound.

"Yeah," I continued, "I was the boss of the missile crew and I wore a very handsome uniform with impressive insignia-not the bully old stripes I got on my chest now-and I was very young and handsome myself. We were all very young in that line of service, though a few of the men under me were a little older. Young and dedicated. I remember feeling a very deep and grim-and *clean* —responsibility. But I wonder sometimes just how deep it went or how clean it really was.

"I had an uncle flew in the war they fought to lick fascism, bombardier on a Flying Fortress or something, and once when he got drunk he told me how some days it didn't bother him at all to drop the eggs on Germany; the buildings and people down there seemed just like toys that a kid sets up to kick over, and the whole business about as naive fun as poking an anthill.

"*I* didn't even have to fly over at seven miles what I was going to be aiming at. Only I remember sometimes getting out a map and looking at a certain large dot on it and smiling a little and softly saying, 'Pow!' —and then giving a little conventional shudder and folding up the map quick.

"Naturally we told ourselves we'd never have to do it, fire the thing, I mean, we joked about how after twenty years or so we'd all be given jobs as museum attendants of this same bomb, deactivated at last. But naturally it didn't work out that way. There came the day when our side of the world got hit and the orders started cascading down from Defense Coordinator Bigelow —"

"Bigelow?" Pop interrupted. "Not Joe Bigelow?"

"Joseph A., I believe," I told him, a little annoyed.

"Why he's my boy then, the one I was telling you about-the skinny runt had this horn-handle! Can you beat that?" Pop sounded startlingly happy. "Him and you'll have a lot to talk about when you get together."

I wasn't so sure of that myself, in fact my first reaction was that the opposite would be true. To be honest I was for the first moment more than a little annoyed at Pop interrupting my story of my Big Grief-for it was that to me, make no mistake. Here my story had finally been teased out of me, against all expectation, after decades of repression and in spite of dozens of assorted psychological blocks-and here was Pop interrupting it for the sake of a lot of trivial organizational gossip about Joes and Bills and Georges we'd never heard of and what they'd say or think!

But then all of a sudden I realized that I didn't really care, that it didn't feel like a Big Grief any more, that just starting to tell about it after hearing Pop and Alice tell their stories had purged it of that unnecessary weight of feeling that had made it a millstone around my neck. It seemed to me now that I could look down at Ray Baker from a considerable height (but not an angelic or contemptuously superior height) and ask myself *not* why he had grieved so much-that was understandable and even desirable-but why he had grieved so *uselessly* in such a stuffy little private hell.

And it *would* be interesting to find out how Joseph A. Bigelow had felt.

"How does it feel, Ray, to kill a million people?"

I realized that Alice had asked me the question several seconds back and it was hanging in the air.

"That's just what I've been trying to tell you," I told her and started to explain it all over again-the words poured out of me now. I won't put them down here-it would take too long-but they were honest words as far as I knew and they eased me.

I couldn't get over it: here were us three murderers feeling a trust and understanding and sharing a communion that I wouldn't have believed possible between *any* two or three people in the Age of the Deaders-or in *any* age, to tell the truth. It was against everything I knew of Deathland psychology, but it was happening just the same. Oh, our strange isolation had something to do with it, I knew, and that Pullman-car memory hypnotizing my mind, and our reactions to the voices and violence of Atla-Alamos, but in spite of all that I ranked it as a wonder. I felt an inward freedom and easiness that I never would have believed possible. Pop's little disorganized organization had really got hold of something, I couldn't deny it.

Three treacherous killers talking from the bottoms of their hearts and believing each other! — for it never occurred to me to doubt that Pop and Alice were feeling exactly like I was. In fact, we were all so sure of it that we didn't even mention our communion to each other. Perhaps we were a little afraid we would rub off the bloom. We just enjoyed it.

We must have talked about a thousand things that night and smoked a couple of hundred cigarettes. After a while we started taking little catnaps-we'd gotten too much off our chests and come to feel too tranquil for even our excitement to keep us awake. I remember the first time I dozed waking up with a cold start and grabbing for Mother-and then hearing Pop and Alice gabbing in the dark, and remembering what had happened, and relaxing again with a smile.

Of all things, Pop was saying, "Yep, I imagine Ray must be good to make love to, murderers almost always are, they got the fire. It reminds me of what a guy named Fred told me, one of our boys..."

Mostly we took turns going to sleep, though I think there were times when all three of us were snoozing. About the fifth time I woke up, after some tighter shut-eye, the orange soup was back again outside and Alice was snoring gently in the next seat and Pop was up and had one of his knives out.

He was looking at his reflection in the viewport. His face gleamed. He was rubbing butter into it.

"Another day, another pack of troubles," he said cheerfully.

The tone of his remark jangled my nerves, as that tone generally does early in the morning. I squeezed my eyes. "Where are we?" I asked.

He poked his elbow toward the North America screen. The two green dots were almost one.

"My God, we're practically there," Alice said for me. She'd waked fast, Deathlands style.

"I know," Pop said, concentrating on what he was doing, "but I aim to be shaved before they commence landing maneuvers."

"You think automatic will land us?" Alice asked. "What if we just start circling around?"

"We can figure out what to do when it happens," Pop said, whittling away at his chin. "Until then, I'm not interested. There's still a couple of bottles of coffee in the sack. I've had mine."

I didn't join in this chit-chat because the green dots and Alice's first remark had reminded me of a lot deeper reason for my jangled nerves than Pop's cheerfulness. Night was gone, with its shielding cloak and its feeling of being able to talk forever, and the naked day was here, with its demands for action. It is not so difficult to change your whole view of life when you are flying, or even bumping along above the ground with friends who understand, but soon, I knew, I'd be down in the dust with something I never wanted to see again.

"Coffee, Ray?"

"Yeah, I guess so." I took the bottle from Alice and wondered whether my face looked as glum as hers.

"They shouldn't salt butter," Pop asserted. "It makes it lousy for shaving."

"It was the *best* butter," Alice said.

"Yeah," I said. "The Dormouse, when they buttered the watch."

It may be true that feeble humor is better than none. I don't know.

"What are you two yakking about?" Pop demanded.

"A book we both read," I told him.

"Either of you writers?" Pop asked with sudden interest. "Some of the boys think we should have a book about us. I say it's too soon, but they say we might all die off or something. Whoa, Jenny! Easy does it. Gently, please!"

That last remark was by way of recognizing that the plane had started an authoritative turn to the left. I got a sick and cold feeling. This was it.

Pop sheathed his knife and gave his face a final rub. Alice belted on her satchel. I reached for my knapsack, but I was staring through the viewport, dead ahead.

The haze lightened faintly, three times. I remembered the St. Elmo's fire that had flamed from the cracking plant.

"Pop," I said-almost whined, to be truthful, "why'd the bugger ever have to land here in the first place? He was rushing stuff they needed bad at Atla-Hi —why'd he have to break his trip?"

"That's easy," Pop said. "He was being a bad boy. At least that's my theory. He was supposed to go straight to Atla-Hi, but there was somebody he wanted to check up on first. He stopped here to see his girlfriend. Yep, his girlfriend. She tried to warn him off-that's my explanation of the juice that flared out of the cracking plant and interfered with his landing, though I'm sure she didn't intend the last. By the way, whatever she turned on to give him the warning must still be turned on. But Grayl came on down in spite of it."

Before I could assimilate that, the seven deformed gas tanks materialized in the haze. We got the freeway in our sights and steadied and slowed and kept slowing. The plane didn't graze the cracking plant this time, though I'd have sworn it was going to hit it head on. When I saw we *weren't* going to hit it, I wanted to shut my eyes, but I couldn't.

The stain was black now and the Pilot's body was thicker than I remembered-bloated. But that wouldn't last long. Three or four vultures were working on it.

# Chapter 7

Here now in his triumph where all things falter,
Stretched out on the spoils that his own hand spread,
As a god self-slain on his own strange altar,

Death lies dead.

—A Forsaken Garden,
by Charles Swinburne

Pop was first down. Between us we helped Alice. Before joining them I took a last look at the control panel. The cracking plant button was up again and there was a blue nimbus on another button. For Los Alamos, I supposed. I was tempted to push it and get away solo, but then I thought, *nope, there's nothing for me at the other end and the loneliness will be worse than what I got to face here.* I climbed out.

I didn't look at the body, although we were practically on top of it. I saw a little patch of silver off to one side and remembered the gun that had melted. The vultures had waddled off but only a few yards.

"We could kill them," Alice said to Pop.

"Why?" he responded. "Didn't some Hindus use them to take care of dead bodies? Not a bad idea, either."

"Parsees," Alice amplified.

"Yep, Parsees, that's what I meant. Give you a nice clean skeleton in a matter of days."

Pop was leading us past the body toward the cracking plant. I heard the flies buzzing loudly. I felt terrible. I wanted to be dead myself. Just walking along after Pop was an awful effort.

"His girl was running a hidden observation tower here," Pop was saying now. "Weather and all that, I suppose. Or maybe setting up a robot station of some kind. I couldn't tell you about her before, because you were both in a mood to try to rub out anybody remotely connected with the Pilot. In fact, I did my best to lead you astray, letting you think I'd been the one to scream and all. Even now, to be honest about it, I don't know if I'm doing the right thing telling and showing you all this, but a man's got to take some risks whatever he does."

"Say, Pop," I said dully, "isn't she apt to take a shot at us or something?" Not that I'd have minded on my own account. "Or are you and her that good friends?"

"Nope, Ray," he said, "she doesn't even know me. But I don't think she's in a position to do any shooting. You'll see why. Hey, she hasn't even shut the door. That's bad."

He seemed to be referring to a kind of manhole cover standing on its edge just inside the open-walled first story of the cracking plant. He knelt and looked down the hole the cover was designed to close off.

"Well, at least she didn't collapse at the bottom of the shaft," he said. "Come on, let's see what happened." And he climbed into the shaft.

We followed him like zombies. At least that's how I felt. The shaft was about twenty feet deep. There were foot- and hand-holds. It got stuffy right away, and warmer, in spite of the shaft being open at the top.

At the bottom there was a short horizontal passage. We had to duck to get through it. When we could straighten up we were in a large and luxurious bomb-resistant dugout, to give it a name. And it was stuffier and hotter than ever.

There was a lot of scientific equipment around and several small control panels reminding me of the one in the back of the plane. Some of them, I supposed, connected with instruments, weather and otherwise, hidden up in the skeletal structure of the cracking plant. And there were signs of occupancy, a young woman's occupancy—clothes scattered around in a frivolous way, and some small objects of art, and a slightly more than life-size head in clay that I guessed the occupant must have been sculpting. I didn't give that last more than the most fleeting look, strictly unintentional to begin with, because although it wasn't finished I could tell whose head it was supposed to be-the Pilot's.

The whole place was finished in dull silver like the cabin of the plane, and likewise it instantly struck me as having a living personality, partly the Pilot's and partly someone else's —the personality of a marriage. Which wasn't a bit nice, because the whole place smelt of death.

But to tell the truth I didn't give the place more than the quickest look-over, because my attention was rivetted almost at once on a long wide couch with the covers kicked off it and on the body there.

The woman was about six feet tall and built like a goddess. Her hair was blonde and her skin tanned. She was lying on her stomach and she was naked.

She didn't come anywhere near my libido, though. She looked sick to death. Her face, twisted towards us, was hollow-cheeked and flushed. Her eyes, closed, were sunken and dark-circled. She was breathing shallowly and rapidly through her open mouth, gasping now and then.

I got the crazy impression that all the heat in the place was coming from her body, radiating from her fever.

And the whole place stunk of death. Honestly it seemed to me that this dugout was Death's underground temple, the bed Death's altar, and the woman Death's sacrifice. (Had I unconsciously come to worship Death as a god in the Deathlands? I don't really know. There it gets too deep for me.)

No, she didn't come within a million miles of my libido, but there was another part of me that she was eating at...

If guilt's a luxury, then I'm a plutocrat.

...eating at until I was an empty shell, until I had no props left, until I wanted to die then and there, until I figured I had to die...

There was a faint sharp hiss right at my elbow. I looked and found that, unbeknownst to myself, I'd taken the steel cube out of my pocket and holding it snuggled between my first and second fingers I'd punched the button with my thumb just as I'd promised myself I would if I got to really feeling bad.

It goes to show you that you should never give your mind any kind of instructions even half in fun, unless you're prepared to have them carried out whether you approve later or not.

Pop saw what I'd done and looked at me strangely. "So you had to die after all, Ray," he said softly. "Most of us find out we have to, one way or another."

We waited. Nothing happened. I noticed a very faint milky cloud a few inches across hanging in the air by the cube.

Thinking right away of poison gas, I jerked away a little, dispersing the cloud.

"What's that?" I demanded of no one in particular.

"I'd say," said Pop, "that that's something that squirted out of a tiny hole in the side of the cube opposite the button. A hole so nearly microscopic you wouldn't see it unless you looked for it hard. Ray, I don't think you're going to get your baby A-blast, and what's more I'm afraid you've wasted something that's damn valuable. But don't let it worry you. Before I dropped those cubes for Atla-Hi I snagged one."

And darn if he didn't pull the brother of my cube out of his pocket.

"Alice," he said, "I noticed a half pint of whiskey in your satchel when we got the salve. Would you put some on a rag and hand it to me."

Alice looked at him like he was nuts, but while her eyes were looking her pliers and her gloved hand were doing what he told her.

Pop took the rag and swabbed a spot on the sick woman's nearest buttock and jammed the cube against the spot and pushed the button.

"It's a jet hypodermic, folks," he said.

He took the cube away and there was the welt to substantiate his statement.

"Hope we got to her in time," he said. "The plague is tough. Now I guess there's nothing for us to do but wait, maybe for quite a while."

I felt shaken beyond all recognition.

"Pop, you old caveman detective!" I burst out. "When did you get that idea for a steel hospital?" Don't think I was feeling anywhere near that gay. It was reaction, close to hysterical.

Pop was taken aback, but then he grinned. "I had a couple of clues that you and Alice didn't," he said. "I knew there was a very sick woman involved. And I had that bout with Los Alamos fever I told you. They've had a lot of trouble with it, I believe-some say its spores come from outside the world with the cosmic dust-and now it seems to have been carried to Atla-Hi. Let's hope they've found the answer this time. Alice, maybe we'd better start getting some water into this gal."

After a while we sat down and fitted the facts together more orderly. Pop did the fitting mostly. Alamos researchers must have been working for years on the plague as it ravaged intermittently, maybe with mutations and ET tricks to make the job harder. Very recently they'd found a promising treatment (cure, we hoped) and prepared it for rush shipment to Atla-Hi, where the plague was raging too and they were sieged in by Savannah as well. Grayl was picked to fly the serum, or drug or whatever it was. But he knew or guessed that this lone woman observer (because she'd fallen out of radio communication or something) had come down with the plague too and he decided to land some serum for her, probably without authorization.

"How do we know she's his girlfriend?" I asked.

"Or wife," Pop said tolerantly. "Why, there was that bag of woman's stuff he was carrying, frilly things like a man would bring for a woman. Who else'd he be apt to make a special stop for?

"Another thing," Pop said. "He must have been using jets to hurry his trip. We heard them, you know."

That seemed about as close a reconstruction of events as we could get. Strictly hypothetical, of course. Deathlanders trying to figure out what goes on inside a "country" like Atla-Alamos and *why* are sort of like foxes trying to understand world politics, or wolves the Gothic migrations. Of course we're all human beings, but that doesn't mean as much as it sounds.

Then Pop told us how he'd happened to be on the scene. He'd been doing a "tour of duty", as he called it, when he spotted this woman's observatory and decided to hang around anonymously and watch over her for a few days and maybe help protect her from some dangerous characters that he knew were in the neighborhood.

"Pop, that sounds like a lousy idea to me," I objected. "Risky, I mean. Spying on another person, watching them without their knowing, would be the surest way to stir up in me the idea of murdering them. Safest thing for me to do in that situation would be to turn around and run."

"*You* probably should," he agreed. "For now, anyway. It's all a matter of knowing your own strength and stage of growth. Me, it helps to give myself these little jobs. And the essence of 'em is that the other person shouldn't know I'm helping."

It sounded like knighthood and pilgrimage and the Boy Scouts all over again-for murderers. Well, why not?

Pop had seen this woman come out of the manhole a couple of times and look around and then go back down and he'd got the impression she was sick and troubled. He'd even guessed she might be coming down with Alamos fever. He'd seen us arrive, of course, and that had bothered him. Then when the plane landed she'd come up again, acting out of her head, but when she'd seen the Pilot and us going for him she'd given that scream and collapsed at the top of the shaft. He'd figured the only thing he could do for her was keep us occupied. Besides, now that he knew for sure we were murderers he'd started to burn with the desire to talk to us and maybe help us quit killing if we seemed to want to. It was only much later, in the middle of our trip, that he began to suspect that the steel cubes were jet hypodermics.

While Pop had been telling us all this, we hadn't been watching the woman so closely. Now Alice called our attention to her. Her skin was covered with fine beads of perspiration, like diamonds.

"That's a good sign," Pop said and Alice started to wipe her off. While she was doing that the woman came to in a groggy sort of way and Pop fed her some thin soup and in the middle of his doing it she dropped off to sleep.

Alice said, "Any other time I would be wild to kill another woman that beautiful. But she has been so close to death that I would feel I was robbing another murderer. I suppose there is more behind the change in my feelings than that, though."

"Yeah, a little, I suppose," Pop said.

I didn't have anything to say about my own feelings. Certainly not out loud. I knew that they had changed and that they were still changing. It was complicated.

After a while it occurred to me and Alice to worry whether we mightn't catch this woman's sickness. It would serve us right, of course, but plague is plague. But Pop reassured us. "Actually I snagged three cubes," he said. "That should take care of you two. I figure I'm immune."

Time wore on. Pop dragged out the harmonica, as I'd been afraid he would, but his playing wasn't too bad. "Tenting Tonight," "When Johnnie Comes Marching Home," and such. We had a meal.

The Pilot's woman woke up again, in her full mind this time or something like it. We were clustered around the bed, smiling a little I suppose and looking inquiring. Being even assistant nurses makes you all concerned about the patient's health and state of mind.

Pop helped her sit up a little. She looked around. She saw me and Alice. Recognition came into her eyes. She drew away from us with a look of loathing. She didn't say a word, but the look stayed.

Pop drew me aside and whispered, "I think it would be a nice gesture if you and Alice took a blanket and went up and sewed him into it. I noticed a big needle and some thread in her satchel." He looked me in the eye and added, "You can't expect this woman to feel any other way toward you, you know. Now or ever."

He was right of course. I gave Alice the high sign and we got out.

No point in dwelling on the next scene. Alice and me sewed up in a blanket a big guy who'd been dead a day and worked over by vultures. That's all.

About the time we'd finished, Pop came up.

"She chased me out," he explained. "She's getting dressed. When I told her about the plane, she said she was going back to Los Alamos. She's not fit to travel, of course, but she's giving herself injections. It's none of our business. Incidentally, she wants to take the body back with her. I told her how we'd dropped the serum and how you and Alice had helped and she listened."

The Pilot's woman wasn't long after Pop. She must have had trouble getting up the shaft, she had a little trouble even walking straight, but she held her head high. She was wearing a dull silver tunic and sandals and cloak. As she passed me and Alice I could see the look of loathing come back into her eyes, and her chin went a little higher. I thought, why shouldn't she want us dead? Right now she probably wants to be dead herself.

Pop nodded to us and we hoisted up the body and followed her. It was almost too heavy a load even for the three of us.

As she reached the plane a silver ladder telescoped down to her from below the door. I thought, *the Pilot must have had it keyed to her some way, so it would let down for her but nobody else. A very lovely gesture.*

The ladder went up after her and we managed to lift the body above our heads, our arms straight, and we walked it through the door of the plane that way, she receiving it.

The door closed and we stood back and the plane took off into the orange haze, us watching it until it was swallowed.

Pop said, "Right now, I imagine you two feel pretty good in a screwed-up sort of way. I know I do. But take it from me, it won't last. A day or two and we're going to start feeling another way, the *old* way, if we don't get busy."

I knew he was right. You don't shake Old Urge Number One anything like that easy.

"So," said Pop, "I got places I want to show you. Guys I want you to meet. And there's things to do, a lot of them. Let's get moving."

So there's my story. Alice is still with me (Urge Number Two is even harder to shake, supposing you wanted to) and we haven't killed anybody lately. (Not since the Pilot, in fact, but it doesn't do to boast.) We're making a stab (my language!) at doing the sort of work Pop does in the Deathlands. It's tough but interesting. I still carry a knife, but I've given Mother to Pop. He has it strapped to him alongside Alice's screw-in blade.

Atla-Hi and Alamos still seem to be in existence, so I guess the serum worked for them generally as it did for the Pilot's Woman; they haven't sent us any medals, but they haven't sent a hangman's squad after us either-which is more than fair, you'll admit. But Savannah, turned back from Atla-Hi, is still going strong: there's a rumor they have an army at the gates of Ouachita right now. We tell Pop he'd better start preaching fast-it's one of our standard jokes.

There's also a rumor that a certain fellowship of Deathlanders is doing surprisingly well, a rumor that there's a new America growing in the Deathlands-an America that never need kill again. But don't put too much stock in it. Not *too* much.

# The Moon is Green

*Anybody who wanted to escape death could, by paying a very simple price-denial of life!*

"Effie! What the devil are you up to?"

Her husband's voice, chopping through her mood of terrified rapture, made her heart jump like a startled cat, yet by some miracle of feminine self-control her body did not show a tremor.

*Dear God,* she thought, *he mustn't see it. It's so beautiful, and he always kills beauty.*

"I'm just looking at the Moon," she said listlessly. "It's green."

*Mustn't, mustn't see it.* And now, with luck, he wouldn't. For the face, as if it also heard and sensed the menace in the voice, was moving back from the window's glow into the outside dark, but slowly, reluctantly, and still faunlike, pleading, cajoling, tempting, and incredibly beautiful.

"Close the shutters at once, you little fool, and come away from the window!"

"Green as a beer bottle," she went on dreamily, "green as emeralds, green as leaves with sunshine striking through them and green grass to lie on." She couldn't help saying those last words. They were her token to the face, even though it couldn't hear.

"Effie!"

She knew what that last tone meant. Wearily she swung shut the ponderous lead inner shutters and drove home the heavy bolts. That hurt her fingers; it always did, but he mustn't know that.

"You know that those shutters are not to be touched! Not for five more years at least!"

"I only wanted to look at the Moon," she said, turning around, and then it was all gone-the face, the night, the Moon, the magic-and she was back in the grubby, stale little hole, facing an angry, stale little man. It was then that the eternal thud of the air-conditioning fans and the crackle of the electrostatic precipitators that sieved out the dust reached her consciousness again like the bite of a dentist's drill.

"Only wanted to look at the Moon!" he mimicked her in falsetto. "Only wanted to die like a little fool and make me that much more ashamed of you!" Then his voice went gruff and professional. "Here, count yourself."

She silently took the Geiger counter he held at arm's length, waited until it settled down to a steady ticking slower than a clock-due only to cosmic rays and indicating nothing dangerous-and then began to comb her body with the instrument. First her head and shoulders, then out along her arms and back along their under side. There was something oddly voluptuous about her movements, although her features were gray and sagging.

The ticking did not change its tempo until she came to her waist. Then it suddenly spurted, clicking faster and faster. Her husband gave an excited grunt, took a quick step forward, froze. She goggled for a moment in fear, then grinned foolishly, dug in the pocket of her grimy apron and guiltily pulled out a wristwatch.

He grabbed it as it dangled from her fingers, saw that it had a radium dial, cursed, heaved it up as if to smash it on the floor, but instead put it carefully on the table.

"You imbecile, you incredible imbecile," he softly chanted to himself through clenched teeth, with eyes half closed.

She shrugged faintly, put the Geiger counter on the table, and stood there slumped.

He waited until the chanting had soothed his anger, before speaking again. He said quietly, "I do suppose you still realize the sort of world you're living in?"

---

She nodded slowly, staring at nothingness. Oh, she realized, all right, realized only too well. It was the world that hadn't realized. The world that had gone on stockpiling hydrogen bombs. The world that had put those bombs in cobalt shells, although it had promised it wouldn't, because the cobalt made them much more terrible and cost no more. The world that had started throwing those bombs, always telling itself that it hadn't thrown enough of them yet to make the air really dangerous with the deadly radioactive dust that came from the cobalt. Thrown them and kept on throwing until the danger point, where air and ground would become fatal to all human life, was approached.

Then, for about a month, the two great enemy groups had hesitated. And then each, unknown to the other, had decided it could risk one last gigantic and decisive attack without exceeding the danger point. It had been planned to strip off the cobalt cases, but someone forgot and then there wasn't time. Besides, the military scientists of each group were confident that the lands of the other had got the most dust. The two attacks came within an hour of each other.

After that, the Fury. The Fury of doomed men who think only of taking with them as many as possible of the enemy, and in this case-they hoped-all. The Fury of suicides who know they have botched up life for good. The Fury of cocksure men who realize they have been outsmarted by fate, the enemy, and themselves, and know that they will never be able to improvise a defense when arraigned before the high court of history-and whose unadmitted hope is that there will be no high court of history left to arraign them. More cobalt bombs were dropped during the Fury than in all the preceding years of the war.

After the Fury, the Terror. Men and women with death sifting into their bones through their nostrils and skin, fighting for bare survival under a dust-hazed sky that played fantastic tricks with the light of Sun and Moon, like the dust from Krakatoa that drifted around the world for years. Cities, countryside, and air were alike poisoned, alive with deadly radiation.

The only realistic chance for continued existence was to retire, for the five or ten years the radiation would remain deadly, to some well-sealed and radiation-shielded place that must also be copiously supplied with food, water, power, and a means of air-conditioning.

Such places were prepared by the far-seeing, seized by the stronger, defended by them in turn against the desperate hordes of the dying ... until there were no more of those.

After that, only the waiting, the enduring. A mole's existence, without beauty or tenderness, but with fear and guilt as constant companions. Never to see the Sun, to walk among the trees-or even know if there were still trees.

Oh, yes, she realized what the world was like.

---

"You understand, too, I suppose, that we were allowed to reclaim this ground-level apartment only because the Committee believed us to be responsible people, and because I've been making a damn good showing lately?"

"Yes, Hank."

"I thought you were eager for privacy. You want to go back to the basement tenements?"

*God, no! Anything rather than that fetid huddling, that shameless communal sprawl. And yet, was this so much better? The nearness to the surface was meaningless; it only tantalized. And the privacy magnified Hank.*

She shook her head dutifully and said, "No, Hank."

"Then why aren't you careful? I've told you a million times, Effie, that glass is no protection against the dust that's outside that window. The lead shutter must never be touched! If you make one single slip like that and it gets around, the Committee will send us back to the lower levels without blinking an eye. And they'll think twice before trusting me with any important jobs."

"I'm sorry, Hank."

"Sorry? What's the good of being sorry? The only thing that counts is never to make a slip! Why the devil do you do such things, Effie? What drives you to it?"

She swallowed. "It's just that it's so dreadful being cooped up like this," she said hesitatingly, "shut away from the sky and the Sun. I'm just hungry for a little beauty."

"And do you suppose I'm not?" he demanded. "Don't you suppose I want to get outside, too, and be carefree and have a good time? But I'm not so damn selfish about it. I want my children to enjoy the Sun, and my children's children. Don't you see that that's the all-important thing and that we have to behave like mature adults and make sacrifices for it?"

"Yes, Hank."

He surveyed her slumped figure, her lined and listless face. "You're a fine one to talk about hunger for beauty," he told her. Then his voice grew softer, more deliberate. "You haven't forgotten, have you, Effie, that until last month the Committee was so concerned about your sterility? That they were about to enter my name on the list of those waiting to be allotted a free woman? Very high on the list, too!"

She could nod even at that one, but not while looking at him. She turned away. She knew very well that the Committee was justified in worrying about the birth rate. When the community finally moved back to the surface again, each additional healthy young person would be an asset, not only in the struggle for bare survival, but in the resumed war against Communism which some of the Committee members still counted on.

It was natural that they should view a sterile woman with disfavor, and not only because of the waste of her husband's germ-plasm, but because sterility might indicate that she had suffered more than the average from radiation. In that case, if she did bear children later on, they would be more apt to carry a defective heredity, producing an undue number of monsters and freaks in future generations, and so contaminating the race.

Of course she understood it. She could hardly remember the time when she didn't. Years ago? Centuries? There wasn't much difference in a place where time was endless.

---

His lecture finished, her husband smiled and grew almost cheerful.

"Now that you're going to have a child, that's all in the background again. Do you know, Effie, that when I first came in, I had some very good news for you? I'm to become a member of the Junior Committee and the announcement will be made at the banquet tonight." He cut short her mumbled congratulations. "So brighten yourself up and put on your best dress. I want the other Juniors to see what a handsome wife the new member has got." He paused. "Well, get a move on!"

She spoke with difficulty, still not looking at him. "I'm terribly sorry, Hank, but you'll have to go alone. I'm not well."

He straightened up with an indignant jerk. "There you go again! First that infantile, inexcusable business of the shutters, and now this! No feeling for my reputation at all. Don't be ridiculous, Effie. You're coming!"

"Terribly sorry," she repeated blindly, "but I really can't. I'd just be sick. I wouldn't make you proud of me at all."

"Of course you won't," he retorted sharply. "As it is, I have to spend half my energy running around making excuses for you-why you're so odd, why you always seem to be ailing, why you're always stupid and snobbish and say the wrong thing. But tonight's really important, Effie. It will cause a lot of bad comment if the new member's wife isn't present. You know how just a hint of sickness starts the old radiation-disease rumor going. You've *got* to come, Effie."

She shook her head helplessly.

"Oh, for heaven's sake, come on!" he shouted, advancing on her. "This is just a silly mood. As soon as you get going, you'll snap out of it. There's nothing really wrong with you at all."

He put his hand on her shoulder to turn her around, and at his touch her face suddenly grew so desperate and gray that for a moment he was alarmed in spite of himself.

"Really?" he asked, almost with a note of concern.

She nodded miserably.

"Hmm!" He stepped back and strode about irresolutely. "Well, of course, if that's the way it is ..." He checked himself and a sad smile crossed his face. "So you don't care enough about your old husband's success to make one supreme effort in spite of feeling bad?"

Again the helpless headshake. "I just can't go out tonight, under any circumstances." And her gaze stole toward the lead shutters.

He was about to say something when he caught the direction of her gaze. His eyebrows jumped. For seconds he stared at her incredulously, as if some completely new and almost unbelievable possibility had popped into his mind. The look of incredulity slowly faded, to be replaced by a harder, more calculating expression. But when he spoke again, his voice was shockingly bright and kind.

"Well, it can't be helped naturally, and I certainly wouldn't want you to go if you weren't able to enjoy it. So you hop right into bed and get a good rest. I'll run over to the men's dorm to freshen up. No, really, I don't want you to have to make any effort at all. Incidentally, Jim Barnes isn't going to be able to come to the banquet either-touch of the old 'flu, he tells me, of all things."

He watched her closely as he mentioned the other man's name, but she didn't react noticeably. In fact, she hardly seemed to be hearing his chatter.

"I got a bit sharp with you, I'm afraid, Effie," he continued contritely. "I'm sorry about that. I was excited about my new job and I guess that was why things upset me. Made me feel let down when I found you weren't feeling as good as I was. Selfish of me. Now you get into bed right away and get well. Don't worry about me a bit. I know you'd come if you possibly could. And I know you'll be thinking about me. Well, I must be off now."

He started toward her, as if to embrace her, then seemed to think better of it. He turned back at the doorway and said, emphasizing the words, "You'll be completely alone for the next four hours." He waited for her nod, then bounced out.

---

She stood still until his footsteps died away. Then she straightened up, walked over to where he'd put down the wristwatch, picked it up and smashed it hard on the floor. The crystal shattered, the case flew apart, and something went *zing!*

She stood there breathing heavily. Slowly her sagged features lifted, formed themselves into the beginning of a smile. She stole another look at the shutters. The smile became more definite. She felt her hair, wet her fingers and ran them along her hairline and back over her ears. After wiping her hands on her apron, she took it off. She straightened her dress, lifted her head with a little flourish, and stepped smartly toward the window.

Then her face went miserable again and her steps slowed.

No, it couldn't be, and it won't be, she told herself. It had been just an illusion, a silly romantic dream that she had somehow projected out of her beauty-starved mind and given a moment's false reality. There couldn't be anything alive outside. There hadn't been for two whole years.

And if there conceivably were, it would be something altogether horrible. She remembered some of the pariahs-hairless, witless creatures, with radiation welts crawling over their bodies like worms, who had come begging for succor during the last months of the Terror-and been shot down. How they must have hated the people in refuges!

But even as she was thinking these things, her fingers were caressing the bolts, gingerly drawing them, and she was opening the shutters gently, apprehensively.

No, there couldn't be anything outside, she assured herself wryly, peering out into the green night. Even her fears had been groundless.

But the face came floating up toward the window. She started back in terror, then checked herself.

For the face wasn't horrible at all, only very thin, with full lips and large eyes and a thin proud nose like the jutting beak of a bird. And no radiation welts or scars marred the skin, olive in the tempered moonlight. It looked, in fact, just as it had when she had seen it the first time.

For a long moment the face stared deep, deep into her brain. Then the full lips smiled and a half-clenched, thin-fingered hand materialized itself from the green darkness and rapped twice on the grimy pane.

Her heart pounding, she furiously worked the little crank that opened the window. It came unstuck from the frame with a tiny explosion of dust and a *zing* like that of the watch, only louder. A moment later it swung open wide and a puff of incredibly fresh air caressed her face and the inside of her nostrils, stinging her eyes with unanticipated tears.

The man outside balanced on the sill, crouching like a faun, head high, one elbow on knee. He was dressed in scarred, snug trousers and an old sweater.

"Is it tears I get for a welcome?" he mocked her gently in a musical voice. "Or are those only to greet God's own breath, the air?"

---

He swung down inside and now she could see he was tall. Turning, he snapped his fingers and called, "Come, puss."

A black cat with a twisted stump of a tail and feet like small boxing gloves and ears almost as big as rabbits' hopped clumsily in view. He lifted it down, gave it a pat. Then, nodding familiarly to Effie, he unstrapped a little pack from his back and laid it on the table.

She couldn't move. She even found it hard to breathe.

"The window," she finally managed to get out.

He looked at her inquiringly, caught the direction of her stabbing finger. Moving without haste, he went over and closed it carelessly.

"The shutters, too," she told him, but he ignored that, looking around.

"It's a snug enough place you and your man have," he commented. "Or is it that this is a free-love town or a harem spot, or just a military post?" He checked her before she could answer. "But let's not be talking about such things now. Soon enough I'll be scared to death for both of us. Best enjoy the kick of meeting, which is always good for twenty minutes at the least." He smiled at her rather shyly. "Have you food? Good, then bring it."

She set cold meat and some precious canned bread before him and had water heating for coffee. Before he fell to, he shredded a chunk of meat and put it on the floor for the cat, which left off its sniffing inspection of the walls and ran up eagerly mewing. Then the man began to eat, chewing each mouthful slowly and appreciatively.

From across the table Effie watched him, drinking in his every deft movement, his every cryptic quirk of expression. She attended to making the coffee, but that took only a moment. Finally she could contain herself no longer.

"What's it like up there?" she asked breathlessly. "Outside, I mean."

He looked at her oddly for quite a space. Finally, he said flatly, "Oh, it's a wonderland for sure, more amazing than you tombed folk could ever imagine. A veritable fairyland." And he quickly went on eating.

"No, but really," she pressed.

Noting her eagerness, he smiled and his eyes filled with playful tenderness. "I mean it, on my oath," he assured her. "You think the bombs and the dust made only death and ugliness. That was true at first. But then, just as the doctors foretold, they changed the life in the seeds and loins that were brave enough to stay. Wonders bloomed and walked." He broke off suddenly and asked, "Do any of you ever venture outside?"

"A few of the men are allowed to," she told him, "for short trips in special protective suits, to hunt for canned food and fuels and batteries and things like that."

"Aye, and those blind-souled slugs would never see anything but what they're looking for," he said, nodding bitterly. "They'd never see the garden where a dozen buds blossom where one did before, and the flowers have petals a yard across, with stingless bees big as sparrows gently supping their nectar. Housecats grown spotted and huge as leopards (not little runts like Joe Louis here) stalk through those gardens. But they're gentle beasts, no more harmful than the rainbow-scaled snakes that glide around their paws, for the dust burned all the murder out of them, as it burned itself out.

"I've even made up a little poem about that. It starts, 'Fire can hurt me, or water, or the weight of Earth. But the dust is my friend.' Oh, yes, and then the robins like cockatoos and squirrels like a princess's ermine! All under a treasure chest of Sun and Moon and stars that the dust's magic powder changes from ruby to emerald and sapphire and amethyst and back again. Oh, and then the new children—"

"You're telling the truth?" she interrupted him, her eyes brimming with tears. "You're not making it up?"

"I am not," he assured her solemnly. "And if you could catch a glimpse of one of the new children, you'd never doubt me again. They have long limbs as brown as this coffee would be if it had lots of fresh cream in it, and smiling delicate faces and the whitish teeth and the finest hair. They're so nimble that I—a sprightly man and somewhat enlivened by the dust-feel like a cripple beside them. And their thoughts dance like flames and make me feel a very imbecile.

"Of course, they have seven fingers on each hand and eight toes on each foot, but they're the more beautiful for that. They have large pointed ears that the Sun shines through. They play in the garden, all day long, slipping among the great leaves and blooms, but they're so swift that you can hardly see them, unless one chooses to stand still and look at you. For that matter, you have to look a bit hard for all these things I'm telling you."

"But it is true?" she pleaded.

"Every word of it," he said, looking straight into her eyes. He put down his knife and fork. "What's your name?" he asked softly. "Mine's Patrick."

"Effie," she told him.

He shook his head. "That can't be," he said. Then his face brightened. "Euphemia," he exclaimed. "That's what Effie is short for. Your name is Euphemia." As he said that, looking at her, she suddenly felt beautiful. He got up and came around the table and stretched out his hand toward her.

"Euphemia—" he began.

"Yes?" she answered huskily, shrinking from him a little, but looking up sideways, and very flushed.

"Don't either of you move," Hank said.

The voice was flat and nasal because Hank was wearing a nose respirator that was just long enough to suggest an elephant's trunk. In his right hand was a large blue-black automatic pistol.

---

They turned their faces to him. Patrick's was abruptly alert, shifty. But Effie's was still smiling tenderly, as if Hank could not break the spell of the magic garden and should be pitied for not knowing about it.

"You little—" Hank began with an almost gleeful fury, calling her several shameful names. He spoke in short phrases, closing tight his unmasked mouth between them while he sucked in breath through the respirator. His voice rose in a crescendo. "And not with a man of the community, but a pariah! *A pariah!*"

"I hardly know what you're thinking, man, but you're quite wrong," Patrick took the opportunity to put in hurriedly, conciliatingly. "I just happened to be coming by hungry tonight, a lonely tramp, and knocked at the window. Your wife was a bit foolish and let kindheartedness get the better of prudence—"

"Don't think you've pulled the wool over my eyes, Effie," Hank went on with a screechy laugh, disregarding the other man completely. "Don't think I don't know why you're suddenly going to have a child after four long years."

At that moment the cat came nosing up to his feet. Patrick watched him narrowly, shifting his weight forward a little, but Hank only kicked the animal aside without taking his eyes off them.

"Even that business of carrying the wristwatch in your pocket instead of on your arm," he went on with channeled hysteria. "A neat bit of camouflage, Effie. Very neat. And telling me it was my child, when all the while you've been seeing him for months!"

"Man, you're mad; I've not touched her!" Patrick denied hotly though still calculatingly, and risked a step forward, stopping when the gun instantly swung his way.

"Pretending you were going to give me a healthy child," Hank raved on, "when all the while you knew it would be-either in body or germ plasm —a thing like *that*!"

He waved his gun at the malformed cat, which had leaped to the top of the table and was eating the remains of Patrick's food, though its watchful green eyes were fixed on Hank.

"I should shoot him down!" Hank yelled, between sobbing, chest-racking inhalations through the mask. "I should kill him this instant for the contaminated pariah he is!"

All this while Effie had not ceased to smile compassionately. Now she stood up without haste and went to Patrick's side. Disregarding his warning, apprehensive glance, she put her arm lightly around him and faced her husband.

"Then you'd be killing the bringer of the best news we've ever had," she said, and her voice was like a flood of some warm sweet liquor in that musty, hate-charged room. "Oh, Hank, forget your silly, wrong jealousy and listen to me. Patrick here has something wonderful to tell us."

---

Hank stared at her. For once he screamed no reply. It was obvious that he was seeing for the first time how beautiful she had become, and that the realization jolted him terribly.

"What do you mean?" he finally asked unevenly, almost fearfully.

"I mean that we no longer need to fear the dust," she said, and now her smile was radiant. "It never really did hurt people the way the doctors said it would. Remember how it was with me, Hank, the exposure I had and recovered from, although the doctors said I wouldn't at first-and without even losing my hair? Hank, those who were brave enough to stay outside, and who weren't killed by terror and suggestion and panic-they adapted to the dust. They changed, but they changed for the better. Everything —"

"Effie, he told you lies!" Hank interrupted, but still in that same agitated, broken voice, cowed by her beauty.

"Everything that grew or moved was purified," she went on ringingly. "You men going out-side have never seen it, because you've never had eyes for it. You've been blinded to beauty, to life itself. And now all the power in the dust has gone and faded, anyway, burned itself out. That's true, isn't it?"

She smiled at Patrick for confirmation. His face was strangely veiled, as if he were calculating obscure changes. He might have given a little nod; at any rate, Effie assumed that he did, for she turned back to her husband.

"You see, Hank? We can all go out now. We need never fear the dust again. Patrick is a living proof of that," she continued triumphantly, standing straighter, holding him a little tighter. "Look at him. Not a scar or a sign, and he's been out in the dust for years. How could he be this way, if the dust hurt the brave? Oh, believe me, Hank! Believe what you see. Test it if you want. Test Patrick here."

"Effie, you're all mixed up. You don't know —" Hank faltered, but without conviction of any sort.

"Just test him," Effie repeated with utter confidence, ignoring-not even noticing-Patrick's warning nudge.

"All right," Hank mumbled. He looked at the stranger dully. "Can you count?" he asked.

Patrick's face was a complete enigma. Then he suddenly spoke, and his voice was like a fencer's foil-light, bright, alert, constantly playing, yet utterly on guard.

"Can I count? Do you take me for a complete simpleton, man? Of course I can count!"

"Then count yourself," Hank said, barely indicating the table.

"Count myself, should I?" the other retorted with a quick facetious laugh. "Is this a kindergarten? But if you want me to, I'm willing." His voice was rapid. "I've two arms, and two legs, that's four. And ten fingers and ten toes-you'll take my word for them? —that's twenty-four. A head, twenty-five. And two eyes and a nose and a mouth —"

"With this, I mean," Hank said heavily, advanced to the table, picked up the Geiger counter, switched it on, and handed it across the table to the other man.

But while it was still an arm's length from Patrick, the clicks began to mount furiously, until they were like the chatter of a pigmy machine gun. Abruptly the clicks slowed, but that was only the counter shifting to a new scaling circuit, in which each click stood for 512 of the old ones.

---

With those horrid, rattling little volleys, fear cascaded into the room and filled it, smashing like so much colored glass all the bright barriers of words Effie had raised against it. For no dreams can stand against the Geiger counter, the Twentieth Century's mouthpiece of ultimate truth. It was as if the dust and all the terrors of the dust had incarnated themselves in one dread invading shape that said in words stronger than audible speech, "Those were illusions, whistles in the dark. This is reality, the dreary, pitiless reality of the Burrowing Years."

Hank scuttled back to the wall. Through chattering teeth he babbled, "...enough radioactives ...kill a thousand men ...freak ...a freak ..." In his agitation he forgot for a moment to inhale through the respirator.

Even Effie-taken off guard, all the fears that had been drilled into her twanging like piano wires-shrank from the skeletal-seeming shape beside her, held herself to it only by desperation.

Patrick did it for her. He disengaged her arm and stepped briskly away. Then he whirled on them, smiling sardonically, and started to speak, but instead looked with distaste at the chattering Geiger counter he held between fingers and thumb.

"Have we listened to this racket long enough?" he asked.

Without waiting for an answer, he put down the instrument on the table. The cat hurried over to it curiously and the clicks began again to mount in a minor crescendo. Effie lunged for it frantically, switched it off, darted back.

"That's right," Patrick said with another chilling smile. "You do well to cringe, for I'm death itself. Even in death I could kill you, like a snake." And with that his voice took on the tones of a circus barker. "Yes, I'm a freak, as the gentleman so wisely said. That's what one doctor who dared talk with me for a minute told me before he kicked me out. He couldn't tell me why, but somehow the dust doesn't kill me. Because I'm a freak, you see, just like the men who ate nails and walked on fire and ate arsenic and stuck themselves through with pins. Step right up, ladies and gentlemen-only not too close! —and examine the man the dust can't harm. Rappaccini's child, brought up to date; his embrace, death!

"And now," he said, breathing heavily, "I'll get out and leave you in your damned lead cave."

He started toward the window. Hank's gun followed him shakingly.

"Wait!" Effie called in an agonized voice. He obeyed. She continued falteringly, "When we were together earlier, you didn't act as if..."

"When we were together earlier, I wanted what I wanted," he snarled at her. "You don't suppose I'm a bloody saint, do you?"

"And all the beautiful things you told me?"

"That," he said cruelly, "is just a line I've found that women fall for. They're all so bored and so starved for beauty-as *they* generally put it."

"Even the garden?" Her question was barely audible through the sobs that threatened to suffocate her.

He looked at her and perhaps his expression softened just a trifle.

"What's outside," he said flatly, "is just a little worse than either of you can imagine." He tapped his temple. "The garden's all here."

"You've killed it," she wept. "You've killed it in me. You've both killed everything that's beautiful. But you're worse," she screamed at Patrick, "because he only killed beauty once, but you brought it to life just so you could kill it again. Oh, I can't stand it! I won't stand it!" And she began to scream.

Patrick started toward her, but she broke off and whirled away from him to the window, her eyes crazy.

"You've been lying to us," she cried. "The garden's there. I know it is. But you don't want to share it with anyone."

"No, no, Euphemia," Patrick protested anxiously. "It's hell out there, believe me. I wouldn't lie to you about it."

"Wouldn't lie to me!" she mocked. "Are you afraid, too?"

With a sudden pull, she jerked open the window and stood before the blank green-tinged oblong of darkness that seemed to press into the room like a menacing, heavy, wind-urged curtain.

At that Hank cried out a shocked, pleading, "Effie!"

She ignored him. "I can't be cooped up here any longer," she said. "And I won't, now that I know. I'm going to the garden."

Both men sprang at her, but they were too late. She leaped lightly to the sill, and by the time they had flung themselves against it, her footsteps were already hurrying off into the darkness.

"Effie, come back! Come back!" Hank shouted after her desperately, no longer thinking to cringe from the man beside him, or how the gun was pointed. "I love you, Effie. Come back!"

Patrick added his voice. "Come back, Euphemia. You'll be safe if you come back right away. Come back to your home."

No answer to that at all.

They both strained their eyes through the greenish murk. They could barely make out a shadowy figure about half a block down the near-black canyon of the dismal, dust-blown street, into which the greenish moonlight hardly reached. It seemed to them that the figure was scooping something up from the pavement and letting it sift down along its arms and over its bosom.

"Go out and get her, man," Patrick urged the other. "For if I go out for her, I warn you I won't bring her back. She said something about having stood the dust better than most, and that's enough for me."

But Hank, chained by his painfully learned habits and by something else, could not move.

And then a ghostly voice came whispering down the street, chanting, "Fire can hurt me, or water, or the weight of Earth. But the dust is my friend."

Patrick spared the other man one more look. Then, without a word, he vaulted up and ran off.

Hank stood there. After perhaps a half minute he remembered to close his mouth when he inhaled. Finally he was sure the street was empty. As he started to close the window, there was a little *mew*.

He picked up the cat and gently put it outside. Then he did close the window, and the shutters, and bolted them, and took up the Geiger counter, and mechanically began to count himself.

# Nice Girl with Five Husbands

*Adventure is relative to one's previous experience. Sometimes, in fact, you can't even be sure you're having or not having one!*

To be given paid-up leisure and find yourself unable to create is unpleasant for any artist. To be stranded in a cluster of desert cabins with a dozen lonely people in the same predicament only makes it worse. So Tom Dorset was understandably irked with himself and the Tosker-Brown Vacation Fellowships as he climbed with the sun into the valley of red stones. He accepted the chafing of his camera strap against his shoulder as the nagging of conscience. He agreed with the disparaging hisses of the grains of sand rutched by his sneakers, and he wished that the occasional breezes, which faintly echoed the same criticisms, could blow him into a friendlier, less jealous age.

He had no way of knowing that just as there are winds that blow through space, so there are winds that blow through time. Such winds may be strong or weak. The strong ones are rare and seldom blow for short distances, or more of us would know about them. What they pick up is almost always whirled far into the future or past.

This has happened to people. There was Ambrose Bierce, who walked out of America and existence, and there are thousands of others who have disappeared without a trace, though many of these may not have been caught up by time tornadoes and I do not know if a time gale blew across the deck of the *Marie Celeste*.

Sometimes a time wind is playful, snatching up an object, sporting with it for a season and then returning it unharmed to its original place. Sometimes we may be blown about by whimsical time winds without realizing it. Memory, for example, is a tiny time breeze, so weak that it can ripple only the mind.

A very few time winds are like the monsoon, blowing at fixed intervals, first in one direction, then the other. Such a time wind blows near a balancing rock in a valley of red stones in the American Southwest. Every morning at ten o'clock, it blows a hundred years into the future; every afternoon at two, it blows a hundred years into the past.

Quite a number of people have unwittingly seen time winds in operation. There are misty spots on the sea's horizon and wavery patches over desert sands. There are mirages and will o' the wisps and ice blinks. And there are dust devils, such as Tom Dorset walked into near the balancing rock.

It seemed to him no more than a spiteful upgust of sand, against which he closed his eyes until the warm granules stopped peppering the lids. He opened them to see the balancing rock had silently fallen and lay a quarter buried-no, that couldn't be, he told himself instantly. He had been preoccupied; he must have passed the balancing rock and held its image in his mind.

---

Despite this rationalization he was quite shaken. The strap of his camera slipped slowly down his arm without his feeling it. And just then there stepped around the giant bobbin of the rock an extraordinarily pretty girl with hair the same pinkish copper color.

She was barefoot and wearing a pale blue playsuit rather like a Grecian tunic. But most important, as she stood there toeing his rough shadow in the sand, there was a complete naturalness about her, an absence of sharp edges, as if her personality had weathered without aging, just as the valley seemed to have taken another step toward eternity in the space of an instant.

She must have assumed something of the same gentleness in him, for her faint surprise faded and she asked him, as easily as if he were a friend of five years' standing, "Tell now, do you think a woman can love just one man? All her life? And a man just one woman?"

Tom Dorset made a dazed sound.

His mind searched wildly.

"I do," she said, looking at him as calmly as at a mountain. "I think a man and woman can be each other's world, like Tristan and Isolde or Frederic and Catherine. Those old authors were wise. I don't see why on earth a girl has to spread her love around, no matter how enriching the experiences may be."

"You know, I agree with you," Tom said, thinking he'd caught her idea-it was impossible not to catch her casualness. "I think there's something cheap about the way everybody's supposed to run after sex these days."

"I don't mean that exactly. Tenderness is beautiful, but —" She pouted. "A big family can be vastly crushing. I wanted to declare today a holiday, but they outvoted me. Jock said it didn't chime with our mood cycles. But I was angry with them, so I put on my clothes —"

"Put on —?"

"To make it a holiday," she explained bafflingly. "And I walked here for a tantrum." She stepped out of Tom's shadow and hopped back. "Ow, the sand's getting hot," she said, rubbing the grains from the pale and uncramped toes.

"You go barefoot a lot?" Tom guessed.

"No, mostly digitals," she replied and took something shimmering from a pocket at her hip and drew it on her foot. It was a high-ankled, transparent moccasin with five separate toes. She zipped it shut with the speed of a card trick, then similarly gloved the other foot. Again the metal-edged slit down the front seemed to close itself.

"I'm behind on the fashions," Tom said, curious. They were walking side by side now, the way she'd come and he'd been going. "How does that zipper work?"

"Magnetic. They're on all my clothes. Very simple." She parted her tunic to the waist, then let it zip together.

"Clever," Tom remarked with a gulp. There seemed no limits to this girl's naturalness.

"I see you're a button man," she said. "You actually believe it's possible for a man and woman to love just each other?"

---

His chuckle was bitter. He was thinking of Elinore Murphy at Tosker-Brown and a bit about cold-faced Miss Tosker herself. "I sometimes wonder if it's possible for anyone to love anyone."

"You haven't met the right girls," she said.

"Girl," he corrected.

She grinned at him. "You'll make me think you really are a monogamist. What group do you come from?"

"Let's not talk about that," he requested. He was willing to forego knowing how she'd guessed he was from an art group, if he could be spared talking about the Vacation Fellowships and those nervous little cabins.

"My group's very nice on the whole," the girl said, "but at times they can be nefandously exasperating. Jock's the worst, quietly guiding the rest of us like an analyst. How I loathe that man! But Larry's almost as bad, with his shame-faced bumptiousness, as if we'd all sneaked off on a joyride to Venus. And there's Jokichi at the opposite extreme, forever scared he won't distribute his affection equally, dividing it up into mean little packets like candy for jealous children who would scream if they got one chewy less. And then there's Sasha and Ernest —"

"Who are you talking about?" Tom asked.

"My husbands." She shook her head dolefully. "To find five more difficult men would be positively Martian."

Tom's mind backtracked frantically, searching all conversations at Tosker-Brown for gossip about cultists in the neighborhood. It found nothing and embarked on a wider search. There were the Mormons (was that the word that had sounded like Martian?) but it wasn't the Mormon husbands who were plural. And then there was Oneida (weren't husbands and wives both plural there?) but that was 19th century New England.

"Five husbands?" he repeated. She nodded. He went on, "Do you mean to say five men have got you alone somewhere up here?"

"To be sure not," she replied. "There are my kwives."

"Kwives?"

"Co-wives," she said more slowly. "They can be fascinerously exasperating, too."

---

Tom's mind did some more searching. "And yet you believe in monogamy?"

She smiled. "Only when I'm having tantrums. It was civilized of you to agree with me."

"But I actually do believe in monogamy," he protested.

She gave his hand a little squeeze. "You are nice, but let's rush now. I've finished my tantrum and I want you to meet my group. You can fresh yourself with us."

As they hurried across the heated sands, Tom Dorset felt for the first time a twinge of uneasiness. There was something about this girl, more than her strange clothes and the odd words she used now and then, something almost-though ghosts don't wear digitals-spectral.

They scrambled up a little rise, digging their footgear into the sand, until they stood on a long flat. And there, serpentining around two great clumps of rock, was a many-windowed adobe ranch house with a roof like fresh soot.

"Oh, they've put on their clothes," his companion exclaimed with pleasure. "They've decided to make it a holiday after all."

Tom spotted a beard in the group swarming out to meet them. Its cultish look gave him a momentary feeling of superiority, followed by an equally momentary apprehension-the five husbands were certainly husky. Then both feelings were swallowed up in the swirl of introduction.

He told his own name, found that his companion's was Lois Wolver, then smiling faces began to bob toward his, his hands were shaken, his cheeks were kissed, he was even spun around like blind man's bluff, so that he lost track of the husbands and failed to attach Mary, Rachel, Simone and Joyce to the right owners.

He did notice that Jokichi was an Oriental with a skin as tight as enameled china, and that Rachel was a tall slim Negro girl. Also someone said, "Joyce isn't a Wolver, she's just visiting."

He got a much clearer impression of the clothes than the names. They were colorful, costly-looking, and mostly Egyptian and Cretan in inspiration. Some of them would have been quite immodest, even compared to Miss Tosker's famous playsuits, except that the wearers didn't seem to feel so.

"There goes the middle-morning rocket!" one of them eagerly cried.

Tom looked up with the rest, but his eyes caught the dazzling sun. However, he heard a faint roaring that quickly sank in volume and pitch, and it reminded him that the Army had a rocket testing range in this area. He had little interest in science, but he hadn't known they were on a daily schedule.

"Do you suppose it's off the track?" he asked anxiously.

"Not a chance," someone told him-the beard, he thought. The assurance of the tones gave him a possible solution. Scientists came from all over the world these days and might have all sorts of advanced ideas. This could be a group working at a nearby atomic project and leading its peculiar private life on the side.

---

As they eddied toward the house he heard Lois remind someone, "But you finally did declare it a holiday," and a husband who looked like a gay pharaoh respond, "I had another see at the mood charts and I found a subtle surge I'd missed."

Meanwhile the beard (a black one) had taken Tom in charge. Tom wasn't sure of his name, but he had a tan skin, a green sarong, and a fiercely jovial expression. "The swimming pool's around there, the landing spot's on the other side," he began, then noticed Tom gazing at the sooty roof. "Sun power cells," he explained proudly. "They store all the current we need."

Tom felt his idea confirmed. "Wonder you don't use atomic power," he observed lightly.

The beard nodded. "We've been asked that. Matter of esthetics. Why waste sunlight or use hard radiations needlessly? Of course, you might feel differently. What's your group, did you say?"

"Tosker-Brown," Tom told him, adding when the beard frowned, "the Fellowship people, you know."

"I don't," the beard confessed. "Where are you located?"

Tom briefly described the ranch house and cabins at the other end of the valley.

"Comic, I can't place it." The beard shrugged. "Here come the children."

A dozen naked youngsters raced around the ranch house, followed by a woman in a vaguely African dress open down the sides.

"Yours?" Tom asked.

"Ours," the beard answered.

"C'est un homme!"

"Regardez des vêtements!"

"No need to practice, kids; this is a holiday," the beard told them. "Tom, Helen," he said, introducing the woman with the air-conditioned garment. "Her turn today to companion die Kinder."

One of the latter rapped on the beard's knee. "May we show the stranger our things?" Instantly the others joined in pleading. The beard shot an inquiring glance at Tom, who nodded. A moment later the small troupe was hurrying him toward a spacious lean-to at the end of the ranch house. It was chuckful of strange toys, rocks and plants, small animals in cages and out, and the oddest model airplanes, or submarines. But Tom was given no time to look at any one thing for long.

"See my crystals? I grew them."

"Smell my mutated gardenias. Tell now, isn't there a difference?" There didn't seem to be, but he nodded.

"Look at my squabbits." This referred to some long-eared white squirrels nibbling carrots and nuts.

"Here's my newest model spaceship, a DS-57-B. Notice the detail." The oldest boy shoved one of the submarine affairs in his face.

---

Tom felt like a figure that is being tugged about in a rococo painting by wide pink ribbons in the chubby hands of naked cherubs. Except that these cherubs were slim and tanned, fantastically energetic, and apparently of depressingly high IQ. (What these scientists did to children!) He missed Lois and was grateful for the single little girl solemnly skipping rope in a corner and paying no attention to him.

The odd lingo she repeated stuck in his mind: "Gik-lo, I-o, Rik-o, Gis-so. Gik-lo, I-o...."

Suddenly the air was filled with soft chimes. "Lunch," the children shouted and ran away.

Tom followed at a soberer pace along the wall of the ranch house. He glanced in the huge windows, curious about the living and sleeping arrangements of the Wolvers, but the panes were strangely darkened. Then he entered the wide doorway through which the children had scampered and his curiosity turned to wonder.

A resilient green floor that wasn't flat, but sloped up toward the white of the far wall like a breaking wave. Chairs like giants' hands tenderly cupped. Little tables growing like mushrooms and broad-leafed plants out of the green floor. A vast picture window showing the red rocks.

Yet it was the wood-paneled walls that electrified his artistic interest. They blossomed with fruits and flowers, deep and poignantly carved in several styles. He had never seen such work.

He became aware of a silence and realized that his hosts and hostesses were smiling at him from around a long table. Moved by a sudden humility, he knelt and unlaced his sneakers and added them to the pile of sandals and digitals by the door. As he rose, a soft and comic piping started and he realized that beyond the table the children were lined up, solemnly puffing at little wooden flutes and recorders. He saw the empty chair at the table and went toward it, conscious for the moment of nothing but his dusty feet.

He was disappointed that Lois wasn't sitting next to him, but the food reminded him that he was hungry. There was a charming little steak, striped black and brown with perfection, and all sorts of vegetables and fruits, one or two of which he didn't recognize.

"Flown from Africa," someone explained to him.

These sly scientists, he thought, living behind their security curtain in the most improbable world!

When they were sitting with coffee and wine, and the children had finished their concert and were busy at another table, he asked, "How do you manage all this?"

Jock, the gay pharaoh, shrugged. "It's not difficult."

Rachel, the slim Negro, chuckled in her throat. "We're just people, Tom."

He tried to phrase his question without mentioning money. "What do you all do?"

"Jock's a uranium miner," Larry (the beard) answered, briskly taking over. "Rachel's an algae farmer. I'm a rocket pilot. Lois —"

---

Although pleased at this final confirmation of his guess, Tom couldn't help feeling a surge of uneasiness. "Sure you should be telling me these things?"

Larry laughed. "Why not? Lois and Jokichi have been exchange-workers in China the last six months."

"Mostly digging ditches," Jokichi put in with a smile.

" —and Sasha's in an assembly plant. Helen's a psychiatrist. Oh, we just do ordinary things. Now we're on grand vacation."

"Grand vacation?"

"When all of us have a vacation together," Larry explained. "What do you do?"

"I'm an artist," Tom said, taking out a cigaret.

"But what else?" Larry asked.

Tom felt an angry embarrassment. "Just an artist," he mumbled, cigaret in mouth, digging in his pockets for a match.

"Hold on," said Joyce beside him and pointed a silver pencil at the tip of the cigaret. He felt a faint thrill in his lips and then started back, coughing. The cigaret was lighted.

"Please mutate my poppy seeds, Mommy." A little girl had darted to Joyce from the children's table.

"You're a very dirty little girl," Joyce told her without reproof. "Hold them out." She briefly directed the silver pencil at the clay pellets on the grimy little palm. The little girl shivered delightedly. "I love ultrasonics, they feel so funny." She scampered off.

Tom cleared his throat. "I must say I'm tremendously impressed with the wood carvings. I'd like to photograph them. Oh, Lord!"

"What's the matter?" Rachel asked.

"I lost my camera somewhere."

"Camera?" Jokichi showed interest. "You mean one for stills?"

"Yes."

"What kind?"

"A Leica," Tom told him.

Jokichi seemed impressed. "That is interesting. I've never seen one of those old ones."

"Tom's a button man," Lois remarked by way of explanation, apparently. "Was the camera in a brown case? You dropped it where we met. We can get it later."

"Good, I'd really like to take those pictures," Tom said. "Incidentally, who did the carvings?"

"We did," Jock said. "Together."

Tom was grateful that the scamper of the children out of the room saved him from having to reply. He couldn't think of anything but a grunt of astonishment.

The conversation split into a group of chats about something called a psych machine, trips to Russia, the planet Mars, and several artists Tom had never heard of. He wanted to talk to Lois, but she was one of the group gabbling about Mars like children. He felt suddenly uneasy and out of things, and neither Rachel's deprecating remarks about her section of the wood carvings nor Joyce's interesting smiles helped much. He was glad when they all began to get up. He wandered outside and made his way to the children's lean-to, feeling very depressed.

---

Once again he was the center of a friendly naked cluster, except for the same solemn-faced little girl skipping rope. A rather malicious but not very hopeful whim prompted him to ask the youngest, "What's one and one?"

"Ten," the shaver answered glibly. Tom felt pleased.

"It could also be two," the oldest boy remarked.

"I'll say," Tom agreed. "What's the population of the world?"

"About seven hundred million."

Tom nodded noncommittally and, grabbing at the first long word that he thought of, turned to the eldest girl. "What's poliomyelitis?"

"Never heard of it," she said.

The solemn little girl kept droning the same ridiculous chant: "Gik-lo, I-o, Rik-o, Gis-so."

His ego eased, Tom went outside and there was Lois.

"What's the matter?" she asked.

"Nothing," he said.

She took his hand. "Have we pushed ourselves at you too much? Has our jabbering bothered you? We're a loud-mouthed family and I didn't think to ask if you were loning."

"Loning?"

"Solituding."

"In a way," he said. They didn't speak for a moment. Then, "Are you happy, Lois, in your life here?" he asked.

Her smile was instant. "Of course. Don't you like my group?"

He hesitated. "They make me feel rather no good," he said, and then admitted, "but in a way I'm more attracted to them than any people I've ever met."

"You are?" Her grip on his hand tightened. "Then why don't you stay with us for a while? I like you. It's too early to propose anything, but I think you have a quality our group lacks. You could see how you fit in. And there's Joyce. She's just visiting, too. You wouldn't have to lone unless you wanted."

Before he could think, there was a rhythmic rush of feet and the Wolvers were around them. "We're swimming," Simone announced.

Lois looked at Tom inquiringly. He smiled his willingness, started to mention he didn't have trunks, then realized that wouldn't be news here. He wondered whether he would blush.

Jock fell in beside him as they rounded the ranch house. "Larry's been telling me about your group at the other end of the valley. It's comic, but I've whirled down the valley a dozen times and never spotted any sort of place there. What's it like?"

"A ranch house and several cabins."

---

Jock frowned. "Comic I never saw it." His face cleared. "How about whirling over there? You could point it out to me."

"It's really there," Tom said uneasily. "I'm not making it up."

"Of course," Jock assured him. "It was just an idea."

"We could pick up your camera on the way," Lois put in.

The rest of the group had turned back from the huge oval pool and the dark blue and flashing thing beyond it, and stood gay-colored against the pool's pale blue shimmer.

"How about it?" Jock asked them. "A whirl before we bathe?"

Two or three said yes besides Lois, and Jock led the way toward the helicopter that Tom now saw standing beyond the pool, its beetle body as blue as a scarab, its vanes flashing silver.

The others piled in. Tom followed as casually as he could, trying to suppress the pounding of his heart. "Wonder you don't go by rocket," he remarked lightly.

Jock laughed. "For such a short trip?"

The vanes began to thrum. Tom sat stiffly, gripping the sides of the seat, then realized that the others had sunk back lazily in the cushions. There was a moment of strain and they were falling ahead and up. Looking out the side, Tom saw for a moment the sooty roof of the ranch house and the blue of the pool and the pinkish umber of tanned bodies. Then the helicopter lurched gently around. Without warning a miserable uneasiness gripped him, a desire to cling mixed with an urge to escape. He tried to convince himself it was fear of the height.

He heard Lois tell Jock, "That's the place, down by that rock that looks like a wrecked spaceship."

The helicopter began to fall forward. Tom felt Lois' hand on his.

"You haven't answered my question," she said.

"What?" he asked dully.

"Whether you'll stay with us. At least for a while."

He looked at her. Her smile was a comfort. He said, "If I possibly can."

"What could possibly stop you?"

"I don't know," he answered abstractedly.

"You're strange," Lois told him. "There's a weight of sadness in you. As if you lived in a less happy age. As if it weren't 2050."

"Twenty?" he repeated, awakening from his thoughts with a jerk. "What's the time?" he asked anxiously.

"Two," Jock said. The word sounded like a knell.

"You need cheering," Lois announced firmly.

Amid a whoosh of air rebounding from earth, they jounced gently down. Lois vaulted out. "Come on," she said.

Tom followed her. "Where?" he asked stupidly, looking around at the red rocks through the settling sand cloud stirred by the vanes.

"Your camera," she told him, laughing. "Over there. Come on, I'll race you."

He started to run with her and then his uneasiness got beyond his control. He ran faster and faster. He saw Lois catch her foot on a rock and go down sprawling, but he couldn't stop. He ran desperately around the rock and into a gust of up-whirling sand that terrified him with its suddenness. He tried to escape from the stinging, blinding gust, but there was the nightmarish fright that his wild strides were carrying him nowhere.

Then the sand settled. He stopped running and looked around him. He was standing by the balancing rock. He was gasping. At his feet the rusty brown leather of the camera case peeped from the sand. Lois was nowhere in sight. Neither was the helicopter. The valley seemed different, rawer-one might almost have said younger.

Hours after dark he trailed into Tosker-Brown. Curtained lights still glowed from a few cabins. He was footsore, bewildered, frightened. All afternoon and through the twilight and into the moonlit evening that turned the red rocks black, he had searched the valley. Nowhere had he been able to find the soot-roofed ranch house of the Wolvers. He hadn't even been able to locate the rock like a giant bobbin where he'd met Lois.

During the next days he often returned to the valley. But he never found anything. And he never happened to be near the balancing rock when the time winds blew at ten and two, though once or twice he did see dust devils. Then he went away and eventually forgot.

In his casual reading he ran across popular science articles describing the binary system of numbers used in electronic calculating machines, where one and one make ten. He always skipped them. And more than once he saw the four equations expressing Einstein's generalized theory of gravitation:

$$\text{``}g_{\pm}^{i}K; \ell = 0; \Gamma i = 0; R_{i}k = 0; \varphi, \overset{is}{\underset{s}{V}} = 0\text{''}!$$

He never connected them with the little girl's chant: "Gik-lo, I-o, Rik-o, Gis-so."

# Appointment in Tomorrow

Is it possible to have a world without moral values?
Or does lack of morality become a moral value, also?

The first angry rays of the sun-which, startlingly enough, still rose in the east at 24 hour in-tervals-pierced the lacy tops of Atlantic combers and touched thousands of sleeping Americans with unconscious fear, because of their unpleasant similarity to the rays from World War III's atomic bombs.

They turned to blood the witch-circle of rusty steel skeletons around Inferno in Manhattan. Without comment, they pointed a cosmic finger at the tarnished brass plaque commemorating the martyrdom of the Three Physicists after the dropping of the Hell Bomb. They tenderly touched the rosy skin and strawberry bruises on the naked shoulders of a girl sleeping off a drunk on the furry and radiantly heated floor of a nearby roof garden. They struck green magic from the glassy blot that was Old Washington. Twelve hours before, they had revealed things as eerily beautiful, and as ravaged, in Asia and Russia. They pinked the white walls of the Colonial dwelling of Morton Opperly near the Institute for Advanced Studies; upstairs they slanted impartially across the Pharoahlike and open-eyed face of the elderly physicist and the ugly, sleep-surly one of young Willard Farquar in the next room. And in nearby New Wash-ington they made of the spire of the Thinkers' Foundation a blue and optimistic glory that outshone White House, Jr.

It was America approaching the end of the Twentieth Century. America of juke-box bur-lesque and your local radiation hospital. America of the mask-fad for women and Mystic Chris-tianity. America of the off-the-bosom dress and the New Blue Laws. America of the Endless War and the loyalty detector. America of marvelous Maizie and the monthly rocket to Mars. America of the Thinkers and (a few remembered) the Institute. "Knock on titanium," "Whadya do for black-outs," "Please, lover, don't think when I'm around," America, as combat-shocked and crippled as the rest of the bomb-shattered planet.

Not one impudent photon of the sunlight penetrated the triple-paned, polarizing windows of Jorj Helmuth's bedroom in the Thinker's Foundation, yet the clock in his brain awakened him to the minute, or almost. Switching off the Educational Sandman in the midst of the phrase, "...applying tensor calculus to the nucleus," he took a deep, even breath and cast his mind to the limits of the world and his knowledge. It was a somewhat shadowy vision, but, he noted with impartial approval, definitely less shadowy than yesterday morning.

Employing a rapid mental scanning technique, he next cleared his memory chains of false associations, including those acquired while asleep. These chores completed, he held his finger on a bedside button, which rotated the polarizing window panes until the room slowly filled with a muted daylight. Then, still flat on his back, he turned his head until he could look at the remarkably beautiful blonde girl asleep beside him.

---

Remembering last night, he felt a pang of exasperation, which he instantly quelled by taking his mind to a higher and dispassionate level from which he could look down on the girl and even himself as quaint, clumsy animals. Still, he grumbled silently, Caddy might have had enough consideration to clear out before he awoke. He wondered if he shouldn't have used his hypnotic control of the girl to smooth their relationship last night, and for a moment the word that would send her into deep trance trembled on the tip of his tongue. But no, that special power of his over her was reserved for far more important purposes.

Pumping dynamic tension into his 20-year-old muscles and confidence into his 60-year-old mind, the 40-year-old Thinker rose from bed. No covers had to be thrown off; the nuclear heating unit made them unnecessary. He stepped into his clothing-the severe tunic, tights and sockassins of the modern business man. Next he glanced at the message tape beside his phone, washed down with ginger ale a vita-amino-enzyme tablet, and walked to the window. There, gazing along the rows of newly planted mutant oaks lining Decontamination Avenue, his smooth face broke into a smile.

It had come to him, the next big move in the intricate game making up his life-and mankind's. Come to him during sleep, as so many of his best decisions did, because he regularly employed the time-saving technique of somno-thought, which could function at the same time as somno-learning.

He set his who?-where? robot for "Rocket Physicist" and "Genius Class." While it worked, he dictated to his steno-robot the following brief message:

Dear Fellow Scientist:

A project is contemplated that will have a crucial bearing on man's future in deep space. Ample non-military Government funds are available. There was a time when professional men scoffed at the Thinkers. Then there was a time when the Thinkers perforce neglected the professional men. Now both times are past. May they never return! I would like to consult you this afternoon, three o'clock sharp, Thinkers' Foundation I.

Jorj Helmuth

Meanwhile the who?-where? had tossed out a dozen cards. He glanced through them, hesitated at the name "Willard Farquar," looked at the sleeping girl, then quickly tossed them all into the addresso-robot and plugged in the steno-robot.

The buzz-light blinked green and he switched the phone to audio.

"The President is waiting to see Maizie, sir," a clear feminine voice announced. "He has the general staff with him."

"Martian peace to him," Jorj Helmuth said. "Tell him I'll be down in a few minutes."

---

Huge as a primitive nuclear reactor, the great electronic brain loomed above the knot of hush-voiced men. It almost filled a two-story room in the Thinkers' Foundation. Its front was an orderly expanse of controls, indicators, telltales, and terminals, the upper ones reached by a chair on a boom.

Although, as far as anyone knew, it could sense only the information and questions fed into it on a tape, the human visitors could not resist the impulse to talk in whispers and glance uneasily at the great cryptic cube. After all, it had lately taken to moving some of its own controls-the permissible ones-and could doubtless improvise a hearing apparatus if it wanted to.

For this was the thinking machine beside which the Marks and Eniacs and Maniacs and Maddidas and Minervas and Mimirs were less than Morons. This was the machine with a million times as many synapses as the human brain, the machine that remembered by cutting delicate notches in the rims of molecules (instead of kindergarten paper-punching or the Coney Island shimmying of columns of mercury). This was the machine that had given instructions on building the last three-quarters of itself. This was the goal, perhaps, toward which fallible human reasoning and biased human judgment and feeble human ambition had evolved.

*This was the machine that really thought —a million-plus!*

This was the machine that the timid cyberneticists and stuffy professional scientists had said could not be built. Yet this was the machine that the Thinkers, with characteristic Yankee push, *had* built. And nicknamed, with characteristic Yankee irreverence and girl-fondness, "Maizie."

Gazing up at it, the President of the United States felt a chord plucked within him that hadn't been sounded for decades, the dark and shivery organ chord of his Baptist childhood. Here, in a strange sense, although his reason rejected it, he felt he stood face to face with the living God: infinitely stern with the sternness of reality, yet infinitely just. No tiniest error or wilful misstep could ever escape the scrutiny of this vast mentality. He shivered.

---

The grizzled general-there was also one who was gray-was thinking that this was a very odd link in the chain of command. Some shadowy and usually well-controlled memories from World War II faintly stirred his ire. Here he was giving orders to a being immeasurably more intelligent than himself. And always orders of the "Tell me how to kill that man" rather than the "Kill that man" sort. The distinction bothered him obscurely. It relieved him to know that Maizie had built-in controls which made her always the servant of humanity, or of humanity's right-minded leaders-even the Thinkers weren't certain which.

The gray general was thinking uneasily, and, like the President, at a more turbid level, of the resemblance between Papal infallibility and the dictates of the machine. Suddenly his bony wrists began to tremble. He asked himself: Was this the Second Coming? Mightn't an incarnation be in metal rather than flesh?

The austere Secretary of State was remembering what he'd taken such pains to make everyone forget: his youthful flirtation at Lake Success with Buddhism. Sitting before his *guru*, his teacher, feeling the Occidental's awe at the wisdom of the East, or its pretense, he had felt a little like this.

The burly Secretary of Space, who had come up through United Rockets, was thanking his stars that at any rate the professional scientists weren't responsible for this job. Like the grizzled general, he'd always felt suspicious of men who kept telling you how to do things, rather than doing them themselves. In World War III he'd had his fill of the professional physicists, with their eternal taint of a misty sort of radicalism and free-thinking. The Thinkers were better-more disciplined, more human. They'd called their brain-machine Maizie, which helped take the curse off her. Somewhat.

---

The President's Secretary, a paunchy veteran of party caucuses, was also glad that it was the Thinkers who had created the machine, though he trembled at the power that it gave them over the Administration. Still, you could do business with the Thinkers. And nobody (not even the Thinkers) could do business (that sort of business) with Maizie!

Before that great square face with its thousands of tiny metal features, only Jorj Helmuth seemed at ease, busily entering on the tape the complex Questions of the Day that the high officials had handed him: logistics for the Endless War in Pakistan, optimum size for next year's sugar-corn crop, current thought trends in average Soviet minds-profound questions, yet many of them phrased with surprising simplicity. For figures, technical jargon, and layman's language were alike to Maizie; there was no need to translate into mathematical shorthand, as with the lesser brain-machines.

The click of the taper went on until the Secretary of State had twice nervously fired a cigaret with his ultrasonic lighter and twice quickly put it away. No one spoke.

Jorj looked up at the Secretary of Space. "Section Five, Question Four-whom would that come from?"

The burly man frowned. "That would be the physics boys, Opperly's group. Is anything wrong?"

Jorj did not answer. A bit later he quit taping and began to adjust controls, going up on the boom-chair to reach some of them. Eventually he came down and touched a few more, then stood waiting.

From the great cube came a profound, steady purring. Involuntarily the six officials backed off a bit. Somehow it was impossible for a man to get used to the sound of Maizie starting to think.

---

Jorj turned, smiling. "And now, gentlemen, while we wait for Maizie to celebrate, there should be just enough time for us to watch the takeoff of the Mars rocket." He switched on a giant television screen. The others made a quarter turn, and there before them glowed the rich ochres and blues of a New Mexico sunrise and, in the middle distance, a silvery mighty spindle.

Like the generals, the Secretary of Space suppressed a scowl. Here was something that ought to be spang in the center of his official territory, and the Thinkers had locked him completely out of it. That rocket there-just an ordinary Earth satellite vehicle commandeered from the Army, but equipped by the Thinkers with Maizie-designed nuclear motors capable of the Mars journey and more. The first spaceship-and the Secretary of Space was not in on it!

Still, he told himself, Maizie had decreed it that way. And when he remembered what the Thinkers had done for him in rescuing him from breakdown with their mental science, in rescuing the whole Administration from collapse he realized he had to be satisfied. And that was without taking into consideration the amazing additional mental discoveries that the Thinkers were bringing down from Mars.

"Lord," the President said to Jorj as if voicing the Secretary's feeling, "I wish you people could bring a couple of those wise little devils back with you this trip. Be a good thing for the country."

Jorj looked at him a bit coldly. "It's quite unthinkable," he said. "The telepathic abilities of the Martians make them extremely sensitive. The conflicts of ordinary Earth minds would impinge on them psychotically, even fatally. As you know, the Thinkers were able to contact them only because of our degree of learned mental poise and errorless memory-chains. So for the present it must be our task alone to glean from the Martians their astounding mental skills. Of course, some day in the future, when we have discovered how to armor the minds of the Martians —"

"Sure, I know," the President said hastily. "Shouldn't have mentioned it, Jorj."

Conversation ceased. They waited with growing tension for the great violet flames to bloom from the base of the silvery shaft.

---

Meanwhile the question tape, like a New Year's streamer tossed out a high window into the night, sped on its dark way along spinning rollers. Curling with an intricate aimlessness curiously like that of such a streamer, it tantalized the silvery fingers of a thousand relays, saucily evaded the glances of ten thousand electric eyes, impishly darted down a narrow black alleyway of memory banks, and, reaching the center of the cube, suddenly emerged into a small room where a suave fat man in shorts sat drinking beer.

He flipped the tape over to him with practiced finger, eyeing it as a stockbroker might have studied a ticker tape. He read the first question, closed his eyes and frowned for five seconds. Then with the staccato self-confidence of a hack writer, he began to tape out the answer.

For many minutes the only sounds were the rustle of the paper ribbon and the click of the taper, except for the seconds the fat man took to close his eyes, or to drink or pour beer. Once, too, he lifted a phone, asked a concise question, waited half a minute, listened to an answer, then went back to the grind.

Until he came to Section Five, Question Four. That time he did his thinking with his eyes open.

The question was: "Does Maizie stand for Maelzel?"

He sat for a while slowly scratching his thigh. His loose, persuasive lips tightened, without closing, into the shape of a snarl.

Suddenly he began to tape again.

"Maizie does not stand for Maelzel. Maizie stands for amazing, humorously given the form of a girl's name. Section Six, Answer One: The mid-term election viewcasts should be spaced as follows...."

But his lips didn't lose the shape of a snarl.

Five hundred miles above the ionosphere, the Mars rocket cut off its fuel and slumped gratefully into an orbit that would carry it effortlessly around the world at that altitude. The pilot unstrapped himself and stretched, but he didn't look out the viewport at the dried-mud disc that was Earth, cloaked in its haze of blue sky. He knew he had two maddening months ahead of him in which to do little more than that. Instead, he unstrapped Sappho.

Used to free fall from two previous experiences, and loving it, the fluffy little cat was soon bounding about the cabin in curves and gyrations that would have made her the envy of all back-alley and parlor felines on the planet below. A miracle cat in the dream world of free fall. For a long time she played with a string that the man would toss out lazily. Sometimes she caught the string on the fly, sometimes she swam for it frantically.

After a while the man grew bored with the game. He unlocked a drawer and began to study the details of the wisdom he would discover on Mars this trip-priceless spiritual insights that would be balm to war-battered mankind.

The cat carefully selected a spot three feet off the floor, curled up on the air, and went to sleep.

---

Jorj Helmuth snipped the emerging answer tape into sections and handed each to the appropriate man. Most of them carefully tucked theirs away with little more than a glance, but the Secretary of Space puzzled over his.

"Who the devil would Maelzel be?" he asked.

A remote look came into the eyes of the Secretary of State. "Edgar Allen Poe," he said frowningly, with eyes half-closed.

The grizzled general snapped his fingers. "Sure! Maelzel's Chess player. Read it when I was a kid. About an automaton that was supposed to play chess. Poe proved it hid a man inside it."

The Secretary of Space frowned. "Now what's the point in a fool question like that?"

"You said it came from Opperly's group?" Jorj asked sharply.

The Secretary of Space nodded. The others looked at the two men puzzledly.

"Who would that be?" Jorj pressed. "The group, I mean."

The Secretary of Space shrugged. "Oh, the usual little bunch over at the Institute. Hindeman, Gregory, Opperly himself. Oh, yes, and young Farquar."

"Sounds like Opperly's getting senile," Jorj commented coldly. "I'd investigate."

The Secretary of Space nodded. He suddenly looked tough. "I will. Right away."

---

Sunlight striking through French windows spotlighted a ballet of dust motes untroubled by air-conditioning. Morton Opperly's living room was well-kept but worn and quite behind the times. Instead of reading tapes there were books; instead of steno-robots, pen and ink; while in place of a four by six TV screen, a Picasso hung on the wall. Only Opperly knew that the painting was still faintly radioactive, that it had been riskily so when he'd smuggled it out of his bomb-singed apartment in New York City.

The two physicists fronted each other across a coffee table. The face of the elder was cadaverous, large-eyed, and tender-fined down by a long life of abstract thought. That of the younger was forceful, sensuous, bulky as his body, and exceptionally ugly. He looked rather like a bear.

Opperly was saying, "So when he asked who was responsible for the Maelzel question, I said I didn't remember." He smiled. "They still allow me my absent-mindedness, since it nourishes their contempt. Almost my sole remaining privilege." The smile faded. "Why do you keep on teasing the zoo animals, Willard?" he asked without rancor. "I've maintained many times that we shouldn't truckle to them by yielding to their demand that we ask Maizie questions.

You and the rest have overruled me. But then to use those questions to convey veiled insults isn't reasonable. Apparently the Secretary of Space was bothered enough about this last one to pay me a 'copter call within twenty minutes of this morning's meeting at the Foundation. Why do you do it, Willard?"

The features of the other convulsed unpleasantly. "Because the Thinkers are charlatans who must be exposed," he rapped out. "We know their Maizie is no more than a tealeaf-reading fake. We've traced their Mars rockets and found they go nowhere. We know their Martian mental science is bunk."

"But we've already exposed the Thinkers very thoroughly," Opperly interposed quietly. "You know the good it did."

Farquar hunched his Japanese-wrestler shoulders. "Then it's got to be done until it takes."

Opperly studied the bowl of mutated flowers by the coffee pot. "I think you just want to tease the animals, for some personal reason of which you probably aren't aware."

Farquar scowled. "We're the ones in the cages."

---

Opperly continued his inspection of the flowers' bells. "All the more reason not to poke sticks through the bars at the lions and tigers strolling outside. No, Willard, I'm not counseling appeasement. But consider the age in which we live. It wants magicians." His voice grew especially tranquil. "A scientist tells people the truth. When times are good-that is, when the truth offers no threat-people don't mind. But when times are very, very bad...." A shadow darkened his eyes. "Well, we all know what happened to —" And he mentioned three names that had been household words in the middle of the century. They were the names on the brass plaque dedicated to the martyred three physicists.

He went on, "A magician, on the other hand, tells people what they wish were true-that perpetual motion works, that cancer can be cured by colored lights, that a psychosis is no worse than a head cold, that they'll live forever. In good times magicians are laughed at. They're a luxury of the spoiled wealthy few. But in bad times people sell their souls for magic cures, and buy perpetual motion machines to power their war rockets."

Farquar clenched his fist. "All the more reason to keep chipping away at the Thinkers. Are we supposed to beg off from a job because it's difficult and dangerous?"

Opperly shook his head. "We're to keep clear of the infection of violence. In my day, Willard, I was one of the Frightened Men. Later I was one of the Angry Men and then one of the Minds of Despair. Now I'm convinced that all my reactions were futile."

"Exactly!" Farquar agreed harshly. "You reacted. You didn't act. If you men who discovered atomic energy had only formed a secret league, if you'd only had the foresight and the guts to use your tremendous bargaining position to demand the power to shape mankind's future...."

"By the time you were born, Willard," Opperly interrupted dreamily, "Hitler was merely a name in the history books. We scientists weren't the stuff out of which cloak-and-dagger men are made. Can you imagine Oppenheimer wearing a mask or Einstein sneaking into the Old White House with a bomb in his briefcase?" He smiled. "Besides, that's not the way power is seized. New ideas aren't useful to the man bargaining for power-only established facts or lies are."

"Just the same, it would have been a good thing if you'd had a little violence in you."

"No," Opperly said.

"I've got violence in me," Farquar announced, shoving himself to his feet.

---

Opperly looked up from the flowers. "I think you have," he agreed.

"But what are we to do?" Farquar demanded. "Surrender the world to charlatans without a struggle?"

Opperly mused for a while. "I don't know what the world needs now. Everyone knows Newton as the great scientist. Few remember that he spent half his life muddling with alchemy, looking for the philosopher's stone. Which Newton did the world need then?"

"Now you are justifying the Thinkers!"

"No, I leave that to history."

"And history consists of the actions of men," Farquar concluded. "I intend to act. The Thinkers are vulnerable, their power fantastically precarious. What's it based on? A few lucky guesses. Faith-healing. Some science hocus-pocus, on the level of those juke-box burlesque acts between the strips. Dubious mental comfort given to a few nerve-torn neurotics in the Inner Cabinet-and their wives. The fact that the Thinkers' clever stage-managing won the President a doubtful election. The erroneous belief that the Soviets pulled out of Iraq and Iran because of the Thinkers' Mind Bomb threat. A brain-machine that's just a cover for Jan Tregarron's guesswork. Oh, yes, and that hogwash of 'Martian wisdom.' All of it mere bluff! A few pushes at the right times and points are all that are needed-and the Thinkers know it! I'll bet they're terrified already, and will be more so when they find that we're gunning for them. Eventually they'll be making overtures to us, turning to us for help. You wait and see."

"I am thinking again of Hitler," Opperly interposed quietly. "On his first half dozen big steps, he had nothing but bluff. His generals were against him. They knew they were in a cardboard fort. Yet he won every battle, until the last. Moreover," he pressed on, cutting Farquar short, "the power of the Thinkers isn't based on what they've got, but on what the world hasn't got-peace, honor, a good conscience...."

The front-door knocker clanked. Farquar answered it. A skinny old man with a radiation scar twisting across his temple handed him a tiny cylinder. "Radiogram for you, Willard." He grinned across the hall at Opperly. "When are you going to get a phone put in, Mr. Opperly?"

The physicist waved to him. "Next year, perhaps, Mr. Berry."

The old man snorted with good-humored incredulity and trudged off.

"What did I tell you about the Thinkers making overtures?" Farquar chortled suddenly. "It's come sooner than I expected. Look at this."

He held out the radiogram, but the older man didn't take it. Instead he asked, "Who's it from? Tregarron?"

"No, from Helmuth. There's a lot of sugar corn about man's future in deep space, but the real reason is clear. They know that they're going to have to produce an actual nuclear rocket pretty soon, and for that they'll need our help."

"An invitation?"

Farquar nodded. "For this afternoon." He noticed Opperly's anxious though distant frown. "What's the matter?" he asked. "Are you bothered about my going? Are you thinking it might be a trap-that after the Maelzel question they may figure I'm better rubbed out?"

The older man shook his head. "I'm not afraid for your life, Willard. That's yours to risk as you choose. No, I'm worried about other things they might do to you."

"What do you mean?" Farquar asked.

---

Opperly looked at him with a gentle appraisal. "You're a strong and vital man, Willard, with a strong man's prides and desires." His voice trailed off for a bit. Then, "Excuse me, Willard, but wasn't there a girl once? A Miss Arkady?"

Farquar's ungainly figure froze. He nodded curtly, face averted.

"And didn't she go off with a Thinker?"

"If girls find me ugly, that's their business," Farquar said harshly, still not looking at Opperly. "What's that got to do with this invitation?"

Opperly didn't answer the question. His eyes got more distant. Finally he said, "In my day we had it a lot easier. A scientist was an academician, cushioned by tradition."

Willard snorted. "Science had already entered the era of the police inspectors, with laboratory directors and political appointees stifling enterprise."

"Perhaps," Opperly agreed. "Still, the scientist lived the safe, restricted, highly respectable life of a university man. He wasn't exposed to the temptations of the world."

Farquar turned on him. "Are you implying that the Thinkers will somehow be able to buy me off?"

"Not exactly."

"You think I'll be persuaded to change my aims?" Farquar demanded angrily.

Opperly shrugged his helplessness. "No, I don't think you'll change your aims."

Clouds encroaching from the west blotted the parallelogram of sunlight between the two men.

---

As the slideway whisked him gently along the corridor toward his apartment, Jorj was thinking of his spaceship. For a moment the silver-winged vision crowded everything else out of his mind.

Just think, a spaceship with sails! He smiled a bit, marveling at the paradox.

Direct atomic power. Direct utilization of the force of the flying neutrons. No more ridiculous business of using a reactor to drive a steam engine, or boil off something for a jet exhaust-processes that were as primitive and wasteful as burning gunpowder to keep yourself warm.

Chemical jets would carry his spaceship above the atmosphere. Then would come the thrilling order, "Set sail for Mars!" The vast umbrella would unfold and open out around the stern, its rear or Earthward side a gleaming expanse of radioactive ribbon perhaps only an atom thick and backed with a material that would reflect neutrons. Atoms in the ribbon would split, blasting neutrons astern at fantastic velocities. Reaction would send the spaceship hurtling forward.

In airless space, the expanse of sails would naturally not retard the ship. More radioactive ribbon, manufactured as needed in the ship itself, would feed out onto the sail as that already there became exhausted.

A spaceship with direct nuclear drive-and he, a Thinker, had conceived it completely except for the technical details! Having strengthened his mind by hard years of somno-learning, mind-casting, memory-straightening, and sensory training, he had assured himself of the executive power to control the technicians and direct their specialized abilities. Together they would build the true Mars rocket.

But that would only be a beginning. They would build the true Mind Bomb. They would build the true Selective Microbe Slayer. They would discover the true laws of ESP and the inner life. They would even-his imagination hesitated a moment, then strode boldly forward-build the true Maizie!

And then ... then the Thinkers would be on even terms with the scientists. Rather, they'd be far ahead. No more deception.

He was so exalted by this thought that he almost let the slideway carry him past his door. He stepped inside and called, "Caddy!" He waited a moment, then walked through the apartment, but she wasn't there.

---

Confound the girl, he couldn't help thinking. This morning, when she should have made herself scarce, she'd sprawled about sleeping. Now, when he felt like seeing her, when her presence would have added a pleasant final touch to his glowing mood, she chose to be absent. He really should use his hypnotic control on her, he decided, and again there sprang into his mind the word —a pet form of her name-that would send her into obedient trance.

No, he told himself again, that was to be reserved for some moment of crisis or desperate danger, when he would need someone to strike suddenly and unquestioningly for himself and mankind. Caddy was merely a wilful and rather silly girl, incapable at present of understanding the tremendous tensions under which he operated. When he had time for it, he would train her up to be a fitting companion without hypnosis.

Yet the fact of her absence had a subtly disquieting effect. It shook his perfect self-confidence just a fraction. He asked himself if he'd been wise in summoning the rocket physicists without consulting Tregarron.

But this mood, too, he conquered quickly. Tregarron wasn't his boss, but just the Thinker's most clever salesman, an expert in the mumbo-jumbo so necessary for social control in this chaotic era. He himself, Jorj Helmuth, was the real leader in theoretics and all-over strategy, the mind behind the mind behind Maizie.

He stretched himself on the bed, almost instantly achieved maximum relaxation, turned on the somno-learner, and began the two hour rest he knew would be desirable before the big conference.

---

Jan Tregarron had supplemented his shorts with pink coveralls, but he was still drinking beer. He emptied his glass and lifted it a lazy inch. The beautiful girl beside him refilled it without a word and went on stroking his forehead.

"Caddy," he said reflectively, without looking at her, "there's a little job I want you to do. You're the only one with the proper background. The point is: it will take you away from Jorj for some time."

"I'd welcome it," she said with decision. "I'm getting pretty sick of watching his push-ups and all his other mind and muscle stunts. And that damn somno-learner of his keeps me awake."

Tregarron smiled. "I'm afraid Thinkers make pretty sad sweethearts."

"Not all of them," she told him, returning his smile tenderly.

He chuckled. "It's about one of those rocket physicists in the list you brought me. A fellow named Willard Farquar."

Caddy didn't say anything, but she stopped stroking his forehead.

"What's the matter?" he asked. "You knew him once, didn't you?"

"Yes," she replied and then added, with surprising feeling, "The big, ugly ape!"

"Well, he's an ape whose services we happen to need. I want you to be our contact girl with him."

She took her hands away from his forehead. "Look, Jan," she said, "I wouldn't like this job."

"I thought he was very sweet on you once."

"Yes, as he never grew tired of trying to demonstrate to me. The clumsy, overgrown, bumbling baby! The man's disgusting, Jan. His approach to a woman is a child wanting candy and enraged because Mama won't produce it on the instant. I don't mind Jorj-he's just a pipsqueak and it amuses me to see how he frustrates himself. But Willard is...."

"...a bit frightening?" Tregarron finished for her.

"No!"

"Of course you're not afraid," Tregarron purred. "You're our beautiful, clever Caddy, who can do anything she wants with any man, and without whose...."

"Look, Jan, this is different —" she began agitatedly.

"...and without whose services we'd have got exactly nowhere. Clever, subtle Caddy, whose most charming attainment in the ever-appreciative eyes of Papa Jan is her ability to handle every man in the neatest way imaginable and without a trace of real feeling. Kitty Kaddy, who...."

"Very well," she said with a sigh. "I'll do it."

"Of course you will," Jan said, drawing her hands back to his forehead. "And you'll begin right away by getting into your nicest sugar-and-cream war clothes. You and I are going to be the welcoming committee when that ape arrives this afternoon."

"But what about Jorj? He'll want to see Willard."

"That'll be taken care of," Jan assured her.

"And what about the other dozen rocket physicists Jorj asked to come?"

"Don't worry about them."

---

The President looked inquiringly at his secretary across his littered desk in his homey study at White House, Jr. "So Opperly didn't have any idea how that odd question about Maizie turned up in Section Five?"

His secretary settled his paunch and shook his head. "Or claimed not to. Perhaps he's just the absent-minded prof, perhaps something else. The old feud of the physicists against the Thinkers may be getting hot again. There'll be further investigation."

The President nodded. He obviously had something uncomfortable on his mind. He said uneasily, "Do you think there's any possibility of it being true?"

"What?" asked the secretary guardedly.

"That peculiar hint about Maizie."

The secretary said nothing.

"Mind you, I don't think there is," the President went on hurriedly, his face assuming a sorrowful scowl. "I owe a lot to the Thinkers, both as a private person and as a public figure. Lord, a man has to lean on *something* these days. But just supposing it were true —" he hesitated, as before uttering blasphemy —"that there was a man inside Maizie, what could we do?"

The secretary said stolidly, "The Thinkers won our last election. They chased the Commies out of Iran. We brought them into the Inner Cabinet. We've showered them with public funds." He paused. "We couldn't do a damn thing."

The President nodded with equal conviction, and, not very happily, summed up: "So if anyone should go up against the Thinkers-and I'm afraid I wouldn't want to see that happen, whatever's true-it would have to be a scientist."

---

Willard Farquar felt his weight change the steps under his feet into an escalator. He cursed under his breath, but let them carry him, a defiant hulk, up to the tall and mystic blue portals, which silently parted when he was five meters away. The escalator changed to a slideway and carried him into a softly gleaming, high-domed room rather like the antechamber of a temple.

"Martian peace to you, Willard Farquar," an invisible voice intoned. "You have entered the Thinkers' Foundation. Please remain on the slideway."

"I want to see Jorj Helmuth," Willard growled loudly.

The slideway carried him into the mouth of a corridor and paused. A dark opening dilated on the wall. "May we take your hat and coat?" a voice asked politely. After a moment the request was repeated, with the addition of, "Just pass them through."

Willard scowled, then fought his way out of his shapeless coat and passed it and his hat through in a lump. Instantly the opening contracted, imprisoning his wrists, and he felt his hands being washed on the other side of the wall.

He gave a great jerk which failed to free his hands from the snugly padded gyves. "Do not be alarmed," the voice advised him. "It is only an esthetic measure. As your hands are laved, invisible radiations are slaughtering all the germs in your body, while more delicate emanations are producing a benign rearrangement of your emotions."

The rather amateurish curses Willard was gritting between his teeth became more sulfurous. His sensations told him that a towel of some sort was being applied to his hands. He wondered if he would be subjected to a face-washing and even greater indignities. Then, just before his wrists were released, he felt-for a moment only, but unmistakably-the soft touch of a girl's hand.

That touch, like the mysterious sweet chink of a bell in darkness, brought him a sudden feeling of excitement, wonder.

Yet the feeling was as fleeting as that caused by a lurid advertisement, for as the slideway began to move again, carrying him past a series of depth-pictures and inscriptions celebrating the Thinkers' achievements, his mood of bitter exasperation returned doubled. This place, he told himself, was a plague spot of the disease of magic in an enfeebled and easily infected world. He reminded himself that he was not without resources-the Thinkers must fear or need him, whether because of the Maelzel question or the necessity of producing a nuclear power spaceship. He felt his determination to smash them reaffirmed.

---

The slideway, having twice turned into an escalator, veered toward an opalescent door, which opened as silently as the one below. The slideway stopped at the threshold. Momentum carried him a couple of steps into the room. He stopped and looked around.

The place was a sybarite's modernistic dream. Sponge-carpeting thick as a mattress and topped with down. Hassocks and couches that looked butter-soft. A domed ceiling of deep glossy blue mimicking the night sky, with the constellations tooled in silver. A wall of niches crammed with statuettes of languorous men, women, beasts. A self-service bar with a score of golden spigots. A depth-TV-screen simulating a great crystal ball. Here and there barbaric studs of hammered gold that might have been push-buttons. A low table set for three with exquisite ware of crystal and gold. An ever-changing scent of resins and flowers.

A smiling fat man clad in pearl gray sports clothes came through one of the curtained archways. Willard recognized Jan Tregarron from his pictures, but did not at once offer to speak to him. Instead he let his gaze wander with an ostentatious contempt around the crammed walls, take in the bar and the set table with its many wine glasses, and finally return to his host.

"And where," he asked with harsh irony, "are the dancing girls?"

The fat man's eyebrows rose. "In there," he said innocently, indicating the second archway. The curtains parted.

"Oh, I *am* sorry," the fat man apologized. "There seems to be only one on duty. I hope that isn't too much at variance with your tastes."

She stood in the archway, demure and lovely in an off-the-bosom frock of pale blue skylon edged in mutated mink. She was smiling the first smile that Willard had ever had from her lips.

"Mr. Willard Farquar," the fat man murmured, "Miss Arkady Simms."

---

Jorj Helmuth turned from the conference table with its dozen empty chairs to the two mousily pretty secretaries.

"No word from the door yet, Master," one of them ventured to say.

Jorj twisted in his chair, though hardly uncomfortably, since it was a beautiful pneumatic job. His nervousness at having to face the twelve rocket physicists —a feeling which, he had to admit, had been unexpectedly great-was giving way to impatience.

"What's Willard Farquar's phone?" he asked sharply.

One of the secretaries ran through a clutch of desk tapes, then spent some seconds whispering into her throat-mike and listening to answers from the soft-speaker.

"He lives with Morton Opperly, who doesn't have one," she finally told Jorj in scandalized tones.

"Let me see the list," Jorj said. Then, after a bit, "Try Dr. Welcome's place."

This time there were results. Within a quarter of a minute he was handed a phone which he hung expertly on his shoulder.

"This is Dr. Asa Welcome," a reedy voice told him.

"This is Helmuth of the Thinkers' Foundation," Jorj said icily. "Did you get my communication?"

The reedy voice became anxious and placating. "Why, yes, Mr. Helmuth, I did. Very glad to get it too. Sounded most interesting. Very eager to come. But...."

"Yes?"

"Well, I was just about to hop in my 'copter-my son's 'copter-when the other note came."

"What other note?"

"Why, the note calling the meeting off."

"I sent no other note!"

The other voice became acutely embarrassed. "But I considered it to be from you ... or just about the same thing. I really think I had the right to assume that."

"How was it signed?" Jorj rapped.

"Mr. Jan Tregarron."

Jorj broke the connection. He didn't move until a low sound shattered his abstraction and he realized that one of the girls was whispering a call to the door. He handed back the phone and dismissed them. They went in a rustle of jackets and skirtlets, hesitating at the doorway but not quite daring to look back.

He sat motionless a minute longer. Then his hand crept fretfully onto the table and pushed a button. The room darkened and a long section of wall became transparent, revealing a dozen silvery models of spaceships, beautifully executed. He quickly touched another; the models faded and the opposite wall bloomed with an animated cartoon that portrayed with charming humor and detail the designing and construction of a neutron-drive spaceship. A third button, and a depth-picture of deep star-speckled space opened behind the cartoon, showing a section of Earth's surface and in the far distance the tiny ruddy globe of Mars. Slowly a tiny rocket rose from the section of Earth and spread its silvery sails.

---

He switched off the pictures, keeping the room dark. By a faint table light he dejectedly examined his organizational charts for the neutron-drive project, the long list of books he had boned up on by somno-learning, the concealed table of physical constants and all sorts of other crucial details about rocket physics —a cleverly condensed encyclopedic "pony" to help out his memory on technical points that might have arisen in his discussion with the experts.

He switched out all the lights and slumped forward, blinking his eyes and trying to swallow the lump in his throat. In the dark his memory went seeping back, back, to the day when his math teacher had told him, very superciliously, that the marvelous fantasies he loved to read and hoarded by his bed weren't real science at all, but just a kind of lurid pretense. He had so wanted to be a scientist, and the teacher's contempt had cast a damper on his ambition.

And now that the conference was canceled, would he ever know that it wouldn't have turned out the same way today? That his somno-learning hadn't taken? That his "pony" wasn't good enough? That his ability to handle people extended only to credulous farmer Presidents and mousy girls in skirtlets? Only the test of meeting the experts would have answered those questions.

Tregarron was the one to blame! Tregarron with his sly tyrannical ways, Tregarron with his fear of losing the future to men who really understood theoretics and could handle experts. Tregarron, so used to working by deception that he couldn't see when it became a fault and a crime. Tregarron, who must now be shown the light ... or, failing that, against whom certain steps must be taken.

For perhaps half an hour Jorj sat very still, thinking. Then he turned to the phone and, after some delay, got his party.

"What is it now, Jorj?" Caddy asked impatiently. "Please don't bother me with any of your moods, because I'm tired and my nerves are on edge."

He took a breath. When steps may have to be taken, he thought, one must hold an agent in readiness. "Caddums," he intoned hypnotically, vibrantly. "Caddums...."

The voice at the other end had instantly changed, become submissive, sleepy, suppliant. "Yes, Master?"

---

Morton Opperly looked up from the sheet of neatly penned equations at Willard Farquar, who had somehow acquired a measure of poise. He neither lumbered restlessly nor grimaced. He removed his coat with a certain dignity and stood solidly before his mentor. He smiled. Granting that he was a bear, one might guess he had just been fed.

"You see?" he said. "They didn't hurt me."

"They didn't hurt you?" Opperly asked softly.

Willard slowly shook his head. His smile broadened.

Opperly put down his pen, folded his hands. "And you're as determined as ever to expose and smash the Thinkers?"

"Of course!" The menacing growl came back into the bear's voice, except that it was touched with a certain pleased luxuriousness. "Only from now on I won't be teasing the zoo animals, and I won't embarrass you by asking any more Maelzel questions. I have reached the objective at which those tactics were aimed. After this I shall bore from within."

"Bore from within," Opperly repeated, frowning. "Now where have I heard that phrase before?" His brow cleared. "Oh, yes," he said listlessly. "Do I understand that you are becoming a Thinker, Willard?"

The other gave him a faintly pitying smile and stretched himself on the couch, gazed at the ceiling. All his movements were deliberate, easy.

"Certainly. That's the only realistic way to smash them. Rise high in their councils. Out-trick all their trickeries. Organize a fifth column. Then *strike!*"

"The end justifying the means, of course," Opperly said.

"Of course. As surely as the desire to stand up justifies your disturbing the air over your head. All action in this world is nothing but means."

Opperly nodded abstractedly. "I wonder if anyone else ever became a Thinker for those same reasons. I wonder if being a Thinker doesn't simply mean that you've decided you have to use lies and tricks as your chief method."

---

Willard shrugged. "Could be." There was no longer any doubt about the pitying quality of his smile.

Opperly stood up, squaring together his papers. "So you'll be working with Helmuth?"

"Not Helmuth. Tregarron." The bear's smile became cruel. "I'm afraid that Helmuth's career as a Thinker is going to have quite a setback."

"Helmuth," Opperly mused. "Morgenschein once told me a bit about him. A man of some idealism, despite his affiliations. Best of a bad lot. Incidentally, is he the one with whom...."

"...Miss Arkady Simms ran off?" Willard finished without any embarrassment. "Yes, that was Helmuth. But that's all going to be changed now."

Opperly nodded. "Good-by, Willard," he said.

Willard quickly heaved himself up on an elbow. Opperly looked at him for about five seconds, then, without a word, walked out of the room.

---

The only obvious furnishings in Jan Tregarron's office were a flat-topped desk and a few chairs. Tregarron sat behind the desk, the top of which was completely bare. He looked almost bored, except that his little eyes were smiling. Jorj Helmuth sat across the desk from him, a few feet back, erect and grim-faced, while shadowy in the muted light, Caddy stood against the wall behind Tregarron. She still wore the fur-trimmed skylon frock she'd put on that afternoon. She took no part in the conversation, seemed almost unaware of it.

"So you just went ahead and canceled the conference without consulting me?" Jorj was saying.

---

"You called it without consulting me." Tregarron playfully wagged a finger. "Shouldn't do that sort of thing, Jorj."

"But I tell you I was completely prepared. I was absolutely sure of my ground."

"I know, I know," Tregarron said lightly. "But it's not the right time for it. I'm the best judge of that."

"When will be the right time?"

Tregarron shrugged. "Look here, Jorj," he said, "every man should stick to his trade, to his forte. Technology isn't ours."

Jorj's lips thinned. "But you know as well as I do that we are going to have to have a nuclear spaceship and actually go to Mars someday."

Tregarron lifted his eyebrows. "Are we?"

"Yes! Just as we're going to have to build a real Maizie. Everything we've done until now have been emergency measures."

"Really?"

Jorj stared at him. "Look here, Jan," he said, gripping his knees with his hands, "you and I are going to have to talk things through."

"Are you quite sure of that?" Jan's voice was very cool. "I have a feeling that it might be best if you said nothing and accepted things as they are."

"No!"

"Very well." Tregarron settled himself in his chair.

"I helped you organize the Thinkers," Jorj said, and waited. "At least, I was your first partner."

Tregarron barely nodded.

"Our basic idea was that the time had come to apply science to the life of man on a large scale, to live rationally and realistically. The only things holding the world back from this all-important step were the ignorance, superstition, and inertia of the average man, and the stuffiness and lack of enterprise of the academic scientists-their worship of facts, even when facts were clearly dangerous.

"Yet we knew that in their deepest hearts the average man and the professionals were both on our side. They wanted the new world visualized by science. They wanted the simplifications and conveniences, the glorious adventures of the human mind and body. They wanted the trips to Mars and into the depths of the human psyche, they wanted the robots and the thinking machines. All they lacked was the nerve to take the first big step-and that was what we supplied.

"It was no time for half measures, for slow and sober plodding. The world was racked by wars and neurosis, in danger of falling into the foulest hands. What was needed was a tremendous and thrilling appeal to the human imagination, an Earth-shaking affirmation of the power of science for good.

"But the men who provided that appeal and affirmation couldn't afford to be cautious. They wouldn't check and double check. They couldn't wait for the grudging and jealous approval of the professionals. They had to use stunts, tricks, fakes —*anything to get over the big point*. Once that had been done, once mankind was headed down the new road, it would be easy enough to give the average man the necessary degree of insight to heal the breach with the professionals, to make good in actuality what had been made good only in pretense.

"Have I stated our position fairly?"

---

Tregarron's eyes were hooded. "You're the one who's telling it."

"On those general assumptions we established our hold on susceptible leaders and the mob," Jorj went on. "We built Maizie and the Mars rocket and the Mind Bomb. We discovered the wisdom of the Martians. We *sold* the people on the science that the professionals had been too high-toned to advertise or bring into the market place.

"But now that we've succeeded, now that we've made the big point, now that Maizie and Mars and science do rule the average human imagination, the time has come to take the second big step, to let accomplishment catch up with imagination, to implement fantasy with fact.

"Do you suppose I'd ever have gone into this with you, if it hadn't been for the thought of that second big step? Why, I'd have felt dirty and cheap, a mere charlatan-except for the sure conviction that someday everything would be set right. I've devoted my whole life to that conviction, Jan. I've studied and disciplined myself, using every scientific means at my disposal, so that I wouldn't be found lacking when the day came to heal the breach between the Thinkers and the professionals. I've trained myself to be the perfect liaison man for the job.

"Jan, the day's come and I'm the man. I know you've been concentrating on other aspects of our work; you haven't had time to keep up with my side of it. But I'm sure that as soon as you see how carefully I've prepared myself, how completely practical the neutron-drive rocket project is, you'll beg me to go ahead!"

Tregarron smiled at the ceiling for a moment. "Your general idea isn't so bad, Jorj, but your time scale is out of whack and your judgment is a joke. Oh, yes. Every revolutionary wants to see the big change take place in his lifetime. Tcha! It's as if he were watching evolutionary vaudeville and wanted the Ape-to-Man Act over in twenty minutes.

"Time for the second big step? Jorj, the average man's exactly what he was ten years ago, except that he's got a new god. More than ever he thinks of Mars as a Hollywood paradise, with wise men and yummy princesses. Maizie is Mama magnified a million times. As for professional scientists, they're more jealous and stuffy than ever. All they'd like to do is turn the clock back to a genteel dream world of quiet quadrangles and caps and gowns, where every commoner bows to the passing scholar.

"Maybe in ten thousand years we'll be ready for the second big step. Maybe. Meanwhile, as should be, the clever will rule the stupid for their own good. The realists will rule the dreamers. Those with free hands will rule those who have deliberately handcuffed themselves with taboos.

"Secondly, your judgment. Did you actually think you could have bossed those professionals, kept your mental footing in the intellectual melee? You a nuclear physicist? A rocket scientist? Why, it's —Take it easy now, boy, and listen to me. They'd have torn you to pieces in twenty minutes and glad of the chance! You baffle me, Jorj. You know that Maizie and the Mars rocket and all that are fakes, yet you believe in your somno-learning and consciousness-expansion and optimism-pumping like the veriest yokel. I wouldn't be surprised to hear you'd taken up ESP and hypnotism. I think you should take stock of yourself and get a new slant. It's overdue."

---

He leaned back. Jorj's face had become a mask. His eyes did not flicker from Tregarron's, yet there was a subtle change in his expression. Behind Tregarron, Caddy swayed as if in a sudden gust of intangible wind and took a silent step forward from the wall.

"That's your honest opinion?" Jorj asked, very quietly.

"It's more than that," Tregarron told him, just as unmelodramatically. "It's orders."

Jorj stood up purposefully. "Very well," he said. "In that case I have to tell you that —"

Casually, but with no wasted motion, Tregarron slipped an ultrasonic pistol from under the desk and laid it on the empty top.

"No," he said, "let me tell you something. I was afraid this would happen and I made preparations. If you've studied your Nazi, Fascist and Soviet history, you know what happens to old revolutionaries who don't move with the times. But I'm not going to be too harsh. I have a couple of the boys waiting outside. They'll take you by 'copter to the field, then by jet to New Mex. Bright and early tomorrow morning, Jorj, you're leaving on a trip to Mars."

Jorj hardly reacted to the words. Caddy was two steps nearer Tregarron.

"I decided Mars would be the best place for you," the fat man continued. "The robot controls will be arranged so that your 'visit' to Mars lasts two years. Perhaps in that time you will have learned wisdom, such as realizing that the big liar must never fall for his own big lie.

"Meanwhile, there will have to be a replacement for you. I have in mind a person who may prove peculiarly worthy to occupy your position, with all its perquisites. A person who seems to understand that force and desire are the motive powers of life, and that anyone who believes the big lie proves himself strictly a jerk."

---

Caddy was standing behind Tregarron now, her half-closed, sleepy eyes fixed on Jorj's.

"His name is Willard Farquar. You see, I too believe in cooperating with the scientists, Jorj, but by subversion rather than conference. My idea is to offer the hand of friendship to a selected few of them-the hand of friendship with a nice big bribe in it." He smiled. "You were a good man, Jorj, for the early days, when we needed a publicist with catchy ideas about Mind Bombs, ray guns, plastic helmets, fancy sweaters, space brassieres, and all that other corn. Now we can afford a soldier."

Jorj moistened his lips.

"We'll have a neat explanation of what's happened to you. Callers will be informed that you've gone on an extended visit to imbibe the wisdom of the Martians."

Jorj whispered, "Caddums."

Caddy leaned forward. Her arms snaked down Tregarron's, as if to imprison his wrists. But instead she reached out and took the ultrasonic pistol and put it in Tregarron's right hand. Then she looked up at Jorj with eyes that were very bright.

She said very sweetly and sympathetically, "Poor Superman."

# Bread Overhead

The Staff of Life suddenly and
disconcertingly sprouted wings
—and mankind had to eat crow!

As a blisteringly hot but guaranteed weather-controlled future summer day dawned on the Mississippi Valley, the walking mills of Puffy Products ("Spike to Loaf in One Operation!") began to tread delicately on their centipede legs across the wheat fields of Kansas.

The walking mills resembled fat metal serpents, rather larger than those Chinese paper dragons animated by files of men in procession. Sensory robot devices in their noses informed them that the waiting wheat had reached ripe perfection.

As they advanced, their heads swung lazily from side to side, very much like snakes, gobbling the yellow grain. In their throats, it was threshed, the chaff bundled and burped aside for pickup by the crawl trucks of a chemical corporation, the kernels quick-dried and blown along into the mighty chests of the machines. There the tireless mills ground the kernels to flour, which was instantly sifted, the bran being packaged and dropped like the chaff for pickup. A cluster of tanks which gave the metal serpents a decidedly humpbacked appearance added water, shortening, salt and other ingredients, some named and some not. The dough was at the same time infused with gas from a tank conspicuously labeled "Carbon Dioxide" ("No Yeast Creatures in Your Bread!").

Thus instantly risen, the dough was clipped into loaves and shot into radionic ovens forming the midsections of the metal serpents. There the bread was baked in a matter of seconds, a fierce heat-front browning the crusts, and the piping-hot loaves sealed in transparent plastic bearing the proud Puffyloaf emblem (two cherubs circling a floating loaf) and ejected onto the delivery platform at each serpent's rear end, where a cluster of pickup machines, like hungry piglets, snatched at the loaves with hygienic claws.

A few loaves would be hurried off for the day's consumption, the majority stored for winter in strategically located mammoth deep freezes.

But now, behold a wonder! As loaves began to appear on the delivery platform of the first walking mill to get into action, they did not linger on the conveyor belt, but rose gently into the air and slowly traveled off down-wind across the hot rippling fields.

---

The robot claws of the pickup machines clutched in vain, and, not noticing the difference, proceeded carefully to stack emptiness, tier by tier. One errant loaf, rising more sluggishly than its fellows, was snagged by a thrusting claw. The machine paused, clumsily wiped off the injured loaf, set it aside-where it bobbed on one corner, unable to take off again-and went back to the work of storing nothingness.

A flock of crows rose from the trees of a nearby shelterbelt as the flight of loaves approached. The crows swooped to investigate and then suddenly scattered, screeching in panic.

The helicopter of a hangoverish Sunday traveler bound for Wichita shied very similarly from the brown fliers and did not return for a second look.

A black-haired housewife spied them over her back fence, crossed herself and grabbed her walkie-talkie from the laundry basket. Seconds later, the yawning correspondent of a regional newspaper was jotting down the lead of a humorous news story which, recalling the old flying-saucer scares, stated that now apparently bread was to be included in the mad aerial tea party.

The congregation of an open-walled country church, standing up to recite the most familiar of Christian prayers, had just reached the petition for daily sustenance, when a sub-flight of the loaves, either forced down by a vagrant wind or lacking the natural buoyancy of the rest, came coasting silently as the sunbeams between the graceful pillars at the altar end of the building.

Meanwhile, the main flight, now augmented by other bread flocks from scores and hundreds of walking mills that had started work a little later, mounted slowly and majestically into the cirrus-flecked upper air, where a steady wind was blowing strongly toward the east.

About one thousand miles farther on in that direction, where a cluster of stratosphere-tickling towers marked the location of the metropolis of NewNew York, a tender scene was being enacted in the pressurized penthouse managerial suite of Puffy Products. Megera Winterly, Secretary in Chief to the Managerial Board and referred to by her underlings as the Blonde Icicle, was dealing with the advances of Roger ("Racehorse") Snedden, Assistant Secretary to the Board and often indistinguishable from any passing office boy.

"Why don't you jump out the window, Roger, remembering to shut the airlock after you?" the Golden Glacier said in tones not unkind. "When are your high-strung, thoroughbred nerves going to accept the fact that I would never consider marriage with a business inferior? You have about as much chance as a starving Ukrainian kulak now that Moscow's clapped on the interdict."

---

Roger's voice was calm, although his eyes were feverishly bright, as he replied, "A lot of things are going to be different around here, Meg, as soon as the Board is forced to admit that only my quick thinking made it possible to bring the name of Puffyloaf in front of the whole world."

"Puffyloaf could do with a little of that," the business girl observed judiciously. "The way sales have been plummeting, it won't be long before the Government deeds our desks to the managers of Fairy Bread and asks us to take the Big Jump. But just where does your quick thinking come into this, Mr. Snedden? You can't be referring to the helium-that was Rose Thinker's brainwave."

She studied him suspiciously. "You've birthed another promotional bumble, Roger. I can see it in your eyes. I only hope it's not as big a one as when you put the Martian ambassador on 3D and he thanked you profusely for the gross of Puffyloaves, assuring you that he'd never slept on a softer mattress in all his life on two planets."

"Listen to me, Meg. Today-yes, today! —you're going to see the Board eating out of my hand."

"Hah! I guarantee you won't have any fingers left. You're bold enough now, but when Mr. Gryce and those two big machines come through that door —"

"Now wait a minute, Meg —"

"Hush! They're coming now!"

Roger leaped three feet in the air, but managed to land without a sound and edged toward his stool. Through the dilating iris of the door strode Phineas T. Gryce, flanked by Rose Thinker and Tin Philosopher.

The man approached the conference table in the center of the room with measured pace and gravely expressionless face. The rose-tinted machine on his left did a couple of impulsive pirouettes on the way and twittered a greeting to Meg and Roger. The other machine quietly took the third of the high seats and lifted a claw at Meg, who now occupied a stool twice the height of Roger's.

"Miss Winterly, please-our theme."

The Blonde Icicle's face thawed into a little-girl smile as she chanted bubblingly:

"*Made up of tiny wheaten motes*
*And reinforced with sturdy oats,*
*It rises through the air and floats —*
*The bread on which all Terra dotes!*"

"Thank You, Miss Winterly," said Tin Philosopher. "Though a purely figurative statement, that bit about rising through the air always gets me-here." He rapped his midsection, which gave off a high musical *clang*.

"Ladies —" he inclined his photocells toward Rose Thinker and Meg —"and gentlemen. This is a historic occasion in Old Puffy's long history, the inauguration of the helium-filled loaf ('So Light It Almost Floats Away!') in which that inert and heaven-aspiring gas replaces old-fashioned carbon dioxide. Later, there will be kudos for Rose Thinker, whose bright relays genius-sparked the idea, and also for Roger Snedden, who took care of the details.

"By the by, Racehorse, that was a brilliant piece of work getting the helium out of the government-they've been pretty stuffy lately about their monopoly. But first I want to throw wide the casement in your minds that opens on the Long View of Things."

Rose Thinker spun twice on her chair and opened her photocells wide. Tin Philosopher coughed to limber up the diaphragm of his speaker and continued:

"Ever since the first cave wife boasted to her next-den neighbor about the superior paleness and fluffiness of her tortillas, mankind has sought lighter, whiter bread. Indeed, thinkers wiser than myself have equated the whole upward course of culture with this poignant quest. Yeast was a wonderful discovery-for its primitive day. Sifting the bran and wheat germ from the flour was an even more important advance. Early bleaching and preserving chemicals played their humble parts.

"For a while, barbarous faddists-blind to the deeply spiritual nature of bread, which is recognized by all great religions-held back our march toward perfection with their hair-splitting insistence on the vitamin content of the wheat germ, but their case collapsed when tasteless colorless substitutes were triumphantly synthesized and introduced into the loaf, which for flawless purity, unequaled airiness and sheer intangible goodness was rapidly becoming mankind's supreme gustatory experience."

"I wonder what the stuff tastes like," Rose Thinker said out of a clear sky.

"I wonder what taste tastes like," Tin Philosopher echoed dreamily. Recovering himself, he continued:

"Then, early in the twenty-first century, came the epochal researches of Everett Whitehead, Puffyloaf chemist, culminating in his paper 'The Structural Bubble in Cereal Masses' and making possible the baking of airtight bread twenty times stronger (for its weight) than steel and of a lightness that would have been incredible even to the advanced chemist-bakers of the twentieth century —a lightness so great that, besides forming the backbone of our own promotion, it has forever since been capitalized on by our conscienceless competitors of Fairy Bread with their enduring slogan: 'It Makes Ghost Toast'."

"That's a beaut, all right, that ecto-dough blurb," Rose Thinker admitted, bugging her photocells sadly. "Wait a sec. How about? —

*"There'll be bread*
*Overhead*
*When you're dead —*
*It is said."*

Phineas T. Gryce wrinkled his nostrils at the pink machine as if he smelled her insulation smoldering. He said mildly, "A somewhat unhappy jingle, Rose, referring as it does to the end of the customer as consumer. Moreover, we shouldn't overplay the figurative 'rises through the air' angle. What inspired you?"

She shrugged. "I don't know-oh, yes, I do. I was remembering one of the workers' songs we machines used to chant during the Big Strike —

*"Work and pray,*
*Live on hay.*
*You'll get pie*
*In the sky*
*When you die —*
*It's a lie!*

"I don't know why we chanted it," she added. "We didn't want pie-or hay, for that matter. And machines don't pray, except Tibetan prayer wheels."

Phineas T. Gryce shook his head. "Labor relations are another topic we should stay far away from. However, dear Rose, I'm glad you keep trying to outjingle those dirty crooks at Fairy Bread." He scowled, turning back his attention to Tin Philosopher. "I get whopping mad, Old Machine, whenever I hear that other slogan of theirs, the discriminatory one —'Untouched by Robot Claws.' Just because they employ a few filthy androids in their factories!"

Tin Philosopher lifted one of his own sets of bright talons. "Thanks, P.T. But to continue my historical resume, the next great advance in the baking art was the substitution of purified carbon dioxide, recovered from coal smoke, for the gas generated by yeast organisms indwelling in the dough and later killed by the heat of baking, their corpses remaining *in situ*. But even purified carbon dioxide is itself a rather repugnant gas, a product of metabolism whether fast or slow, and forever associated with those life processes which are obnoxious to the fastidious."

Here the machine shuddered with delicate clinkings. "Therefore, we of Puffyloaf are taking today what may be the ultimate step toward purity: we are aerating our loaves with the noble gas helium, an element which remains virginal in the face of all chemical temptations and whose slim molecules are eleven times lighter than obese carbon dioxide-yes, noble uncontaminable helium, which, if it be a kind of ash, is yet the ash only of radioactive burning, accomplished or initiated entirely on the Sun, a safe 93 million miles from this planet. Let's have a cheer for the helium loaf!"

---

Without changing expression, Phineas T. Gryce rapped the table thrice in solemn applause, while the others bowed their heads.

"Thanks, T.P.," P.T. then said. "And now for the Moment of Truth. Miss Winterly, how is the helium loaf selling?"

The business girl clapped on a pair of earphones and whispered into a lapel mike. Her gaze grew abstracted as she mentally translated flurries of brief squawks into coherent messages. Suddenly a single vertical furrow creased her matchlessly smooth brow.

"It isn't, Mr. Gryce!" she gasped in horror. "Fairy Bread is outselling Puffyloaves by an infinity factor. So far this morning, *there has not been one single delivery of Puffyloaves to any sales spot*! Complaints about non-delivery are pouring in from both walking stores and sessile shops."

"Mr. Snedden!" Gryce barked. "What bug in the new helium process might account for this delay?"

Roger was on his feet, looking bewildered. "I can't imagine, sir, unless-just possibly-there's been some unforeseeable difficulty involving the new metal-foil wrappers."

"Metal-foil wrappers? Were *you* responsible for those?"

"Yes, sir. Last-minute recalculations showed that the extra lightness of the new loaf might be great enough to cause drift during stackage. Drafts in stores might topple sales pyramids. Metal-foil wrappers, by their added weight, took care of the difficulty."

"And you ordered them without consulting the Board?"

"Yes, sir. There was hardly time and —"

"Why, you fool! I noticed that order for metal-foil wrappers, assumed it was some sub-secretary's mistake, and canceled it last night!"

Roger Snedden turned pale. "You canceled it?" he quavered. "And told them to go back to the lighter plastic wrappers?"

"Of course! Just what is behind all this, Mr. Snedden? *What* recalculations were you trusting, when our physicists had demonstrated months ago that the helium loaf was safely stackable in light airs and gentle breezes-winds up to Beaufort's scale 3. *Why* should a change from heavier to lighter wrappers result in complete non-delivery?"

---

Roger Snedden's paleness became tinged with an interesting green. He cleared his throat and made strange gulping noises. Tin Philosopher's photocells focused on him calmly, Rose Thinker's with unfeigned excitement. P.T. Gryce's frown grew blacker by the moment, while Megera Winterly's Venus-mask showed an odd dawning of dismay and awe. She was getting new squawks in her earphones.

"Er ...ah ...er...." Roger said in winning tones. "Well, you see, the fact is that I...."

"Hold it," Meg interrupted crisply. "Triple-urgent from Public Relations, Safety Division. Tulsa-Topeka aero-express makes emergency landing after being buffeted in encounter with vast flight of objects first described as brown birds, although no failures reported in airway's electronic anti-bird fences. After grounding safely near Emporia-no fatalities-pilot's windshield found thinly plastered with soft white-and-brown material. Emblems on plastic wrappers embedded in material identify it incontrovertibly as an undetermined number of Puffyloaves cruising at three thousand feet!"

Eyes and photocells turned inquisitorially upon Roger Snedden. He went from green to Puffyloaf white and blurted: "All right, I did it, but it was the only way out! Yesterday morning, due to the Ukrainian crisis, the government stopped sales and deliveries of all strategic stockpiled materials, including helium gas. Puffy's new program of advertising and promotion, based on the lighter loaf, was already rolling. There was only one thing to do, there being only one other gas comparable in lightness to helium. I diverted the necessary quantity of hydrogen gas from the Hydrogenated Oils Section of our Magna-Margarine Division and substituted it for the helium."

"You substituted ...hydrogen ...for the ...helium?" Phineas T. Gryce faltered in low mechanical tones, taking four steps backward.

"Hydrogen is twice as light as helium," Tin Philosopher remarked judiciously.

"And many times cheaper-did you know that?" Roger countered feebly. "Yes, I substituted hydrogen. The metal-foil wrapping would have added just enough weight to counteract the greater buoyancy of the hydrogen loaf. But —"

"So, when this morning's loaves began to arrive on the delivery platforms of the walking mills...." Tin Philosopher left the remark unfinished.

"Exactly," Roger agreed dismally.

"Let me ask you, Mr. Snedden," Gryce interjected, still in low tones, "if you expected people to jump to the kitchen ceiling for their Puffybread after taking off the metal wrapper, or reach for the sky if they happened to unwrap the stuff outdoors?"

"Mr. Gryce," Roger said reproachfully, "you have often assured me that what people do with Puffybread after they buy it is no concern of ours."

"I seem to recall," Rose Thinker chirped somewhat unkindly, "that dictum was created to answer inquiries after Roger put the famous sculptures-in-miniature artist on 3D and he testified that he always molded his first attempts from Puffybread, one jumbo loaf squeezing down to approximately the size of a peanut."

---

Her photocells dimmed and brightened. "Oh, boy-hydrogen! The loaf's unwrapped. After a while, in spite of the crust-seal, a little oxygen diffuses in. An explosive mixture. Housewife in curlers and kimono pops a couple slices in the toaster. Boom!"

The three human beings in the room winced.

Tin Philosopher kicked her under the table, while observing, "So you see, Roger, that the non-delivery of the hydrogen loaf carries some consolations. And I must confess that one aspect of the affair gives me great satisfaction, not as a Board Member but as a private machine. You have at last made a reality of the 'rises through the air' part of Puffybread's theme. They can't ever take that away from you. By now, half the inhabitants of the Great Plains must have observed our flying loaves rising high."

Phineas T. Gryce shot a frightened look at the west windows and found his full voice.

"Stop the mills!" he roared at Meg Winterly, who nodded and whispered urgently into her mike.

"A sensible suggestion," Tin Philosopher said. "But it comes a trifle late in the day. If the mills are still walking and grinding, approximately seven billion Puffyloaves are at this moment cruising eastward over Middle America. Remember that a six-month supply for deep-freeze is involved and that the current consumption of bread, due to its matchless airiness, is eight and one-half loaves per person per day."

Phineas T. Gryce carefully inserted both hands into his scanty hair, feeling for a good grip. He leaned menacingly toward Roger who, chin resting on the table, regarded him apathetically.

"Hold it!" Meg called sharply. "Flock of multiple-urgents coming in. News Liaison: information bureaus swamped with flying-bread inquiries. Aero-expresslines: Clear our airways or face law suit. U. S. Army: Why do loaves flame when hit by incendiary bullets? U. S. Customs: If bread intended for export, get export license or face prosecution. Russian Consulate in Chicago: Advise on destination of bread-lift. And some Kansas church is accusing us of a hoax inciting to blasphemy, of faking miracles —I don't know *why*."

The business girl tore off her headphones. "Roger Snedden," she cried with a hysteria that would have dumfounded her underlings, "you've brought the name of Puffyloaf in front of the whole world, all right! Now do something about the situation!"

Roger nodded obediently. But his pallor increased a shade, the pupils of his eyes disappeared under the upper lids, and his head burrowed beneath his forearms.

"Oh, boy," Rose Thinker called gayly to Tin Philosopher, "this looks like the start of a real crisis session! Did you remember to bring spare batteries?"

---

Meanwhile, the monstrous flight of Puffyloaves, filling midwestern skies as no small fliers had since the days of the passenger pigeon, soared steadily onward.

Private fliers approached the brown and glistening bread-front in curiosity and dipped back in awe. Aero-expresslines organized sightseeing flights along the flanks. Planes of the government forestry and agricultural services and 'copters bearing the Puffyloaf emblem hovered on the fringes, watching developments and waiting for orders. A squadron of supersonic fighters hung menacingly above.

The behavior of birds varied considerably. Most fled or gave the loaves a wide berth, but some bolder species, discovering the minimal nutritive nature of the translucent brown objects, attacked them furiously with beaks and claws. Hydrogen diffusing slowly through the crusts had now distended most of the sealed plastic wrappers into little balloons, which ruptured, when pierced, with disconcerting *pops*.

Below, neck-craning citizens crowded streets and back yards, cranks and cultists had a field day, while local and national governments raged indiscriminately at Puffyloaf and at each other.

Rumors that a fusion weapon would be exploded in the midst of the flying bread drew angry protests from conservationists and a flood of telefax pamphlets titled "H-Loaf or H-bomb?"

Stockholm sent a mystifying note of praise to the United Nations Food Organization.

Delhi issued nervous denials of a millet blight that no one had heard of until that moment and reaffirmed India's ability to feed her population with no outside help except the usual.

Radio Moscow asserted that the Kremlin would brook no interference in its treatment of the Ukrainians, jokingly referred to the flying bread as a farce perpetrated by mad internationalists inhabiting Cloud Cuckoo Land, added contradictory references to airborne bread booby-trapped by Capitalist gangsters, and then fell moodily silent on the whole topic.

Radio Venus reported to its winged audience that Earth's inhabitants were establishing food depots in the upper air, preparatory to taking up permanent aerial residence "such as we have always enjoyed on Venus."

---

New York made feverish preparations for the passage of the flying bread. Tickets for sight-seeing space in skyscrapers were sold at high prices; cold meats and potted spreads were hawked to viewers with the assurance that they would be able to snag the bread out of the air and enjoy a historic sandwich.

Phineas T. Gryce, escaping from his own managerial suite, raged about the city, demanding general cooperation in the stretching of great nets between the skyscrapers to trap the errant loaves. He was captured by Tin Philosopher, escaped again, and was found posted with oxygen mask and submachine gun on the topmost spire of Puffyloaf Tower, apparently determined to shoot down the loaves as they appeared and before they involved his company in more trouble with Customs and the State Department.

Recaptured by Tin Philosopher, who suffered only minor bullet holes, he was given a series of mild electroshocks and returned to the conference table, calm and clear-headed as ever.

But the bread flight, swinging away from a hurricane moving up the Atlantic coast, crossed a clouded-in Boston by night and disappeared into a high Atlantic overcast, also thereby evading a local storm generated by the Weather Department in a last-minute effort to bring down or at least disperse the H-loaves.

Warnings and counterwarnings by Communist and Capitalist governments seriously interfered with military trailing of the flight during this period and it was actually lost in touch with for several days.

At scattered points, seagulls were observed fighting over individual loaves floating down from the gray roof-that was all.

A mood of spirituality strongly tinged with humor seized the people of the world. Ministers sermonized about the bread, variously interpreting it as a call to charity, a warning against gluttony, a parable of the evanescence of all earthly things, and a divine joke. Husbands and wives, facing each other across their walls of breakfast toast, burst into laughter. The mere sight of a loaf of bread anywhere was enough to evoke guffaws. An obscure sect, having as part of its creed the injunction "Don't take yourself so damn seriously," won new adherents.

The bread flight, rising above an Atlantic storm widely reported to have destroyed it, passed unobserved across a foggy England and rose out of the overcast only over Mittel-europa. The loaves had at last reached their maximum altitude.

The Sun's rays beat through the rarified air on the distended plastic wrappers, increasing still further the pressure of the confined hydrogen. They burst by the millions and tens of millions. A high-flying Bulgarian evangelist, who had happened to mistake the up-lever for the east-lever in the cockpit of his flier and who was the sole witness of the event, afterward described it as "the foaming of a sea of diamonds, the crackle of God's knuckles."

---

By the millions and tens of millions, the loaves coasted down into the starving Ukraine. Shaken by a week of humor that threatened to invade even its own grim precincts, the Kremlin made a sudden about-face. A new policy was instituted of communal ownership of the produce of communal farms, and teams of hunger-fighters and caravans of trucks loaded with pumpernickel were dispatched into the Ukraine.

World distribution was given to a series of photographs showing peasants queueing up to trade scavenged Puffyloaves for traditional black bread, recently aerated itself but still extra solid by comparison, the rate of exchange demanded by the Moscow teams being twenty Puffyloaves to one of pumpernickel.

Another series of photographs, picturing chubby workers' children being blown to bits by booby-trapped bread, was quietly destroyed.

Congratulatory notes were exchanged by various national governments and world organizations, including the Brotherhood of Free Business Machines. The great bread flight was over, though for several weeks afterward scattered falls of loaves occurred, giving rise to a new folk-lore of manna among lonely Arabian tribesmen, and in one well-authenticated instance in Tibet, sustaining life in a party of mountaineers cut off by a snow slide.

Back in NewNew York, the managerial board of Puffy Products slumped in utter collapse around the conference table, the long crisis session at last ended. Empty coffee cartons were scattered around the chairs of the three humans, dead batteries around those of the two machines. For a while, there was no movement whatsoever. Then Roger Snedden reached out wearily for the earphones where Megera Winterly had hurled them down, adjusted them to his head, pushed a button and listened apathetically.

After a bit, his gaze brightened. He pushed more buttons and listened more eagerly. Soon he was sitting tensely upright on his stool, eyes bright and lower face all a-smile, muttering terse comments and questions into the lapel mike torn from Meg's fair neck.

The others, reviving, watched him, at first dully, then with quickening interest, especially when he jerked off the earphones with a happy shout and sprang to his feet.

---

"Listen to this!" he cried in a ringing voice. "As a result of the worldwide publicity, Puffy-loaves are outselling Fairy Bread three to one-and that's just the old carbon-dioxide stock from our freezers! It's almost exhausted, but the government, now that the Ukrainian crisis is over, has taken the ban off helium and will also sell us stockpiled wheat if we need it. We can have our walking mills burrowing into the wheat caves in a matter of hours!

"But that isn't all! The far greater demand everywhere is for Puffyloaves that will actually float. Public Relations, Child Liaison Division, reports that the kiddies are making their mothers' lives miserable about it. If only we can figure out some way to make hydrogen non-explosive or the helium loaf float just a little —"

"I'm sure we can take care of that quite handily," Tin Philosopher interrupted briskly. "Puffy-loaf has kept it a corporation secret-even you've never been told about it-but just before he went crazy, Everett Whitehead discovered a way to make bread using only half as much flour as we do in the present loaf. Using this secret technique, which we've been saving for just such an emergency, it will be possible to bake a helium loaf as buoyant in every respect as the hydrogen loaf."

"Good!" Roger cried. "We'll tether 'em on strings and sell 'em like balloons. No mother-child shopping team will leave the store without a cluster. Buying bread balloons will be the big event of the day for kiddies. It'll make the carry-home shopping load lighter too! I'll issue orders at once —"

---

He broke off, looking at Phineas T. Gryce, said with quiet assurance, "Excuse me, sir, if I seem to be taking too much upon myself."

"Not at all, son; go straight ahead," the great manager said approvingly. "You're" —he laughed in anticipation of getting off a memorable remark —"rising to the challenging situation like a genuine Puffyloaf."

Megera Winterly looked from the older man to the younger. Then in a single leap she was upon Roger, her arms wrapped tightly around him.

"My sweet little ever-victorious, self-propelled monkey wrench!" she crooned in his ear. Roger looked fatuously over her soft shoulder at Tin Philosopher who, as if moved by some similar feeling, reached over and touched claws with Rose Thinker.

This, however, was what he telegraphed silently to his fellow machine across the circuit so completed:

"Good-o, Rosie! That makes another victory for robot-engineered world unity, though you almost gave us away at the start with that 'bread overhead' jingle. We've struck another blow against the next world war, in which–as we know only too well! —we machines would suffer the most. Now if we can only arrange, say, a fur-famine in Alaska and a migration of long-haired Siberian lemmings across Behring Straits ...we'd have to swing the Japanese Current up there so it'd be warm enough for the little fellows....Anyhow, Rosie, with a spot of help from the Brotherhood, those humans will paint themselves into the peace corner yet."

Meanwhile, he and Rose Thinker quietly watched the Blonde Icicle melt.

# Bullet with His Name

Before passing judgment, just ask yourself
one question: Would you like answering for
humanity any better than Ernie Meeker did?

The Invisible Being shifted his anchorage a bit in Earth's gravitational field, which felt like a push rather than a pull to him, and said, "This featherless biped seems to satisfy Galaxy Center's requirements. I'd say he's a suitable recipient for the Gifts."

His Coadjutor, equally invisible and negatively massed, chewed that over. "Mature by his length and mass. Artificial plumage neither overly gaudy nor utterly drab-indicating median social level, which is confirmed by the size of his bachelor nest. Inward maps of his environment not fantastically inaccurate. Feelings reasonably meshed-at least neither volcanic nor frozen. Thoughts and values in reasonable order. Yes, I agree, a satisfactory test subject. Except...."

"Except what?"

"Except we can never be sure of that 'reasonable' part."

"Of course not! Thank your stars *that's* beyond the reach of Galaxy Center's keenest telepathy, or even ours on the spot. Otherwise you and I'd be out of a job."

"And have to scheme up some other excuse for free-touring the Cosmos with backtracking permitted."

"Exactly!" The Being and his Coadjutor understood each other very well and were the best of friends. "Well, how many Gifts would you suggest for the test?"

"How about two Little and one Big?" the Coadjutor ventured.

"Umm ... statistically adequate but spiritually unsatisfying. Remember, the fate of his race hangs on his reactions to them. I'd be inclined to increase your suggestion by one each and add a Great."

"No-at least I question the last. After all, the Great Gifts aren't as important, really, as the Big Gifts. Besides...."

"Besides what? Come on, spit it out!" The Invisible Being was the bluff, blunt type.

"Well," said his less hearty but unswervingly honest companion, "I'm always afraid that you'll use the granting of a Great Gift as an excuse for some sardonic trick-that you'll put a sting in its tail."

"And why shouldn't I, if I want to? Snakes have stings in their tails (or do they on this planet?) and I'm a sort of snake. If he fails the test, he fails. And aren't both of us malicious, plaguing spirits, eager to knock holes in the inward armor of provincial entities? It's in the nature of our job. But we can argue about that in due course. What Little Gifts would you suggest?"

"That's something I want to talk about. Many of the Little Gifts are already well within his race's reach, if not his. After all, they've already got atomic power."

"Which as you very well know scores them nothing one way or the other on a Galaxy Center test. We're agreed on the nature and the number of our Gifts-three Little, two Big, and one Great?"

"Yes," his Coadjutor responded resignedly.

"And we're agreed on our subject?"

"Yes to that too."

"All right, then, let's get started. This isn't the only solar system we have to visit on this circuit."

---

Ernie Meeker-of Chicago, Illinois, U.S. of A., Occident, Terra, Sol, Starswarm 37, Rim Sector, Milky Way Galaxy-rubbed his chin and slanted across the street to a drugstore.

"Package of blades. Double edge. Five. Cheapest."

At one point during the transaction, the clerk lost sight of the tiny packet he'd placed on the coin-whitened glass between them. He gave a suspicious look, as if the customer had palmed them.

Ernie blinked. After a moment, he pointed toward the center of the counter.

"There they are," he said, dropping a coin beside them.

The clerk's face didn't get any less suspicious. Customer who could sneak something without your seeing could sneak it back the same way. He rang up the sale and closed the register fast.

Ernie Meeker went home and shaved. Five days-and-shaves-later, he pushed the first blade, uncomfortably dull now, through the tiny slot beside the bathroom mirror. He unwrapped the second blade from the packet.

Five shaves later, he cut himself under the chin with the second blade, although he was drawing it as gently through his soaped beard as if it were only his second shave with it, or at most his third. He looked at it sourly and checked the packet. Wouldn't have been the first time he'd absentmindedly changed blades ahead of schedule.

But there were still three blades in their waxed wrappings.

Maybe, he thought, he'd still had one of the blades from the last packet and shuffled it into this series.

Or maybe-although the manufacturers undoubtedly had inspectors to prevent it from happening-he'd got a decent blade for once.

Two or three shaves later, it still seemed as sharp as ever, or almost so.

"Funny thing," he remarked to Bill at lunch, "sometimes you get a blade that shaves a lot better. Looks exactly like the others, but shaves better. Or worse sometimes, of course."

"And sometimes," his office mate said, "you wear out a blade fast by not soaking your beard enough. For me, one shave with a stiff beard and the blade's through. On the other hand, if you're careful to soak your beard real good-four, five minutes at least-have the water steaming hot, get the soap really into it, one blade can last a long time."

"That's true, all right," Ernie agreed, trying to remember how well he had been soaking his beard lately. Shaving was a good topic for light conversation, warm and agreeable, like most bathroom and kitchen topics.

---

But next morning in the bathroom, looking at the reflection of his unremarkable face, there was something chilly in his feelings that he couldn't quite analyze. He flipped his razor open and suspiciously studied the bright metal wafer, then flipped it closed with an irritated shrug.

As he shaved, it occurred to him that a good detective-story murder method would be to substitute a very sharp razor blade for one the victim knew was extremely dull. He'd whip it across his throat, putting a lot of muscle into the stroke to get through the tangle, and —urrk!

Ridiculous, of course. Wouldn't work except with a straight razor. Wouldn't even work with a straight razor, unless ... oh, well.

He told himself the blade was noticeably duller today.

Next morning, he was still using the freak blade, but with a persistent though very slight uneasiness. Things should behave as you expected them to, in accordance with their flimsy souls, he told himself at the barely conscious level. Men should die, hearts should break, girls should tell, nations perish, curtains get dirty, milk sour ... and razor blades grow dull. It was the comfortable, expected, reassuring way.

He told himself the blade was duller still. Just a bit.

The third morning, face lathered, he flipped open the razor and lifted it out.

"You're through," he said to it silently. "I've had the experience before of getting bum shaves by trying to save a penny by pretending to myself that a wornout blade was still sharp enough, when it obviously couldn't be. Or maybe —" he grinned a little wryly —"maybe I'd almost get one more shave out of you and then you'd fall to pieces like the Wonderful One Horse Shay and leave me with a chin full of steel porcupine quills. No, thanks."

So Ernie Meeker pushed through the little slot beside the mirror and heard tinkle faintly down and away the first of the Little Gifts, the Everlasting Razor Blade. One hundred and fifty thousand years later, it turned up, bright and shining, in the midst of a small knob of red iron oxide excavated by an archeological expedition of multi-brachs from Antares Gamma. Those wise history-mad beings handed it about wonderingly, from tentacle to impatient tentacle.

---

That day, Ernie felt a little sick, somehow. After dinner, he decided it was the Thuringer sausage he'd eaten at lunch. He hurried up to the bathroom with a spoon, but as he clutched the box of bicarbonate of soda, preparatory to plunging the spoon into it, it seemed to him that the box said distinctly, in a small inward-outward voice:

"No, no, no!"

Ernie sat down suddenly on the toilet seat. The spoon rattled against the porcelain finish of the washbowl as he laid it down. He held the box firmly in both hands and studied it.

Size, shape, materials, blue color, closure, etc., were exactly as they should be. But the white lettering on the blue background read:

### AQUEOUS FUEL CATALYST

Dissociates $H_2O$ into hemi-quasi-stable H and O, furnishing a serviceable fuel-and-oxydizer mix for most motorcycles, automobiles, trucks, motorboats, airplanes, stationary motors, torque-twisters, translators, and rockets (exhaust velocity up to 6000 meters per second). Operates safely within and outside of all normal atmospheres. No special adaptor needed on oxygenizer-atmosphere motors.

*Directions*: Place one pinch in fuel tank, fill with water. Add water as needed.

A-F Catalyst should generally be renewed when objective tests show fuel quality has deteriorated 50 per cent.

U.S. and Foreign Patents Pending

After reading that several times, with suitable mind-checking and eye-testing in between, Ernie took up a little of the white powder on the end of a nailfile. He had thought of tasting it, but had instantly abandoned the notion and even refrained from sniffing the stuff-after all, the human body is mostly water.

After reducing the quantity several times, he gingerly dumped at most four or five grains on the flat edge of the washbowl and then used the broad end of the nailfile to maneuver a large bead of water over to the almost invisible white deposit. He closed the box, put it and the nailfile carefully on the window ledge, lit a match and touched it to the drop, at the last moment ducking his head a little below the level of the washbowl.

Nothing happened. After a moment, he slowly withdrew the match, shaking it out, and looked. There was nothing to see. He reached out to touch the stupid squashed ovoid of water.

Ouch! He withdrew his fingers much faster than the match, shook them more sharply. Something was there, all right. Heat. Heat enough to hurt.

---

He cautiously explored the boundaries of the heat. It became noticeable about eighteen inches above the drop and almost an inch to each side-an invisible slim vertical cylinder. Crouching close, eyes level with the top of the washbowl, he could make out the flame —a thin finger of crinkled light.

He noticed that a corner of the drop was seething-but only a corner, as if the heat were sharply bounded in that direction and perhaps as if the catalyst were only transforming the water to fuel a bit at a time.

He reached up and tugged off the light. Now he could see the flame-ghostly, about four inches high, hardly thicker than a string, and colored not blue but pale green. A spectral green needle. He blew at it softly. It shimmied gracefully, but not, he thought, as much as the flame of a match or candle. It had character.

He switched on the light. The drop was more than half gone now; the part that was left was all seething. And the bathroom was markedly warmer.

"Ernie! Are you going to be much longer?"

The knock hadn't been loud and his widowed sister's voice was more apologetic than peremptory, but he jumped, of course.

"I am testing something," he started to say and changed it mid-way. It came out, "I am be out in a minute."

He turned off the light again. The flame was a little shorter now and it shrank as he watched, about a quarter inch a second. As soon as it died, he switched on the light. The drop was gone.

He scrubbed off the spot with a dry washrag, on second thought put a dab of vaseline on the washrag, scrubbed the spot again with that-he didn't like to think of even a grain of the powder getting in the drains or touching any water. He folded the washrag, tucked it in his pocket, put the blue box-after a final check of the lettering-in his other coat pocket, and opened the door.

"I was taking some bicarb," he told his sister. "Thuringer sausage at lunch."

She nodded absently.

―――――――――――――――――――

Sleep refused even to flirt with Ernie, his mind was full of so many things, especially calculations involving the distance between his car and the house and the length of the garden hose. In desperation, as the white hours accumulated and his thoughts began to squirm, he grabbed up the detective story he'd bought at the corner newsstand. He had read thirty pages before he realized that he was turning them as rapidly as he could focus just once on each facing page.

He jumped out of bed. My God, he thought, at that rate he'd finish the book under three minutes and here it wasn't even two o'clock yet!

He selected the thickest book on the shelf, an overpoweringly dull historical treatise in small print. He turned two pages, three, then closed it with a clap and looked at the wall with frightened eyes. Ernie Meeker had discovered, inside the birthday box that was himself, the first of the Big Gifts.

The trouble was that in that wee-hour, lonely bedroom, it didn't seem like a gift at all. How would he ever keep himself in books, he wondered, if he read them so fast? And think how full to bursting his mind would get-right now, the seven pages of fine-print history were churning in it, vividly clear, along with the first chapters of the new detective story. If he kept on absorbing information that fast, he'd have to be revising all his opinions and beliefs every couple of days at least-maybe every couple of hours.

It seemed a dreadful, literally maddening prospect-his mind would ultimately become a universe of squirming macaroni. Even the wallpaper he was staring at, which imitated the grain of wood, had in an instant become so fully part of his consciousness that he felt he could turn his back on it right now and draw a picture of it correct to the tiniest detail. But who would ever want to do such a thing, or want to be able to?

It was an abnormal, dangerous, temporary sensitivity, he told himself, generated by the excitement of the crazy discovery he'd made in the bathroom. Like the thoughts of a drowning man, riffling an infinity-paneled adventure-comic of his life as he bolts his last rough ration of air. Or like the feeling a psychotic must have that he's on the verge of visualizing the whole universe, having its ultimate secrets patter down into the palm of his outstretched hand-just before the walls close in.

Ernie Meeker was not a drinking man, then. A pint had stood a week on his closet shelf and only been diminished three shots. But now he did a good job on the sturdy remainder.

Pretty soon the unbearable, edge-of-doom clarity in his mind faded, the universe-macaroni cooked down to a thick white soup uniform as fog, and the words of the detective story were sliding into his mind individually, or at most in strings of three and four. Which, if it wasn't as it ideally should be in an ambitious man's mind, was at least darn comfortable.

He had not rejected the Big Gift of Page-at-a-Glance Reading. Not quite. But he had dislocated for tonight at least the imposed nervous field on which it depended.

---

For want of a better place, Ernie dropped the rubber tube from the bathtub spray into the scrub bucket half full of odorous pink fluid and stared doubtfully at the uncapped gas tank. The tank had been almost empty when he'd last driven his car, he knew, because he'd been waiting until payday to gas up. Now he had used the tube to siphon out what he could of the remainder (he still could taste the stuff!) and he'd emptied the fuel line and carburetor, more or less.

Further than that, in the way of engine hygiene, Ernie's strictly kitchen mechanics did not go, but he felt that a catalyst used in pinches shouldn't be too particular about contaminants. Besides, the directions on the box hadn't said anything about cleaning the fuel tank, had they?

He hesitated. At his feet, the garden hose gurgled noisily over the curb into the gutter; it had vindicated his midnight estimate, proving just long enough. He looked uneasily up and down the dawning street and was relieved to find it still empty. He wished fervently, not for the first time this Saturday morning, that he had a garage. Then he sighed, squared his shoulders a little, and lifted the box out of his pocket.

Making to check the directions the umpteenth time, he received a body blow. The white lettering on the box had disappeared. The box didn't proclaim itself sodium bicarbonate again-there was just no lettering at all, only blue background. He turned it over several times.

Right there died his tentative plan of eventually sharing his secret with some friend who knew more than himself about motors (he hadn't decided anyway who that would be). It would be just too silly to approach anyone he knew with a more-than-wild story and featureless blue box.

For a moment, he came very close to dropping the box between the wide-set bars of the street drain and pouring the pink gas back in the tank. It had hit him, in a way for the first time, just how *crazy* this all was, how jarringly implausible even on such hypotheses as practical jokes, secret product perhaps military, or mad inventor (except himself).

For how the devil should the stuff get into his bathroom disguised as bicarb? That circumstance seemed beyond imagination. Green flames ... vanishing letters ... "torque-twisters, translators" ... a box that talked....

---

At that point, simple faith came to Ernie's rescue: in the same bathroom, he *had* seen the green flame; it had burned his fingers.

Quickly he dipped up a little of the white powder on the edge of a fifty-cent piece, dumped it in the gas tank without quibbling as to quantity, rapped the coin on the edge of the opening, closed and pocketed the blue box, and picked up the spurting hose and jabbed it into the round hole.

His heart was pounding and his breath was coming fast. That had taken real effort. So he was slow in hearing the footsteps behind him.

His neighbor's gate was open and Mr. Jones stood open-mouthed a few feet behind him, all ready for his day's work as streetcar motorman and wearing the dark blue uniform that always made him look for a moment unpleasantly like a policeman.

Ernie swung the hose around, flipping his thumb over the end to make a spray, and nonchalantly began to water the little rectangle of lawn between sidewalk and curb.

The first things he watered were the bottoms of Mr. Jones's pants legs.

Mr. Jones voiced no complaint. He backed off several steps, stared intently at Ernie, rather palely, it seemed to the latter. Then he turned and made off for the streetcar tracks at a very fast shuffle, shaking his feet a little now and then and glancing back several times over his shoulder without slowing down.

Ernie felt light-headed. He decided there was enough water in the gas tank, capped it, and momentarily continued to water the lawn.

"Ernie! Come on in and have breakfast!"

He heeded his sister's call, telling himself it would be a good idea "to give the stuff time to mix" before testing the engine.

He had divined her question and was ready with an answer.

"I've just found out that we're supposed to water our lawns only before seven in the morning or after seven in the evenings. It's the law."

---

It was the day for their monthly drive out to Wheaton to visit Uncle Fabius. On the whole, Ernie was glad his sister was in the car when he turned the key in the starter-it forced him to be calm and collected, though he didn't feel exactly right about exposing her to the danger of being blown up without first explaining to her the risk. But the motor started right up and began purring powerfully. Ernie's sister commented on it favorably.

Then she went on to ask, "Did you remember to buy gas yesterday?"

"No," he said without thinking; then, realizing his mistake, quickly added, "I'll buy some in Wheaton. There's enough to get us there."

"You didn't think so yesterday," she objected. "You said the tank was nearly empty."

"I was wrong. Look, the gauge shows it's half full."

"But then how ... Ernie, didn't you once tell me the gauge doesn't work?"

"Did I?"

"Yes. Look, there's a station. Why don't you buy gas now?"

"No, I'll wait for Wheaton —I know a place there I can get it cheaper," he insisted, rather lamely, he feared.

His sister looked at him steadily. He settled his head between his shoulders and concentrated on driving. His feeling of excitement was spoiled, but a few minutes of silence brought it back. He thought of the blur of green flashes inside the purring motor. If the passing drivers only knew!

Uncle Fabius, retired perhaps a few years too early and opinionated, was a trial, but he did know something about the automobile industry. Ernie chose a moment when his sister was out of the room to ask if he'd ever heard of a white powder that would turn water into gasoline or some usable fuel.

"Who's been getting at you?" Uncle Fabius demanded sharply, to Ernie's surprise and embarrassment. "That's one of the oldest swindles. They always tell this story about how this man had a white powder or something and demonstrated it once with a pail of water and then disappeared. You're supposed to believe that Detroit or the big oil companies got rid of him. It's just another of those malicious legends, concocted-by Russia, I imagine-to weaken your faith in American Industry, like the everlasting battery or the razor blade that never gets dull. You're looking pale, Ernie-don't tell me you've already put money in this white powder? I suppose someone's approached you with a proposition, though?"

---

With considerable difficulty, Ernie convinced his uncle that he had "just heard the story from a friend."

"In that case," Uncle Fabius opined, "you can be sure some fuel-powder swindler has been getting at *him*. When you see him-and be sure to make that soon-tell him from me that —" and Uncle Fabius began an impassioned ninety-minute defense of big business, small business, prosperity, America, money, know-how, and a number of other institutions that defended pretty easily, so that the situation was wholly normal when Ernie's sister returned.

As soon as the car pulled away from the curb on their way back to Chicago, she reminded him about the gas.

"Oh, I've already done that," he assured her. "Made a special trip so I wouldn't forget. It was while you were out of the room. Didn't you hear me?"

"No," she said, "I didn't," and she looked at him steadily, as she had that morning. He similarly retreated to driving.

Stopping for a railroad crossing, he braked too hard and the car stalled. His sister grabbed his arm. "I knew that was going to happen," she said. "I knew that for some reason you lied to me when —" The motor, starting readily again, cut short her remark and Ernie didn't press his small triumph by asking her what she was about to say.

To tell the truth, Ernie wasn't feeling as elated about today's fifty-mile drive as he'd imagined he would. Now he thought he could put his finger on the reason: It was the completely ...well, *arbitrary* way in which the white powder had come into his possession.

If he'd concocted it himself, or been given it by a shady promoter, or even seen the box fall out of the pocket of a suspicious-looking man in a trenchcoat, *then* he'd have felt more able to *do* something about it, whether in the general line of starting a fuel-powder company or of going to the F.B.I.

But just having the stuff drop into his hands from the sky, so to speak, as if in a crazy dream, and for that same reason not feeling able to talk about it and assure himself he wasn't going crazy ...oh, it is rough when you can't share things, really rough; not being able to share depressing news corrodes the spirit, but not being able to share exciting news can sometimes be even more corroding.

Maybe, he told himself, he could figure out someone to tell. But who? And how? His mind shied away from the problem, rather decisively.

---

When he checked the blue box that night, the original sodium bicarbonate lettering had returned with all its humdrum paragraphs. Not one word about exhaust velocities.

From that moment, the fuel-powder became a trial to Ernie rather than a secret glory. He'd wake in the middle of the night doubting that he had ever really read the mind-dizzying lettering, ever really tested the stuff-perhaps he'd bring from sleep the chilling notion that in the dimness and excitement of Saturday morning he'd put the water in some other car's gas tank, perhaps Mr. Jones's. He could usually argue such ideas away, but they kept coming back. And yet he did no more bathroom testing.

Of course the car still ran. He even fueled it once again with the garden hose, sniffing the nozzle to make sure it hadn't somehow got connected to the basement furnace oil-tank. He picked three o'clock in the morning for the act, but nevertheless as he was returning indoors he heard a window in Mr. Jones's house slam loudly. It unsettled him. Coming home the next day, he caught his sister and Mr. Jones consulting about something on the latter's doorsteps, which unsettled him further.

He couldn't decide on a safe place to keep the box and took to carrying it around with him day and night. Bill spotted it once down at the office and by an unhappy coincidence needed some bicarb just then for a troubled stomach. Ernie explained on the spur of the moment that he was using the box to carry plaster of Paris, which involved him in further lies that he felt were quite unconvincing as well as making him appear decidedly eccentric, even butter-brained. Bill took to calling him "the sculptor."

Meanwhile, besides the problem of the white powder, Ernie was having other unsettling experiences, stemming (though of course he didn't know that) from the other Gifts-and not just the Big Gift of Page-at-a-Glance Reading, though that still returned from time to time to shock his consciousness and send him hurrying for a few quick shots.

---

Like many another car-owning commuter, Ernie found the traffic and parking problems a bit too much for comfort and so used the fast electric train to carry him five times a week to the heart of the city. During those brief, swift, crowded trips Ernie, generally looking steadily out the window at the brown buildings and black stanchions whipping past, enjoyed a kind of anonymity and privacy more refreshing to his spirit than he realized. But now all that had been suddenly changed. People had started to talk to him; total strangers struck up conversations almost every morning and afternoon.

Ernie couldn't figure out the reason and wasn't at all sure he liked it-except for Vivian.

She was the sort of girl Ernie dreamed about, improperly. Tall, blonde and knowing, excitedly curved but armored in a black suit, friendly and funny but given to making almost cruelly deflating remarks, as if the neatly furled short umbrella dangling from her wrist might better be a black dog whip.

She worked in an office too, a fancier one than Ernie's, as he found out from their morning conversations. He hadn't got to the point of asking her to lunch, but he was prodding himself.

Why such a girl should ever have asked him for a match in the first place and then put up with his clumsy babblings on subsequent mornings was a mystery to him. He finally asked her about it in what he hoped was a joking way, though she seemed to know a lot more about joking than he did.

"Don't you know?" she countered. "I mean what makes you attractive to people?"

"Me attractive? No."

"Well, I'll tell you then, Ernie, and I've got to admit it's something quite out of the ordinary. *I've* never noticed it in anyone else. Ernie, I'm sure your knowledge of romantic novels is shamefully deficient, it's clear from your manners, but in the earlier ones-not in style now-the hero is described as tall, manly, broad-shouldered, Anglo-Saxon features, etcetera, etcetera, but there's one thing he always has, something that sounds like poetic over-enthusiasm if you stop to analyze it, a physical impossibility, but that I have to admit you, Ernie, actually have. Flashing eyes."

"Flashing eyes? Me?"

She nodded solemnly. He thought her long straight lips trembled on the verge of a grin, but he couldn't be sure.

"How do you mean, flashing eyes?" he protested. "How *can* eyes flash, except by reflecting light? In that case, I guess they'd seem to 'flash' more if a person opened them wide but kept blinking them a lot. Is that what I do?"

"No, Ernie, though you're doing it now," she told him, shaking her head. "No, Ernie, your eyes just give a tiny flash of their own about every five seconds, like a lighthouse, but barely, *barely* bright enough for another person to notice. It makes you irresistible. Of course I've never seen you in the dark; maybe they wouldn't flash in the dark."

"You're joking."

Vivian frowned a little at that remark, as if she were puzzled herself.

"Well, maybe I am and maybe I'm not," she said. "In any case, don't get conceited about your Flashing Eyes, because I'm sure you'll never know how to take advantage of them."

When he parted from her downtown, pausing a moment to watch her walk away with feline majesty, he muttered "Flashing Eyes!" with a shrug of the shoulders and a skeptical growl. Just the same, he ducked his head as he moved off and he pulled the brim of his hat down sharply.

Afternoons, hurtling home in the five o'clock rush, it was not Vivian but Verna who frequently occupied the seat beside him, taking up rather more space in it than the Panther Princess. Verna was another of his newly acquired and not altogether welcome conversation-pals, along with Jacob the barber, Mr. Willis the druggist and Herman the health-food manufacturer, inventor of Soybean Mush-conquests of his Flashing Eyes or whatever it was.

Verna was stocky, pasty-faced, voluble (with him), coy, and had bad breath-he could see the tiny triangles of pale food between her incisors and canines whenever her conversations became particularly vehement and confidential, which was often. She always had a stack of books hugged to her stomach. She worked in a fur-storage vault, she said, and could snatch quite a bit of time for reading-rather heavy reading, it seemed.

It wasn't very long before Verna was head-over-heels (fearful picture!) infatuated with him. Somehow his friendliness had touched a hidden spring in this ugly, friendless, clumsy girl and for once she had lost her fear of the world's ridicule and opened her hulking heart to another human being. It was touching but rather overpowering, especially since she always opened her mouth too. He learned a great deal about herself, her invalid father, Elizabethan and Restoration poetry, paleontology, an organization known as the Working Girls' Front, Mr. Abrusian, and a brassy Miss Minkin who sounded like a fiendish caricature of Vivian.

He felt that deliberately avoiding Verna would be a dirtier trick than he liked to think himself capable of. Nevertheless there were times when he seriously wished he'd never acquired whatever power it was-except for Vivian, of course. What the devil, he asked himself for the $n$th time, could that power be?

That night, in the bathroom, the question came back to him and he impulsively switched off the light and looked into the mirror. He gasped and seemed on the point of shrieking out something, but he only grasped the washbowl more tightly and stared into the mirror more intently.

After about a minute, he tugged on the light again. He was pale. He had convinced himself of the actual existence of the phenomenon that was in reality the third of the Little Gifts: Flashing Eyes.

He couldn't notice anything in the light, but in the dark his eyes gave off a faint blue flash about every five seconds, just as Vivian had said, lighting up his cheeks and eyebrows like some comic-book vampire!

It might be attractive by day, when it just registered as an impalpable hint, but it was damn sinister in the dark! It wasn't much, but it was *there* —unless the flashes were inside his head and he was projecting them ...blue ...something called the Purkinje effect? ...but then Vivian had actually seen ...oh, damn!

Suddenly he wildly looked around, a little like a trapped animal. Why did it always have to happen in the *bathroom*, he asked himself-the bicarb, the flame, the blade (if that counted), and now this? Could there be something wrong about the bathroom, something either in the room itself or in his childhood associations?

But neither the bathroom walls nor his minutely searched memory returned an answer.

It was dark in the hall outside and he almost bumped into his sister. He recoiled, stared at her a moment, then threw his hand over his eyes, darted into his bedroom and shut the door.

"Is there something wrong, Ernie?" she called after him.

"Wrong?"

The door muffled his voice. "How do you mean?"

"I mean about your eyes."

"My *eyes*?" It was almost a scream. "What about my eyes?"

"Don't shout, Ernie. I mean are they painful?"

"Painful? Why should they be painful?"

"I really don't know, Ernie." She was being very patient and calm.

"I mean did you *notice* anything about them?" He was trying to be the same without much success.

"Just that you put your hand up to them as if they hurt."

"Oh." Great relief. "Yes, they do smart a little. I guess I've been using them too much. I'm putting some eye-drops in them now."

"Can I help you, Ernie? And shouldn't you see an opto ... ocu ... optha ... I mean an eye doctor?"

Ernie answered "No" to both those questions, but of course it took a lot more lying and improvising and general smoothing out before his sister would even pretend to be satisfied and stop her general nagging for the evening. She was getting uncomfortably cagy and curious lately, addicted to asking such questions out of a blue sky as:

"Ernie, when we were visiting Uncle Fabius, did you actually believe that you went out and bought gas?"

That one momentarily brought Ernie's stammer back, something which hadn't troubled him for years.

And when she wasn't asking questions, her quiet studying of him for long minutes was even more upsetting.

---

Next morning, on the way to the electric train, Ernie made a purchase at the drugstore. When he sat down beside Vivian, she took one look at him and gave a very deliberate-sounding hollow laugh.

"Black glasses!" she said. "I tell him he's attractive because he has Flashing Eyes and within two days he's wearing black glasses. I suppose I should have guessed it."

"But my eyes hurt," Ernie protested. "Sensitive to sunlight, I think." He wished he could explain to her that he'd bought the glasses not only in case he got caught out at night, but also to convince his sister he hadn't been lying about sore eyes. He hadn't intended to wear them by day and hardly knew why he'd put them on before joining Vivian.

"Spare me your rationalizations," she said. "Your motives are clear to me, Ernie, and they happen to be very commonplace."

She leaned toward him and her voice, little more than a whisper, took on an unexpectedly gloomy, chilling, hopeless tone.

"See these people all around us, Ernie? They're suicides, every one of them. Day by day, in every way, they're killing themselves. People love them, admire them, and it only makes them uneasy. They have abilities and charms by the bushel-yes, they do, even that man with the wen on his neck-and they only try to hide them. The spotlight turns their way and they goof. They think they're running away from failure, but actually they're running away from success."

Ernie looked at them, he couldn't help it, her voice made him, and the ability of Page-at-a-Glance Reading chose that moment to come back to him, only applied to faces instead of letters, and there seemed to be another ability along with it, unclear as yet but frightening. He felt like a very old detective scanning the lineup for the thousandth time.

The black glasses didn't interfere a bit-the dozens of faces in this speeding electric car were suddenly as familiar as the court cards in a deck-and he had the feeling that, like a bunch of pink pasteboards, they were about to be hurled in his face.

My God, he asked himself, flinching, how could you go on living with so many faces so close to you, so completely known? —each street you turned into, each store you entered, each gathering you joined, another deluge of unique features. Ugly, pretty, strong, weak-those words didn't mean anything any more in this drenching of individuality he was getting, and that showed no signs of stopping.

So he hardly heard Vivian saying, "And it's true of you, Ernie-in spades, for your black glasses," and he hardly remembered parting from her, and when he found himself alone he did something unprecedented for him at that time of day-he went to a bar and drank two double whiskies.

---

The drinks brought the downtown landscape back to normal and stopped the faces printing themselves on his mind, but they left him very disturbed, and the suspiciousness with which he was treated at the office didn't improve that, and Ernie began to wish for ordinariness and commonplaceness in himself more than anything in the whole world. If only, he silently implored, there were some way of junking everything that had happened to him in the past few weeks-except maybe Vivian.

Verna on the train home positively terrified him. She was unusually talkative and engulfing this evening and he thought that if the faces-forever feeling came to him just as she was baring her food-triangles and all, he wouldn't be able to stand it. Somehow, it didn't. Yet the very intensity of his distaste frightened him. Not for the first time, the word "insanity" appeared in his mind, pulsing in pale yellowish-green.

Half a block from home, passing his parked car (with an unconscious little veer of avoidance), he spotted three figures in close conference in front of his house: his sister, a man in dark blue-yes, Mr. Jones, and ...a man in a white coat.

Almost before he knew it, he was in his car and driving away. He truly didn't know what he was going to do, only that he was going to do it, and found a trivial interest in trying to guess what it was going to be. Whatever it was, it was going to dim that yellowish-green word, decrease its type-size, make him a little more able to face the crisis waiting him at home ... or somewhere.

He had a picture of himself getting on an airplane, another of renting a room in a slum, another of stopping the car on a lonely, treeless country road and getting out and looking up to the coldly glimmering Milky Way-why?

That last picture was the most vivid, and when he realized he had actually stopped his car, it was a moment before it would go away. Then he saw he was parked in front of a demolished old apartment building a few blocks from his home. Only yesterday he'd watched the last wall going down. Now, just across the littered sidewalk from him, the old cellar gaped, flimsily guarded in front by a makeshift rail and surrounded on the other three sides by great hillocks of battered bricks. Tomorrow probably (and in fact that was the way it happened) a bulldozer would tumble them forward, filling the cellar with old bricks and brick-dust, leveling the lot.

---

Now he knew what he was going to do. He unlatched the top over the windshield and pushed the button. Slowly the top folded back over his head, showing the smoke-dark sky, almost night. He hitched up a little in the seat, reached inside his coat, pulled out the blue box he always carried and pitched it into the dark pit across the sidewalk.

He was driving away almost before it landed. Yet through the hum of the motor he thought he heard something call faintly, "Good-by."

The material of the filled-in cellar stayed fairly dry for many years and the atom-bombing, when it finally came, created a partial surface-seal of fused stone over that area. However, the bicarb box fell apart in time; water reached it in little seepings and was accumulated as a non-evaporating fuel-and-oxydizer mix. The amount of this strange fluid grew and grew, eventually invading and filling a now-blind section of the city's old sewer system.

Many tens of thousands of years after that, the buried pool was sensed by the fuel-finders of a spaceship from up Polaris way, which had made an emergency landing on the ruined planet. A well was drilled and the mix pumped up and the centipedal Polarians, scuttling about the bleak landscape, had a fine time trying to explain how such a sophisticated fluid should occur in a seeming state of nature. However, they were grateful to the Cosmic All-Father.

Long before that, Ernie had arrived home in something of a daze. He told himself that he had cast off the most tangible element of his "insanity," but he didn't feel any the better for it. In fact, he felt distinctly apathetic when his sister confronted him and only with an effort did he manage to brace himself for the trial he knew she had in store for him.

"Ernie," she said hesitatingly, "I've come to a decision about something-about a change in our arrangements here, to tell you the truth-and I've gone ahead with it without consulting you. I do hope you won't mind."

"No," he said heavily, "I guess I won't mind."

"I'm doing it partly on Mr. Jones's advice," she added slowly. "As a matter of fact he suggested it."

Ernie nodded. "Yes, I've noticed the two of you conferring together."

"You have? Then maybe you know what I'm talking about."

"Oh, yes." Ernie nodded again and smiled grimly. "The man in white?"

She laughed. "Exactly, the man in white. For a long time, I've thought it was just too much bother for either of us to carry the milk home, and the eggs and my yogurt too. So I decided to have the milkman that Mr. Jones uses make deliveries. Mr. Jones brought him over half an hour ago and it's all arranged. Four quarts a week, one dozen eggs, and yogurt Tuesdays and Fridays."

---

The Invisible Being and his Coadjutor, backtracking for a checkup, summarized the situation.

The latter said, "So he's already thrown away the Everlasting Cosmetic Knife and the Water Splitter; he seems to be trying to reject the third Little Gift and the first Big One, while he still isn't even conscious of the other two Gifts."

"Cheer up," said the Invisible Being. "It's his life and he's doing what he thinks best."

"Yes," the Coadjutor said, "but he doesn't know he's making these decisions for his race as well as himself. Sometimes I think Galaxy Center makes it too hard for chaps like him. For instance, that trick of having the images on the box fade back to the old ones."

"Nonsense! We have to take all reasonable precautions that our activities remain secret. He knew that the powder worked. He should have had faith."

"Sometimes it takes a lot of faith."

"You're right, it does." The Invisible Being smiled his Cheshire smile. "You feel a lot for these test subjects, don't you? That's fine, but you've got to remember you can't accept the Gifts for them; that's one thing they have to do themselves, however long they take about it. Which reminds me, I think we ought to set up a recorder here to report the final outcome of the test to Galaxy Center."

"Good idea."

"And cheer up, I say. This test isn't over yet and our featherless biped isn't necessarily licked. If he thinks to link up the third Little Gift with the two Big Ones, he has a pretty sweet setup for making psychic progress-and his race will be Galactic Citizens in a jiffy."

"You're right."

"Moreover, it stands to reason he's soon going to become aware of the Great Gift, and that generally gives a person a jolt and makes him think seriously about other things."

"True enough-though I still have the feeling you intend some sardonic trick in conjunction with the Great Gift. Are you sure you're not planning to leave some other setup here along with the recorder? I notice you've got a spare Juxtaposer in the ship and it bothers me."

"That, dear Coadjutor, is my business. Whatever I do, it won't interfere in any way with the fairness of the tests."

"Sometimes I think the tests are *too* fair," the Coadjutor observed. "I'd like to be able to ease them up a bit in special cases."

"Confidentially, my friend, so would I."

---

The Great Gift announced itself to Ernie next morning at 7:53 sharp, when the Special slowed to forty miles an hour to swing past the platform on which he was waiting for the Express.

One moment he was standing morning-weary on the thick wooden planks, looking down through the quarter-inch gaps between them at the cinders five feet below, vaguely conscious of a woman's white-polka-dotted black skirt on one side of his field of vision and a man's brown shoes and briefcase to the other.

Next moment he was in a small cab under which steel rails were vanishing at an alarming speed, and way ahead he could just make out the platform on which he was standing, and something was hurting his head and he was slumping forward and everything was darkening and the cab was leaping forward more swiftly still.

The third moment he was back on the platform, running furiously to get off it. He didn't care who yelled at him or whom he bumped, so long as it didn't slow him down. The people were just blurs anyway and soon he was beyond them. He took in two strides the short flight of wooden steps leading down off the platform proper and spurted the last sixty feet to the stairs leading down to street level. There he stumbled, recovered himself, and chanced a hasty backward look.

There was a tall man at his heels, hugging a briefcase and panting hard. Then, beyond the tall man, he saw the platform rear up like a wooden caterpillar, spilling people against the bright gray morning sky. There was a cosmic crunch and the battered Special, still coming strong, burst through the upreared platform in a blossoming broken-matchstick crown of planks and beams-and big blue sparks where a writhing power wire, snagged by the uprearing platform, was grounding against the first car.

---

Ernie ducked his head and plunged down the steps ahead.

(That was how I came to meet Ernie Meeker. I was the tall man. As you can imagine, it's quite strange to be standing in a huddle of fresh-washed morning commuters and have the one beside you close his eyes and slump a little and then take off like a bat out of hell-without a word spoken or a thing happened to explain it. I started to laugh, but then I got the funniest feeling of curiosity and terror and I took off after him. It saved my life.

(Afterward, Ernie and I went back to help with the ghastliness, but pretty soon there were more than enough trainmen, firemen, police, and what not, and we got chased off. We had a couple of drinks together and met a few times after and that's how I got some of this story. But my chief sources of information I am not permitted to disclose.)

---

As the Invisible Being had predicted, Ernie's first brush with the Great Gift gave him a considerable jolt, though he didn't suspect at first that it was a permanent gift.

He analyzed what had happened, quite reasonably, I believe, as a case of second sight. Some-how his mind had been projected into the brain of the motorman of the Special just at the moment the latter had his stroke (the final official explanation too) and blindly put on more speed instead of reducing it for the approaching curve and station. His second sight saved his life by getting him off the platform before the Special jumped the tracks and ploughed through it.

It certainly gave a jolt to Ernie's habit patterns, as it temporarily did of a great many other people. He started driving his car to work, for one thing, and he took to drinking regularly in the evenings, though not excessively as yet.

He also had the feeling, which he did not try to analyze, that his miraculous escape marked the end of the "strange weeks" in his life, when he'd had such odd illusions or been the victim of such odd circumstances; and, true enough, that first week or so there were no recurrences of his chillingly weird experiences.

---

But jolts have their infallible Law of Diminishing Effects.

After a few days, Ernie found the traffic and parking problems as nervous and wearisome as ever and he grew envious of the snug commuters meditating luxuriously in their electric coaches. Come the first morning of the third week and he was standing on the rebuilt platform, studying the new planks, ties and rails with a pleasantly morbid interest.

Vivian was not in her accustomed seat nor on the train, as far as he could tell, which did not surprise him, though it disappointed him sharply; the Panther Princess had a stronger hold on his feelings, or at least on his imagination, than he'd realized.

But Verna was on the train home all right; in fact, she gave a small whoop of pleasure when she spotted him. And he had barely sat down beside her when who should come prowling smoothly along but Vivian in a charcoal version of her tailored black armor.

Ernie jumped up and blurted out introductions. Vivian accepted his seat with a certain deliberateness and with a smile that seemed to Ernie to say, "So I'm his morning light-badinage girl, but this is the girl Mr. Meeker goes home with. It's another instance of 'black-glasses' behavior, don't you think? He puts her on whenever he gets afraid he's getting attractive."

---

The two women started to chat easily enough, however, and shortly Ernie got over his confusion and, smiling down at them from where he swayed in his aisle with his hand lightly touching the back of the seat ahead, was even thinking quite smugly that here in one seat, by gosh, were the woman he wanted and the woman who wanted him. Very interesting to be the man in the middle.

Just at that moment, the power came back to him that made everything feverishly real, expanding his center of attention to his visual horizons, and this time it was only a prelude, for a second gateway opened behind the first —a window into all human hearts and minds, the power of human insight fantastically sharpened and enlarged. He could "read minds," or at least he knew the motives-the core of values and consciousness-of any person he cared to look at. Most especially, he knew the motives of Verna and Vivian almost as if he *were* them.

The big thing about Vivian was her fear-no, her conviction, that she wasn't attractive. Every glance her way knocked a hole in the armor of artificial attractiveness she built around herself, and all the hours she devoted to perfecting it, even the desperate worship she lavished on her body, were all utterly lost. A simple relationship with another human being was unthinkable; her armor got in the way and under her armor she knew she was worthless. A man was sometimes attracted to her armor-never to herself! —but as soon as he started to scrutinize it, it began to tarnish and crumple.

She hoped that other people, men especially, had a trace of her own weaknesses, and she sniped away at them constantly to get under the armor to find out. Ernie was one in a long series of such men. She was actually in love with him, but only as one loves a dream, not the real Ernie at all. Physically he was disgusting to her, like most men.

---

Verna, on the other hand, had absolute confidence that she was sufficiently attractive for all practical purposes. She wasn't in love with Ernie at all. She wanted to make an intellectual conquest of him, add him to her private Brain Trust, her cultured entourage that won Mr. Abrusian's seldom-tendered admiration and broke Miss Minkin's heart, and finally get Ernie to join the Working Boys' Front. He was one of her projects. If it became tactically necessary during her campaign, she knew that Ernie would be only too happy to jump in bed with her, food-triangles and all.

Now in other circumstances (who really knows?), Ernie might have found the courage to accept Vivian and Verna as they really were and work on from there, ruthlessly discarding his false pictures of them–and of himself. He might conceivably have found the strength to accept all people not as shadowy projections of himself, fabricated targets of his desires and aversions, puppets in his private chess games and circuses, but as complete persons with inexhaustible surprises and contradictions, each a microcosm, a universe-in-little with his or her own earth and stars, spaceflight and crawling, heaven and hell.

But under the present circumstances, Ernie was confused. His knowledge of the real Vivian spoiled completely the titillating picture of the Panther Princess, who might submit to him contemptuously in the end–he needed that sex idol more than he needed truth. As for Verna, her stalwart self-reliance and her accurate appraisal of his own motives and possible future behavior were both unbearably humiliating to him. And the delight of really knowing people was completely outweighed, in his tired spirit, by the thought of the lifetime of work that would be involved in adjusting himself to this new knowledge. It was so much more comfortable to work with stereotypes.

The Express was slowing for his station. Both girls were looking at him puzzledly.

"Good-by, Verna. Good-by, Vivian," he said in a set sort of voice. "This is where I get off."

He moved stiffly toward the door. They watched him go, and turned to each other with a frown.

---

That evening marked the beginning of Ernie's serious drinking. He never saw either of the V-girls again. He took his car or the bus to work; then, for a short period, he took taxicabs, then he lost his job and was working in another part of the city. He became mixed up with a number of other women and crowds, but they are not part of this or any story.

Among other things, his drinking eventually completely confused his memories of abnormal personal powers with his entirely normal illusions of alcoholic ones. And it also seemed to be blotting out the former. Once, at a party, he bet twenty dollars that his eyes glowed in the dark. Next morning he was relieved to discover, after making several anxious phone calls, that he'd lost his bet.

When he finally pulled out of it, some five years later, because of a growing aversion to liquor that he only understood later, the two Big Gifts of Page-at-a-Glance and Mind Reading were gone forever.

The Great Gift had a more durable lodgment in him. From his alcoholic years, he brought hazy memories of accidents avoided because of sudden wrong-ended visions of onrushing cars, alley rollings missed because he'd seen himself reeling along a block away through the eyes of lounging hoodlums. Now, sober again, he had a clear confirmation of it when he left a banquet on a trumped-up excuse because of a disturbing vision of inexplicable rodlike shapes–and read the next day that a hundred of the guests, of whom four finally died, had come down with bacterial food poisoning. Another time, hiking in dry woods, he'd smelled smoke that his companions couldn't —and persuaded them to turn back, avoiding a disastrous flash fire that broke out soon afterward.

He had to admit to himself that he certainly seemed to have the gift of second sight, warning him against threats to his life.

"All right," he told himself, "so forget it. Gifts are upsetting. Even as a kid, you sweated more about your birthday presents than you ever got fun out of them."

Our story has already jumped five years; now it must jump twenty. Ernie is living with his sister again; while he was drinking, they pulled apart, and now they've once more pulled together. They're having dinner, have arrived at dessert, a big piece of chocolate cake each with satiny thick creamy frosting and filling.

Ernie looks at his piece-and sees himself climbing stairs and clutching at his heart. He thinks of warning his sister, but she's already halfway through her piece. Then she goes on and eats Ernie's.

---

Ernie's sister didn't get food poisoning, she only got fat, but the incident of the chocolate cake was for Ernie the beginning of a series of peculiar food revulsions and diet experiments that eventually made Ernie instead of his sister the family yogurt-fiend and a regular customer of his old acquaintance, Herman, the health-food manufacturer.

Herman had to admit that Ernie had cooked himself up a pretty good longevity diet for an amateur, though there were some items in it that made the old man shake his head-and he always asserted that Ernie was passing up a good thing in Soybean Mush.

Ernie got his diet tailored to fit his tastes and stuck to it. He had a strong suspicion of what had happened, though he tried not to think about it too often: that his gift of second sight had taken to warning him of the longer-range dangers to his existence; after all, chocolate cake can be as deadly as atomic bombs in the long run.

More years passed. Friends and relatives began to remark quietly to each other that his sister was aging faster. Ernie, they had to admit, was a remarkably well-preserved old gent. Ironic, considering what a drunk he'd been and what strange junk he insisted on eating now.

One day Ernie's self-styled health diet began to pall on him. It didn't revolt him; it merely left him unsatisfied, yet with no yearning for any particular food he could think of. He lived with this yearning for some weeks, meditating on it and trying to guess its nature. Finally he had an inspiration. He headed for Mr. Willis' drugstore.

The bent, silvery-haired man greeted him eagerly; somehow there was a special warmth about the friendships Ernie had made during the "strange weeks" (Verna and Vivian excepted) that put them in a different class from any other of his human relationships.

---

"Now what can I give you, Ernie?" Mr. Willis asked. "Anything in the place within reason."

"I'll tell you, Bert I'd like to go back in your dispensary-you with me, if you want-and just shop around."

"That's a sort of screwy idea, Ernie. I couldn't sell you any narcotics or sleeping pills, of course-well, maybe a few sleeping pills."

"I wouldn't want any."

"What's the idea, Ernie? Getting interested in chemistry in your old ... You know, Ernie, you just don't look your years."

"Secret of mine. Yes, in a way I've got interested in chemistry."

"Won't talk, eh? I remember, when I first met you, I tagged you for an evening inventor. Well, come on back and shop around. Just don't ask me for *elixer vitae, aurum potabile,* or ground philosophers' stone."

"Not unless I see 'em."

Afterward, Bert Willis used to say it was one of the most mystifying experiences of his life. For a good half a day, Ernie Meeker studied the rows of jars, canisters and glass-stoppered bottles, sometimes lifting two down together and contemplating them, one in each hand, as if he could weigh the difference. Often he'd take out a stopper and sniff, and maybe, asking permission of Bert with a glance, take up a dab of some powder and taste it.

"You know that game," Bert would say, "where someone goes out of the room and you all decide on an object, or hide one, and he comes back and tries to find it by telepathy or muscle-reading or something? That was exactly the way Ernie was acting. Dog on a difficult scent."

A couple of times, especially when the customers came in, Bert wanted to chase him out, except that Ernie was such a special friend and Bert was so darn curious about it all himself.

In the end, Ernie made a good twenty purchases, including a mortar and pestle and two poisons for which Bert made him sign, though the amounts were less than a lethal dose.

"Actually none of the chemicals he bought were very dangerous," Bert would say. "And none of them were terribly unusual. The thing about them was that, put together, they just didn't make sense-as a medicine or anything else. Let me see, there was sulphur, bismuth, a bit of mercury, one of the sulfa drugs, a tiny packet of auric chloride, and ... I had 'em all on a list once, but I've lost it."

After that, Ernie always mixed a little grayish paste in his cup of yogurt at suppertime. Ernie stopped aging altogether.

---

After his sister's coffin was lowered past the margins of green matting into the ground, Ernie shook hands with the minister, walked Bert Willis and Herman Schover to their car and told them he thought he'd better drive home with some relatives who'd turned up. Actually he just wanted to stay behind a while. It was a beautiful blue-and-white summer day; the tidy suburban cemetery had caught his fancy, and now he felt like a quiet stroll.

Ernie followed his little impulses these days. As he sometimes said, "I figure I've got plenty of time. I just don't feel the pressure like I used to."

The last car chugged away. Ernie stretched and started to stroll, slowly, but not like an old man, now that he was alone. His hair had grown whiter in the last few years and his face a little wrinkled, but that was due to the very judicious use of silvering and theatrical liner-people's comments about his youthfulness had gotten wearisome and would, he knew, eventually become suspicious.

Keeping himself oriented by a white tower at the cemetery gate, he arrived at an area that had no graves as yet, no trees either, just lawn. He made his way to the center of it, where there was a gently swelling hummock, and sat down in the warm crinkly grass, resting his back against the slope. The sky was lovely, enough clouds to be interesting, but a great oval of pure blue just overhead —a pear-shaped gateway to space.

He felt no grief at his sister's death, only the desire to think a bit, have a quiet look at his past and another at the great future.

Alone like this, he dared to face his fate for a moment and admit to himself that, all wishful thinking aside, it really began to look as if he were going to live forever, or at least for a very long time.

Live forever! That was a phrase to give you a chill, he told himself. And what to do, he asked himself, with all that time?

Back in the "strange weeks," he'd have had little trouble in answering that question-if only he'd known then what he did now and realized what was being offered him. For, during his sober decades, Ernie had gradually come to a shrewdly accurate estimate of what had happened to him then. He thought of it in terms of having been offered six Gifts and turned down five of them.

---

Back in the "strange weeks" and armed with the five rejected Gifts (Page-at-a-Glance and Mind Reading were the only ones that counted, though), he could easily have said, "Live forever by all means! Increase your knowledge and understanding until your mind bursts or is transfigured. Plunge forever into the unending variety of the Cosmos. Open yourself to everything."

But now, equipped to travel only as a snail....

Still, even snails get somewhere. With forever to work with, even four-words-at-a-glance gets you through many, many books. Patient love and dispassionate thought give you human insight in the end, can finally open the tightest shutter on the darkest human heart.

But that would take so very long and Ernie felt tired. Not old, just tired, tired. Best simply to watch the soft clouds-the pear-shaped gateway had become almost circular. To do anything but drift through life, a stereotype among stereotypes, was simply ... too ... much ... work....

At that very moment, as if his thought had summoned the experience into being, another scene filmed over the blue sky and white clouds above him. The sudden humming in his ears —a kind of "audible silence" —informed him that his second sight was at work, warning him of some deadly danger. But this was a more gentle instance of it, for not all his consciousness jumped somewhere else. All through the experience, he was still aware of himself leaning against the grassy hummock, of the restful melancholy of the scene around him, and of the sky overhead. The second scene only superimposed itself on the first.

He was poised many hundreds of miles above the Earth, a ghost-Ernie immune to the airlessness and the Sun's untempered beams. At his back was black night filled with stars. Below him stretched the granulated dry brown of Earth's surface, tinged here and there with green, clumped with white cloud, and everywhere faintly hazed with blue.

---

Up there in space with him, right at his elbow, so close that he could reach out and touch it, was a tiny silver cylinder about as big as a hazelnut, domed at one end, reflecting sunlight from one point in a way that would have been blinding enough except that Ernie's ghost eyes were immune to brightness.

As he reached out to examine it, the thing darted away from him as if at some imperious summons, like a bit of iron jumping through a magnetic field.

But in spite of its enormous acceleration, Ernie's ghost was able to follow it in its downward plunge. It kept just ahead of his outstretched fingertips.

The brown granules that were Earth's surface grew in size. The tiny metal cylinder began to glow with more than reflected sunlight. It turned red, orange, yellow and then blazing white as atmospheric friction transformed it into a meteor.

Ernie's ghost, immune to friction and incandescence alike, followed it as it dove toward its target-for even though Ernie had never heard of a Juxtaposer and how it brought objects together, he had the feeling, from the dizzy speed of the meteor's plunge, that it yearned for something.

He knew most meteors vaporized or exploded, but this did not, even when Earth's brown surface grew rivers and roads. Suddenly there was a cloudbank ahead; then, in the white, there appeared an almost circular hole toward the very center of which the meteorite plunged.

Everything was happening very fast now, but his ghost senses were able to keep pace. As they plunged through the cloud-ring and the green landscape below grew explosively, he saw the white tower, the trees, the curving drives, and the clearing which was now the target.

There was still time to escape. Lying on the warm grass, with death lancing down from the sky at miles a second, he had merely to roll over.

But it was simply ... too ... much ... work....

---

Elsewhere near Earth, a recorder sped toward Galaxy Center a message which ended, "Six Gifts tendered, all finally refused. I will now sign off and await pickup with one Juxtaposer."

A little later, a Receiver in Galaxy Center passed the message to a Central Recorder, which filed it in the Starswarm 37 section with this addition: "Spiritual immaturity of Terran bipeds indicated. Advise against enlightenment and admission to Galactic citizenship. Test subject humanely released."

---

Police, digging into the turf under Ernie's shattered head two days later found the bright bullet, cold now, of course, and untarnished.

"Looks like silver!" one cop said, scratching his head. "Haven't I heard somewhere that the Mafia use silver bullets? So bright, though."

Lieutenant Padilla, later on, lifting the bullet in his forceps to re-examine it for rifling marks, had the same thought about its brightness. By now, however, he knew it was not silver. (What alloy was never satisfactorily determined. Actually it was made of the same substance as the Everlasting Razor Blade.)

This time, although he still found no rifling marks, a tiny dull stretch on the flat end of the cylinder caught his attention. He took up a magnifier and examined it carefully.

A moment later, he put down the magnifier, snatched up the pocketbook found on the dead man and rechecked some cards in it. The bullet dropped from the forceps, rolled a few inches. The lieutenant sat back in his chair, breathing a little hard.

"This is one for the books, all right!" he told himself. "I've heard a lot of people, soldiers especially, talk about such bullets, but I never expected to see one!"

For under the magnifying glass, finely engraved in very tiny letters, he had read the words: ERNEST WENCESLAUS MEEKER.

# The Big Engine

Have you found out about the Big
Engine? It's all around us, you
know-can't you hear it even now?

There are all sorts of screwy theories (the Professor said) of what makes the wheels of the world go round. There's a boy in Chicago who thinks we're all of us just the thoughts of a green cat; when the green cat dies we'll all puff to nothing like smoke. There's a man in the west who thinks all women are witches and run the world by conjure magic. There's a man in the east who believes all rich people belong to a secret society that's a lot tighter and tougher than the Mafia and that has a monopoly of power-secrets and pleasure-secrets other people don't dream exist.

Me, I think the wheels of the world just go. I decided that forty years ago and I've never since seen or heard or read anything to make me change my mind.

I was a stoker on a lake boat then (the Professor continued, delicately sipping smoke from his long thin cigarette). I was as stupid as they make them, but I liked to think. Whenever I'd get a chance I'd go to one of the big libraries and make them get me all sorts of books. That was how guys started calling me the Professor. I'd get books on philosophy, metaphysics, science, even religion. I'd read them and try to figure out the world. What was it all about, anyway? Why was I here? What was the point in the whole business of getting born and working and dying? What was the use of it? Why'd it have to go on and on?

And why'd it have to be so complicated?

Why all the building and tearing down? Why'd there have to be cities, with crowded streets and horse cars and cable cars and electric cars and big open-work steel boxes built to the sky to be hung with stone and wood-my closest friend got killed falling off one of those steel boxkites. Shouldn't there be some simpler way of doing it all? Why did things have to be so mixed up that a man like myself couldn't have a single clear decent thought?

More than that, why weren't people a real part of the world? Why didn't they show more honest-to-God response? When you slept with a woman, why was it something you had and she didn't? Why, when you went to a prize fight, were the bruisers only so much meat, and the crowd a lot of little screaming popinjays? Why was a war nothing but blather and blowup and bother? Why'd everybody have to go through their whole lives so dead, doing everything so methodical and prissy like a Sunday School picnic or an orphan's parade?

---

And then, when I was reading one of the science books, it came to me. The answer was all there, printed out plain to see only nobody saw it. It was just this: Nobody was really alive.

Back of other people's foreheads there weren't any real thoughts or minds, or love or fear, to explain things. The whole universe-stars and men and dirt and worms and atoms, the whole shooting match-was just one great big engine. It didn't take mind or life or anything else to run the engine. It just ran.

Now one thing about science. It doesn't lie. Those men who wrote those science books that showed me the answer, they had no more minds than anybody else. Just darkness in their brains, but because they were machines built to use science, they couldn't help but get the right answers. They were like the electric brains they've got now, but hadn't then, that give out the right answer when you feed in the question. I'd like to feed in the question, "What's Life?" to one of those machines and see what came out. Just figures, I suppose. I read somewhere that if a billion monkeys had typewriters and kept pecking away at them they'd eventually turn out all the Encyclopedia Brittanica in trillions and trillions of years. Well, they've done it all right, and in jig time.

They're doing it now.

A lot of philosophy and psychology books I worked through really fit in beautifully. There was Watson's *Behaviorism* telling how we needn't even assume that people are conscious to explain their actions. There was Leibitz's *Monadology*, with its theory that we're all of us lonely atoms that are completely out of touch and don't effect each other in the slightest, but only seem to ... because all our little clockwork motors were started at the same time in pre-established harmony. We *seem* to be responding to each other, but actually we're just a bunch of wooden-minded puppets. Jerk one puppet up into the flies and the others go on acting as if exactly nothing at all had happened.

So there it was all laid out for me (the Professor went on, carefully pinching out the end of his cigarette). That was why there was no honest-to-God response in people. They were machines.

The fighters were machines made for fighting. The people that watched them were machines for stamping and screaming and swearing. The bankers had banking cogs in their bellies, the crooks had crooked cams. A woman was just a loving machine, all nicely adjusted to give you a good time (sometimes!) but the farthest star was nearer to you than the mind behind that mouth you kissed.

See what I mean? People just machines, set to do a certain job and then quietly rust away. If you kept on being the machine you were supposed to be, well and good. Then your actions fitted with other people's. But if you didn't, if you started doing something else, then the others didn't respond. They just went on doing what was called for.

It wouldn't matter what you did, they'd just go on making the motions they were set to make. They might be set to make love, and you might decide you wanted to fight. They'd go on making love while you fought them. Or it might happen the other way-seems to, more often!

Or somebody might be talking about Edison. And you'd happen to say something about Ingersoll. But he'd just go on talking about Edison.

You were all alone.

---

Except for a few others-not more than one in a hundred thousand, I guess-who wake up and figure things out. And they mostly go crazy and run themselves to death, or else turn mean. Mostly they turn mean. They get a cheap little kick out of pushing things around that can't push back. All over the world you find them-little gangs of three or four, half a dozen-who've waked up, but just to their cheap kicks. Maybe it's a couple of coppers in 'Frisco, a schoolteacher in K.C., some artists in New York, some rich kids in Florida, some undertakers in London-who've found that all the people walking around are just dead folk and to be treated no decenter, who see how bad things are and get their fun out of making it a little worse. Just a mean *little* bit worse. They don't dare to destroy in a big way, because they know the machine feeds them and tends them, and because they're always scared they'd be noticed by gangs like themselves and wiped out. They haven't the guts to really wreck the whole shebang. But they get a kick out of scribbling their dirty pictures on it, out of meddling and messing with it.

I've seen some of their fun, as they call it, sometimes hidden away, sometimes in the open streets.

You've seen a clerk dressing a figure in a store window? Well, suppose he slapped its face. Suppose a kid stuck pins in a calico pussy-cat, or threw pepper in the eyes of a doll.

No decent live man would have anything to do with nickel sadism or dime paranoia like that. He'd either go back to his place in the machine and act out the part set for him, or else he'd hide away like me and live as quiet as he could, not stirring things up. Like a mouse in a dynamo or an ant in an atomics plant.

(The Professor went to the window and opened it, letting the sour old smoke out and the noises of the city in.)

---

Listen (he said), listen to the great mechanical symphony, the big black combo. The airplanes are the double bass. Have you noticed how you can always hear one nowadays? When one walks out of the sky another walks in.

Presses and pumps round out the bass section. Listen to them rumble and thump! Tonight they've got an old steam locomotive helping. Maybe they're giving a benefit show for the old duffer.

Cars and traffic-they're the strings. Mostly cellos and violas. They purr and wail and whine and keep trying to get out of their section.

Brasses? To me the steel-on-steel of streetcars and El trains always sounds like trumpets and cornets. Strident, metallic, fiery cold.

Hear that siren way off? It's a clarinet. The ship horns are tubas, the diesel horn's an oboe. And that lovely dreadful french horn is an electric saw cutting down the last tree.

But what a percussion section they've got! The big stuff, like streetcar bells jangling, is easy to catch, but you have to really listen to get the subtleties-the buzz of a defective neon sign, the click of a stoplight changing.

Sometimes you do get human voices, I'll admit, but they're not like they are in Beethoven's *Ninth* or Holst's *Planets*.

*There's* the real sound of the universe (the Professor concluded, shutting the window). That's your heavenly choir. That's the music of the spheres the old alchemists kept listening for-if they'd just stayed around a little longer they'd all have been deafened by it. Oh, to think that Schopenhauer was bothered by the crack of carters' whips!

And now it's time for this mouse to tuck himself in his nest in the dynamo. Good night, gentlemen!

# A Bad Day for Sales

*Don't wait to "Get 'em while they're hot."*
*By then, it is too late to get them of all!*

The big bright doors of the office building parted with a pneumatic *whoosh* and Robie glided onto Times Square. The crowd that had been watching the fifty-foot-tall girl on the clothing billboard get dressed, or reading the latest news about the Hot Truce scrawl itself in yard-high script, hurried to look.

Robie was still a novelty. Robie was fun. For a little while yet, he could steal the show. But the attention did not make Robie proud. He had no more emotions than the pink plastic giantess, who dressed and undressed endlessly whether there was a crowd or the street was empty, and who never once blinked her blue mechanical eyes. But she merely drew business while Robie went out after it.

For Robie was the logical conclusion of the development of vending machines. All the earlier ones had stood in one place, on a floor or hanging on a wall, and blankly delivered merchandise in return for coins, whereas Robie searched for customers. He was the demonstration model of a line of sales robots to be manufactured by Shuler Vending Machines, provided the public invested enough in stocks to give the company capital to go into mass production.

The publicity Robie drew stimulated investments handsomely. It was amusing to see the TV and newspaper coverage of Robie selling, but not a fraction as much fun as being approached personally by him. Those who were usually bought anywhere from one to five hundred shares, if they had any money and foresight enough to see that sales robots would eventually be on every street and highway in the country.

---

Robie radared the crowd, found that it surrounded him solidly, and stopped. With a carefully built-in sense of timing, he waited for the tension and expectation to mount before he began talking.

"Say, Ma, he doesn't look like a robot at all," a child said. "He looks like a turtle."

Which was not completely inaccurate. The lower part of Robie's body was a metal hemisphere hemmed with sponge rubber and not quite touching the sidewalk. The upper was a metal box with black holes in it. The box could swivel and duck.

A chromium-bright hoopskirt with a turret on top.

"Reminds me too much of the Little Joe Paratanks," a legless veteran of the Persian War muttered, and rapidly rolled himself away on wheels rather like Robie's.

His departure made it easier for some of those who knew about Robie to open a path in the crowd. Robie headed straight for the gap. The crowd whooped.

Robie glided very slowly down the path, deftly jogging aside whenever he got too close to ankles in skylon or sockassins. The rubber buffer on his hoopskirt was merely an added safeguard.

The boy who had called Robie a turtle jumped in the middle of the path and stood his ground, grinning foxily.

Robie stopped two feet short of him. The turret ducked. The crowd got quiet.

"Hello, youngster," Robie said in a voice that was smooth as that of a TV star, and was, in fact, a recording of one.

The boy stopped smiling. "Hello," he whispered.

"How old are you?" Robie asked.

"Nine. No, eight."

"That's nice," Robie observed. A metal arm shot down from his neck, stopped just short of the boy.

The boy jerked back.

"For you," Robie said.

The boy gingerly took the red polly-lop from the neatly fashioned blunt metal claws, and began to unwrap it.

"Nothing to say?" asked Robie.

"Uh-thank you."

After a suitable pause, Robie continued. "And how about a nice refreshing drink of Poppy Pop to go with your polly-lop?" The boy lifted his eyes, but didn't stop licking the candy. Robie waggled his claws slightly. "Just give me a quarter and within five seconds —"

A little girl wriggled out of the forest of legs. "Give me a polly-lop, too, Robie," she demanded.

"Rita, come back here!" a woman in the third rank of the crowd called angrily.

Robie scanned the newcomer gravely. His reference silhouettes were not good enough to let him distinguish the sex of children, so he merely repeated, "Hello, youngster."

"Rita!"

"Give me a polly-lop!"

Disregarding both remarks, for a good salesman is single-minded and does not waste bait, Robie said winningly, "I'll bet you read *Junior Space Killers*. Now I have here —"

"Uh-uh, I'm a girl. *He* got a polly-lop."

---

At the word "girl," Robie broke off. Rather ponderously, he said, "I'll bet you read *Gee-Gee Jones, Space Stripper*. Now I have here the latest issue of that thrilling comic, not yet in the stationary vending machines. Just give me fifty cents and within five —"

"Please let me through. I'm her mother."

A young woman in the front rank drawled over her powder-sprayed shoulder, "I'll get her for you," and slithered out on six-inch platform shoes. "Run away, children," she said nonchalantly. Lifting her arms behind her head, she pirouetted slowly before Robie to show how much she did for her bolero half-jacket and her form-fitting slacks that melted into skylon just above the knees. The little girl glared at her. She ended the pirouette in profile.

At this age-level, Robie's reference silhouettes permitted him to distinguish sex, though with occasional amusing and embarrassing miscalls. He whistled admiringly. The crowd cheered.

Someone remarked critically to a friend, "It would go over better if he was built more like a real robot. You know, like a man."

The friend shook his head. "This way it's subtler."

No one in the crowd was watching the newscript overhead as it scribbled, "Ice Pack for Hot Truce? Vanadin hints Russ may yield on Pakistan."

Robie was saying, "...in the savage new glamor-tint we have christened Mars Blood, complete with spray applicator and fit-all fingerstalls that mask each finger completely except for the nail. Just give me five dollars-uncrumpled bills may be fed into the revolving rollers you see beside my arm-and within five seconds —"

"No, thanks, Robie," the young woman yawned.

"Remember," Robie persisted, "for three more weeks, seductivizing Mars Blood will be unobtainable from any other robot or human vendor."

"No, thanks."

Robie scanned the crowd resourcefully. "Is there any gentleman here ..." he began just as a woman elbowed her way through the front rank.

"I told you to come back!" she snapped at the little girl.

"But I didn't get my polly-lop!"

"...who would care to...."

"Rita!"

"Robie cheated. Ow!"

Meanwhile, the young woman in the half bolero had scanned the nearby gentlemen on her own. Deciding that there was less than a fifty per cent chance of any of them accepting the proposition Robie seemed about to make, she took advantage of the scuffle to slither gracefully back into the ranks. Once again the path was clear before Robie.

He paused, however, for a brief recapitulation of the more magical properties of Mars Blood, including a telling phrase about "the passionate claws of a Martian sunrise."

But no one bought. It wasn't quite time. Soon enough silver coins would be clinking, bills going through the rollers faster than laundry, and five hundred people struggling for the privilege of having their money taken away from them by America's first mobile sales robot.

But there were still some tricks that Robie had to do free, and one certainly should enjoy those before starting the more expensive fun.

So Robie moved on until he reached the curb. The variation in level was instantly sensed by his under-scanners. He stopped. His head began to swivel. The crowd watched in eager silence. This was Robie's best trick.

Robie's head stopped swiveling. His scanners had found the traffic light. It was green. Robie edged forward. But then the light turned red. Robie stopped again, still on the curb. The crowd softly *ahhed* its delight.

It was wonderful to be alive and watching Robie on such an exciting day. Alive and amused in the fresh, weather-controlled air between the lines of bright skyscrapers with their winking windows and under a sky so blue you could almost call it dark.

(But way, way up, where the crowd could not see, the sky was darker still. Purple-dark, with stars showing. And in that purple-dark, a silver-green something, the color of a bud, plunged down at better than three miles a second. The silver-green was a newly developed paint that foiled radar.)

Robie was saying, "While we wait for the light, there's time for you youngsters to enjoy a nice refreshing Poppy Pop. Or for you adults-only those over five feet tall are eligible to buy-to enjoy an exciting Poppy Pop fizz. Just give me a quarter or-in the case of adults, one dollar and a quarter; I'm licensed to dispense intoxicating liquors-and within five seconds...."

But that was not cutting it quite fine enough. Just three seconds later, the silver-green bud bloomed above Manhattan into a globular orange flower. The skyscrapers grew brighter and brighter still, the brightness of the inside of the Sun. The windows winked blossoming white fire-flowers.

The crowd around Robie bloomed, too. Their clothes puffed into petals of flame. Their heads of hair were torches.

---

The orange flower grew, stem and blossom. The blast came. The winking windows shattered tier by tier, became black holes. The walls bent, rocked, cracked. A stony dandruff flaked from their cornices. The flaming flowers on the sidewalk were all leveled at once. Robie was shoved ten feet. His metal hoopskirt dimpled, regained its shape.

The blast ended. The orange flower, grown vast, vanished overhead on its huge, magic beanstalk. It grew dark and very still. The cornice-dandruff pattered down. A few small fragments rebounded from the metal hoopskirt.

Robie made some small, uncertain movements, as if feeling for broken bones. He was hunting for the traffic light, but it no longer shone either red or green.

He slowly scanned a full circle. There was nothing anywhere to interest his reference silhouettes. Yet whenever he tried to move, his under-scanners warned him of low obstructions. It was very puzzling.

The silence was disturbed by moans and a crackling sound, as faint at first as the scampering of distant rats.

A seared man, his charred clothes fuming where the blast had blown out the fire, rose from the curb. Robie scanned him.

"Good day, sir," Robie said. "Would you care for a smoke? A truly cool smoke? Now I have here a yet-unmarketed brand...."

But the customer had run away, screaming, and Robie never ran after customers, though he could follow them at a medium brisk roll. He worked his way along the curb where the man had sprawled, carefully keeping his distance from the low obstructions, some of which writhed now and then, forcing him to jog. Shortly he reached a fire hydrant. He scanned it. His electronic vision, though it still worked, had been somewhat blurred by the blast.

"Hello, youngster," Robie said. Then, after a long pause, "Cat got your tongue? Well, I have a little present for you. A nice, lovely polly-lop.

"Take it, youngster," he said after another pause. "It's for you. Don't be afraid."

His attention was distracted by other customers, who began to rise up oddly here and there, twisting forms that confused his reference silhouettes and would not stay to be scanned properly. One cried, "Water," but no quarter clinked in Robie's claws when he caught the word and suggested, "How about a nice refreshing drink of Poppy Pop?"

The rat-crackling of the flames had become a jungle muttering. The blind windows began to wink fire again.

---

A little girl marched, stepping neatly over arms and legs she did not look at. A white dress and the once taller bodies around her had shielded her from the brilliance and the blast. Her eyes were fixed on Robie. In them was the same imperious confidence, though none of the delight, with which she had watched him earlier.

"Help me, Robie," she said. "I want my mother."

"Hello, youngster," Robie said. "What would you like? Comics? Candy?"

"Where is she, Robie? Take me to her."

"Balloons? Would you like to watch me blow up a balloon?"

The little girl began to cry. The sound triggered off another of Robie's novelty circuits, a service feature that had brought in a lot of favorable publicity.

"Is something wrong?" he asked. "Are you in trouble? Are you lost?"

"Yes, Robie. Take me to my mother."

"Stay right here," Robie said reassuringly, "and don't be frightened. I will call a policeman." He whistled shrilly, twice.

Time passed. Robie whistled again. The windows flared and roared. The little girl begged, "Take me away, Robie," and jumped onto a little step in his hoopskirt.

"Give me a dime," Robie said.

The little girl found one in her pocket and put it in his claws.

"Your weight," Robie said, "is fifty-four and one-half pounds."

"Have you seen my daughter, have you seen her?" a woman was crying somewhere. "I left her watching that thing while I stepped inside —*Rita!*"

"Robie helped me," the little girl began babbling at her. "He knew I was lost. He even called the police, but they didn't come. He weighed me, too. Didn't you, Robie?"

But Robie had gone off to peddle Poppy Pop to the members of a rescue squad which had just come around the corner, more robotlike in their asbestos suits than he in his metal skin.

# The Last Letter

*Who or what was the scoundrel that kept
these couriers from the swift completion
of their handsomely appointed rondos?*

On Tenthmonth 1, 2457 A.D., at exactly 9 A.M. Planetary Federation Time-but with a permissible error of a millionth of a second either way-in the fifth sublevel of NewNew York Robot Postal Station 68, Black Sorter gulped down ten thousand pieces of first-class mail.

This breakfast tidbit did not agree with the mail-sorting machine. It was as if a robust dog had been fed a large chunk of good red meat with a strychnine pill in it. Black Sorter's innards went *whirr-klunk*, a blue electric glow enveloped him, and he began to shake as if he might break loose from the concrete.

He desperately spat back over his shoulder a single envelope, gave a great *huff* and blew out toward the sorting tubes a medium-size snowstorm consisting of the other nine thousand, nine hundred and ninety-nine pieces of first-class mail chewed to confetti. Then, still convulsed, he snapped up a fresh ten thousand and proceeded to chomp and grind on them. Black Sorter was rugged.

The rejected envelope was tongued up by Red Subsorter, who growled deep in his throat, said a very bad word, and passed it to Yellow Rerouter, who passed it to Green Rerouter, who passed it to Brown Study, who passed it to Pink Wastebasket.

Unlike Black Sorter, Pink Wastebasket was very delicate, though highly intuitive-the machine equivalent of a White Russian countess. She was designed to scan in 3,137 codes, route special-delivery spacemail to interplanetary liners by messenger rocket, and distinguish 9s from upside-down 6s.

Pink Wastebasket haughtily inhaled the offending envelope and almost instantly turned a bright crimson and began to tremble. After a few minutes, small atomic flames started to flicker from her mid-section.

White Nursemaid Seven and Greasy Joe both received Pink Wastebasket's distress signal and got there as fast as their wheels would roll them, but the high-born machine's malady was beyond their simple skills of oilcan and electroshock.

---

They summoned other machine-tending-and-repairing machines, ones far more expert than themselves, but all were baffled. It was clear that Pink Wastebasket, who continued to tremble and flicker uncontrollably, was suffering from the equivalent of a major psychosis with severe psychosomatic symptoms. She spat a stream of filthy ions at Gray Psychiatrist, not recognizing her old friend.

Meanwhile, the paper blizzard from Black Sorter was piling up in great drifts between the dark pillars of the sublevel, and flurries had reached Pink Wastebasket's aristocratic area. An expedition of sturdy machines, headed by two hastily summoned snowplows, was dispatched to immobilize Black Sorter at all costs.

Pink Wastebasket, quivering like a demented hula dancer, was clearly approaching a crisis. Finally Gray Psychiatrist-after consulting with Green Surgeon, and even then with an irritated reluctance, as if he were calling in a witch-doctor —summoned a human being.

The human being walked respectfully around Pink Wastebasket several times and then gave her a nervous little poke with a rubber-handled probe.

Pink Wastebasket gently regurgitated her last snack, turned dead white, gave a last flicker and shake, and expired. Black Coroner recorded the immediate cause of death as tinkering by a human being.

The human being, a bald and scrawny one named Potshelter, picked up the envelope responsible for all the trouble, stared at it incredulously, opened it with trembling fingers, scanned the contents briefly, gave a great shriek and ran off at top speed, forgetting to hop on his perambulator, which followed him making anxious clucking noises.

The nearest human representative of the Solar Bureau of Investigation, a rather wooden-looking man named Krumbine, also bald, recognized Potshelter as soon as the latter burst gasping into his office, squeezing through the door while it was still dilating. The human beings whose work took them among the Top Brass, as the upper-echelon machines were sometimes referred to, formed a kind of human elite, just one big nervous family.

"Sit down, Potshelter," the SBI Man said. "Hold still a second so the chair can grab you. Hitch onto the hookah and choose a tranquilizer from the tray at your elbow. Whatever deviation you've uncovered can't be that much of a danger to the planets. I imagine that when you leave this office, the Solar Battle Fleet will still be orbiting peacefully around Luna."

"I seriously doubt that."

---

Potshelter gulped a large lavender pill and took a deep breath. "Krumbine, a letter turned up in the first-class mail this morning."

"Great Scott!"

"It is a letter from one person to another person."

"Good Lord!"

"The flow of advertising has been seriously interfered with. At a modest estimate, three hundred million pieces of expensive first-class advertising have already been chewed to rags and I'm not sure the Steel Helms-God bless 'em! —have the trouble in hand yet."

"Judas Priest!"

"Naturally the poor machines weren't able to cope with the letter. It was utterly outside their experience, beyond the furthest reach of their programming. It threw them into a terrible spasm. Pink Wastebasket is dead and at this very instant, if we're lucky, three police machines of the toughest blued steel are holding down Black Sorter and putting a muzzle on him."

"Great Scott! It's incredible, Potshelter. And Pink Wastebasket dead? Take another tranquilizer, Potshelter, and hand over the tray."

Krumbine received it with trembling fingers, started to pick up a big pink pill but drew back his hand from it in sudden revulsion at its color and swallowed two blue oval ones instead. The man was obviously fighting to control himself.

He said unsteadily, "I almost never take doubles, but this news you bring-Good Lord! I seem to recall a case where someone tried to send a sound-tape through the mails, but that was before my time. Incidentally, is there any possibility that this is a letter sent by one *group* of persons to another group? A hive or a therapy group or a social club? That would be bad enough, of course, but —"

"No, just one single person sending to another." Potshelter's expression set in grimly solicitous lines. "I can see you don't quite understand, Krumbine. This is not a sound-tape, but a letter written in letters. You know, letters, characters-like books."

"Don't mention books in this office!" Krumbine drew himself up angrily and then slumped back. "Excuse me, Potshelter, but I find this very difficult to face squarely. Do I understand you to say that one person has tried to use the mails to send a printed sheet of some sort to another?"

"Worse than that. A written letter."

"Written? I don't recognize the word."

"It's a way of making characters, of forming visual equivalents of sound, without using electricity. The writer, as he's called, employs a black liquid and a pointed stick called a pen. I know about this because one hobby of mine is ancient means of communication."

---

Krumbine frowned and shook his head. "Communication is a dangerous business, Potshelter, especially at the personal level. With you and me, it's all right, because we know what we're doing."

He picked up a third blue tranquilizer. "But with most of the hive-folk, person-to-person communication is only a morbid form of advertising, a dangerous travesty of normal newscasting-catharsis without the analyst, recitation without the teacher—a perversion of promotion employed in betraying and subverting."

The frown deepened as he put the blue pill in his mouth and chewed it. "But about this pen-do you mean the fellow glues the pointed stick to his tongue and then speaks, and the black liquid traces the vibrations on the paper? A primitive non-electrical oscilloscope? Sloppy but conceivable, and producing a record of sorts of the spoken word."

"No, no, Krumbine." Potshelter nervously popped a square orange tablet into his mouth. "It's a hand-written letter."

Krumbine watched him. "I never mix tranquilizers," he boasted absently. "Hand-written, eh? You mean that the message was imprinted on a hand? And the skin or the entire hand afterward detached and sent through the mails in the fashion of a Martian reproach? A grisly find indeed, Potshelter."

"You still don't quite grasp it, Krumbine. The fingers of the hand move the stick that applies the ink, producing a crude imitation of the printed word."

"Diabolical!" Krumbine smashed his fist down on the desk so that the four phones and two-score microphones rattled. "I tell you, Potshelter, the SBI is ready to cope with the subtlest modern deceptions, but when fiends search out and revive tricks from the pre-Atomic Cave Era, it's almost too much. But, Great Scott, I dally while the planets are in danger. What's the sender's code on this hellish letter?"

"No code," Potshelter said darkly, proferring the envelope. "The return address is-hand-written."

Krumbine blanched as his eyes slowly traced the uneven lines in the upper left-hand corner:

*from* Richard Rowe
215 West 10th St. (horizontal)
2837 Rocket Court (vertical)
Hive 37, NewNew York 319, N. Y.
Columbia, Terra

"Ugh!" Krumbine said, shivering. "Those crawling characters, those letters, as you call them, those *things* barely enough like print to be readable-they seem to be on the verge of awakening all sorts of horrid racial memories. I find myself thinking of fur-clad witch-doctors dipping long pointed sticks in bubbling black cauldrons. No wonder Pink Wastebasket couldn't take it, brave girl."

---

Firming himself behind his desk, he pushed a number of buttons and spoke long numbers and meaningful alphabetical syllables into several microphones. Banks of colored lights around the desk began to blink like a theatre marquee sending Morse Code, while phosphorescent arrows crawled purposefully across maps and space-charts and through three-dimensional street diagrams.

"There!" he said at last. "The sender of the letter is being apprehended and will be brought directly here. We'll see what sort of man this Richard Rowe is-if we can assume he's human. Seven precautionary cordons are being drawn around his population station: three composed of machines, two of SBI agents, and two consisting of human and mechanical medical-combat teams. Same goes for the intended recipient of the letter. Meanwhile, a destroyer squadron of the Solar Fleet has been detached to orbit over NewNew York."

"In case it becomes necessary to Z-Bomb?" Potshelter asked grimly.

Krumbine nodded. "With all those villains lurking just outside the Solar System in their invisible black ships, with planeticide in their hearts, we can't be too careful. One word transmitted from one spy to another and anything may happen. And we must bomb before they do, so as to contain our losses. Better one city destroyed than a traitor on the loose who may destroy many cities. One hundred years ago, three person-to-person postcards went through the mails-just three postcards, Potshelter! —and *pft* went Schenectady, Hoboken, Cicero, and Walla Walla. Here, as long as you're mixing them, try one of these oval blues —I find them best for steady swallowing."

Bells jangled. Krumbine grabbed up two phones, holding one to each ear. Potshelter automatically picked up a third. The ringing continued. Krumbine started to wedge one of his phones under his chin, nodded sharply at Potshelter and then toward a cluster of microphones at the end of the table. Potshelter picked up a fourth phone from behind them. The ringing stopped.

The two men listened, looking doped, Krumbine with an eye fixed on the sweep second hand of the large wall clock. When it had made one revolution, he cradled his phones. Potshelter followed suit.

"I do like the simplicity of the new on-the-hour Puffyloaf phono-commercial," the latter remarked thoughtfully. "The Bread That's Lighter Than Air. Nice."

Krumbine nodded. "I hear they've had to add mass to the leadfoil wrapping to keep the loaves from floating off the shelves. Fact."

---

He cleared his throat. "Too bad we can't listen to more phono-commercials, but even when there isn't a crisis on the agenda, I find I have to budget my listening time. One minute per hour strikes a reasonable balance between duty and self-indulgence."

The nearest wall began to sing:

> Mister J. Augustus Krumbine,
> We all think you're fine, fine, fine, fine.
> Now out of the skyey blue
> Come some telegrams for you.

The wall opened to a small heart shape toward the center and a sheaf of pale yellow envelopes arced out and plopped on the middle of the desk. Krumbine started to leaf through them, scanning the little transparent windows.

"Hm, Electronic Soap ... Better Homes and Landing Platforms ... Psycho-Blinkers ... Your Girl Next Door ... Poppy-Woppies ... Poopsy-Woopsies...."

He started to open an envelope, then, after a quick look around and an apologetic smile at Potshelter, dumped them all on the disposal hopper, which gargled briefly.

"After all, there *is* a crisis this morning," he said in a defensive voice.

Potshelter nodded absently. "I can remember back before personalized delivery and rhyming robots," he observed. "But how I'd miss them now-so much more distingué than the hives with their non-personalized radio, TV and stereo advertising. For that matter, I believe there are some backward areas on Terra where the great advertising potential of telephones and telegrams hasn't been fully realized and they are still used in part for personal communication. Now me, I've never in my life sent or received a message except on my walky-talky." He patted his breast pocket.

Krumbine nodded, but he was a trifle shocked and inclined to revise his estimate of Potshelter's social status. Krumbine conducted his own social correspondence solely by telepathy. He shared with three other SBI officials a private telepath —a charming albino girl named Agnes.

"Yes, and it's a very handsome walky-talky," he assured Potshelter a little falsely. "Suits you. I like the upswept antenna." He drummed on the desk and swallowed another blue tranquilizer. "Dammit, what's happened to those machines? They ought to have the two spies here by now. Did you notice that the second-the intended recipient of the letter, I mean-seems to be female? Another good Terran name, too, Jane Dough. Hive in Upper Manhattan." He began to tap the envelope sharply against the desk. "Dammit, where *are* they?"

"Excuse me," Potshelter said hesitantly, "but I'm wondering why you haven't read the message inside the envelope."

---

Krumbine looked at him blankly. "Great Scott, I assumed that at least *it* was in some secret code, of course. Normally I'd have asked you to have Pink Wastebasket try her skill on it, but...." His eyes widened and his voice sank. "You don't mean to tell me that it's —"

Potshelter nodded grimly. "Hand-written, too. Yes."

Krumbine winced. "I keep trying to forget that aspect of the case." He dug out the message with shaking fingers, fumbled it open and read:

> *Dear Jane,*
>
> *It must surprise you that I know your name, for our hives are widely separated. Do you recall day before yesterday when your guided tour of Grand Central Spaceport got stalled because the guide blew a fuse? I was the young man with hair in the tour behind yours. You were a little frightened and a groupmistress was reassuring you. The machine spoke your name.*
>
> *Since then I have been unable to forget you. When I go to sleep, I dream of your face looking up sadly at the mistress's kindly photocells. I don't know how to get in touch with you, but my grandfather has told me stories his grandfather told him that his grandfather told him about young men writing what he calls love-letters to young ladies. So I am writing you a love-letter.*
>
> *I work in a first-class advertising house and I will slip this love-letter into an outgoing ten-thousand-pack and hope.*
>
> *Do not be frightened of me, Jane. I am no caveman except for my hair. I am not insane. I am emotionally disturbed, but in a way that no machine has ever described to me. I want only your happiness.*
>
> *Sincerely,*
>
> *Richard Rowe*

Krumbine slumped back in his chair, which braced itself manfully against him, and looked long and thoughtfully at Potshelter. "Well, if that's a code, it's certainly a fiendishly subtle one. You'd think he was talking to his Girl Next Door."

Potshelter nodded wonderingly. "I only read as far as where they were planning to blow up Grand Central Spaceport and all the guides in it."

"Judas Priest, I think I have it!" Krumbine shot up. "It's a pilot advertisement-Boy Next Door or-that kind of thing-printed to look like hand-writtening, which would make all the difference. And the pilot copy got mailed by accident-which would mean there is no real Richard Rowe."

At that instant, the door dilated and two blue detective engines hustled a struggling young man into the office. He was slim, rather handsome, had a bushy head of hair that had somehow survived evolution and radioactive fallout, and across the chest and back of his paper singlet was neatly stamped: "Richard Rowe."

When he saw the two men, he stopped struggling and straightened up. "Excuse me, gentlemen," he said, "but these police machines must have made a mistake. I've committed no crime."

Then his gaze fell on the hand-addressed envelope on Krumbine's desk and he turned pale.

Krumbine laughed harshly. "No crime! No, not at all. Merely using the mails to communicate. Ha!"

The young man shrank back. "I'm sorry, sir."

"Sorry, he says! Do you realize that your insane prank has resulted in the destruction of perhaps a half-billion pieces of first-class advertising? —in the strangulation of a postal station and the paralysis of Lower Manhattan? —in the mobilization of SBI reserves, the de-mothballing of two divisions of G. I. machines and the redeployment of the Solar Battle Fleet? Good Lord, boy, why did you do it?"

Richard Rowe continued to shrink but he squared his shoulders. "I'm sorry, sir, but I just had to. I just had to get in touch with Jane Dough."

"A girl from another hive? A girl you'd merely gazed at because a guide happened to blow a fuse?" Krumbine stood up, shaking an angry finger. "Great Scott, boy, where was Your Girl Next Door?"

Richard Rowe stared bravely at the finger, which made him look a trifle cross-eyed. "She died, sir, both of them."

"But there should be at least six."

"I know, sir, but of the other four, two have been shipped to the Adirondacks on vacation and two recently got married and haven't been replaced."

Potshelter, a faraway look in his eyes, said softly, "I think I'm beginning to understand —"

But Krumbine thundered on at Richard Rowe with, "Good Lord, I can see you've had your troubles, boy. It isn't often we have these shortages of Girls Next Door, so that temporarily a boy can't marry the Girl Next Door, as he always should. But, Judas Priest, why didn't you take your troubles to your psychiatrist, your groupmaster, your socializer, your Queen Mother?"

"My psychiatrist is being overhauled, sir, and his replacement short-circuits every time he hears the word 'trouble.' My groupmaster and socializer are on vacation duty in the Adirondacks. My Queen Mother is busy replacing Girls Next Door."

"Yes, it all fits," Potshelter proclaimed excitedly. "Don't you see, Krumbine? Except for a set of mischances that would only occur once in a billion billion times, the letter would never have been conceived or sent."

"You may have something there," Krumbine concurred. "But in any case, boy, why did you-er-written this letter to this particular girl? What is there about Jane Dough that made you do it?"

"Well, you see, sir, she's —"

Just then, the door re-dilated and a blue matron machine conducted a young woman into the office. She was slim and she had a head of hair that would have graced a museum beauty, while across the back and-well, "chest" is an inadequate word-of her paper chemise, "JANE DOUGH" was silk-screened in the palest pink.

Krumbine did not repeat his last question. He had to admit to himself that it had been answered fully. Potshelter whistled respectfully. The blue detective engines gave hard-boiled grunts. Even the blue matron machine seemed awed by the girl's beauty.

But she had eyes only for Richard Rowe. "My Grand Central man," she breathed in amazement. "The man I've dreamed of ever since. My man with hair." She noticed the way he was looking at her and she breathed harder. "Oh, darling, what have you done?"

"I tried to send you a letter."

"A letter? For me? Oh, darling!"

Krumbine cleared his throat. "Potshelter, I'm going to wind this up fast. Miss Dough, could you transfer to this young man's hive?"

"Oh, yes, sir! Mine has an over-plus of Girls Next Door."

"Good. Mr. Rowe, there's a sky-pilot two levels up-look for the usual white collar just below the photocells. Marry this girl and take her home to your hive. If your Queen Mother objects refer her to-er-Potshelter here."

He cut short the young people's thanks. "Just one thing," he said, wagging a finger at Rowe. "Don't written any more letters."

"Why ever would I?" Richard answered. "Already my action is beginning to seem like a mad dream."

"Not to me, dear," Jane corrected him. "Oh, sir, could I have the letter he sent me? Not to do anything with. Not to show anyone. Just to keep."

"Well, I don't know —" Krumbine began.

"Oh, *please*, sir!"

"Well, I don't know why not, I was going to say. Here you are, miss. Just see that this husband of yours never writtens another."

He turned back as the contracting door shut the young couple from view.

"You were right, Potshelter," he said briskly. "It was one of those combinations of mischances that come up only once in a billion billion times. But we're going to have to issue recommendations for new procedures and safeguards that will reduce the possibilities to one in a trillion trillion. It will undoubtedly up the Terran income tax a healthy percentage, but we can't have something like this happening again. Every boy must marry the Girl Next Door! And the first-class mails must not be interfered with! The advertising must go through!"

"I'd almost like to see it happen again," Potshelter murmured dreamily, "if there were another Jane Dough in it."

---

Outside, Richard and Jane had halted to allow a small cortege of machines to pass. First came a squad of police machines with Black Sorter in their midst, unmuzzled and docile enough, though still gnashing his teeth softly. Then-stretched out horizontally and borne on the shoulders of Gray Psychiatrist, Black Coroner, White Nursemaid Seven and Greasy Joe-there passed the slim form of Pink Wastebasket, snow-white in death. The machines were keening softly, mournfully.

Round about the black pillars, little mecho-mops were scurrying like mice, cleaning up the last of the first-class-mail bits of confetti.

Richard winced at this evidence of his aberration, but Jane squeezed his hand comfortingly, which produced in him a truly amazing sensation that changed his whole appearance.

"I know how you feel, darling," she told him. "But don't worry about it. Just think, dear, I'll always be able to tell your friends' wives something no other woman in the world can boast of: that my husband once wrote me a letter!"